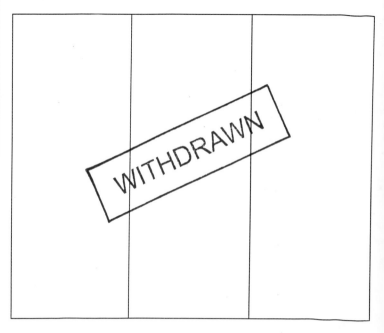

Nightshade

E. S. Thomson

CONSTABLE

CONSTABLE

First published in Great Britain in 2021 by Constable
This paperback edition published in 2021 by Constable

Copyright © E. S. Thomson, 2021

The moral right of the author has been asserted.

*All characters and events in this publication, other than
those clearly in the public domain, are fictitious
and any resemblance to real persons,
living or dead, is purely coincidental.*

All rights reserved.

No part of this publication may be reproduced, stored in a retrieval system,
or transmitted, in any form, or by any means, without the prior permission
in writing of the publisher, nor be otherwise circulated in any form of
binding or cover other than that in which it is published and without a
similar condition including this condition being imposed
on the subsequent purchaser.

A CIP catalogue record for this book
is available from the British Library.

ISBN: 978-1-47213-151-5

Typeset in ITC New Baskerville by SX Composing DTP, Rayleigh, Essex
Printed and bound in Great Britain by Clays Ltd, Elcograf S.p.A.

Papers used by Constable are from well-managed forests
and other responsible sources.

Constable
An imprint of
Little, Brown Book Group
Carmelite House
50 Victoria Embankment
London EC4Y 0DZ

An Hachette UK Company

www.hachette.co.uk

www.littlebrown.co.uk

For Sharon Corrall.
Hairdresser. Reader. Friend.

Notes on the poisonous nightshades (Solanaceae).

ATROPA BELLADONNA

Also known as deadly nightshade, banewort, Devil's cherries, belladonna lily, dwale.

Description

Dingy purple flowers appear from June and July through to September. Afterwards, the plants become studded with small, sweet berries the size and colour of sloes but shiny as polished jet. The dull, darkish leaves have downy hairs on the obverse, and a bitter taste, whether fresh or dried.

The roots are thick, fleshy and white, and characteristically some eight inches in length. It is a temperamental perennial, though once established plants can last for many years, and may grow up to six feet tall. When crushed, the fresh leaves give off a repulsive, corrupt odour.

A lover of shade and dim light, the deadly nightshade prefers well-drained soil, favouring freshly turned earth – often graves, or old ruins.

Toxicity

All parts of the plant are poisonous, the roots especially. The leaves and flowers are less so, the berries least of all.

Symptoms

The poison is fast acting. Symptoms include dilated pupils, blurred vision, increased heart rate. The skin turns hot, dry and red. Disorientation, hallucinations, impaired vision are notable symptoms. Behaviour often turns aggressive, sometimes wildly so. Dilated pupils are a distinctive characteristic. The effects of the toxin may linger for some time, and there are instances of those who have lost their wits completely, so terrifying are the hallucinations experienced while under its influence.

Antidotes

The stomach contents must be evacuated, and the stomach washed clean. Stimulants, such as strong coffee, might also be administered. Death is certain if the herb is taken without care.

Medical applications

Powdered roots and leaves can be efficacious against colic, asthma, problems with the menses, seasickness, and an excess of stomach acid.

Miscellanea

According to legend, the plant belongs to the Devil, who tends it at his leisure. The name 'Belladonna' is said to refer to an ancient superstition, whereby at certain times of the year the plant takes the form of an enchantress of extraordinary beauty upon whose face it is dangerous to look, though the name is more usually associated with the mediaeval Italian practice of using the tincture to brighten ladies' eyes.

Belladonna is fabled to be one of the principal ingredients of 'flying ointment', a salve beloved by witches and applied internally via the blunt end of a broomstick.

Chapter One

❦

Mother Nature has divined many ways to kill the uninitiated. The sap of the curare vine will leave you a living corpse awaiting death by asphyxiation. The tubers of the blood root cause suffocation and coma. The crimson berries of the yew – succulent mid-winter fruits, as tempting as sweeties – would have your heart fail by the time you reached the lychgate. Death lurks in every hedgerow, every garden, every lover's bouquet. Monkshood will turn your veins to ice, cuckoopint will blister your innards until you bleed to death. The water in which you sit your bunch of spring daffodils, or your lily-of-the-valley nosegay, if sipped, will stop your heart in an instant.

Some years ago I started work on a *Treatise on Poisons*, my old friend Dr Bain my companion amongst the toxins. But Dr Bain died, and our work was never completed. I could not bear to look at it when he was gone, as it brought back memories upon which I had no wish to dwell. Of course, time works its deft magic on us all, and that which we were once unable to contemplate without our heart breaking becomes endurable as the months and years pass. I had always known I owed it to Dr Bain to continue our work and, that winter, I took out our manuscript, and the notes we had taken, and resolved to complete what we had started. It was that, above all else, that had led us to where we were now, the two of us – Will and I – standing side by side in the physic garden, looking down at a corpse.

It was Will, along with my apprentices Gabriel and Jenny, who found it. At first, they thought it was nothing but stones, old roots, bits of pipe. But Will had unearthed more corpses than any of us, having once been commissioned to empty St Saviour's graveyard, and for him there could be no mistaking it. 'Bones, Jem,' he said, wiping his hands on his gardening apron. 'Human bones.' At that I had left my work in the glasshouse and come to see for myself: a ridge of ribs, dark with earth, gripped tightly by the roots of the deadly nightshade, as if the poison were determined to keep the corpse for its own.

Will and Gabriel had removed what parts of the plant they could, both of them wearing the thick leather gloves and aprons that the job demanded, for every part of *Atropa belladonna* is poisonous. The soil beneath seemed darker than the surrounding stuff, as if the flesh that had given the bones grace and form had leached into the ground in a dark ooze.

Once a part of St Saviour's Infirmary in the dirty heart of London, the physic garden I now owned had been tended by my family for as long as anyone could remember. Its history was my history, and I could not help but feel that whatever crimes were hidden in its earth were mine to answer. I said nothing of this at that time, however, and we turned our faces to the ground, scraping carefully so as not to disturb the lie of the body. Overhead, the sky darkened. Gabriel lit a lantern and set it beside the hole. Beside the grave. The light shone yellow on our hands, and on the bones as we dug away the dirt.

'It's in a curious position,' said Will. 'There's nothing restful about the way this person met their end.'

I could not disagree, for what we had uncovered was monstrous in appearance, the back arched, the chest flung upwards, the ribs splintered as if something had burst from its heart. The bones of the hands, still manacled by the night-shade's roots, were claw-like, the fingers bent and clutching, the arms drawn up as if warding off an attacker. The head was thrown back, the dislocated jaw yawning wide. A fist of dark earth and a great tangle of roots plugged its scream.

'We should send Gabriel for the constable,' said Will. 'The Watch goes down St Saviour's Street at six and it's almost that time—'

'Wait,' I said. 'Let's not be rash.'

'Rash?' said Will. 'We've found a corpse. What is there to hesitate over?'

'Evidently it's been here for some time. Another few hours will make no difference. And I want to look at it more closely, to see what we can learn about it. The constable will do a very brisk job and all manner of observations will be obliterated by his clod-hopping feet.' I bent my face close to the skull, the lantern in my hand. A thick, pale root, hairy and obscene, snaked in and out of the eye sockets. I saw a scrap of something damp and sticky-looking adhering to the left temple, and a wiry tuft of hair. Another root had forced the bones of the jaw apart, and they were thickly matted about the head and neck, the chest and ribs. The bones themselves were entirely without flesh, for although the heavy clay of London is the enemy of decay, my garden has been tended by apothecaries for centuries. Its earth is well drained and friable, its worms fat and healthy. Dead flesh would not last long in it.

'When might the body have gone into the ground?' said Will. 'The same time this belladonna was planted, I presume?'

'I imagine so,' I replied. 'The deadly nightshade has always been here, for as long as I can remember. It's a lover of disturbed soil – graves are its speciality.'

Will looked down at the contorted figure. 'It looks as though the bones themselves have spawned the weeds,' he muttered.

'Belladonna is not a weed.' I could not help myself, though I knew what he meant. There was something grotesque about the way the pale roots gripped the bones, forcing them apart. The plant itself, pulled from the earth, lay wilting guiltily beside the hole.

'Had the seeds been ingested?' he added. 'The berries? They look tempting enough. Until I met you I had no idea how poisonous they are.'

'And you a country boy too. Did you not see them in the hedgerows of whatever yokel's backwater you grew up in?'

'Fortunately I only ate blackberries as a boy.' He pulled his gloves back on. 'And Bath is *not* a backwater, though I admit it is full of yokels. As for this noxious weed – and I *will* call it that – why do you grow it if it's so toxic? I assume it has some medicinal uses?'

'Pain relief, menstrual problems, peptic ulcers, inflammation. Motion sickness. It's not without its uses though the dose must be carefully measured.'

'What happens when you take too much?'

'Madness and death,' I replied. 'The usual things.'

'And you know this how?' said Will. 'Have you tried it?'

'No,' I said. I was lying, of course. I had taken deadly nightshade with Dr Bain during an evening of experimentation that still haunted me, and I had no wish to resurrect the memory. The demons I had seen, conjured up by my own imagination, were recorded in our notes. Even now, years later, I still could not bear to read them. I had recovered, but Dr Bain, fascinated and – as was his way – jealous that I had experienced what he had not, had taken an even larger dose. I had watched him run screaming into the night pursued, in his mind, by devils and creatures more diabolical than anything hell had to offer. In the end, to protect him from himself, I had held him down while the superintendent from Angel Meadow Asylum strapped him into a straitjacket. He raved for two days, so that we both thought his wits might be lost for ever. After that, he lay exhausted, hardly able to speak, too terrified to sleep for fear of what awaited him there. But I said nothing of this to Will. He already knew that I wanted to continue the work on poisons that I had started with Dr Bain, but as we were standing looking down at the bones of a corpse now did not seem the best time to share my anecdotes.

The skeleton itself was easy enough to disinter. We started at the skull and worked our way down, carefully removing the loose soil from about the bones with trowels and boot brushes. At the feet, however, we came to a halt. Will stood back, appalled.

'Jem,' he whispered. 'I think there are other bones here too. Small ones.' I peered into the hole. Five tiny finger bones grasped the dirt, the way a sleeping baby might hold tight to its coverlet.

Jenny, my junior apprentice, gasped as she peeped over Will's shoulder. 'A baby! Oh, the poor little mite.' Jenny had come to us only recently. A refugee from a brothel on the waterfront near the docks, she had originally found a new home as apprentice apothecary on the Seamen's Floating Hospital. When her master died she had come to live with us. She was, I guessed, no more than thirteen years of age, but I knew she had seen and done things that would make others blench. Dead babies were something with which she was sadly familiar.

'It's not a baby, Jenny,' I said. 'Not unless it's a baby with a tail.' I bent down, and from the small mass of bones we had unearthed I plucked up a skull – small, with gaping eye sockets and sharp pointed teeth. 'It's a monkey, though I'm not sure what kind.'

There was more too. 'Look at those,' said Will. 'I've never seen anything like those before. Have you?'

I picked from the soil one of the objects he was pointing to. It was made of ivory, no bigger than a crab apple, smooth and globe-like in my hand. A perfect imitation of a human skull: rounded cranium, deep eye sockets, grinning teeth set in a carved, angular jawbone. More macabre still, there appeared to be a considerable number of them. I told Gabriel to fetch a pail of water from the pump near the glasshouse and he and Jenny washed them free of dirt. When we set them out side by side, I could see that their expressions varied slightly – this one had closer eye sockets, that one a missing tooth, another was without teeth altogether. Every one of them had a small hole, blocked with dirt, at each temple, as if they had once been strung up, one beside the other. All together there were some forty-five of them. The sight left all of us without words. I stuffed them in a sack so that we did not have to look at them, though even the *clack, clack, clack* they made as they rolled and shifted made me uneasy.

'And what about this?' said Gabriel. 'Looks like a soup dish. Do you think it is?'

'No,' I said. Could the lad think of nothing but food? 'I don't think this was for soup. But it does look familiar.' We had found it lying against the right leg of the skeleton, as if it had been tossed into the grave along with the skulls and the monkey: a shallow bowl, some twelve inches wide and three inches deep. Perhaps made of silver, it had grown black during its time underground, the patterns on its rim choked with dirt.

'It's for blood,' said Jenny. She was wearing one of my old stovepipe hats, as she always was, and her eyes were dark beneath its crooked brim and the rough fringe of her hair. 'When the physician comes.'

'Is it?' said Will.

'Perhaps,' I said. It certainly reminded me of the basins used by physicians when they bled a patient. Some bowls had an indentation, or lip of some kind, where the patient's arm might rest. Some, like this one, did not. We'd had pewter ones at St Saviour's that were just the same size and shape. 'If the patient is lanced, or scarified, the blood might be collected in a vessel such as this,' I said. 'But we can't be certain that's what this one was for.'

'What else might it be?' said Will.

I shrugged. 'I have no idea. I don't want to jump to conclusions, that's all.'

Night had fallen, the lantern light throwing long shadows across the grass. A mist was creeping up from the river, as it so often did during the winter, and the garden had taken on a gritty, indistinct appearance. I felt a sickness in my stomach that my physic garden, the one place I had always looked upon as a sanctuary from the evils of the city, was now tainted by death. And I could not turn my back on our discovery either, for it was *my* garden, *my* belladonna bushes, this skeleton was a part of *my* family's past. If I had known where my questions would lead I would have pushed it straight back into the cold dark earth and stamped the sod down hard. But I did neither of those things. And so it began.

I told Jenny to bring around the handcart so that we might take the bones and other items back to the apothecary. I sent Gabriel to fetch the Watch, though there was little to be done at that hour of the night. The constable Gabriel brought to the physic garden showed little interest in our findings. 'It's remains, sir,' he said, as if I had no idea what I was looking at. 'Them's human bones.' He looked tired and uncomfortable. His hat, a black chimney pot lined with steel to deflect an assailant's cudgel, seemed to weigh him down. He took it off and set it on the ground. Its sturdy construction meant that it might also be used to stand on, to see over a wall or in at a window, perhaps. This constable chose to use his as a stool, however, and he lowered himself onto it with a sigh, gingerly touching his finger to the red mark the thing had left on his forehead. 'Oh dear, sir,' he said, gazing at the tiny bones of the monkey. 'Baby, is it, sir? P'raps this is a girl what's fallen, sir. If you take my meaning. It's not uncommon.'

'It's a monkey,' I said. 'These are monkey bones.'

'I never liked monkeys,' he replied. 'And these other things.' He gestured to the bowl and the collection of ivory skulls. 'What might these be? Looks like his swag to me, sir. Some travelling gypsy fellow, no doubt. Stole some things, p'raps from a doctor? Who else might have a bag o' little skulls? And we are in the old physic garden for St Saviour's, you know.'

'Are we?' I said. The man was an idiot. Did he not know I had once been apothecary to St Saviour's Infirmary? And what sort of a doctor owned 'a bag of little skulls'? None that I had ever met, and I'd seen them all!

'Why, yes sir.' He gave me a pitying look. 'This fellow'll just be some sneak thief what came a cropper. Been dead a long time too, sir. Not much hope of finding anything out about him now, is there?' He looked pleased with himself at having so readily dismissed the matter. 'I'll tell the magistrate, but I'm sure he'll agree with me. Besides, we've enough to do with the recent dead, sir, never mind a set of old bones what's probably come from the Infirmary. I mean, must be twenty, thirty years this'n's been in the ground, judging by the state of him. Get the sexton at St Saviour's to put him in the proper place. Graveyard's just along the road.'

'Might you be able to put this in the *Police Gazette*?' said Will. 'Someone might know something and come forward.'

'We might be in the *Gazette*!' breathed Gabriel. 'Did you hear that, Jenny? Why, we'll be famous across all London!'

'Well? Might it be possible?' I addressed the constable, but he was shaking his head.

'Bless you sir, these bones ain't important enough for *that*. Best just pass them over to the sexton like I said.' He stood up and put his hat back on. 'Lord, but this thing's a burden. Makes my head ache. Chafes somethin' rotten too.'

'Try this.' I fumbled in my satchel and pulled out a small pot of salve. 'Comfrey, lavender, arnica in a base of beeswax and honey. Rub it on at night where your hat rubs the skin. I have a tincture of feverfew, skullcap and laudanum that you can try for the headaches too, if the salve doesn't work, but that's at the apothecary. Call in next time you're passing. Fishbait Lane.'

'Oh! Thank you, sir!' He took the pot and sniffed warily at the contents. A smile creased his face. 'Lavender! Reminds me of the smell of my mam's laundry cupboard, sir. Loved hiding in the laundry, especially when she was after me with the strap.' He pocketed the salve and pulled his tunic straight. 'Well then, sir, I'll see what I can do. If we're lucky these here bones'll be in the *Gazette* tomorrow. Might produce a bit of interest. These things usually do.'

Chapter Two

❧

We were all relieved to get back to my apothecary on Fishbait Lane. The air was warm, and sweet with the scent of cardamom, camomile and rose petals. Mrs Speedicut, who had once worked with me as the matron at St Saviour's Infirmary, was sitting in front of the fire with her legs stretched out before her. She had been out of work for some months, and I had finally caved in and offered her temporary employment looking after Will while he was sick. Will had suffered a dose of whooping cough, combined with a bronchial infection, and it was a surprise to us all that he had recovered. Since then, I had employed the woman as a cleaner, though it seemed to me that she had done little more than doze in front of the fire, and complain that I would not let her smoke her evil-smelling tobacco in the shop.

I kicked the slattern's chair. 'Madam,' I said. 'Do I pay you to sleep?'

She opened her eyes and regarded us from between

narrowed lids. 'Mr Jem,' she said. 'And Mr Quartermain too. Ain't *you* workin', sir?'

'No,' said Will. 'You may recall I am recovering from an illness.'

She grunted. 'Whooping cough? That ain't much to speak of. I've 'ad that many times. And the cholera. Not to mention the nirls, the bots, and the phlegm. Black phlegm,' she said. 'That were the *worst*.'

'If you smoked less, madam, I believe your phlegm would be less black and cause you less trouble,' said Will.

'Stop your bickering,' I said. 'We have work to do. Clear this table, please. And close the shop. It is too late for customers now.'

On the apothecary table I set the bones out in order, from the cranium, to the phalanges, in the shape of the person they had once been. The monkey too I laid out as best I could. I wanted to examine them both as closely as possible, and I put lanterns about the table, and hung them from the ceiling, so that everything was illuminated. I took out my magnifying glass, and my notebook. The others watched in silence as I bent to my task.

'Well,' I said after a while. 'It's definitely a man.'

'How can you tell?' said Will.

'A number of things. The bones of a male tend to be thicker, the areas of muscle attachment more defined than in females. It's the cranium especially, though – forehead, eyes, jaw.' I held up the skull, turning it this way and that. 'Viewed in profile, female skulls have a more rounded forehead. You can see this one tends to slope backwards. And look at the supraorbital ridge—'

'Supraorbital?'

'The ridge along the brow. It's more prominent in males.

The eye sockets of women are rounder, with sharp edges to the upper borders, whereas a male has squarer orbits. See here?' I pointed the skull towards him. 'The jaw too is square, the line between the outer edge and the ear is vertical. In females the edge of the jaw slopes more gently.'

'Anything else?'

'Well, he was some six feet tall. Judging by the scrap of flesh and hair at his temple he had dark hair. The skull also tells us that he'd had a violent life.' I ran my finger over the right eye socket, pressing down on a deep depression in the bone. 'The bone has been crushed. Splintered. A violent blow to the head, across the eye. His cheek bone shows evidence of trauma too. And the nose.'

'Perhaps a fall?'

'Perhaps, though a fall might result in a broader area of trauma, especially on the eye socket. And it would have to be a pretty bad fall.' I shrugged. 'Either way I would expect this man to have been either blind in one eye, or to have lost the eye altogether. Probably the latter.'

'And this is what killed him?'

'No. This is an older injury. You can see where the bone has healed itself. There's other evidence of violence too, also from some time before he died. A broken leg, a broken foot, a broken arm, shoulder, knee. Fingers missing from the right hand – well, half of the fingers. He would have had stumps at least.'

'Perhaps we left some tiny finger bones in the ground,' said Gabriel. 'You know. The end bits.'

'I think not,' I said. 'The bones I have here tell me that the fingers were lost some time ago. Some time before he met his end.'

'Don't like having a body on the table like that,' said

Mrs Speedicut suddenly. 'Should be buried proper. Right away too!' She eyed the blackened bleeding bowl, and the collection of ivory skulls which Jenny had set out before her in a grinning row upon the hearth. 'Them especially,' she said. 'Ain't Christian. Ain't civilised.'

'Christian?' said Will. 'What on earth does that have to do with it?'

'Them skulls. That bowl. Them *bones*. Heathen, that's what they are!'

'This man will have been quite distinctive,' I said. 'Even in London. He was blind in one eye, and judging by the bones of his legs, he was a cripple too. He will have walked with a pronounced limp, or more likely with a stick or a crutch – perhaps two crutches. His front teeth were missing. He travelled with a monkey, and he was probably a beggar, or at least impoverished, as what man can work without the fingers of his right hand?'

'Perhaps he was left-handed,' said Gabriel. 'I am.'

'Perhaps,' I said. 'Though the balance of probability rests with his being right-handed, as most people are. The monkey might have been a way of earning money, as he was unable to earn it himself. Unless it was a companion.'

'No wedding ring?' said Will.

'No. But that's not uncommon.'

'So how did he die if it was not by these wounds?'

'I'm not sure,' I replied. 'This is the part that perplexes me. You recall the arrangement of the bones as we found them? The head thrown back, the arms clutched upwards, the spine arched so as to be bent towards the heels?'

'Recall it?' said Will. 'I will never forget it.'

'From the way his jaw was torn apart and writhed about with roots I suspect his mouth was filled with nightshade berries, though I cannot be certain. As for the position in which he was lying there are only two things that might cause a body to spasm in such a way. The first is lockjaw. The second is strychnine poisoning.'

'And which interpretation do you favour?'

'Lockjaw would suggest misadventure,' I said. 'Dirt enters a wound. Certainly there may well be tetanus somewhere in the ground in the garden. But the illness doesn't manifest immediately, and what is noticeable about tetanus is that the muscles relax after death. This man's muscles had not relaxed.'

'Perhaps he was buried alive,' said Will.

'I think not, but I'll come to that in a moment.'

'And strychnine?'

'Strychnine is a different matter entirely.'

'So he was poisoned?'

'Quite likely. Strychnine is found in the fruits of *Strychnos nux-vomica*. The plant is native to India but can be grown in many other places. I have some in the glasshouse. It's one of my most poisonous.'

'Why on earth do you grow it if it's so poisonous?'

I shrugged. 'We use it to kill the rats.'

'It has no medicinal uses?'

'It can improve athletic performance if used in strictly controlled doses and administered by an expert, but it has no real medicinal value. The poison acts quickly too, so you have no time to go anywhere or do anything. The point I'm trying to make is that the victim dies in agony, the body spasming back and forth uncontrollably while the poison courses through the veins. I have heard of the bones snapping under the strain, so vicious are the contractions of the muscles. It's a terrible and agonising way to die, and a fearful death to behold. And, unlike tetanus, the body remains in its contorted position after death. For that reason alone, I think that is what we're looking at here.'

'And there's no antidote?'

'Not really. An emetic *might* work if only a little of the fruit, or the poison, was ingested.'

'But it could be an accident?' Will persisted.

'You're suggesting he went into the glasshouse, plucked the admittedly attractive orange fruit of the *strychnos*, and ate a few to see how they tasted?'

'It's possible, isn't it?'

'It's *possible*,' I said. 'Though they smell and taste horrible. But is it probable? Anyway, there's more.' I put the skull down and picked up one of the ribs. 'There are a number of more recent wounds. This is the third rib on the right-hand side. You see this?' I pointed to a small v-shaped mark on the edge of the bone. 'This is the mark of a knife blade. You can see that it's recent, or at least was done immediately prior to, or after, death, as the bone has not healed itself. Sternum, ribs, the bones of the lower arm – all bear marks like this.'

'Meaning what?'

'Meaning, Will, that this man was stabbed. Over and over again. I have counted five wounds, at least. Five places where the blade of a knife nicked the bones. Some are deeper than others, as if some of the blows were more forceful, but there is no mistaking them. I cannot say what sort of knife it was – my guess, given the location, would be that it was a pruning knife, not unlike this one.' I held up my own knife. It was one that my father had given me. I kept it in my satchel, but we had many such blades in the shed at the physic garden, in the glasshouse, in the apothecary. 'Would he stab himself? No, he would not. So, he was poisoned, and *then* stabbed.'

'Perhaps . . . perhaps he ate the *strychnos* fruit by mistake, started to have these violent spasms you describe, and somebody . . . somebody put him out of his misery.'

I knew we had to consider all possibilities, but even Will must realise that he was clutching at straws. 'Surely no one would stab a dying man five times or more to put him out of his misery, Will.'

I put the rib back onto the table. The man's skull stared up at me, his gaping eye sockets and broken-apart jaw made him look as though he found the whole thing wildly funny. But it was not funny. It was not funny at all. 'This man was murdered,' I said. 'He was poisoned, and then he was stabbed, and then he was buried in my garden. And I want to know why.'

Chapter Three

To give the others something to do I handed Mrs Speedicut the blackened bowl and pointed Gabriel and Jenny to the skulls. 'Give them a clean, can you? See what we can learn from them.' But Mrs Speedicut refused to touch the bowl, and I had to give the job to Gabriel. He scrubbed it with sand, lemon juice and vinegar. 'It's come up nice,' he said, holding it up. It was wide and shallow, with a broad flat rim. It had been tarnished black, with its time spent under the earth, but it was now gleaming, a shimmering circle as lustrous as the moon. It was heavy, its bowl smooth to the touch and bearing not even the faintest evidence of the silversmith's hammer.

'It's finely crafted for a bleeding bowl,' said Will. 'And what are these markings?' He ran his fingers around the flat face of the rim where a pattern had been engraved, a frieze of stylised star-shaped five-petalled flowers, alongside curling shapes resembling waves and tears.

'And these? What about these, Mr Jem?' Jenny held up one of the ivory skulls. Washed clean of earth it glowed stark white in the lamplight. I felt Mrs Speedicut's eyes upon me. She opened her mouth to speak, but then a look passed between us and she closed it again. She had seen one just like it, I knew. So had I, but I did not want to speak of it. Not then. Not in front of Gabriel and Jenny. It was my secret and I would share it when I was ready.

'I don't know,' I said, which was true enough. 'Put it down and go to bed.'

Gabriel and Jenny were subdued. Both were used to death and decay but having the bones of a stranger we had dug from our own garden lying on the apothecary table was upsetting both of them. In two minutes Gabriel was snoring. Jenny, however, was quite the opposite. After quarter of an hour I could see that she was still awake, the light from her candle flickering beneath the door to the herb drying room where she slept. I pushed it open, slowly and silently. The herb drying room was a small cell that backed onto the chimney flue. The air was forever drowsy with the scent of summer's end – fennel, lavender, mint, sandalwood. I had loved it when I was a child, and my father had thrashed me more than once for falling asleep in there. Now, I lowered myself silently onto an upturned tea chest and watched her as she held something up to the candlelight.

'Hadn't you better give that to me?' I said after a moment.

She jumped, dropping the thing she had been looking

at into her rumpled bedding. 'Don't creep up on a body like that, Mr Jem!'

I held out my hand. 'What is it?'

'Don't know,' she said, not meeting my gaze.

'Where did you get it?' I said, though I already knew the answer as I had seen her palm something when we were in the physic garden.

'Found it in the monkey's paw,' she said. 'His little bones were clutching it.'

I held it up between my finger and thumb. It was a token of some kind, slightly smaller than a penny, almost smooth to the touch and greenish black in colour. 'Why did you take it?'

'Thought it might be lucky.'

'Aren't you already lucky?'

'Yes, Mr Jem.' Her tone suggested otherwise.

'Well, it evidently wasn't very lucky for the monkey,' I said. 'Or his owner, come to that, as they both ended up dead.' I held the thing up to the candle, angling it towards the light, the way she had done. I saw that it was engraved – clumsily, as though by an unsteady hand, but competently done. At the top was the word 'SAUL', beneath this, the letter 'N', and below that what looked like a star, or perhaps the rough approximation of a compass, the 'N' corresponding to where north might be. At the very bottom was the word 'ANGEL'.

'My mother's name was Angel,' said Jenny. 'At least, when I was at Mrs Lovibond's house down on the waterfront, there was one of the girls called Angel, and she was nice to me, so I decided it was her what was my mother. She died, so they said. Don't know where she really went.'

'And that's why you took it?'

She nodded. 'She had one like this. She said a man give it her.'

'A man called Saul?'

'So she told me.'

'Did she indeed?' I turned the thing over. The back of it bore no inscription at all. I knew it was common for love-sick sailors to fashion tokens for their sweethearts out of a smoothed-down ha'penny, but this was too small for a ha'penny and too big for a farthing. Besides, why smooth both sides and engrave only one? I slipped it into my pocket. 'Go to sleep, Jenny,' I said. 'We'll talk about this in the morning.'

Will and I sat on either side of the apothecary stove, watching the embers flicker and glow. It was cold. A frost was coming – we had been lucky to make progress in the garden while the earth was still soft, for when the frost came the ground would be like stone. I shook some coal onto the embers, banking up the stove for the night.

'What is it, Jem?' Will was sitting in my father's old chair. 'There is something bothering you, I can see it.'

'We have just unearthed a body from my garden,' I said stiffly. 'Isn't that enough to bother anyone?'

'Yes, but there's more, I can tell. I know you.'

I jabbed at the coals but did not answer.

'Jem,' he said, 'leave that fire. You'll make it burn like a furnace with all that levering and poking, and it will be dead by the morning.' He reached forward and took the poker from my hand. 'Tell me what it is.' He was right. There *was* something else, something I had told no one. It concerned my mother.

My mother had died of fever, not two weeks after I, and my dead twin brother, were born. As the wrong child had survived, my father had brought me up as the son he'd wanted. He never mentioned her – unless I brought the subject up. I had done so often when I was younger, when my menses had started and I had no one to guide me, no one to speak to about who I might grow up to be. I was a girl in boy's apparel, destined to run the apothecary that had had the name 'Flockhart' over the door for two hundred years; a girl schooled to say nothing about who she really was, so that it might give her licence to say anything she pleased. I lived that contradiction every day with all its benefits and regrets. Had she lived would my mother have agreed with his deception? I had no idea. I had no idea what she was like. And so I had asked him, 'What sort of a person was she, Father? Was she clever? Was she kind? Do I look like her? Do I sound like she did?' The one question, always unspoken, that I longed to ask above all others, was 'Did she love me?'

'You are nothing like her,' he always replied. 'Apart from your stubbornness.'

My father had kept mementoes of her – a day dress, and a miniature, both kept in a chest in his room. Peering at her likeness in a miniature no bigger than the palm of my hand, I had searched her features looking for an echo of my own. But I am blighted by a birthmark, a patch of scarlet skin that covers my eyes and nose like a blindfold. She had no such disguise and the face that looked out at me from that tiny painting seemed to regard me with mingled pity and horror. Between her fingers she held a sprig of greenery, something with small purple-green leaves and tiny black berries set against a star of sepals. I used to think she held a sprig of blackthorn. Now I knew it to be the leaves and fruit of the deadly nightshade. And there was one other object. I had found it nestled deep in the pocket of her day dress, hidden from sight, perhaps hidden even from him, as he had said nothing about it to me. It was a small human skull, no bigger than a crab apple, carved from ivory. I had always assumed it to be a *memento mori*, something unsurprising for the wife of a hospital apothecary. It was clear that she had rubbed it again and again, like a rosary, or a worry bead, as it was smooth and lustrous as alabaster, its features, if one could call them that, softened from where her fingers had nursed it. I had not dared to take it and I did not like to look at it. But I had always wondered. And now, it seemed, my questions were at least partly answered, for it was exactly the same as the other ivory skulls we had found in the grave beneath the deadly nightshade. I went to my room to fetch it.

'This belonged to my mother,' I said, handing the thing over.

At first, he said nothing, but caressed its domed crown with his thumb thoughtfully. 'Well,' he said at last, 'we mustn't jump to conclusions.'

'It is hard not to,' I replied. 'My mother is connected to this man, and to his death. His murder. There can be no other conclusion we might draw, though how and why she was involved we have no way of knowing.'

Will frowned. 'She was instrumental in the design of the garden, I believe. When it was laid out in its current form?'

'Yes.'

'But she was not alone, was she? She had help. There were others.' He struggled to his feet. He hardly filled his clothes as he had lost so much weight during his illness, and he looked frail. I watched him as he shuffled to the back of the apothecary, to his drawing board and his stool, his box of writing tools, rulers, compasses. We were an incongruous partnership by anyone's estimation – me the apothecary who had once run one of London's great infirmaries, now the owner of a shop on a narrow street near the slums of Prior's Rents. Will the jobbing architect, surveyor and draughtsman, only three years in London and still innocent of its ways. His first commission in the city had been to empty the graveyard of St Saviour's Infirmary where I had once worked. Now, with the Infirmary razed to the ground to make way for a railway bridge, he and I were the best of friends. But London can be unkind to those who are not used to it, and Will had recently spent more time sick in bed than he had at his drawing board. I knew he was finding his convalescence frustrating. It was one of the reasons why I had asked him to help me redesign the physic garden, and he had leaped at the chance. 'Your garden is a lung, Jem,' he'd said to me. 'And I need air.' It was true, for he was often short of breath, the choking atmosphere of the city lying heavy on his chest. I was glad of his assistance, and his company, in the garden. Unlike Gabriel, Jenny and Mrs Speedicut, he was not given to prattle, and there is much to be said for a companion who knows when to speak and when to remain silent.

'I found the plans to the garden a while ago, plans from when it was designed, landscaped and planted,' he said. 'I thought nothing of it at the time, but now—' Beside his stool was a tea chest bristling with rolled-up papers and drawings. He ran pale slender fingers over them, before selecting one and pulling it out. 'You know I always like to have a plan, Jem.' He flourished it like a sword before him. 'I think our search for the truth might start here.'

I knew where everything was in the garden. I had worked in it all my life, and it was the one place on earth I loved above all others. And yet I'd had no idea that a plan of it existed. Feeling rather put out, I asked Will where he had found it. 'There are boxes and boxes of stuff in the attic from when we left the Infirmary,' he said. 'I'm an architect. A draughtsman. I can spot a rolled-up plan a mile away and when I see one I'm overcome with the irresistible urge to unfurl.' He grinned. 'Don't worry, Jem. I won't tell anyone that there was a tiny bit of your own garden's history that you knew nothing about.'

But I did not share his good humour, and I bent over the thick sheet of paper he unrolled on the table-top without answering. Perhaps if it was *his* garden in which the skeleton had been found, *his* mother who was implicated in the violent death of an unknown man, he might be in a less buoyant mood.

The hand that had drawn the plan was bold. Was it a man's handiwork I was looking at? I could not be certain. What I *was* certain of was how little the place had changed in the years since it had been laid down. My fingers traced the outline of familiar friends – the lavender bushes, the glasshouse, the beds where we grew comfrey, feverfew, camomile, calendula. The deadly nightshade, situated at the edge of the poison garden, was marked with nothing more than its own name, *Atropa belladonna*.

'It seems there has been belladonna on this spot since 1820,' said Will, pointing to the date at the top. 'That's a long time.' He pored over the plan, my magnifying glass in his hand. I wanted to snatch it off him, to push him aside and tell him it was *my* garden, the plan belonged to *me*, and *I* would look at it first. But I bit my tongue and remained silent. 'I thought so,' he said after a moment.

'What?'

'Here.' He pointed to the top right-hand corner and handed me the glass, though I could see well enough with my own eyes what he was alluding to. Written in the same bold copperplate were the words *St Saviour's Physic Garden. Improved and Extended, 1820.* Beneath this, in a list, as though in order of importance, were six names.

B. Wilde

Dr R. Christian

Mr J. Flockhart

Mrs D. Christian

C. Underhill

J. Spiker

'My mother was Catherine Underhill,' I said. 'Before she got married.'

'Who are the others? Do you know? I wonder why some of them have no title.'

'I don't know. I've never heard of J. Spiker. Dr Christian, however, I *have* heard of. He was Dr Bain's mentor in recklessness amongst the poisons,' I said. 'He used to work at St Saviour's Infirmary. I heard the man left in some disgrace, though I never knew him myself. A highly regarded physician and botanist at one time, though rumoured to be a man who would put nothing into his publications that he had not tried himself. He's the author of a book on Indian *materia medica*. His wife too is – or was – a well-respected botanist with her own publications.'

'He sounds a good place to start. What about the others? What about "B. Wilde"?'

'She's dead,' I said. 'As far as I know.'

'She?' said Will.

'Of course,' I replied. 'Women understand horticulture too, you know.'

'Yes, but . . . well, never mind. Are you sure she's dead? Have you met her? When did you last see her?'

'When I was a child,' I said. 'She came to the apothecary once when my father was out.'

I had been perhaps twelve years old. My father had been doing his ward rounds and had left me to set up the condenser and clean the floor. I recalled the way she had stood in the doorway, the light behind her. She had watched me for a while before saying, 'You must be Jemima.'

'I'm Jem,' I had stammered, keenly aware that my secret must be kept at all costs. 'After my father.'

'That's not what I heard.' She had stalked forward, her gait brisk and business-like. She was some six foot in height, tall for a woman, her hair cut as short as a man's so that it stood out from her head in a dark bush. Her skin was brown, tanned by the weather, her eyes a bright, sparkling blue, as if they had spent so long staring out at tropical seas that they had absorbed some of their azure colour. 'Where's your mother?' she had said. 'I need to speak with her.'

'She's dead,' I replied.

She looked surprised. 'I'm sorry to hear it. She wrote to me,' she said after a moment. 'She told me about you and your brother.'

'Then you'll know that my brother was stillborn,' I said. 'My mother died of fever a week later. My father decided he would rather his daughter had died and his son had lived. So *I am* Jem Flockhart. I am named after my father.'

I remembered the resentment I had felt, resentment that my mother had so carelessly died and left me to live my brother's life, resentment too that this woman, who claimed to know my mother, had been unaware that she had left me and my father alone some twelve years earlier. She had affected not to notice my surly face, but bent to open the large carpet bag she had dropped at her feet, and drew out a thick leather gardening glove. Next, using her gloved hand she produced a plant – dark green leaves and pale soily roots – from a pouch of waxed cotton. 'This is Indian Balsam,' she said. 'Would you like it? Your mother always wanted some. Plant it in full sun. Cover it with straw in the winter or better still bring it inside. But don't touch it. Its poison will kill you. There! Use that cloth to take it. Are you afraid?'

'No,' I said.

'Good,' she replied. 'Neither was your mother.'

'How did you know her?'

'Your father hasn't told you?'

'I don't know who you are so I cannot say.'

And that's when she told me. 'I am Bathsheba Wilde.'

'My father has never mentioned you.'

'I suppose he wouldn't have,' she said sharply. 'He never approved.' She removed her leather gauntlet and stuffed it back into her bag. 'Don't forget to tell him I called.'

At that she had turned and walked out into the blazing sunlight. I remembered bounding over to the door to call her back, to ask her to stay and tell me more – but she was gone, nothing remaining of her but her scent: cloves, cardamom, hemp, wood-smoke.

'It was a long time ago, but a memorable encounter,' I said now. 'I never told my father about her visit, but I learned from Dr Bain that she lived out near Islington Fields, was a well-known traveller and plant collector and had spent years abroad, in India, Ceylon, Burma. When I was older, and able to escape from the Infirmary now and again, I tried to visit her. But the house was shut up. I learned that she'd gone travelling again. And then one day I read of her death in *The Times*, a note amongst the obituaries describing her as "lost at sea" off the coast of Africa.' I shrugged. 'In fact, I credit her with sparking my interest in poisons, as I kept the Indian Balsam for myself. But perhaps Dr Christian will be able to tell us more – if he's still alive. Mrs Speedicut keeps me up to date with the deaths of St Saviour's medical men, and as she has never yet mentioned him, we have reason to hope for the best. My father kept the names and addresses of all the physicians and surgeons who worked there in a ledger, so unless the man has moved to a new house it should be easy enough to find him.'

Will rolled up the plan. 'Well then,' he said, securing it with its faded pink ribbon, 'I think we should pay Dr Christian a visit as soon as we can.'

Excerpts from the diary of Catherine Underhill.

20th May 1818

I am to go to Nightshade House. My father insists upon it. He seems to think I have not heard of the place, but I have. Anyone with an interest in botany or physic, anyone who is curious about plants or materia medica *has heard of Nightshade House. I think he has a plan for me, though I don't know what it is. I know he disapproves of the attentions I receive from Dr Bain – no longer 'Dr Bain' to me, but Alexander (at least in the pages of this diary). Father thinks him unreliable and reckless, and he may well be right. But he is* my *Alexander and I will make up my own mind about whether to accept him or not.*

I am to go to Nightshade alone. Apparently, the woman there does not receive male visitors.

What a peculiar afternoon! Nightshade is to the north, near Islington, within sight of the city but beyond it, the land round about still fields and smallholdings. A large box of a house with shuttered windows, its gardens are laid out like Kew, systematically, with lawns and trees and flowerbeds and ponds. I saw oak and birch and beech, laburnum and yew, along with many more species I did not recognise at all. I would have liked to stop and look around, but the coachman had his instructions and he was not for stopping. 'Miss Wilde does not like waiting,' he said. And he shook the reins so that the carriage hurtled along the drive as if the Devil himself were waiting.

She greeted me in person. 'I sent the servants away,' she said, noticing the surprise on my face that the mistress of the house should pull open her own front door. 'I'm leaving soon, so there is no one but Jane here now. Didn't your father tell you? It's why I wanted you. You will be travelling with us. Did you bring your things?'

She is as tall as a man, with wild dark hair and a disdainful, imperious manner. Her clothes were not the clothes of any lady I have ever seen but were loose folds and drapes of exotic silks. I had no idea what she was talking about, so I said, 'What things were you expecting, Miss Wilde?'

'Your travelling things, of course.' She looked at the small bag that I carried, and into which my father had made me put the work on poisonous plants that I had completed so far. 'No? Well, well, not to worry. I suppose there is some time yet.'

She led me into a lofty hall more exotic, more opulent, than anything I have ever seen. The ceilings were painted with azure skies, coloured birds and leaves, the walls set about with sculptures in marble, and display cases of stuffed birds; golden plates and bowls; bejewelled statues of curious many-armed figures. I tried not to stare, but I could hardly help myself. She saw my surprise, my fascination, and she smiled.

I followed her down the hall. Despite the opulence, there was a curious, disagreeable smell on the air. Sweetish and familiar, it reminded me of the wards at St Saviour's, or of the smell of Alexander's coat after he has been in the mortuary. But there was another smell too. It was smoky, like incense or burning leaves or herbs. I did not recognise it at all. The combination of the two was far from pleasant, though I did not like to say anything. And then she pushed open a pair of tall, oak panelled doors and there we were in her glasshouse. What a place it is! I have never in my entire life seen such a collection, such a building, and I am no stranger to glasshouses. As tall and broad as a church, and so entirely filled with plants – bromeliads, orchids, vines, ferns – that I cried out in pleasure. I could not help myself. She looked at me again, and I could see that my reaction had pleased her once more.

'It is a place like no other,' she said. 'You're right to be delighted by it.'

I caught a movement in the foliage and saw a maid, perhaps the 'Jane' she had mentioned earlier, setting out cups and saucers on a small table. Miss Wilde led me towards it.

We talked for a while and sipped our tea. She asked about my father, about his book on natural history, his work as a physician at St Saviour's. She asked about my interests in toxic plants, medicines and herbalism. She had heard that I too was writing a book, she said. Would I consider myself to be an expert on the matter?

I told her that I had brought my work with me if she would like to see it. I made to pull out the pages of my manuscript, but she waved her hand. 'I will look at it later,' she said. 'There's plenty of time.'

She assumed a bored expression then, and said that she had tired of England, that London was growing apace and encroaching upon her home the way a cancer consumed and blighted anything that stood in its way. India, she said, that was where she must go. It was where her father had made his money, where adventure and opportunity lay. She told me she could speak Hindi, as well as Pashtu, Urdu and some other languages the names of which I cannot recall. Languages were her forte. I said I was glad of it, for I had nothing but English, and the Latin and Greek my botany required of me.

'Your father suggested I take you with me,' she said. 'As a companion. An assistant. I am looking for new plants and I need someone knowledgeable to help.' Her lip curled. 'He said you are in love. A Dr Bain?'

'Yes,' I replied.

'Well, love is one thing. Getting married is another. I hope you are not thinking of that.' She did not wait for my answer. 'Anyone who marries before the age of twenty-five is a fool. Any woman with a fortune who gets married at all is an even bigger one.'

But I was not about to discuss my feelings for Alexander with a woman I had only just met, and so I rattled my cup back into its saucer and said, 'What on earth is that smell?' I covered my nose and mouth with my handkerchief – something I had been longing to do since I had entered the place.

She rose to her feet. 'You will have to get used to it if you are in love with a man who works at St Saviour's Infirmary.' She gave a smile I did not like, and said, 'It's rotting flesh. Come, I'll show you.'

She moved quickly, so that if she had not been pulling me by the hand I would have lost her in the greenery.

Is that what it will be like if I go with her to India? Forever trailing in her wake, dragged towards who-knows-what, even if it stinks like the very Devil? I will have to watch her – and myself – she is as bossy as a school mistress, and as beguiling as a

Siren, for I am intrigued by her, I cannot deny it. I do not think she has my best interests at heart, but only her own – whatever those might be. Father tells me that I say this only because she is different. Bathsheba Wilde is a spirited woman, he says, spirited and wealthy. I believe he thinks that a spell abroad with her will cure me of my feelings for Alexander. And yet, when my father asked, 'But what makes you mistrust her, Cathy? Did something happen at Nightshade today?' I did not answer him.

I still have the stink of that glasshouse in my nostrils, even as I write. I remember the cold touch of wet fronds brushing against my cheek. On my left the resinous glint of sap oozing from a lesion in the bark of a tree I did not recognise; on my right, the flabby leaves and petals of orchids as fat and pale as the fingers of dead men. Bathsheba Wilde spoke to me over her shoulder, gesturing first to one plant and then to another. I could not quite hear what she said, and so I did not reply. No doubt she thought I was a dolt, a stupid ignorant girl who hardly knew how to speak to her betters, no matter what my father might have told her to the contrary.

We emerged into a clearing. The smell of corruption was thicker there, the light that filtered through the dirty glass panes overhead dim and murky. On all sides there was a multitude of queer little plants, scores of short fleshy tubes and thick-lipped trumpets, moist and glistening and threaded with scarlet veins.

'These are my carnivores,' she said, spreading her arms wide. 'I have over three hundred, each with their cluster of little open mouths, their wet waiting throats. My brother loved them.' She put out a finger and caressed a fat pendulous bladder streaked with crimson. 'But they are mine now, every one of them. He was ill. His heart, you know. It killed him in the end.' She sighed. 'And

*so I fed a tiny morsel of his most beloved flesh to each of them.'
Her face was in shadow, though I knew she was watching me.
'No doubt you think it bizarre.'*

*I did not trust myself to speak. I knew her brother was recently
dead. I knew she had inherited everything. How she had chosen to
deal with his remains was no concern of mine. But she was clearly
waiting for an answer, and so I shook my head. 'No, Miss Wilde.'
It was not the first lie I had told, and she knew it.*

*'Come, come,' she said. 'We must be honest with one another
if we are to make a success of things. You think it bizarre that I
should feed my brother to my plants?'*

*'Surely you exaggerate, Miss Wilde.' I tried to sound blunt.
Unemotional. A little impatient, even, at her sensational claim.
'One could not feed an entire man to a collection this size. You
would need far more. Thousands more.'*

*She seemed pleased at my answer. 'A measured and logical
response, Miss Underhill,' she said. 'Most of him I left intact,
obviously. But I did take certain . . . parts. The soft parts. The
parts that had meant so much to him. That mean so much to any
man.' Her face was a mask.*

*The soft parts? I felt my stomach squirm. 'Well,' I said, 'certainly
it is without doubt a most singular practice to feed any human
parts to a plant.' And then added, 'But if his plants were his
passion, and if the . . . dissection and the . . . the distribution of
the flesh were done with love—'*

*'Ah, my dear Miss Underhill.' She raised her hand and stroked
my cheek with the back of her fingers. 'How much you still have
to learn.'*

Chapter Four

Dr Christian's address was to the west of Fishbait Lane. We would have been able to walk the half mile easily but noting Will's pale cheeks and bloodless lips I bundled him into a hansom. We sat in silence, side by side, as the cab trundled through the crowded streets. Will put his head back against the hard leather of the seat and closed his eyes. He had been working hard in the garden for the past three days and the work had done him good, but I could tell he was as unsettled as I was to have dug a corpse from beneath his own feet. Might there be more? What other secrets were we to unearth? As much as I hoped we would find Dr Christian alive and well and keen to talk to us, part of me wished he was dead, and the mystery might remain forever unsolved.

The cab turned into a broad thoroughfare lined with tall stone walls. The house we were after stood at the end, behind gates of black iron flanked by towering sandstone gateposts, each carved with fruits and vines, and crowned with a grinning skull. Soot had gathered thickly in the stone eye sockets, streaking down the cheeks like the coursing of foul tears. Beyond, behind an unkempt yew hedge and the tangled branches of oak and hazel, I could see a house. Dark and box-like, its façade was mottled with damp and clutched by snaking fingers of ivy. The building seemed curiously low in the ground, though this was merely an optical illusion caused by a high, flat apron of lawn to the front, which gave the impression that the place had sunk into the moist earth up to its ground floor window frames. We could see a light, dim and yellow, as if from a single candle, at an upstairs window. Smoke trickled from only one of the numerous chimneys. Overhead a rook screamed, nests clotting the high branches of a row of tall trees that lined the rutted drive.

I asked the cabby to wait for us in the street. He seemed reluctant, peering up at the weeping black skulls, though he agreed to it readily enough once I had presented him with another few shillings and the promise of more if he was still there when we returned. 'But if we don't come out after an hour you may leave.'

He pulled out his pocket watch and examined its face. 'One hour, and not a moment longer.'

Will pushed at one of the heavy iron gates. It screamed our arrival, sending rooks cawing and flapping into the muddy sky like scraps of cloth whirled in a storm drain.

Close up the house was no less sinister. The windows were dirty and unlit, those on the upper storeys thickly barred, as if to prevent whoever might be up there from throwing the casement wide and leaping out. My satchel bumped against my hip as we approached, so that for the first time I wondered at the wisdom of bringing the skull of the dead man with me. But it was too late now, and I had no intention of showing the thing to Dr Christian if it did not seem appropriate to do so.

The door was opened by a woman, a housekeeper, the great bundle of keys at her waist proclaiming her role and responsibilities. 'Good afternoon,' I began, sweeping off my hat. 'My name is Jeremiah Flockhart, from the apothecary on Fishbait Lane. I wonder if we might speak with Dr Christian?'

'The doctor?' She smiled a little. 'I doubt it. But you can speak to the mistress.' She did not bother with the deferential 'sir' that was customary amongst servants, but stared at me, her expression insolent. I could see she was gazing at the red birthmark on my face, as so many people did, ignoring the person beneath and focusing solely on the distracting mask of crimson skin that covered my eyes and nose. She pulled open the door. 'But not him.' She gestured to Will.

'We come together, madam,' I said. 'Where I go, Mr Quartermain goes. And I insist that we both speak to Mrs Christian. At once, if you please.' She shrugged at that, as if she had said what she had been told to say and did not care one way or the other what the outcome might be. We stepped into the hall. It was illuminated by candles – cheap, homemade ones – and the stink of tallow was heavy in the air. The wicks needed trimming, and each dismal taper released a trembling wraith of smoke. There was an odour of age and the passing of time about the place – dust, yellowed pages, stale ink. The smell of drains and chamber pots too reminded me uncomfortably of the Infirmary, which had always reeked of the privy, no matter how often I had thrown open the windows or made the orderlies scrub the place with lime wash.

The woman took up a candle and moved off into the gloom. She led us past the foot of a broad staircase, its uncarpeted treads as dark and sticky looking as molasses, and down a long hall. The walls on either side were hung with formless landscapes and pale, expressionless faces. Up ahead, a crimson glow told where a fire danced and flickered. There was now another smell on the air, sweetish, musty, familiar. Opium.

Like the rest of the house, the room was dark, save for the fire and a candle that burned on the mantelpiece. The wall at the back was lined from floor to ceiling with books. In the middle of the floor was a large mahogany table, leather topped, its surface scuffed and stained with ink blots. Books, papers, pens, penknives, blotter and inkstand were set out side by side in order of size. A chair with a threadbare cushion on its seat showed where someone had been sitting. On the table before it was a page of cheap yellow paper covered in a tiny copperplate handwriting. Beside it, a multitude of other, similarly covered pages were neatly stacked in a ream some three inches high. A book lay open, the type annotated with the same tiny handwriting. In the corner of the room stood a tall screen, decorated with flowers and leaves, but stained and darkened with years of dust and smoke.

The housekeeper led us towards the fire, where a man sat, unmoving, in a wing-backed chair. Without a word of introduction she vanished back the way she had come. I shivered. It was a room that would be as cold and dark as a cave no matter what the season, or the time of day. No wonder the man we had come to see had his chair pulled as close as possible to the smouldering mound of coals in the grate.

'Dr Christian?' I said. The man remained where he was, his eyes fixed upon the flames, his body like a collection of twigs swathed in a black wool suit that had once clothed a much bigger man.

There was a movement in the shadows, and a voice said, 'Miss Flockhart?'

'Mr.' I looked towards the direction of the voice. '*Mr* Flockhart, former apothecary to—'

'St Saviour's, yes.' A woman stepped forward from where she had been standing beside the half-shuttered window. 'I know who you are.'

'Evidently not, ma'am,' said Will. 'If you think you are speaking to a lady.'

The woman stared at him. 'I have no idea who *you* are, young man.'

'Forgive me, Mrs Christian, I'm—'

'I was not asking to be enlightened,' she said. 'I was simply stating a fact.' She pointed to the back wall, to the shelves of books. 'Stand over there. That's it. In the corner. Now don't speak again, if you please. If you must stay, then you will stay in silence.' Will threw me a bemused glance and did as he was instructed. Once he was in the shadows I could hardly see him at all.

Mrs Christian was tall and thin. She was clothed entirely in black, her dress high at the neck and close at the bodice. Her waist and arms were tightly sheathed so that she reminded me of a spider, its soft innards encased in a stiff, inflexible exoskeleton of starched and pin-tucked silk. On top of this she wore an apron of rough canvas, and, bizarrely, a pair of leather gardening gloves, as if she was about to begin pruning bushes outside. Her face was so pale, however, it was clear she had not been out in the sun for years. She waved me towards a chair that stood empty before the fire, positioned so that the afternoon light – what there was of it – might illuminate my face whilst keeping my interlocutor in the shadows. 'I have come to see Dr Christian,' I said. I looked at the figure slumped before the fire. 'Is this he?'

'What remains of him,' she replied. She held her hand to her throat, as if to steady her racing heart. 'And I am his wife. What is it you want from us, *Mr* Flockhart? We get very few visitors these days.'

'How do you know who I am?' I said.

'Because I knew your mother,' she replied. 'And you look just like her.' I hardly knew what to say. I had always assumed I took after my father. Was I really like her? But then Mrs Christian was speaking again. 'What do you want? I have a lot of work to do.'

'We found a skeleton beneath the deadly nightshade in my physic garden. The nightshade has been growing in that spot since the garden was laid out some thirty years ago.'

For a moment I thought she was about to faint. It was hardly possible for her complexion to grow paler, but it did, her lips turning bloodless, her flesh taking on a glimmering, sweaty appearance, visible even in that dim light of that dark room. 'Thirty-two,' she said. She put her hand to her breastbone. 'Winter and early spring, 1820.'

'That's correct. We've a plan of the garden that bears that date as well as your husband's name. I wondered what he could remember—'

Her eyes flickered, like those of a snake, though I was sure she had not blinked. She smiled, though there was neither humour nor love in it. 'By all means ask him any question you please.' She turned to the man who still sat motionless in his chair. 'Robert!' she cried. 'Robert! It's Cathy's child come to see you.' Her voice was loud, as if she were calling to someone far away. 'Robert!' He did not move. She clicked her tongue. 'You try,' she said.

'Dr Christian.' I pulled my chair around so that I might face him. 'Dr Christian, do you remember my father, Jeremiah Flockhart the apothecary at St Saviour's? Perhaps you recall Dr Bain? He always spoke so highly of you. Or my mother, Catherine. She was Catherine Underhill then.'

Like a man moving under water, Dr Christian slowly turned his head. I saw then that there was nothing left of him, nothing left at all. His mind, once sharp and enquiring, was gone and what remained was a husk, an empty shell with vacant staring eyes. His mouth hung slack and drooling, his gaze dead. Could he see me? What visions was he lost in, trapped inside his head behind those pin-prick pupils?

'I fear he remembers nothing about anything or anyone,' said Mrs Christian. 'His mind is destroyed beyond all hope of redemption. His soul too, no doubt.'

'By what, madam?' I whispered. 'What's caused this?'

'There's only so much the mind can take,' she said. 'Testing what nature and experience know to be poison, searching for the body's responses – the accelerated beating of the heart, the rapturous reaction of the mind, the diminishment of pain. The pursuit of knowledge has led him to the brink of madness. Now, without opium, he is quite insane. With it he is as you see him, a gaunt wraith trapped in a world no one but he can see.' She sighed. 'I would put him in Angel Meadow Asylum but, when all is said and done, we can watch him well enough here. And there are moments when he is almost lucid.' She peered at him. 'But not today.'

'Dr Christian—' I tried again. This time I pulled the skull from my satchel and held it up before him. His eyes shifted slightly in his ashen face. The whites were yellowish, the irises blank grey discs, the pupils at their centre so small as to be barely visible. I could not tell whether he was seeing me or not, though his gaze appeared to be trained in my direction.

'How long has he been like this?' I said.

'On this occasion? Two days. Usually he's lying on the *charpoi*.' She indicated a low bed that was pushed to one side in the shadows. Before it, a red glow proclaimed the position of the opium lamp and pipe. No wonder the air was thick with the smell of it. 'I'm surprised we managed to rouse him sufficiently to get him into this chair.' Dr Christian's skin had taken on an oily sheen, and in the warmth from the fire the smell of him was sickening.

I put the skull down on the table beside him and slipped my hand into my satchel. The movement caused him to flinch, as if he feared I was about to produce another body part, another bone. He turned his dreadful gaze upon me, and then all at once his expression of gaunt emptiness vanished and his face resolved into a look of sheer terror. He reared up, screaming out a babble of words and throwing up his arms as if warding off blows, though I had not moved a muscle towards him. I staggered back, shocked by his transformation. 'What's he saying?' I said. 'What does he want? I was only going to leave you something to purge his bowels.'

'He's speaking Hindi,' she said. 'Sometimes it is Urdu, sometimes Pathan, or Maratha, sometimes a mixture. And he doesn't want anything, not even your purgatives.'

'He said my mother's name. He said Catherine, didn't you hear him? In amongst the other words. It was quite distinct.'

'No,' she said, 'I did not hear any such thing.'

Dr Christian sank back into his chair. I could see I would get nothing from him, so I turned to his wife. 'Then perhaps, Mrs Christian, *you* might be able to help me.'

'Oh, you want *my* help now, do you? Now that the great Robert Christian's brain has proved too addled to be of use? It is a pity you didn't ask me first. I'd have thought someone like *you* would not just assume that because *he* is a man and *I* am a woman that his opinion is worth seeking out first.'

'I'm sorry—'

'It's no good being *sorry*. Everyone is *sorry*. But they don't mean it. The only thing they are sorry about is that they have to listen to a woman talking, a woman giving them the answers they are looking for.'

'I just thought that as the author of Christian's *Materia Medica*, he—'

'Ha!' she spat. 'Why, he would never have written *any* of that if it wasn't for me.' She looked in disgust at her husband. 'He's weak. Always has been. Weak, but reckless. He never had the strength for the things he did to himself.'

'I believe the body in my physic garden is a man,' I said, deciding to plunge onwards, and unwilling to be distracted by 'things' Dr Christian had done to himself.

'Dark hair, some six feet in height, walking with a limp, or on crutches, judging by the condition of his bones.' Mrs Christian's face, etiolated from a life indoors, glimmered like an alabaster death's-head in the firelight. 'He was travelling with a monkey. And he had one eye.' I held up the skull again. 'You can see the gash here from the wound that caused the loss of his eye. He will have been a very distinctive character, I believe.' I was babbling, I knew, but I could not stop. 'Your name was on the plan for the physic garden too. I just wondered if you could tell us – tell me—'

'Tell you what?'

'Anything.'

'Are you accusing me of murder?'

'No.'

'Then what?'

'Did you know him?'

One of the coals in the fire let off a *crack*, as loud as a pistol shot. I jumped, though neither Dr nor Mrs Christian moved a muscle. There was silence once more, interrupted only by the slow tick of an unseen clock.

'I have no knowledge of such a man,' she said at last.

'But surely you must remember—'

'I think I *would* remember someone who looked as you have described.'

'He had a monkey,' I said desperately. 'Would you not remember a one-eyed man with a monkey?'

'Such a sight is hardly remarkable in this city.'

'But—'

'I remember your mother though.'

I felt my heart leap inside me. At the same time I knew I was being deflected from following a more awkward line of questioning. In the shadows, at the periphery of the room, I saw Will reach up and slide a book off one of the shelves. 'Did you?' I said. 'What was she like?'

'She was not married when I knew her. She married your father later.'

'What was she like?' I repeated. Might Mrs Christian have something she could tell me about her? Perhaps a tale that would make her human, alive, something more than a painted face in a locket, an empty dress, a signature on the flyleaf of a book. 'She died when I was a baby. I have always wondered—'

'She was hard-working. Knew as much about medicinal plants, and about botany, as anyone. As much as Dr Christian and myself. She looked just like you,' she went on. 'Though not so tall.'

'There must be more,' I said. 'Please—'

'She was secretive.' Mrs Christian turned ice blue eyes upon me. 'And rather aloof. I have no idea why. She kept her own counsel – unless she was talking about plants, of course. I suppose that was all she was *supposed* to talk about, so perhaps she might be forgiven for not joining in more. But she was one of us nonetheless, we saw to that. She had to be. She came to India with us, you know. Years ago.'

'She did?' Another thing my father had never mentioned. 'I had no idea.'

'Oh yes. We were looking for plants – medicines, mainly – for the gardens at St Saviour's, and Chelsea, for Kew – all the finest places. Your mother was an able botanist and a keen observer.'

'An observer?' I said. 'Of what?'

'Of everything, Mr Flockhart.' All at once she stood up.

'I can give you something that was hers. A folio. I've had it since . . . well, for a long time. There was a mix up with the baggage on the way home and some of her books came to me. I thought I had returned them all, but somehow this one is still here.' She went to the desk.

'May I ask what you are writing, ma'am?' I said, glancing at the desk.

'It is a monograph about how we might find God in nature.'

'Oh!' I said. I could not keep the surprise out of my voice. The dusty apron, the gardening gloves, and pruning knife that lay on the table – I had expected her to be writing about botany. 'But you are known for your books on flora and fauna,' I said. 'Your *Flowers of India and the Himalaya* is a very fine work. It cemented your reputation as both a botanist and an explorer and was a welcome change to all those "ladies' books" on horticulture.'

She waved a dismissive hand. '*Flowers of India* was a manual, no more. These days I'm more interested in the way the natural world reflects and embodies the plan of the Creator. We are closest to God when we are in the garden. Think of Eden. Gethsemane.'

'I see,' I said, though in fact the only thing I could see was that she never went into the garden and had not been in it for a number of years.

'Your mother was a woman of great independence, great strength of character and determination. Her mind was sharp, enquiring, adventurous. These are the reasons she was chosen. I imagine you're very similar, why else would you have found your way here?'

'Chosen?' I said quickly. 'For what? By whom?'

'By your father, of course.' I had the feeling this was not

what she had meant at all, but the moment had passed, and she was thrusting into my hands a large folio, bound in dark blue fabric and tied with a black silk ribbon. 'Here. Take it.'

'May I look?'

She shrugged, her eyes darting to her husband. 'If you must.'

It was a large volume, some twelve inches by ten, the boards cloth-bound, with the words *An Indian Poison Garden* embossed in gold on the spine and the front cover. To my delight, it contained some twenty-five hand-painted botanical illustrations. Expensive to produce, quite possibly unique, it was undated, and without a named author. I turned the thick pages. The colours seemed to leap out at me, bringing with them the warmth and vibrancy of that distant continent: thick, sensual strawberry-and-cream petals of *Nerium oleander*; tall, pale furls and spiked, quartered pods of the *Datura stramonium*; the round orange fruits of our old friend *Strychnos nux-vomica*. *Parthenium, cassava, aconite, Ricinus* . . . Page after page of death in its most exquisite guises. For reasons I could not fully explain I felt tears prick at my eyes. To see such flowers in their natural habitat would be a delight indeed. Had my mother felt the same? Had she seen these plants when she was in India? Why had my father never mentioned that she had travelled? I felt a familiar stab of rage against him. I had never understood this silence, and I did not believe I ever would. Something small and membranous that had been hidden between the pages fluttered to the floor – a pressed flower, a memory of something I could only guess at. I held it up. It was hard to see what it was in that dark cave of a room.

'Looks like Indian Nightshade,' said Mrs Christian. '*Atropa acuminata*. You see it was once a yellowish colour? The deadly nightshade flowers most of us are familiar with are purple. It's a different strain, *Atropa belladonna*, though the effects of both are the same.'

But I could not reply. I was staring at a small cluster of words, written on the inside cover of the folio Mrs Christian had given me. The date was some seven years before my parents' marriage.

20ᵗʰ May 1818.

For my darling Cathy.
Something to remember me by.
With love, always,
Alexander.

Mrs Christian had already turned away, so she did not notice how distracted I was. I slammed the book closed and stuffed it into my satchel alongside the skull before she could change her mind and ask for it back. She was at the desk again, looking down at her work and I knew she was itching to return to it. 'Your mother is dead, *Mr* Flockhart,' she said as she sat back down. 'She took her secrets with her, and you will not find any of them here.' She nodded towards the door. I had not noticed her tugging a bell-pull, but a maid had appeared all the same. 'I have told you all I can. Please don't come to this house again.'

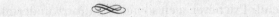

Will followed me out of the room in silence. His expression was stony. 'A medical man enslaved by his own addiction, his mind destroyed by the wilful testing of poisons?' he said as the door closed behind us. 'This is a warning, Jem. You see what you may become if you start working on that *Treatise on Poison* you're always talking about?' I saw his glance dart to my satchel, the way the skull inside distorted the leather, and I knew he wished more than anything that he had never found that twisted skeleton, that it had been left forever hidden in the cold dark earth. If only he had not dug so deep.

I was about to tell him I was *not* always talking about it, and that our visit had been more than worthwhile, as I now had in my bag a folio that had been gifted to my mother by Dr Bain, but Will was still talking. 'And there's something else too,' he muttered. 'While you were waving that skull in Dr Christian's face and being babbled at in Hindi, I took the opportunity to browse the bookshelves. Every single book from A to P is filled with scribblings, exclamation marks, question marks, underlined words. I could make no sense of it at all. My overall impression was of someone searching for an idea too elusive ever to be found.'

'And after P?' I said.

'Nothing. I can only assume she has only just reached Q.' He shook his head. 'They were all books on natural history, plants and flowers mostly, but also fungi, moss, lichen, geography, history. It was the same on her desk. All those pages scribbled with ink. She was writing out the bits she had underlined. Nothing more! To what end? I've never seen so much industry undertaken for no useful purpose. She might say it's about God's presence in the garden, but it looks like the obsessive ravings of a madwoman to me!'

'Let's look about the grounds a little,' I said.

'But why?' He pulled out his watch. 'Our cabby will be gone in ten minutes, and this is a horrible place.'

'I'm curious, that's all.'

'I want to go home. I want a cup of tea. You see she did not even offer us refreshment? I had to stand at the back where it was cold and draughty, like a naughty schoolboy. I'm surprised she didn't make me wear a pointed hat with the letter D painted on it!'

'I can make you one, if you would like,' I said.

'I can make my own. I will be sure to bring it with me next time.'

'Let's see what's at the back of the house. It's south facing, I think there might be something of interest there.' Ignoring his objections, I ushered him into the shrubbery, so that we might be concealed from view as we made our way round the side of the building.

The rear of the house looked out over a courtyard, a small scrubby patch of grass and a wall darkly cloaked from top to bottom with ivy. It rustled gently, as if the leaves whispered to one another in the gathering dusk. Half hidden by the greenery was a small door, ribbed and weathered with age, and bearing a dark patina where hands and shoulders had shoved it open time and again. 'Come along,' I whispered. 'We'll just have a peep.'

'What if it's locked?'

'Then I will stand on your shoulders,' I said. What was the matter with him, I thought? He was usually game for anything. 'Or I can climb up the ivy. It looks strong enough to support me.'

The door was not locked, but neither was I able to get it open. It moved no more than an inch, something on the other side preventing it from opening further. At our back, the house loomed, its windows yawning down at us. 'Someone might be watching, Jem,' hissed Will.

'Let me stand on your shoulders,' I said.

'Certainly not! This is a new topcoat, I don't want your filthy boots all over it.'

'Then take it off.'

'I will not take it off!'

'Shh!' I said. 'Do you want them to hear us? You can at least give me a leg up. Come along, Will!'

He sighed. He put his hat to one side, took off his new coat, and made a stirrup of his hands. I stepped into it, dragging myself up the ivy, searching for a foothold against the gnarled and looped branches so that I might haul myself higher. I peered over the top.

Below me was a giant walled garden. I could see that once, a long time ago, the garden had been truly glorious. Even in decay there was still a semblance of order, the remains of raised beds, the ground set out in meandering terraces, a rock garden. Now, however, whatever order and beauty had once existed had been consumed by a wilderness, a tangled thicket of weeds and grass that grew everywhere in monstrous profusion. The door which we had been unable to open was gripped by the tangled claws of a clematis. The wall upon which I was perched was unstable, the mortar loose from the depredations of ivy and jasmine. I saw the decayed remains of nettles standing some five feet tall, and brambles in huge prickly arches. Crowds of opium poppy seed-heads peered out over the tangled vista, like curious stick-men. Amongst it all I recognised more rarefied species: the late flowering aconite, protected from frost by the walls, had still not died back. I saw hogweed, laburnum, yew, dogbane. And over everything a creeping sea of rustling bindweed. At its heart, like a monstrous glass lung, a once-magnificent glasshouse sagged. Its windows were glittering spikes of broken glass, a wild mass of green and brown lurking within. I had never seen such a vision of decay and neglect.

I clambered down, taking care not to stand on Will's precious hat, which he had foolishly placed almost directly in my path. 'I don't think anyone has been in there for decades,' I said.

'Why did you want to look?'.

'Dr Christian was once extremely capable, and his wife was as good a botanist as he, perhaps better. I could not believe that they did not have their own garden. She was dressed as though she had just been out in it, or was about to go, and yet clearly no one here does any gardening at all.' I brushed twigs and leaves from off my person and handed Will my handkerchief to wipe his hands. 'But the decay in this garden is not recent,' I said. 'It is not just neglected, it is abandoned. And I suspect from the pallor of both of them that neither ever leaves the house. You noted that the ivy covered the whole of the front of the building?'

'I did. And yet one window is kept clear – the one from which Mrs Christian can see the gates when she is seated at her table.'

'Exactly!' I clapped him on the shoulder. 'My dear Will, who, or what, is she waiting for?'

'I have no idea, but it is evidently important that she remain vigilant.'

'Dr Christian's condition perplexes me too,' I said. 'As does the fact that his wife was determined that we should see him in so pitiable a state. Most women would be at pains to hide their husband's addiction to opium, not show it off.'

'You think she drugs him?'

'No, though I suspect she colludes in his habit.'

'Perhaps to keep him biddable, as she suggested.'

'That may well be true, but she could have told us that he was asleep, made excuses for his absence. Why let us see him like that?'

'I suppose it would have been kinder of her to pretend he was indisposed,' said Will. 'We are strangers, after all.'

'Ah, but that might risk us coming back at a later date when we might find him coherent. I think she wanted us to see him as a hopeless wreck of a man, Will, unable to think or speak. I have no doubt that Dr Christian is not the man he used to be, but I suspect there is still enough of his mind left for him to tell us something about the corpse we have exhumed, and how and why it came to be buried in our garden. He knows *something*, Will. So does she, I am certain of it. The only question that perplexes me is how she knew we were coming? We only found the body yesterday.'

'I think I can answer that, Jem. This was on the floor beside the desk.' He put his hand in his pocket, and drew out a crumpled piece of paper. Thick, luxurious note-paper, it had neither watermark nor address. Across it, in a bold scrawl, were four words: *He has been found.*

Excerpts from the diary of Catherine Underhill.

20th May 1818

Evening

When I arrived at Nightshade House I was determined to go nowhere with Miss Wilde. At least, I was determined to go nowhere that took me away from London. By the time I left I had changed my mind. Bathsheba Wilde is the most unusual woman I have ever met. She makes me feel as though I could do anything and go anywhere; that there should be no restrictions on women, that we should be as free as men to do as we please, so that by the time I left today I had agreed to everything she wanted. How had I become so changed? I am not irresolute. Nor am I easily swayed – Father says I am the most stubborn woman he ever knew. When I think about what happened I am glad I can confide it to this diary, as I do not think I could ever explain it to anyone. And yet I must write it down, for already what occurred seems like a dream to me. By tomorrow morning I may well be unable to recall it at all. I still feel strange inside – dizzy and curiously hungry – though this may be because I have come to bed without any supper. Father asked me what ails me, but I told him it is nothing.

I remember being in the greenhouse, sipping tea with her. How luxurious it had felt sitting on silk cushions surrounded by orchids, amaryllis, lotus flowers. I remember how mesmerised I was by her birds, her plants, her silks, the sound of water somewhere in the greenery. She had lolled back on a divan and put a hookah pipe to her lips. The bottle bubbled as she sucked.

'Will you not try some?' Her eyes were so dark, I could not see their pupils. She had laughed when I refused. 'Very well, Cathy,' she said. 'But we will make a native of you yet, won't we, Jane?' She smiled at a dark-faced girl standing amongst the foliage. 'Jane is my maid and companion,' she added. 'Country born, of course. We both are. It's something much misprized in the Company's India, I'm afraid, but I have not let it stop me. I tell Jane it should not stop her either. It is her first trip to London. She will be returning with us, of course.' She smiled and lay back on her mound of silken cushions. I asked her what 'country born' meant and she told me it meant that one had been born in India. She told me that British people in India all called England 'home' no matter whether they had been born there or not. Many of those who were country born had never even set foot in the place they called 'home'. 'But India is home to me, as much as this place is. I am a true hybrid. Come,' she said, offering me the pipe once more. 'There is nothing to fear.'

This time I put it to my lips. I had no idea what it was. It was not opium, for I know the smell of opium well enough from my father. I breathed in the smoke. What was it? She did not tell me, and after that first time I no longer cared. Her face smiled down at me as if from behind a veil of gauze, her hair wild about her shoulders in a great dark halo. Its tendrils seemed to move, writhing about her head as if she were crowned by a nest of snakes. And yet I felt no fear. Instead, a warmth seemed to seep into my bones. My senses felt sharpened, and I found that I was gazing at her, marvelling at the way the coloured silks draped across her body, cool and comfortable and light as gossamer. I could see the curve of her breasts and belly, her strong arms and long, slender thighs, and the rhythmic rise and fall of her breathing, and it seemed to me that she was clothed in the wings of butterflies. Not like me, constrained in my corset, as stiff and unyielding as a beetle. I remember hearing the gold bracelets that encircled her wrists chime as they struck against each other, the rare London sunlight piercing through the foliage like knives. And then I felt cool hands at my neck, her fingers against mine as she helped me to loosen my dress. I took a gasp of air and, with a sense of such blessed release that I could not find it in myself to protest, I felt my corset part. I lay back. The pipe was against my lips once more.

'I prefer this place to any other room in the house,' I heard her say. 'It makes me think of home, and I don't mean England when I say that. But the corset is a continual reminder of London. The sooner you can rid yourself of it, the better.' She sighed, and closed languid eyes, the smoke trailing in tendrils from her nostrils. 'Oh, but the warmth is glorious, don't you think? Jane keeps the boiler going, as we must maintain the correct temperature for the orchids.' She sank lower into the cushions. 'Of course it's nothing like the heat up country. That is a different matter altogether. You will beg me to undo your corset long before we even reach Calcutta.'

'Is that our destination?' I heard a voice say. It sounded familiar to me, but I could not say with any confidence that it was my own. I recall looking about to see whether there was anyone else there; whether the girl Jane had spoken. But she had disappeared.

'Oh,' said Bathsheba (I must not call her Miss Wilde, she says), 'Calcutta is just the start. You will see soon enough once we get there.'

Somehow, I felt entirely satisfied by so inadequate a reply. I still do, though my rational self tells me I ought to feel only concern.

Thinking back, I can recall little but the foliage. So thick and green, pulsing and throbbing with life so that I could not tear my gaze away. I felt as though I could hear the plants themselves breathing, hear the sound of moisture oozing from their pores, gathering in oily droplets on their firm, succulent flesh. I tried to put up a hand, to touch one of them, but although my body felt as light as air, I found I could not move a muscle. Even now, sitting at this table in the light of my candle, my hands feel as though they are not my own, as though I am watching someone else move the pen across the page, and back and forth to the inkstand.

'This smoke is from the seeds of the Cannabis indica,' she said. Her voice seemed very far away. 'Do you like it? I mix it with a little something of my own.' She smiled again. 'What I have in this hookah is the stuff of princes. Beloved by fakirs and philosophers.'

I have no idea how long I slept. When I awoke it was from a deep, warm slumber. Lamps had been lit, and set down amongst the greenery, where they glowed like the ghostly lights of ships lost in the deep.

'Good evening,' said a voice behind me as I stirred. 'I didn't like to wake you. You looked so peaceful and happy. Were you dreaming about your Dr Bain?'

'No, Miss Wilde,' I replied.

'Bathsheba,' she said. 'I am Bathsheba. I insist upon it.'

I struggled to my feet, and found I was standing in my underthings. My dress was draped on a chair beneath a tangled mass of vines on the far side of the clearing. I saw that she had taken out my manuscript, and had been looking through its pages, though she did not say anything about it to me. I reached up to pull my corset tight once more, to adjust the pins in my hair.

'You might want to cut that off,' she said casually. 'Short hair makes everything much easier.'

'I haven't said I am coming with you,' I said.

'Oh, but you will,' she replied. 'Travel will do you good, my dear. Travel does everyone good.'

Bathsheba Wilde strikes me as a singular character, and although I did not warm to her – in fact I find her provoking and macabre – I must confess to feeling intrigued. She told me she had known my father many years ago in Bengal, when he was a young man. She said she had much to thank him for, as it was he who had encouraged her love of botany. The revelation that she had once had some sort of relationship with my father makes me feel – what? I hardly know how to describe it – it is not jealousy, more a possessiveness. He is my father, all I have in the world. She does not know him as I do.

I have agreed to go to India with her.

Chapter Five

The following day was busy in the apothecary. Winter was our most lucrative season. I had allowed my stock of remedies to dwindle somewhat while I had been distracted with Will's illness, and there was much to make up for. We had bronchial mixture to boil, and cough drops to prepare. I had a new recipe I wanted to try for a eucalyptus and clove liniment, and a tincture of echinacea and sage to be applied to inflamed tonsils needed my full attention. The shop bustled with activity, Jenny grinding cloves, Gabriel boiling honey, Mrs Speedicut stitching muslin bags that we would fill with spike lavender to be used against the moths. Even Will was at work, sugaring the pills of senna that we sold in the hundreds to our wealthiest constipated lady customers. The air was warm and sweet, filled with the scents of summer and autumn and the fragrance of lands far from ours where the sun always shone. At the back of the apothecary the bones lay in the shadows in a dark heap. I could not stop thinking about them.

At half past eleven I went out with Will to deliver some medicines. We were gone for a couple of hours. When we came back, I was surprised to find the street outside the apothecary thronged with people. They stood about murmuring and pointing, men, women and children peering in at my windows while they waited to shove their way inside. I saw urchins amongst them, their thieving hands reaching for purses and pocketbooks. In unexpected contrast, a private coach with a coat of arms emblazoned on its doors was just moving away from our door. 'Word of your warm tonsil tincture has evidently reached the gentry already, Jem,' murmured Will. 'Perhaps the Queen will arrive at any moment. I hope you'll make her wait in line, like everyone else.'

'They aren't waiting in line though, are they?' I said. 'This is more like a scrum! What on earth is going on?' I turned to address a woman who was standing in the doorway. She was balanced on her tiptoes trying to see over the shoulder of the man in front of her. 'Madam,' I said, 'why are you here?'

'The bones, sir,' she replied. 'In the *Police Gazette*. I came for a look. They say it's witchcraft!'

'Do they indeed!' I pushed my way inside. The shop was packed, but there was little talking. Instead, everyone was listening, rapt, to the voice that came from behind the counter. 'Found in our very own physic garden, ladies and gen'men, his mouth a-filled with deadly nightshade, his bones bent and twisted with poison . . . ' It was Gabriel. Gabriel! My own apprentice, standing on an upturned box and holding the skull of the dead man in one hand, and the silver bowl in the other. Beside him, Jenny flourished a pair of ivory skulls. A dozen more of the things were lined up along the counter in front of her. 'What dark end did he suffer?' he cried. 'What torments of pain? How long has he laid in the earth, trapped in silence while our feet walked above his head? *Unknowing* feet, ladies and gen'men. Did he collect the blood of others in this here bowl? Did he dance an evil dance an' juggle these here tiny skulls? P'raps he were a warlock, or a witch, a-castin' spells and hexes. Or a one-eyed pirate, on the run with his monkey, fleein' from vengeful shipmates. We will never know his secrets, ladies and gen'men. But look upon his bones and think on your own end, your own sins, your own *mortality*!'

'Gabriel,' I roared. 'Stop your foolery this instant!'

A hubbub broke out and cries of 'no!' and 'shame!' rippled through the crowd. People turned from Gabriel, and clustered around me. Was I the proprietor? Were the bones my property? Was there a reward for their identification? One woman declared that we had found the skeleton of the missing husband she had last seen in Ludlow some thirty years earlier. Another claimed it was her father, a notorious rogue and drunkard, but a clergyman too, who had vanished from Putney with the church's collection money in 1836. One after another they came at me, not one of them with anything useful or constructive to say, not one of them with information I could take seriously. I saw a man pluck the skull from Gabriel's grasp, so that for a moment it was borne aloft on the crowd, like a coconut bobbing on a restless sea. Two well-dressed women stood arm in arm beside me, watching the spectacle with serious faces. They wore bonnets adorned with flowers, their hair neatly parted in the middle and looped about their ears.

'How did you come by him?' asked one. 'Was there nothing else in the grave but the monkey, the ivory and the bowl?'

'How long was he there?' asked the other. 'Will you be able to find out what happened?'

A boy who was clambering on the shelves knocked a jar of sulphur powder to the floor. The stink of brimstone filled our nostrils. I saw another reaching for the liquorice root.

'A penny to touch his bones!' cried Gabriel. The crowd surged.

'Stop!' I shouted. 'Gabriel Locke, stop this *at once*!' Gabriel's cheeks turned bright red. He snatched the skull and shoved it out of sight beneath the counter. Jenny shot him an 'I told you so' look, and I heard the *clack . . . clack* of the two ivory skulls she held being dropped back into the sack with the others.

I was about to inform the crowd that the show was now over, and unless anyone had something they wished to buy would they all kindly leave the premises, when there was a commotion out in the street. I heard a raised voice, scuffling feet and the rattle of cab wheels. A man's face appeared at the window, pale as a ghost, the eyes wild and dark-ringed. Hatless, and without overcoat, he battered his hands upon the pane. 'Sir!' he screamed, his eyes staring straight at me. 'Sir!'

I pushed through the crowd and plunged back out into the street. 'Dr Christian,' I cried. 'What are you doing here?' But my words were drowned out by the noise of a carriage and pair hurtling towards us. Its driver was muffled up to the eyes in a dark scarf, his hat pulled down low. The vehicle seemed to fill the lane. The sound of wheels and hooves reverberated off the buildings, the crack of the whip sharp as a pistol shot in the air. I tried to usher Dr Christian into the shop, but the doorway was clogged with sightseers. Besides, he seemed to be rooted to the spot in fear and I could not get him to move an inch. The driver forced his horses to a standstill and sprang down. He seized the old man by the shoulders. At the coachman's touch, Dr Christian burst into life. 'No!' he screamed. 'No!'

'I know this man, sir,' I shouted, trying to push the coachman away. 'He is Dr Christian, and he has come to see me. Let him go!' At the sound of my voice Dr Christian began to thrash about in his captor's arms, twisting around and digging his yellow nails into the flesh of the man's cheeks. The fellow staggered back, his hands to his face. Released, Dr Christian plunged forward and seized my lapels.

'Cathy!' His voice was a hoarse whisper. 'Cathy!'

'Cathy was my mother,' I said. 'I am—'

'They've found him, Cathy!' he hissed. 'She'll be coming for us now!'

The coachman came forward once again, dashing the blood from his cheeks with the back of his hand and grabbing hold of Dr Christian's arms. By this time the crowd that had been inside the apothecary had surged outside, everyone wanting to see what was going on.

'Come along now, Dr Christian,' the coachman said. He was huge and burly, his caped coat straining over broad shoulders and back. There was nothing Dr Christian or I could do if such a man chose to bundle him, or anyone, into the carriage. Dr Christian maintained his grip upon my lapels, his eyes staring into mine. And then all at once his gaze slithered from my face to look over my shoulder and he cried out in fear. I looked behind me – who, or what, had he seen? A crowd of faces stared back – I saw the urchin who had reached for the liquorice root, the two women in bonnets standing arm in arm, the lady whose husband had gone missing from Ludlow. Was one of them familiar to him? I had no way of knowing, not unless he told me. Dr Christian had sunk to the ground in terror as if his legs had turned to rubber. I bent to haul him to his feet, the coachman and I pulling his limp body this way and that, like a pair of children fighting over a broken puppet. And then all at once Dr Christian recovered himself. He grabbed hold of my arms, his fingers as thin and sharp as sticks. He stared into my eyes, and for a moment his gaze was as clear and focused as mine.

He grinned, and said, 'The Devil is loose again now, Flockhart. Have a care what path you follow. You might not like what you find.' And then he flung himself from me, scrambling into the open door of the carriage. The coachman slammed it closed. 'Lock it!' screamed Dr Christian from inside. He stared out at the crowd in terror. '*Lock it!*' But the coachman had already produced a key from his pocket. He locked the door, sprang back up onto his seat and whipped his horses into motion. The carriage lurched forward, racing down the lane and out into St Saviour's Street as if Satan himself were after it.

At last everyone was gone. I made Gabriel clean out the leech tank, and then sent him and Jenny out with another delivery of medications. I was furious with them both and wanted them out of my sight for the rest of the day. I sent Mrs Speedicut out on a number of grocery-related errands. The silence was a relief as there was always one or other of them talking or making a noise or dropping something. Now, other than the snap and pop of the fire and the gentle ticking of the apothecary clock there was nothing. I had two bottles of ale I'd picked up from Sorley's on the way back to the apothecary, and two slices of game pie – on this occasion not from Sorley's – some apples, some relish. I set out our meal on pewter plates.

We had just begun when the door was shoved open, the bell dancing wildly on its spring as three women marched in. The light from the open door kept them silhouetted, though I recognised two of them as being the women who had stood arm in arm beside me earlier that day, asking me questions about the bones. The other I could not make out, though somehow she too was familiar. She was taller than her companions and had an air of authority. She stood before us with the two others at her back, the apothecary door wide open as if she expected someone else to close it. I had the feeling that she had deliberately chosen the time of day, when she knew the sun would be shining through the apothecary windows behind her, when I was most likely to be sitting down to lunch, so that she might loom over me, inspecting me at her leisure the way a naturalist might study a moth he had caught in his killing bottle. I squinted up at her, my mouth full of pheasant pie, and cursed myself for not locking the apothecary door while we ate.

I sensed rather than saw her critical appraisal, the smile that curved her lips. 'Well, well,' she said at last. 'This is not quite what I expected.'

'May I help you, madam?' said Will.

The woman did not reply. In fact, she ignored him entirely, and continued to stare at me. I swallowed my pie and took a swig of ale, before dabbing my lips and saying, 'I thought you were dead.'

'Certainly not,' said the woman. She turned to the two who had accompanied her. They were not young, both of them being over thirty years of age, though she addressed them as 'girls'. 'Girls,' she said. 'Come and meet Jemima Flockhart. Her mother was a friend of mine.' I darted a glance at Will, but he seemed not to have heard.

'*Jem* Flockhart,' I said. 'After my father.'

The woman inclined her head. 'As you wish, my dear. Clara, Bella, come along now, make yourselves known! And close the door, can't you?'

One of the 'girls' was sallow, her complexion made dull and greyish by the dreary English weather, her eyes large and dark above a sad, unsmiling rosebud mouth. The other was pale and fattish, her face pasty, her eyes wide-set above a flattened bridge to her nose. The hair that peeped out from beneath their bonnets was dark, though I suspected one of them had only achieved this by the application of black walnuts. The woman introduced them as 'Miss Clara Foster, my employee and companion, and Miss Belladonna Wilde, my late brother's daughter.' Miss Clara Foster kept her gaze fixed upon her gloves, her expression unsmiling. The other, Miss Belladonna Wilde, looked about her at my shelves, as if she had never seen such delights. She giggled and nibbled coyly at one of her gloved fingers with little stubby teeth.

'Will, this is Miss Bathsheba Wilde,' I began. 'Miss Wilde, this is—'

But she waved a dismissive hand and said, 'I know who he is.' She looked about the apothecary, and I knew I was being judged. 'Well,' she said after a moment, 'isn't this *nice*? But something of a change in circumstances, after so many generations as apothecary to St Saviour's Infirmary?' She raised her eyes to scan my shelves appraisingly. 'I remember your father *very* well and I hardly think he would approve of this. You're a doctor, not a jobbing apothecary. Is this the best you can do?' She turned to look at me. 'I know he made some interesting decisions about your upbringing, so I suppose he must have had something worthwhile about him,' and then, gesturing towards Will, 'can't you send this fellow away? I want to talk to you.'

'No,' I said. '"This fellow" stays exactly where he is. This is his house as much as it is mine and he comes and goes when he chooses.' I sat back and put my feet up on the stove top. I took an apple and cut a piece off it with my knife. I had the feeling that my casual manner and apparent indifference rather annoyed her, and I was glad about that. I suspected she wanted information, about the bones, about the other items we had found, and I was not prepared to give it. She cut an imposing figure in her long coat and high-heeled boots, with her ebony cane and her hair piled upon her head like a mass of snakes – quite the opposite of the flat, oily styles favoured by most ladies, including the two companions she had brought with her. Not that Bathsheba Wilde cared much for convention, I could see that. I waited in silence for her to speak.

'I knew your mother,' she said at last.

'I believe so,' I replied. I thought about her visit to St Saviour's apothecary, some fifteen years earlier, my efforts to find her. 'Though you have chosen to tell me nothing about her. But, no matter. Mrs Christian was most illuminating.'

For a moment I thought I saw a wariness in her eyes. Her gaze flickered from me, to Will, and back again. But it was a moment only, and then her superior manner returned. 'I'm sure she wasn't,' she said. There was silence.

Will cleared his throat. 'Would you care for some tea, ladies? Or perhaps some other refreshment? We have peppermint, camomile, or herbal mixtures for the digestion. Miss Foster? Miss Wilde?'

'Oh, call them Clara and Bella,' Bathsheba said without taking her eyes off me. 'All this formality! Quite unnecessary. And I will be Bathsheba. I need no other appellation. And no, we will not take tea.'

'You are an artist, Miss Clara?' I said.

'Yes.' She looked at me for the first time, her expression surprised. 'How did you know?'

'There is a smear of green paint on your wrist, and the smell of turpentine from a recent spillage – I fear the stuff leached into your skirts. Plus the satchel you carry. By the weight and shape of the thing I'd say it contains notebooks, drawing instruments, anything you might need to continue your craft. A far cry from the fashionable lady's reticule carried by Miss Bella.' I pointed to my own large bag, which lay on a chair beside me. 'I am never without mine. One simply never knows, does one?'

She smiled at me, her sallow face lighting up, her eyes sparkling. 'Indeed, sir, one never does.'

'May I offer you my condolences, madam,' I continued.

She coloured. 'How—'

'Your gloves,' I said. 'The ribbons in your bonnet, your dress.'

'My mother,' she muttered.

'Months ago now, Clara,' said Bathsheba. Her voice was as loud as a man's. 'I'm not saying you must forget about her, but is it not time you did something to dispense with your dolorous air?'

'I find her dolorous air quite soothing,' said Bella. 'And Clara has the complexion for mourning, she is so sallow.'

'I am here to see whether you are managing, *Mr* Flockhart,' said Bathsheba.

'Managing?' I blinked. 'Managing with what?

'I promised your mother I would make sure you were never in want. I'm your godmother. Did your father not tell you that?'

'My father never mentioned you,' I replied. I found it hard to believe he would have permitted a woman as tall and domineering as Bathsheba Wilde to be a godparent to his only child.

'I cannot say I'm surprised. Certainly, he never approved of me.'

'And I have never been in want of anything,' I said stiffly. 'Apart from a mother.'

'You blame me for that?'

'Why should I blame you for anything? I don't even know you.'

'You think I should have had more input into your upbringing?'

'On the contrary. I'm glad you held back.' I glanced at the 'girls' Clara and Bella. If these two were the product of her 'input' I considered myself fortunate to have been spared.

'I have always watched you. I know you remember me from when you were a child. Did you tell your father I had been that time? No? I thought it unlikely. That was as it should be.' She smiled. 'Our secret.'

'My father never mentioned you, so I chose to do the same,' I said. 'In fact, no one at St Saviour's mentioned you.' She struck me as the kind of woman who expected everyone to have heard of her. I saw her cheeks flush slightly and I was pleased to have riled her again.

'That may be so,' she said. 'Though I see you have my book up on your shelves.'

'Do I?'

'Wilde's *Poisons*. Up there.'

'Oh, that. That's James Wilde, is it not?'

'My brother.' She pressed her lips together. 'A vain, selfish man who published *my* work under *his* name. Bella is his daughter. Illegitimate, of course.' Her gaze continued to sweep the shelves. 'I was sorry your mother died.' She turned to look at me again. A cold hard stare. She had to be some sixty or more years old but was still tall and muscular, her shoulders square, her legs strong beneath her sweeping skirts. Her eyes were dark and piercing, and heavily lined with kohl, her lips stained crimson. 'I said I would look after you and I have always done so. I know *who* you are, and *what* you are. I have kept you from harm, always. I have influence about the streets and have saved you from yourself, and from others, on many occasions.' She held up a hand, as if to forestall me. 'I expect no thanks for it.'

'Saved me?' I scoffed. 'How so?'

'I had you watched. As a child. As a youth.' She shrugged. 'It was all done in the most clandestine of ways, so I hardly expect you to recall.'

'I don't recall.'

'And now I think it is about time you learned about your mother. Your father would not speak of her, would he?' I said nothing. 'Do you know why?'

'It was too painful for him,' I muttered.

'Is that what you tell yourself?' She smiled. Her teeth had a diabolical pinkish hue to them. 'Yes, I can see how that sort of interpretation would give you some solace. He loved her, certainly. Did she deserve your father's devotion? I see from your face, that you suspect she did not, and that what you *think* you knew of her, what you have held onto as your most precious memory, may be nothing more than a fiction you have created for yourself.' She looked down at me, her expression pitying. 'Your entire life is a lie, Jem Flockhart, but you fear that your belief in your mother as good and kind and selfless may well be the biggest invention of all.' She waited as the clock ticked away the empty seconds. I felt my red birthmark flaming, the blood pulsing in my cheeks like liquid fire. I looked at Will, but he had his head down as if he wished he were not witness to such cruel words, and I could not see his face.

'Oh, this does not involve *him*,' said Bathsheba softly. 'It's no use looking at *him*. This is all about *you*. You think it becoming to make me stand here while you slouch before me munching apples? You think to insult me with your denials about my books, and your implied deprecation of my character? What have I done to deserve your contempt, your insolence? What did Dorothea Christian tell you? Nothing much, I imagine. That's because it is *I* who knew Catherine Underhill, and *I* who know what she did.'

'Tell me then,' I said. 'Or have you come all this way just to taunt me?'

'Oh, I will do more than *tell* you,' she cried. Her face had turned dark with fury. 'But you need to learn some manners first.' She turned on her heel and stalked towards the door. 'Girls!' she shouted. 'Come along! *Jaldi! Jaldi!* You will hear from me,' she said over her shoulder. 'And you will do as I say or your mother will remain dead to you.'

'I don't think she liked me much,' said Will as the door slammed shut behind them.

'I wouldn't let it bother you.'

'Do you believe her? About your mother?'

'I'm not sure what to believe. Clearly she's used to getting her own way.'

'She comes here offering you something, but whatever it is that she has for you – information, memories, knowledge – will only come at a price. What that price might be remains to be seen. Do you trust her?'

'Not a bit.'

'And what did you make of her companions?'

'Bella Wilde – an interesting subject. You noted that she was "my dead brother's child" not "my niece"? A curious turn of phrase, that might suggest a dislike of the brother – that much was evident – or perhaps a disdain for her relationship with the girl *per se*. She seeks to distance herself from Bella, and yet she lives with her, and goes about the town with her. Bathsheba Wilde is Anglo-Indian, I believe her brother was only a half-brother. That alone might account for the obvious similarities between the two Miss Wildes – the ears, the oval face, the broad shoulders, the shape of the eyes. But there is something else that keeps them together, a bond that is stronger than any obligation to a "dead brother's child".' I shrugged. 'Perhaps it is because they are both illegitimate. Miss Bella's childish mannerisms too I find rather perplexing.

Is the girl simple? I would need to see more of her to decide what I make of *that*.'

'And Miss Clara?'

'Miss Bella and Miss Bathsheba share common blood. For that reason Miss Clara is the outsider. But it was always Clara whom Bathsheba spoke of first, she who was foremost in her mind. We were introduced to Clara before we were introduced to Bella. And yet did you see the bruises at her wrists? Small and circular. Someone has been pinching her – hard too. She held herself apart, her eyes downcast. Miss Bella might take her arm as they walk, but she did not respond to it, if anything she appeared to recoil a little. Is she being abused? Bullied? If so, then why, and by whom? It's quite possible for a paid companion to be so beholden to her mistress that she is obliged to endure all manner of insults just to keep a roof over her head, and perhaps Miss Clara does not have the means to make her own way in the world. And yet she is a painter. An artist. If she was possessed of any degree of skill she might be able to support herself. And yet she does not do so. So what, precisely, is the relationship between these women?' I sat back and closed my eyes. 'I shall mull it over,' I said. 'And see what comes to mind.'

Excerpts from the diary of Catherine Underhill.

21ˢᵗ May 1818

Miss Wilde told me that the seasons in India are of great significance, and if one is to avoid the rains, or the heat and dust, or a certain type of flying insect the name of which I cannot remember, then there are particular times of year when travelling is most desirable. If we are to go this year, it is better to go now. 'I will give you five days,' she said. 'And on the fifth day, at seven in the morning, I will send a coach.'

She has advised me to 'pack with every economy', to come with 'the stoutest of boots and an open mind, for you will not find me and my companions anything like the women you might commonly be used to'. I have hardly had time to think what she means. I admit (though only to the pages of this journal) that I am more concerned about ants and hornets and snakes, than about clothes and other necessities. I shall just have to hope for the best.

My father has just sent Mary in to tell me that Dr Bain is waiting for me in the drawing room. 'You must tell him you are going away,' he said yesterday. 'Tell him not to wait for you.'

In fact, I intend to tell Alexander that I will wait for him, though whether he might wait for me is a different matter. I know he is often at one of those disreputable Houses on Wicke Street. They all are! Why is there one rule for men and another for women? But I know he is upset that I have decided so abruptly to go abroad. And yet why must I ask his approval for my adventure? We are not married yet! Sometimes I begin to see what Bathsheba means.

26ᵗʰ May 1818

We are all aboard! I am lodged in a small cabin in the body of the ship, with Bathsheba next door. Jane is further aft. We are to catch the tide in the next hour or so, so we do not have long to wait. Bathsheba is in her cabin, and so I took the opportunity of writing this short entry. I must admit I am excited. Bathsheba was most welcoming and has been very attentive to my comfort. She has prepared a mixture to allay the seasickness. 'Tincture of laudanum, ginger and peppermint,' she said. 'Five drops every hour. It is best taken in a little brandy.' She smiled, her teeth glittering in the dim light of the quarterdeck as she dripped it into a pewter snifter she had produced from her luggage. 'Drink, my pretty,' she said. 'Drink it down.' I did as she asked, as she was watching me so closely that I could do nothing else. The taste was as bitter as wormwood, even with the brandy. I think that tincture did not contain any of the things she said it did.

Our ship is a 'tea clipper' on its return journey, and thus as speedy a vessel as we are likely to find. It is mostly filled with cargo. The passengers are few in number and take up less space than the freight we are carrying. Those who travel first class have the best cabins. Bathsheba says we must needs get used to the rougher side of things, and as long as we have our own cabins we should not mind any discomforts. She says we will have nothing half so opulent in the dak *bungalows we will be staying in when we travel up country. (The* dak *is the mail coach. It is, she tells me, the most efficient way to travel anywhere through the Company's India.) I am looking forward to our journey. Our accommodation on board seems perfectly adequate to me, though I imagine those in second and third class can expect a very rough passage indeed.*

Afternoon

Bathsheba is displeased with her cabin – or her 'hutch' as she calls it, as it is no more than eight feet by six. She has been to see the captain, a tall man with a disappointed air. She also took issue with the smell of the place, or 'the vile fetor' which admittedly pervades the whole atmosphere, but which emanates from 'the bilges' and about which there is nothing that can be done. 'Has someone died in it?' I heard her shout.

'Not yet, madam!' the captain roared back at her. 'Not yet!'

I heard angry footsteps and the slamming of doors to my right as she returned. 'Jane!' she screamed. 'Jane!' Footsteps signalled the approach of poor Jane, whose complexion had turned green the moment she had stepped aboard. 'My pipe. Where is it? And my tobacco. And my herbal mix.' I could not hear Jane's muttered reply. She seems a surly girl, cross faced and sullen. At first I was not sure why Bathsheba retained her, though I am beginning to see what a hard mistress she is to please. But Jane seems to know all her requirements, and soon I heard the sound of the girl's footsteps returning, and when I opened my door I saw her struggling up the gangway with a hookah in her arms, the long pipe coiled about her neck like a sleeping snake. Against her skirts a bag swung – the 'herbal mix', no doubt. The same stuff she had given me, perhaps, at Nightshade House? She lurched into her mistress's cabin and the door slammed closed. I bent to my work once more. Bathsheba has tasked me with putting her notes on poisons into some kind of coherence. I have decided on alphabetical by genus, then species, beginning with Atropa acuminata, *common name Indian Belladonna, a variant of the deadly nightshade.*

10th *June 1818*

Another lady botanist has joined our company. She came aboard at Southampton, where we stopped briefly while some provisions were brought up. Her name is Mrs Christian. She is an old friend of Bathsheba's and will be travelling with us. She is going out to meet up with her husband, who is already in Calcutta. He previously had a post at the medical school, lecturing in botany. He now has a position at the Botanical Gardens, she says, though he is not intending to stay there once the cold season begins. The 'cold season' lasts from November to March, and we will arrive at the best time to travel. Mrs Christian knows Bathsheba well, as they have been up country together on a number of occasions.

Chapter Six

The following afternoon we had another unexpected visitor; this time it was Dr Anderson from Angel Meadow Asylum. A long-faced, morose man, he viewed those under his care at the madhouse with a dismal fatalism. They were insane, yes, and madness took many forms, but whether they would recover or not was in God's hands, a statement which always struck me as a convenient excuse for doing very little. Still, an asylum superintendent who was concerned only with keeping his patients no worse than when they entered the place was better than many others, and his bland husbandry seemed to serve them all well enough. I knew Dr Anderson professionally rather than socially. My father had lived his last days at Angel Meadow and, fearing his insanity was a hereditary affliction, I too had spent time there being tested and examined. For his part, Dr Anderson trusted my knowledge and expertise as an apothecary, and sent down an orderly with a list of required prescriptions twice a week. I never took the medications up there myself – I'd had enough of the place to last me for the rest of my life, whether I ran mad or not. Unlike Dr Anderson.

'This is the first time I have left Angel Meadow in over a month!' he said. 'At least there's no Mrs Anderson to complain about it, though I fear I have got into bad habits, and work longer hours than I need to. It's easier just to stay at the Asylum, to be honest, as I have all I need there. Still,' he took a deep draught of his beer. 'It's good to be out.' He was sitting on Jenny's stool at the counter with a pot of ale in his hand – Gabriel and Mrs Speedicut had taken to brewing the stuff in the back yard. The results were cloudy, but not unpleasant, though I tended to buy ale for Will and me from Sorley's all the same. 'You're still looking rather pale, Quartermain,' he added. 'Can't you get Flockhart here to rustle you up an iron tonic?'

Will pointed to a bottle on the table. 'You mean like this stuff here?'

'Ah, yes. Mind and take some senna too. Any iron tonic'll turn your bowels solid in no time.'

'My bowels are in perfect order, sir,' said Will. 'Though I thank you for your solicitations.'

'Yes, well, you'd be surprised. The bowels should be kept as free as possible. I've noticed that the mad generally run costive. Some of them hoard it, you know. I've one chap who does all he can *not* to defecate at all. Says the Devil lives up there and must be kept *inside* at all costs. I have to sneak purgatives into his food and make sure someone is standing by when the stuff works its way through.' He shook his head. 'The screaming! Another of them thinks he's actually possessed by his own faeces. Used to dig the matter out with a spoon and throw it out of the window.

When we took away the cutlery and locked him in a room without a window he used his fingers instead, and tried to force the stuff out through the keyhole. Fellow can't be let out of the straitjacket. You'd be surprised how many of them obsess about it – keeping it in, getting it out . . . And yet it's not something we talk about much, is it?'

'No,' I said.

'Can't think why,' muttered Will.

'And we are not here to talk about it now, Anderson,' I added. 'What is it that brings you here?'

'I have a patient I'd like you to see,' he said. 'Not because I need your opinion as a medical man, Flockhart, I'm quite happy with my own diagnosis and treatment, which, to be honest is the same as my predecessor's.'

'And what is your diagnosis and treatment?' I said.

'She has intellectual monomania. An *idée-fixe*. But you will see that for yourself if you come up. I usually leave her to her own devices, and she is biddable enough when left alone.'

'And she was committed to the asylum for that?' said Will.

'Oh, she was not committed,' said Dr Anderson. 'At least, it was no physician who insisted she be placed there. Oh no, she is not *quite* what one might call insane.' He paused, as if to allow this information to sink in. 'She put *herself* in Angel Meadow. Years ago, and she refuses to leave. Even the suggestion that she might leave for a few minutes – for a walk, for some fresh air – is met with a flat refusal – screaming, fighting, fainting. It is not something I care to witness again. And therein lies her madness. An irrational terror of the outside world, and an obsession with its wickedness in all its many forms.'

I thought about the streets around Angel Meadow and found I could hardly blame anyone for refusing to walk in them. Fresh air could not be found anywhere nearby either, for the stink of the brewery, the vinegar works, and the tanning factory pervaded the entire neighbourhood. Plus there were any number of footpads who roamed the place after dark. 'She won't set foot outside,' went on Dr Anderson. 'She prefers not even to *see* the outside; indeed, she's in a room that allows her no view at all.'

'No window?' I said, appalled. I had seen the windowless cells at Angel Meadow – the darkly stained walls, the heavy wooden doors, the rings affixed to the wall for those whose madness drove them to violence. 'She's in the basement?' My voice was almost a whisper.

'No, no, sir,' he said. 'She is nowhere near *that* bad. But she has covered the window of her room, even though there was little but the sky and a brick wall that was visible from it. She has not seen the city for the last three decades. But her bills are paid on time, and so I allow her to stay. She's no trouble as long as she is kept inside.'

'Who is she?' I said. 'Do I know her?'

'Her name is Jane Spiker.'

I felt my heart leap inside me. J. Spiker was the last name on the plan to the physic garden. Would the woman be able to shed light on the bones and why they were there? I glanced at Will. I saw from his face that he recognised the name too, though he said nothing. I decided to say none of this to Dr Anderson. Instead I shook my head. 'No,' I said. 'I have never heard of a Jane Spiker.'

'I thought not,' said Dr Anderson. 'But that hardly matters. What matters is that I believe you have recently uncovered a collection of bones from your garden.'

'Yes,' I said.

'Mrs Spiker has become . . . somewhat restless since she heard of it.'

'She heard about it in the asylum? I'm surprised the news reached inside. Specially if she's so averse to the outside world,' said Will.

'Ah, she might not want to *see* the outside world, Mr Quartermain, but she is exceptionally interested in knowing about it. She takes *The Times* and the *Police Gazette*. She scours them from cover to cover. I can see no logic to it, and she cannot, or possibly *will* not, explain. But it occupies her time well enough, although there are occasions when I fear it is doing more ill than good. This morning, for instance. She is usually no trouble at all.'

'And how was she this morning?' I said.

'Raving,' said Dr Anderson. 'I've never seen her behave so wildly. We have managed to calm her down, and she is back to her old habits. But I wondered if perhaps you might speak to her? If you could tell her something about these bones, about the garden and how you found them, she may well be reassured.' He shrugged. 'It would connect her to the outside world, at least. Seems worth a try, gentlemen. Unless I just ignore it. I suppose I could do that.'

If there was ever a man who wanted an easy life, who favoured inertia over action, it was Dr Anderson. He drained his glass and made to stand up. I could see that he was about to apologise for bothering us and take his leave, and I leaped to my feet. 'But no, Dr Anderson. I think we should *not* just ignore it.' I grabbed my coat and hat. 'I think we should see whether we can help you, and your Mrs Spiker, and it is a pleasure to be of service. It sounds a most fascinating case. Might Mr Quartermain accompany us? He has been assisting me of late and was with me when we found the bones. Gabriel! Look after the shop.' Before anyone could object, I had ushered Dr Anderson and Will out into the lane.

The sight of Angel Meadow Asylum never failed to unnerve me. It was as ancient as Newgate and almost as forbidding, a great dark block of a building with thick walls and high small windows. The main entrance looked friendly enough, if one overlooked the tall spiked iron railings that topped its walls, for it had large windows that looked out onto an apron of well-tended grass. Its gates stood open, as if in welcome, though in reality it was in readiness to receive a racing carriage – perhaps one of the Asylum's own box-like wheeled cells, as secure as a Black Maria, with bars on the windows and leather restraints inside.

The front of the building looked out over the grass towards the entrance gates. It housed the superintendent's quarters, along with reception rooms, an attendants' sitting room and a high-ceilinged wood-panelled hall – chambers that the sane might inhabit, or into which relatives might be shepherded so that they did not have to see what they did not wish to know about. To the rear of this edifice, beyond a square of scrubby grass and a cobbled stable yard, lay the asylum proper, with men quartered in one wing and women in another. Beyond that, on the far side of a small courtyard, were the low squalid structures that housed the criminally insane.

The women's wing was a long gloomy corridor. On one side it looked out onto a quadrangle of grass. The other side, where the patients' rooms were located, looked out at a tall black wall topped with spikes. The windows were barred so that escape was impossible. Those with sufficient funds were able to pay for a room and board and there were many who had been inside for more years than they had lived outside. If their bills were paid, and they remained insane, what else might be done with them? The corridor was cheerless, the floor a dismal drugget, the walls half panelled in dark oak, half painted in a drab olive. They were garnished with paintings depicting dim, formless landscapes, bland hills or lustreless pools designed to calm the turbulent minds of those who stared bleakly upon them. I understood that the purpose of this was to create what Dr Anderson called a 'drawing room feel to their environment', as 'what more tranquil place is there than a drawing room?' Here and there against the walls stood a table of varnished oak, screwed to the floor with iron brackets should the drawing room tranquillity prove insufficient, and the inmates take to violence.

The patients in the women's wing at Angel Meadow Asylum were not considered to be a menace to themselves, or to others, and were generally allowed out of their rooms during the day. They drifted up and down their corridor or stood staring blankly out at the sky or the grass. They had a common room, from which came the sound of a piano. The instrument was played well, and I was about to remark upon it, when it stopped abruptly to be replaced by screaming, and the sound of fists hammering randomly on the keys.

'Mrs Ampleforth is an excellent pianist,' said Dr Anderson. 'And yet every time she reaches the middle of the final movement of Beethoven's Sonata Pathétique—' He raised his hands in wordless incomprehension. 'This happens. I have no idea why, though I admit the piece holds numerous challenges to the amateur. And yet she will play nothing else.'

'At least it is pleasant music while it lasts,' said Will.

'I beg to differ,' muttered Dr Anderson. 'It is the only tune she will play, and it always ends in violence. Over and over and over again. I'd take the confounded instrument away, but she is ungovernable without it. She is quite mad, of course. They are all, Mr Quartermain.'

'I should hope they are sir,' replied Will, 'given where they are housed.'

'And Mrs Spiker?' I said. 'May I ask, what is the precise nature of her monomania?'

'She is fixated on one thing, and one thing only: a morbid fear of violent crime. Her terror of the outside world is quite prodigious. And yet if we deny her the pleasure of knowing about the crimes of London – her particular enthusiasm – then she becomes completely unmanageable. Violent, foul mouthed, filthy.'

'And your treatment?' said Will.

'Why, I do what my predecessor had always done.' He sighed. 'I indulge her. She's a wealthy patient, and that counts for something, as you can imagine. She can seem quite normal – in her dress and elocution, at least. Her habits, however, are a different matter.'

'And she has no desire to leave, to step outside?'

'She does not. She has no desire even to leave her cell, never mind leave the building.'

'Could you make her leave?'

'I dare say we could force her out. She is a danger neither to herself, nor to others, as far as I can tell. And yet she has been here so long now it is hard to imagine she was once free. Besides, when you try to *make* her go, then she really *does* behave like a lunatic! She has a daughter,' he continued. 'No idea who the father was. Someone told me she was married to a fellow out in India, a Company man, though it's my belief that she was never really anyone's wife, and the "Mrs" is a purely fictitious title. The girl was brought up elsewhere, though she has maintained close contact with her mother. Comes every week in fact.'

By this time we had reached Mrs Spiker's room. All the rooms occupied by the private patients on the women's wing were the same: some twelve feet wide by sixteen feet long, a window – barred, of course – and a bed against the wall, a washstand, a chair and a table. Inmates were permitted to adorn their rooms according to their taste, especially those whose families paid for the best accommodation. Small items, such as a mirror or hairbrush, or a colourful counterpane, were favourite touches. Angel Meadow was known for its sympathetic treatment of the insane, and various activities – dancing, music, gardening, painting – were encouraged. Some women painted watercolours and hung the walls of their chamber with framed daubs. Others made desultory attempts at needlework, under supervision, of course, and badly embroidered cushions were to be found all over the place. Most, however, made little attempt to claim the space for their own. Most hoped not to be staying there for long. Most were not like Mrs Spiker.

Jane Spiker's room at Angel Meadow Asylum was something I will never forget. The woman had laid claim to every inch of her wall space. Gone were the olive walls, the dark oak panelling and grubby yellowish cornice. Not an inch of wallpaper or wainscoting could be seen for every scrap of it was concealed beneath layer upon layer of newspaper cuttings. She had stuck them to the walls, to the windows, to the door. The only reason they were not on the ceiling was because she could not reach it, even when standing on a chair. Year after year, for the thirty years she had been there, ripping and pasting, ripping and pasting, so that the whole room had taken on a leathery, spongy look, like the inside of some monstrous termite's lair. Some sections of her handiwork were yellowed with age, and had a pale, dry look to them, like shreds of dead flesh. More recent additions appeared damp and membranous, the tiny type almost transparent where the glue had not yet dried. Some areas she had favoured more than others, and the walls undulated with bulges and whorls, waves, ridges and ripples.

Dr Anderson nodded. He could see my surprise. 'You see how it is, Flockhart? The woman is completely deranged. Intelligent, I grant you that, for she has nothing of the idiot about her, and yet *this* is where she chooses to live. This is *how* she chooses to live. If we drag her out, or attempt to take it all away – and believe me, sir, we have tried both – she becomes a wildcat. Almost took an attendant's eye out with her glue brush, on one occasion.'

Will was peering at the wall. 'This is *The Times*, is it not?'

'Yes,' said Dr Anderson. 'Morning and evening editions. She has them sent in.' He sighed. 'I have so many patients, Mr Flockhart, and so little time, and those who are stable – who do not attract my notice – receive scant attention. Mrs Spiker is one such. Would that I had the time to understand her more, but we are no different to other places. The city-bound madhouses are struggling everywhere.' I made no comment. With so many living in poverty, so many uprooted and forced to work in crowded, impersonal warrens, was it any wonder that they ran mad for lack of rest and solace? As for the more well-to-do – the idle housewife driven hysterical with boredom, the husband crushed by care and responsibilities – the wonder was that there were not more people clamouring at the gates of the country's asylums.

'She's something of a fixture,' he went on. 'To be honest, Flockhart, no one has tried anything with the woman for years. When she first came I believe they tried to persuade her to go outside, but she became so agitated that all efforts ceased. She avoids sleep too, as far as she can, for she is afflicted with the most fearful nightmares. I attempted various sedatives, but she refused them all. It would not be too much to say that her entire existence is based on fear, though fear of what or whom I cannot say. Fear of being done to death by violent means, I take it, though by whom, and why, remains a mystery.'

Will was still peering up at the walls. 'It's the *Police Gazette* too. Cuttings, all of them. What can she have been looking for?'

'Murders,' said Dr Anderson. 'Murders of any kind. And missing persons, whom she presumes have been murdered unless she hears otherwise. She sits at the table all day long and combs both editions of *The Times* every day. Anything she finds, she cuts and pastes to the wall so that she can see it. So that she can remember it.' He looked around at the yellow, spongy walls. 'As you can see, life is cheap in London.'

'And the *Police Gazette*?'

'She takes every edition, including the special supplements.'

'"Crimes committed, information wanted",' read Will, poring over the walls. 'And I see she has numerous entries from the fortnightly supplement on "Active Travelling Criminals, Wanted Aliens, Absentees and Deserters", not to mention "Deaths Of Those Who Have Previously Appeared In The Police Gazette". These last seem to be concentrated in this corner, where they have resulted in this great lobe of paper.' He ran his hand over a section of wall beside the washstand. He rubbed his fingers together. 'This patch here is still damp. A recent addition, I see. Jack Wentworth of Dagenham hanged at Newgate three days ago. Well, well. She is thorough, if nothing else.' Will gazed in amazement at the swollen, papery walls. 'It's as though she daren't let it go. Can't bear to lose sight of it, just in case one day it matters.'

'What she is looking for she won't say. She's never said. And, as far as I am aware, she's never found it. I have no idea whether I should be glad or sorry.'

'And then she read of the corpse we had found in our garden,' I said.

'Precisely. That's when everything changed, though as you can see now, she seems to be settled once more.'

The woman, Mrs Spiker, was seated at a desk, which was itself partly embedded in the wall of newspaper cuttings, as if the whole thing would one day be entirely consumed by it. She had not turned around when we came in, and seemed oblivious to our presence, and our conversation, remaining hunched over her work as unmoving as a sack of laundry. She was of average height, some five feet and two inches tall I surmised, though it was hard to tell as her bulk was so distracting. A shapeless blob of a woman, she was a stranger to all forms of corsetry or hygiene, dressed in a voluminous gown of verdigris-coloured waxy-looking cloth. Her hair was a greasy grey mass, half caught up in pins, half hanging down, as though a nest of rats was crouched upon her head, their tails swinging. Patches of it had come away to reveal her white, oily scalp. She had sores about her mouth and nose, her big flabby face as pale as suet, her cheeks two slabs of white flesh that drooped like melted wax on either side of a sharp, thread-veined nose. She smelled of sweat and urine, stale breath and rotten teeth. Beneath that the room exhaled the acrid metallic smell of newsprint and glue. There were other smells too, fighting for prominence in that small room, and I recognised immediately the ammonia sting of chamber pots and sickness.

'Look at the mess she makes,' said Dr Anderson, still making no effort to lower his voice, as if he hardly cared whether the woman heard him or not. 'Perhaps I shouldn't let the patients do as they please to their cells like this, no matter how well they pay to stay here.' At that moment a figure appeared in the doorway behind us. Dr Anderson's manner changed instantly, from exasperated asylum superintendent to unctuous toady. 'Ah, Miss Spiker, my dear lady what a great pleasure it is to see you!' He plunged forward to seize her gloved hand, so that for a moment I thought he was about to kiss it. 'I had quite forgotten it was your visiting day, please forgive me.' I wondered whether he was this obsequious to all those who paid their bills on time. 'You find your mother well settled in her tasks today. Mrs Spiker!' he shouted, as if the old woman were deaf as well as mad. 'Mrs Spiker! Your daughter is here to see you.' Still Mrs Spiker did not move.

Miss Spiker was a small, youngish woman. Her face was a pale oval, her eyes green and sparkling above a sharp nose and rosebud lips. Her hair was dark, but flat and dispirited beneath her bonnet, which she had enlivened with artificial flowers and leaves. Her dress was of bottle green silk, nipped in at the waist to show off her trim figure. 'Good afternoon, Dr Anderson,' she said. Her voice was deep and melodious, but she looked at Will and me with ill-concealed hostility. 'And who are these gentlemen?'

'This is Mr Flockhart, Miss Spiker, and his companion Mr Quartermain. They are friends of Angel Meadow and its residents. I was hoping they might be able to shed some light on your mother's condition.' Miss Spiker's cheeks had coloured a little as Dr Anderson droned out his explanation.

'You are welcome, sirs,' she said, half interrupting him, and sounding as though we were anything but welcome. 'If you can do anything to help my mother, please advise us, though I am surprised at you, Dr Anderson. I understood allowing strangers in to view the mad is not something usually permitted at this asylum, and certainly not in these enlightened times.'

Dr Anderson looked surprised at his, and attempted to bluster out an apology, but I stepped in.

'If I may, Dr Anderson, perhaps if I might be permitted to tell Miss Spiker why we are here.' I told her about the skeleton, the *Police Gazette*, her mother's frenzy on reading of the discovery. 'Dr Anderson merely thought we might be able to calm her.'

'And yet you see she is quite calm,' replied Miss Spiker. 'Whatever it was that perturbed her is forgotten, and I see no reason for either of you to be here. Mother,' she said, turning her attention to the fat woman who was still poring over her newspaper and appeared indifferent to everything that was being said about her. 'Are you unable to greet me today?'

Mrs Spiker said nothing. Indeed, she seemed not even to hear, so engrossed was she in her task. She was sitting on a straight-backed chair, a newspaper was spread out before her on the desk, the surface of which bore evidence of much industry. A pot of glue stood at her right hand, a wooden ruler, curls and fragments of discarded paper at her left. Around her ankles rustled the torn and sliced remains of whatever parts of the morning edition of *The Times* she no longer required. Her hands, black with ink and sticky with glue, moved constantly, back and forth across the newspaper. Clamped between her teeth was a thick paintbrush, the handle of which she gnawed absently, the way a child might chew on a stick of liquorice, while she bent to her endless task.

'Oh Mother,' cried Miss Spiker. 'Stop that! You'll get a splinter on your tongue.' She tried to snatch the brush away, but the old woman lashed out at her.

'Get off! I need that!' It was the first time she had spoken or responded in any way, and even as she batted her daughter's hand away she still did not take her eyes off the newspaper. All at once something she was reading caught her eye, and her whole body tensed. Using her ruler like a paperknife, she began to tear at the paper.

She was quick, but skilful, her fingers moving with a dextrous accuracy born of long practice. Once the piece was ripped clear, she reached an ink-stained paw for the glue pot. She removed the thick-handled brush from between her teeth, daubed the back of the paper, and put the brush back into her mouth. She lurched to her feet and blundered across the room, barging past us as if we were invisible. Scanning the wall from side to side and top to bottom, she found a spot she evidently considered to be the right one – though to the casual observer there was no discernible difference between that place and any other – and slapped her handiwork into position. I saw that it concerned the murder of a woman at Seven Dials who had been beaten to death with a flat iron. The husband was being held at Bow Street Magistrates and was due to hang at the end of the week.

Mrs Spiker lowered herself back down into her chair with a sigh of relief and applied herself once more to her task.

'Mrs Spiker,' shouted Dr Anderson. 'Here are some gentlemen who may be able to help you.'

The woman did not give any indication that she had heard. 'Mother,' cried Miss Spiker. She stepped forward and put her hand on the woman's arm. She bent to whisper in her mother's ear: 'There are some men here.'

Mrs Spiker froze. 'Men?' she said. 'What men?'

'This is Mr Flockhart,' said Dr Anderson. He was beginning to perspire with frustration. 'It is he who found the body in St Saviour's physic garden.'

What happened next surprised us all, for the moment the garden's name was mentioned Mrs Spiker sprang to her feet and plunged out into the passage. Dr Anderson was after her in a trice. He seized the woman's dress, but rather than bring her to a halt, he merely succeeded in swinging her around so that she crashed clumsily into a wall. He held her there with his arm at her neck while she screamed and thrashed, her face wild with terror, her eyes rolling, searching for a means of escape. At the commotion, a hubbub broke out. Other patients approached to watch, some began clapping their hands and shouting, others started to cry. One commenced screaming in short sharp bursts, her hands over her ears. Mrs Spiker started shouting, 'Let me go! Let me go! Let me go!' beating at Dr Anderson with clenched fists. Two attendants sprang forward, and Mrs Spiker was wrestled to the ground.

'Oh Mother!' Miss Spiker stood with her hands pressed to her face in horror. 'Dr Anderson, please!' But Mrs Spiker continued to scream and thrash. Despite her sedentary life crouched over *The Times* and the *Police Gazette*, fear had given her strength, and she lashed out with yellow fingernails. Hardened with years of dabbling in glue pots, they were as hard as flint, and she slashed Dr Anderson across the face.

'Damn your eyes, woman!' he roared as blood beaded his cheek. 'Straitjacket! Someone! *Anyone! Now!*' Two more attendants bounded forward to grab the woman's arms, half a dozen more of them swarming out of the sitting room and along the corridor towards us.

'Please!' cried Miss Spiker. She pushed the attendants aside and crouched beside her mother. 'Don't worry, Mother,' she said, patting awkwardly at the old woman's nest of hair. 'Don't worry.'

All at once Mrs Spiker lay still. She eyed her daughter craftily, her lips moving in a whisper. Miss Spiker bent her head, her ear to the old woman's lips. I had no idea what she said, but after she had delivered her message she lay back, like a seal on a beach. 'Words, words, words, words . . . ' her voice rose in a crescendo. 'She wrote it all down. All of it. And he will lead them to it, you'll see! She will hang us all!'

All at once a straitjacket appeared, though I could not see where it had come from. Mrs Spiker screamed at the sight of it and began to writhe and thrash once more. The attendants bore down upon her. They rolled the woman over and over, their hands working quickly, so that I was reminded of the way a doomed fly might be spooled by a dextrous spider. And then, as if by magic, for I hardly saw how they had done it, Mrs Spiker was swaddled in grubby canvas, a collar of leather tight about her neck, her hands bound across her body and tied behind her waist. She wriggled and screeched, foam gathering at the corners of her mouth. Her booted foot shot out like a piston, her heel connecting sharply with Dr Anderson's knee and he shouted in pain. The patients who had flocked towards us to watch the spectacle were now in complete uproar, so that the whole asylum seemed to echo with screams, the sound of crying, and wild, ungoverned laughter. I glanced at Will, shocked at the turn events had taken and at how quickly it had all happened. He was looking stunned, his eyes wide, his hands held gingerly to his head as if he had been boxed on the ears.

Dr Anderson limped to the edge of the fray, one hand clamped to his kneecap, the other dabbing at the claw-mark on his cheek with the corner of a pristinely laundered handkerchief. His face was thunderous. 'Don't just stand there!' he shouted as the attendants stood back to admire their handiwork. 'Get her into the basement!' The patients around us screamed and gibbered louder than ever. Some of them wailed like children, another had torn an aspidistra from its pot – the pot itself was bolted to the tabletop which was, in turn, screwed to the floor – and was rhythmically dashing its soily roots against a doorframe.

'Order!' shouted Dr Anderson. 'Order!' Miss Spiker had subsided onto a chair and was fanning herself with her handkerchief. She looked dazed. I saw her pull a small bottle from her reticule and take a deep draught from it. She closed her eyes.

'I think we should leave,' I murmured to Will. I took his arm and steered him down the corridor.

Excerpts from the diary of Catherine Underhill.

24ᵗʰ June 1818

*I have done what Bathsheba asked and I have written up as
much as I know about the poisonous plants of India. I have used
my own knowledge, as well as the books I brought with me from
my father's library. She has asked that I might supplement this
with new information I might glean from Dr Christian, whom
we will meet in Calcutta. He is to travel with us, and Bathsheba
does not seem pleased with this arrangement. 'Dora insists upon
it,' she said. It appears that 'Dora' is Mrs Christian. 'I would
rather we left him behind, for he is not worth the trouble he
makes, but Dora will not have it. It is a pity. He will only get
in the way.'*

*I saw Jane again today. She has been keeping to her hutch for
much of the time. She was looking unwell. I think seafaring does
not agree with her.*

30th June 1818

I find the sea does not agree with me either and I have been confined to my bunk these last two days. I was not taking the tincture Bathsheba gave me, though when she asked, I said that I was. But she mixed it for me herself and made me drink it while she watched, so I think she did not believe me. I don't like the stuff at all, for although it takes away the sickness it gives me the most fearful dreams, and last night was the worst yet. I refuse to describe them, for the sooner they are gone from my mind, the better.

8th July 1818

This morning I heard Bathsheba shouting at Jane again, and the sound of something breaking. 'Get out, Spiker!' she screamed. She always calls Jane by her surname when she is furious. I think it is to remind her of her place – as if the girl might be in any doubt about it. 'You have mixed it all wrong! Get out, and take Miss Underhill with you, I swear I can hear the infernal scritch scritch scritch *of her pen through these paper-thin walls and it is like rats scratching at my brain.' I put down my pen and sat back. I had been writing, but it had surely not been audible. Perhaps it was indeed the rats she could hear, for they are present about the ship in considerable numbers, no matter what measures are taken to catch them.*

A moment later there was a knock at my door. Jane stood before me, her expression grim. All at once she grinned – she is an attractive girl when she smiles. 'She's a harpy,' she whispered, 'but she's not so bad when all is said and done. Lets me do what I please much of the time. You too, I'll bet, if you tried it. Want to come on deck with me? There's soldiers!'

I admit I was surprised. I didn't want to go with her, but it seemed better to be in her good books rather than not, and if I stayed in my hutch but did not write, then what would I do? Jane's lips were wet, and her eyes had a saucy look. 'Good,' she said when I said I would come and turned to fetch my shawl. 'Makes us look respectable if there's two.'

When she took my arm as we emerged onto the ship's deck, I allowed it. I decided I might as well ask her a few questions.

'How long have you been Miss Wilde's maid?' I said.

'Maid!' she laughed. 'I'm her assistant. I assist. Since I was fifteen, since you ask. I'm twenty-one now.' Her gaze slid past me to rest hungrily on one of the soldiers who were sauntering up and down the deck. I saw her appraise his figure, the tightness of his britches, and fit of his tunic, and she smiled. She propelled me along the deck, her arm hooked through mine, her shawl dangling artfully behind her in the manner of the girls of Wicke Street when they are looking for business. 'Bathsheba doesn't mind what I do when I'm not assisting. She's not like other mistresses. Not a bit. Suppose I'm lucky about that.'

'How is she different?' I asked.

'You'll see. You've already seen – if you were looking.' As we walked past the soldiers she allowed her shawl to fall from her hands. The lieutenant she had been eyeing sprang round and plucked it from the deck. 'Miss,' he cried. 'Allow me.' And he placed it back around her shoulders. She smiled up at him. His friend, an ensign with a shaggy blond moustache, leered at me and stepped forward, though the look of horror on my face stopped him before he could say anything. Jane and her chosen soldier walked away arm in arm. I made to follow but felt a hand upon my arm, and there was Bathsheba standing behind me. She was smoking a small clay pipe and was wearing a pair of spectacles, the lenses made of dark glass so that her eyes were completely

hidden. Her hair was unbound, streaming out behind her in the wind, like seaweed. 'Leave her,' she said, seeing me about to go after the girl.

'But her reputation,' I stammered.

'In England, perhaps that would be a consideration.' She blew out a plume of smoke. 'But we are not in England now, are we? England is a long way away. Jane follows my rules, and I permit the passions. Besides,' now it was her turn to take my arm, 'I have been putting bindii in her tea for months.'

'Bindii?' I said. 'Tribulus terrestris? The Devil's eyelashes?'

She laughed. 'I've not heard it called that for a long time. What do you know of it?' She gave me an appraising glance. 'I can see I chose well when I chose you.'

'Native to the warm regions, southern Europe, Asia, India. Thrives on poor soil. Tiny yellow flowers, April to October. Graves and disturbed ground are its preferred location. It is highly invasive. The seeds have sharp spines that pierce the flesh—'

'Yes, yes,' she sounded impatient. 'But what are its uses, my dear Cathy, what are its uses?'

'As a diuretic mainly,' I said. 'Also used as a tonic. And as—' I felt myself blush, and then blushed some more for shame. I could surely utter the word without embarrassment, and yet here I was with my cheeks as red as any parlour maid.

'An aphrodisiac,' she said. 'Is that what you are struggling to say? I hope so, for that is what I use it for. Mixed it with saffron and cinnamon to enhance its effects, of course. She drinks it every day. I told her it is a tonic, to ease wind and bloating and guard against the seasickness.'

'You encourage her?'

She shrugged. 'She follows her passions. Her instincts. I don't see that I should stop her, and so I give her a little something to enhance what she already feels. And there are other preparations to bring on the menses if she is unlucky or careless. You see how happy she is? Such rosy cheeks and lips! Why might she not take pleasure in so natural an act? It is only the hypocrisy of the drawing room and the pulpit, along with the fears of the medical profession, that have decided how a woman should or should not behave in the company of men.' She took my arm and drew me away. Her grip was strong and masculine, her body against mine warm and firm. The smoke from her pipe was familiar, a sweetish, musty aroma, which I recognised as the same smell that often drifted out from her 'hutch', and which I had noted in her house at Islington.

'But her reputation.' I could not let it drop.

'She cares nothing for such things. Neither do I. I urge you to do the same. Where we are going such reputations do not signify. Now, let us leave her. I have provided her with sheaths.'

Notes on the poisonous nightshades (Solanaceae).

HYOSCYAMUS NIGER

Also known as henbane, stinking nightshade, symponica, black henbane.

Description

Annual or biennial, the plant is bushy, and may grow up to four feet in height. The leaves are sticky to the touch, stalkless, lobed, and up to ten inches long. The flowers too are stalkless. A gloomy yellow in colour, they are marbled by lurid purple veins. The roots are thick, fleshy and pale, the seed pods curious lidded urn-shaped vessels. The whole plant gives off a powerful, nauseating odour. Henbane favours waste ground and old rubbish heaps. An escapee from ancient herb gardens, it was commonly used as physic in Queen Elizabeth's reign, though has fallen into disfavour in more recent times. The seeds are much used by the Mohammedan doctors of India.

Toxicity

All of the plant is poisonous, though the seeds are particularly potent. Drying or boiling makes no difference to its power. The odour of the leaves alone, when fresh, can produce dizziness and stupor.

Symptoms

Consuming the leaves or roots can produce a maniacal delirium followed by coma and death. The symptoms are the same as those of the other poisonous nightshades: rapid pulse, dilated pupils, restlessness, flushed skin, hallucinations. Effects may last for many days.

Antidotes

Washing out the stomach and consuming strong coffee may help to counter its effects. The Calabar bean has been shown to have an antidote effect, but is itself so violent a poison that the correct dose is almost impossible to measure.

Medical applications

Efficacious in spasms of the digestive tract, insomnia, and epilepsy and the convulsive diseases. Culpeper recommends it for gout, sciatica, pains of the joints and headaches. The oil might be used for deafness, and worms in the ear. The seeds might be smoked instead of opium, though insanity may ensue if not undertaken with care.

Miscellanea

Henbane has a long association with witchcraft and malefic practices. It is used in magic and diabolism by witches as an ointment to aid in raising the dead, summoning demons or communing with the Devil. In mythology, the dead wear a crown of henbane as they wander without purpose beside the Styx.

Chapter Seven

We walked briskly down St Saviour's Street to Sorley's Chop House. The stink of the vinegar works and the ordure in the streets acted like ammonia salts and in a few breaths our heads had cleared. Neither of us spoke until we were in a booth beside the fire at Sorley's and had placed an order for two pots of ale and two pheasant pies.

'God, what a place that Asylum is,' said Will. He closed his eyes. 'Talk about a Bedlam! We seem no further on in our enquiries, and all we have done is enrage a madwoman and had her strapped into a straitjacket and condemned to the basement.'

'Oh, but we *are* further on,' I said. 'Whatever is happening at Angel Meadow is a consequence of the disinterring of that body. *Something* has been awoken by it, something that lay sleeping, watching and waiting perhaps, but which is now awake.'

'Perhaps we should visit Bathsheba Wilde.' He pulled the plan of the garden from his satchel and unrolled it onto the table, pushing our plates aside and tossing a scrap to Sorley's dog, who waited patiently beneath the table. 'I admit to being somewhat intrigued by her, and her name is first here, before Dr Christian's.' His skin had a clammy look to it, and I wondered whether I had been wrong to drag him here and there, marching him up to the Asylum and back again. He saw my look and he smiled. 'I am quite well, Jem,' he said. 'Just a little tired. But you – you are preoccupied, I can see it. You are worried that your mother might be a murderer.'

'I must find the truth.'

'Always an elusive commodity in this town.' He coughed, his cheeks glowing pink like a consumptive. I made a mental note to put some balsam on his pillow and handkerchief to aid easeful breathing. Might I be able to take him into the country? I had hoped that spending time in the physic garden might suffice, and yet look where that had got us. I sighed, and began to search my satchel for the lozenges I had made for him. 'Stop rooting, Jem, and listen to me.' He sounded irritable. 'You will not find the truth because you are too emotional. Too involved. And too frightened of what you might find to see clearly. This, I fear, will blind you to any truth that does not fit the picture you wish to have of the past.'

'Since when did you become so wise?' I muttered.

He shrugged. 'It is easy to be so when you are objective. You, on this occasion, are not objective. Eat your pie,' he said. 'The truth is always easier to see on a full stomach. At least, it is when Mrs Sorley has been doing the cooking.'

'Indeed,' I said. 'Unfortunately, on this occasion the only truth to which this pie will lead anyone is indigestion, and the certainty that it is Sorley who has been doing the cooking, and not his wife. What an abomination!'

Will looked over his shoulder with a hunted expression. 'I know. He asked me how it was, and I had not the heart to tell him. It seems he is quite proud of the thing! Does he not wonder why his dog has become so fat? It is being fed by everyone who comes here! And this is not the first time. Mrs Sorley has been away for over ten days now, and the matter is getting out of hand. I tossed that mutton chop I had two days ago onto the fire as it was so badly cooked. Like a piece of inch-thick leather! Look! You can still see it there at the back. I believe it has not burned away even yet!'

I looked over my shoulder too. I had the feeling that we were being watched, and not by Mr Sorley. The chop house was full, as it usually was, the low-ceilinged room noisy with talk and laughter, the air fogged with pipe smoke and heavy with the reek of fat, burned pastry and beer. I watched the pot boy carry a plate of oysters and two tankards of ale across the room. A maid wiped a table top and gathered up some plates, emptying chop bones and gristle into one pail, and oyster shells into another. No one was looking at us. And yet something still did not seem right to me.

Sorley came over to clear our plates. 'Well, sirs, how was it?' He beamed at us.

'Splendid!' cried Will. 'Absolutely splendid. What meat was it again?'

'Mutton and pheasant.'

'Mutton!' Will clapped his hands. 'I knew it. Nothing else has quite that . . . flavour.' I put my hand into my pocket. 'No, Jem, I think it is my turn,' he said.

I waved him away. 'When you are fit and well and working, *then* you can pay my bill. Make the most of my generosity while you can.' I turned to Sorley. 'I need a bottle of that cheap gin you get from the place near the blacking factory. It's for Mrs Speedicut. Take this, will you? It's so heavy I think it's about to pull my britches down.' And I cupped my hands, full of pennies, ha'pennies, shillings, sixpences and held it out to him.

He laughed, counting out what he needed. Then, 'My, Mr Jem, where on earth did you get that?' He held a coin up between his finger and thumb.

'What is it?' said Will.

'Something Jenny found in the physic garden,' I said. 'Do you know what it is, Sorley?'

'Of course!' he replied. 'It's a token.'

'I know that much,' I said. 'A sailor's love token to his doxy, perhaps. Jenny thinks it's to her mother. She said she'd seen it before – I didn't believe her of course.'

'It's quite possible she *has* seen it before,' replied Sorley. 'Or one just like it. Especially coming from the docks. And her mother might well have been called Angel – ain't they all called that? Those what's not called Polly or Sarah or Dolores.' He laughed.

'I don't know what you mean,' I said.

'This is a token,' he said. 'A house token. I used them myself instead of money for regulars when I was in my other place. It made them use their money in my ale house rather than someone else's. Mine had "Jas. Sorley" across the top, and "Green Man" across the bottom. That was when I had the Green Man, obviously. I've moved up in the world since then, o' course, mainly thanks to Mrs Sorley. Don't use tokens anymore though there's plenty of places that do.'

'And this particular token?' said Will.

'This one's from the North Star Angel down near the East India Docks. A man called Solomon Saul runs it, or at least he used to. You see his name "Saul" at the top? The north star drawn in the middle, and "Angel" at the bottom.' He laughed. 'It's definitely no love token. Not that I know much about the place now, and Saul's probably long dead. At least, I hope he is. This city's full o' places to drink, Mr Jem, thousands of 'em. There's only one reason why you'd find yourself in the North Star Angel, and that's if you'd nowhere else to go.'

I slept hardly a wink that night but lay in my bed beneath the eaves, my eyes staring. At my customary hour I arose and went downstairs. Gabriel was still asleep on his truckle bed beneath the table, though I could hear Jenny moving around in the herb drying room. I put a pot of coffee on the stove top and flung a shovel full of coal into its mouth, levering some life into the embers with a poker. The night had been a cold one, bitterly icy, and I could see my own breath in the air. Gabriel was supposed to bank the stove up at night so that the shop was kept warm, but he had done a poor job of it. I pulled my gloves on – a fingerless pair Mrs Speedicut had knitted for me the previous winter – and turned to kick the lad's bed. As I did so, something caught my eye – a shadow, it seemed to me, an impression that someone was watching. I glanced up at the door and gave such a shriek that Gabriel sat bolt upright, banging his head with a *crack* on the apothecary table. Jenny burst out of the herb drying room, her boots half on, half off. 'What is it? What's happened?'

I pointed. Outside the door, pressed against one of the glass panes, was a face. It was white with frost, the eyes dead, and grey as snails. The mouth was open, as if caught mid scream, the hands' long thin fingers spread wide, and frozen to the window like pale, spindly starfish. Frost had sheathed him in a crystalline crust, the rime on the panes and upon his hair, his shoulders, adhering to his brows and clinging to the flesh of his sunken cheeks giving him a ghostly, luminous appearance. He was bare headed, and clothed in nothing but his nightshirt, so I could only conclude that he had come to us in the night, running through the cold and freezing streets to batter on our door. Finding it locked, as all doors were in the small hours of the morning, he had died where he stood. Worst of all, however, was his mouth. It was stuffed full of something black and shiny. What it was I could not yet tell, though whatever it was it had to be coated with oil or alcohol, something that had prevented ice from forming, as it remained untainted by frost, a dark purple mass framed by his white gaping lips. A blackish exudate had dribbled down his chin like congealed blood. With his crystalline face and staring dead eyes I could not recall a more hideous sight.

I unlocked the door and pulled it open as Will appeared beside me. 'Dear God!' he whispered. 'What in heaven's name has happened to him?' I went out into Fishbait Lane. The dawn would not break for well over an hour, and the street was still dark. I could see no one else nearby, and there were no signs of life, even from my fellow shop-keepers. The freezing air drifted into the apothecary. Dr Christian remained unmoving, caught in that final desperate position with his hands up to the window. On the smattering of snow that covered the pavement leading to the apothecary door I could see the faintest outline of footprints, I presumed from the dead man's final steps. They were curiously truncated, only the balls of the feet in contact with the ground, as if he had tiptoed up to the door. I thought I detected other footprints around and about, but they had been deliberately scuffed and obliterated, as well as now being partly obscured by my own, and I cursed my own carelessness.

Will and I manhandled the frozen corpse into the apothecary. Why had he come? What was it that he had been so desperate to tell us? Something so urgent that he must needs cross the city in the dead of night wearing nothing but his nightshirt? His feet were bare and muddy. Beside them, as if it had fallen from his hand, was a small ivory skull, bone-white against the grime and dirt of the street. I picked it up and put it into my pocket.

We brought the body inside and laid it down on the apothecary table. 'It's not exactly good for the appetite to have a corpse on the table, Mr Jem,' said Jenny. 'It's put me right off.' She reached over the body and seized the coffee pot. 'How long do you think he was there?'

'Long enough for his flesh to freeze,' I replied. 'There's not much to him as he's skin and bone, and he will have cooled down pretty quickly as it was bitter last night, the cold wind making it even worse. I'd say he's been here for maybe five hours. Perhaps since one o'clock in the morning. There's little that's virtuous happening at such an hour. I assume you were so bundled up beneath your blankets that you did not hear him knocking.' I looked at the old man's sunken features and thin, talon-like fingers. 'If he even had the strength to knock. I suspect he was able to do little more than raise his hands to the glass. I wonder his wife has not come looking for him. Or at least the coachman.'

'And that stuff in his mouth?' said Will.

'I believe they are the berries of the deadly nightshade,' I said. 'Preserved in alcohol and stuffed into his mouth before rigor mortis set in.'

'How can you tell?'

'Because any apothecary worth his salt could recognise a belladonna berry. And unless he died with his mouth gaping, which is unlikely, then whoever did this would have had to use force to break his jaw open and get the berries in if rigor was present. I see no evidence of force, so we might assume that the berries were stuffed in as he expired, or shortly afterwards. It's possible they were put in while he was still alive, but that he was unable to offer any resistance. Certainly he was either alive or not long dead when they went in.'

I sent Gabriel for the constable. It was the same one that had come to the physic garden two days earlier and he raised his eyebrows at the sight of the dead man. 'You know him, sir?'

'We have not conversed,' I said, which was true enough, 'though I know who he is.'

'And who is he, sir?'

'Dr Robert Christian.'

'And why is he at your door?'

'I have no idea.'

'Needs a post-mortem,' he said, staring at the icy corpse. 'And what's that stuff in his mouth?'

'Deadly nightshade berries,' I replied.

'You seem to know an awful lot,' he said.

'I know that he is dead, and that he has belladonna berries in his mouth,' I said sharply. 'If that sounds like a lot, then I assume you will be able to tell us what happened in no time at all.'

The constable shrugged with evident relief that his line of probing questions had been completed. 'Don't mind me, sir,' he said. 'I have to ask, that's all. I have to be suspicious.'

'And you did it admirably,' I said. 'Had I been guilty, I would have confessed straight away.'

He blushed. 'Thank you, sir. Dr Graves is in the mortuary this morning. He'll be along for the body as soon as he's ready.'

'Dr Christian's wife will be wondering where he has got to,' I said. 'This gentleman, her husband, was once a physician at St Saviour's Infirmary, where I worked as apothecary. I wonder whether I might be permitted to break the news to her?'

'I don't see why not, sir,' said the constable. 'I never like that job, especially when I have to break the news to a lady. But she'll have to arrange to take the body as soon as Dr Graves is finished with it. The mortuary is busy at this time of year and we can't have him hanging around. So many vagrants and beggars, sir. This cold weather finishes 'em off.'

I decided to wait for Dr Graves, the most notorious anatomist in all London. I was sure I could already hear the wheels of his corpse-wagon rattling on the road as it turned down the lane, and as it turned out I was correct, for not a minute later there was Dr Graves, sitting atop the corpse-wagon box like the Reaper himself, black cloak flying, sunken eyes hidden beneath the dark brim of his tall hat. He had come post-haste, unwilling to let a dead body be examined by anyone else. As there was a premium on corpses, especially during the winter months when the anatomy classes were taking place, he had to be particularly prompt if he was to beat the medical students to it. He kept abreast of deaths in and around the city with great alacrity, street sweepers and urchins – as well as constables – keeping him aware of who had died where and when – for a small fee.

'Well, well, Flockhart,' he said as he sprang down. His assistant corpse-carrier, a burly, silent, bald-headed man known only as Bloxham, clambered down after him. 'So this is where you are these days.' Dr Graves had not been to my shop before, though he had known me well at St Saviour's Infirmary and had spent many an hour in the apothecary there gossiping about his colleagues. Since I had become a 'shop keeper' and spent my days 'prising pennies from the fat fists of costive widows' as he put it, he had disdained ever to visit me. Now, he shook my hand, his grasp as cold and damp as the corpses he loved, and looked about him. 'Quite a comprehensive range of powders and salts, I see.' His gaze travelled along the bottles and jars that lined my shelves. 'I know just where to come if I need a good purgative or find myself with a dose of worms.' He shook his head and muttered, 'You are better than this, Flockhart. You're a doctor. You're the last of a family of great apothecaries who ran St Saviour's for years. Your poor father must be turning in his grave.' But his interest lay elsewhere, and his attention was immediately focused on the apothecary table and the stick-like cadaver that lay upon it. 'You've been gathering corpses, I hear, Flockhart. One in the garden, one at the door. Where next, sir? In your bed?' He gave a bark of laughter.

'I hope not, sir,' I said, more primly than I intended. Though I did not like to admit it, his remarks about my father stung.

'Step aside then, sir! Let the dog see the rabbit!' Dr Graves snatched the lantern from beside the stove and held it up, peering down at the corpse. His face was so close that I thought he was about to kiss it. 'This is Robert Christian,' he said after a moment.

'Yes,' I said. 'Did you know him?'

'Not well,' he replied. 'I knew him at St Saviour's, and before that he taught me botany and *materia medica* at the university up in Edinburgh. He was very knowledgeable about both. A great traveller, too, him and his wife. Went all over the world collecting plants, exploring the potential of foreign medications.'

'In recent years he seems to have become something of a recluse,' I said. 'I saw him the other day, as a matter of fact, and he was a shadow of the man he must once have been.'

'Really?' Dr Graves sounded uninterested. 'I never *actually* worked with him, of course. I'm more of a bodies-and-bones man myself, not leeches and tonics and that sort of thing. He was a great friend of your man Bain. All that "pushing back the boundaries of knowledge".' He shook his head. 'Rather a gamble, if you ask me. I mean, it's all very well having an emetic standing by to make you sick the stuff up, or a bath of iced water to jolt you back to life, but it's a risky business. "All in the name of science, Graves!" That's what your friend used to say to me. "How else can one find out anything?" Use a dog, man!

was always my answer, but no, no, no! A dog would never do. "A dog does not have the physiology of a man, sir!" Well *that's* true enough, I dare say, but where did all this "pushing back the boundaries" business actually get either of them? This chap here ends up a recluse, the other one is strung up in your shop like a fairground attraction!' He eyed the skeleton of Dr Bain with distaste. 'I never liked either of them. Arrogant, self-indulgent, glory seekers, both of 'em.' He bent down to sniff at the black mush in Dr Christian's mouth. 'What's this stuff?' he said. 'Looks like damson jam, but I don't think it is.' Dr Graves was an advocate of using all the senses in a post-mortem, and he put out his tongue to give the black matter a little lick.

'I believe it's deadly nightshade,' I said.

He withdrew his tongue, forgoing the taste test. 'And it was there when you found him?'

'It was.'

Dr Graves grunted. 'I see. Well, we'll soon find out if that was the stuff that finished him off.' He rubbed his hands together. 'But that's enough talk, let's see what the body can tell us, eh? Bloxham? The shroud!' With a well-practised move, Dr Graves's lumpen assistant produced a stained winding sheet from one of his bulging pockets. In a single dramatic flourish, he swathed Dr Christian's corpse from head to foot. He made to pick up the body, but Dr Graves put out his hand. 'I'll do it, Bloxham. You open the door.' He picked up Dr Christian's corpse from the apothecary table as tenderly as he might lift a sleeping lover. 'Come along to the mortuary when you're ready, Flockhart,' he said to me over his shoulder. 'We can have a spot of lunch after I'm done.' The door slammed closed behind him.

Chapter Eight

❧❧❧

Will and I took a cab back up to Dr Christian's house. It was still dark, the midwinter sun hardly more than a bloody blur against the eastern sky. We arrived at the house as the sun rose, its first crimson rays striking through the dark evergreen of the clustering yews. The place seemed deserted, the frost that had gripped the city during the night painting everything white and silver. Here and there I could see what might have been a footprint, but whether it was leading to or from the property I could not say, as the ground was so hard with frost that nothing but the wheels of a carriage would have made any impact on it. Dr Christian had been wearing only his nightshirt. Had he climbed down from his chamber window, or run out into the night from his front door?

I looked up at the façade of the house, and the casement on the top floor was wide, the curtains billowing in the breeze. The window was barred, so it would have been impossible for him to come out that way, even if he

117

had wanted to. It surprised me that Mrs Christian had not come looking for her husband. Perhaps she had no idea that he had disappeared. The chimneys, dark fingers against the crimson sky, were all of them dead and cold. Not even a wraith of smoke from the kitchens told where an exhausted housemaid was preparing her mistress's breakfast. I imagined Mrs Christian sitting in her chair before her fire's meagre coals until they were nothing but ash, poring over a book on plants looking for the word of God. I seized the knocker and crashed it up and down. The sound echoed about the hall. We waited, for the scuffle of approaching footsteps, for a voice muttering about the earliness of the hour, anything that might suggest there was somebody coming. I had been struck by the lack of servants in the Christian household on our previous visit; other than the housekeeper, the place had seemed almost devoid of them. Now, it appeared as though there were none at all.

'It shouldn't be this quiet,' I said.

Will nodded. He put out a hand and gave the door a shove. It swung open to reveal a dark and cavernous vestibule. Will's face was tense and pale, his eyes dark and worried. We looked at one another and nodded. Will seized a spade that had been standing beside the front door, and, holding it so that he might jab any waiting assailant in the midriff with it, we crept forward.

The hall was dark, darker than it had been when we had last visited. The candles had burned down to their dregs, long drools of melted tallow hanging where it had solidified, like thick gobs of frozen pus. The whole place was lustreless, everything coated with a pall of coal dust and grime, years of half-hearted housekeeping giving it a sticky grey patina of neglect.

She was lying at the foot of the stairs. At first glance it looked as if she had broken every bone in her body as she fell. Her skirt was thrown up to reveal legs twisted awry. One was bent in the opposite way to its natural articulation. I felt my stomach lurch at the sight, even though I am neither a fainter nor a vomiter when it comes to a corpse. As apothecary to St Saviour's Infirmary I had seen all manner of dead bodies, not to mention the horrific injuries I had mended or treated – limbs torn off by the winding gear at the docks, flesh eaten away by the pox, drunks raw from the burns they had sustained falling into the fire. Will, however, was not so inured, and when he saw the woman's broken body he cried out and stepped back. His spade clattered to the floor as his hand flew to cover his mouth. Mrs Christian lay on her front, though her face was directed towards the ceiling. Her eyes gazed up, wide and sightless. Her jaw had been smashed and her mouth hung open in grotesque mockery of a smile, like a puppet cut from its strings and caught in a cackle of horrible laughter. Her head had twisted almost right round, her neck completely snapped. Her arms were flung out at her sides, one broken at the elbow. The whole effect was so horrifying, such a monstrous shattered parody of the human form, that for a moment I felt slightly lightheaded. It was as though she had fallen from a great height, had been smashed and broken and left where she fell. A gash to her left temple had oozed darkly, the blood seeping into her left eye was blackened and dried, the other stared up at us glassily. Her mouth, like her husband's, was filled with a mass of black, shining berries. I did not bother to feel for a pulse, for no human could lie at such an angle and live.

At that moment a door creaked open behind us and a woman came towards us. Her grubby apron and fatigued demeanour, along with the heavy coal scuttle she carried, proclaimed her to be a housemaid. She froze when she saw us, the coal scuttle slipping from her hand with a crash and flinging its contents across the floor. The noise tore through the silence. She put her hands to her face in fear at the sight of us, two strangers standing in the hall, and she made as if to scurry back the way she had come.

'Miss,' I said, hastily tearing off my coat and tossing it over the corpse which, fortunately, she had not yet noticed. 'There's been an accident. If you could send someone for the constable.'

'An accident?' she said. 'What kind of accident? And who are you?' She backed away, recoiling further into the shadows.

'We are friends of Mrs Christian,' I said. I held out my hands to her in a placatory gesture, but she shrank away from me. 'I am Mr Flockhart from the apothecary on Fishbait Lane, and this is my friend Mr Quartermain. We are acquainted with Dr and Mrs Christian – we were here the other day. We had an important matter we wished to discuss with Mrs Christian this morning.'

She seemed suddenly to notice the mess she had made on the floor, and she crouched down, anxiously plucking up lumps of coal and dropping them back into her scuttle.

'Never mind those,' said Will. He stepped forward, but she sprang back from him, her hands to her face. 'Please,' he said. 'Could you send someone for the constable? Quickly now?'

'Someone?' she said. 'Why, there's no one here, sir. She sent everyone away. Gave us all the night off. Said I was to leave out a cold supper and to go to see my sister, so that's what I did, sir, and just back this moment.'

'Mrs Christian and the doctor were both alone last night?'

'The master was in his room early, sir,' she replied. 'I left here about four. They both seemed well enough then, though I didn't see the master.'

'Perhaps you would go next door and ask one of them to send for the constable,' I said.

'Next door, sir?'

'To your neighbours.'

'I don't know them, sir,' she replied. 'Dr and Mrs Christian keeps themselves to themselves.'

'Well, on this occasion I think it's time you made their acquaintance.' I pulled open the front door, anxious to get rid of her. 'This way will be quicker.'

'Yes, sir. Thank you, sir.' She bobbed a curtsey and vanished out into the freezing morning.

I pulled my coat from Mrs Christian's body, and looked down at her. 'Was she attacked?' said Will. 'Or did she fall down the stairs?'

'I believe she fell down the stairs,' I said. 'Whether she fell or was pushed is, as yet, unclear.' I stepped forward and looked up. On the floor above us was a balustrade, another on the floor after that, for the stairs rose up into the darkness, winding about themselves like the whorl of a seashell, up to the top of the house. A dirty glass cupola let in a sickly, greenish light. 'Up there,' I said, pointing. 'If she fell over that banister at the top, she would have landed on her head right at this spot – which would certainly account for the state of her corpse.'

'I doubt she fell with her mouth full of nightshade

berries,' said Will. 'How long do you think she has been here?'

'I'm not sure,' I said. I put my hand to her flesh. It was cold and hard, like the meat in a butcher's shop. 'The house is freezing, so she would not have retained any body heat for long. The main indication of how long she might have lain here is the rigor, and the hypostasis.'

'Hypostasis?'

'Post-mortem hypostasis,' I said. I crouched over the body, lifting its arm, its head, as best I could to look underneath. 'When you die your heart stops. Your blood stills. What happens to it then? Like any other fluid it begins to seep downward, towards the lowest point; usually the point where the body is touching the floor. The smallest vessels fill up first, the capillaries next to the floor, or whatever the body might be resting on. The blood stains the skin as it leaches through. Then it clots, the way blood always does when it dries. It means the red stain becomes fixed. Immovable. After a few hours, two maybe, the stain is permanent. Even if you move the body the stain remains. You see how red her cheek is?'

'I cannot look, Jem.' He turned his head away.

'This is a stain, not a bruise. What that tells us is that she fell, and she lay here for some hours.'

'I see. Anything else?'

'Yes, in fact, there *is* something else. I believe she lay here for approximately two hours before her mouth was filled with poisonous berries.'

'How can you tell?'

'After two hours of lying here on the stairs the body would be so stiff with rigor mortis that opening the jaw would be impossible without force. There may be something lying around—' I looked about, on the floor of the hallway, on the stair treads, behind the front door. I found what I was looking for against the skirting board further down the hall, as if it had been thrown there with some impatience once the job was done. A poker, with an iron shaft and a brass handle. 'This poker was used to prise her jaw open. You see her teeth are broken, the skin damaged, a black mark on her lips from the coal and smuts that coated its tip? So, what can we conclude? That she fell from the second-floor balustrade, and lay here for over two hours, at which time someone broke her jaw and stuffed her mouth with poisonous berries.'

'She must have been expecting a visitor, to send the servants out for the night,' said Will. 'Perhaps she fell before they came. Perhaps they had determined in advance to kill her, and then had to modify the situation to suit themselves? They might have left her corpse alone if they wanted it to look like an accident. The addition of the deadly nightshade makes the whole thing look more like murder.'

'Then perhaps murder it is.'

'But why be so obvious about it? I don't understand.'

'To implicate someone, perhaps?'

'But who might be implicated?'

'Why, me for one,' I said. 'I am an apothecary, after all. And as the constable said earlier, I seem to know an awful lot about it.'

'That's ridiculous.'

'Is it? There is a connection between this death and the body in the physic garden. I connect the two. And now here I am, standing over my third corpse in as many days.'

'Perhaps it's a warning,' said Will. He glanced at Mrs Christian, and then looked away again. 'Though for whom I have no idea as there is no one here to see her.'

'Perhaps you're right,' I said. 'A macabre death like this will not remain a secret for long. Broken bodies flung down stairs and mouths stuffed with poisonous berries? This will be in the *Police Gazette* immediately, all of the newspapers too, I shouldn't wonder. By the end of the day all of London will know of it. *"Mrs D. Christian, wife of the celebrated Dr R. Christian, of Wolfsbane House, was brutally murdered in her own home, her mouth stopped with the fruits of the* Atropa belladonna, *commonly known as deadly nightshade, and one of the most feared poisons in the apothecary's dispensatory."* So perhaps this *is* a warning, or a message of some kind. What else would such a dramatic ending signify? She might have been left at the foot of the stairs, or pushed beneath the wheels of a cab, and nothing but death by misadventure be recorded in the magistrate's ledger. If all that was required was to get rid of the woman then there were myriad ways of doing so.'

'Jem, we should leave this to the police. To the magistrate. It is no concern of ours.'

'Really, Will? You think either the police or the magistrate will have the wit or imagination to deal with this? To work out what might be going on here? They will look for the most obvious and least time-consuming scapegoat – in this case that is most likely to be me.' I sighed. 'An apothecary with a clear connection to the deceased – her husband found frozen stiff at my door. It would not be the first time they jumped to the wrong conclusions.' Not long ago I had spent some time in Newgate, wrongly accused of murder. I had narrowly avoided the gallows. The police, and the magistrate, had shown little determination to find out whether I was innocent or not. Given that, I had no faith in them at all. If the truth was to be arrived at, then I would have to uncover it myself, with or without Will's help. I said as much – and saw his face darken.

'You hardly have cause to doubt either my loyalty or my ability to help get to the bottom of the matter,' he said.

'I'm sorry.' I clapped him on the shoulder. 'It's – it's this situation. That body in *my* garden. My mother's name – after so many years, to hear her spoken of by so many, and in such circumstances—' I felt my crimson birthmark grow hot and prickly, the way it always did when my emotions rose. I prided myself on remaining in control, dispassionate and aloof, no matter what I heard or saw. But never had my own history, and my mother's, been held up to such scrutiny. I hesitated to say what was on my mind, but I had no choice. 'I don't know what's going on, Will, but I think we are in the middle of something very dark, and very dangerous. We are up against someone driven by powerful emotions. This is not about money or fame, it is not about jealousy or greed. I have no idea what it *is* about, but we must be on our guard, Will. Both of us. If poison is involved, we can take no risks.'

He nodded, his face serious. 'Well, then, we must take advantage of our current situation and look around. The police will be here before long.'

He was right. We would not be permitted to poke about the place once the maid returned with the constable. I looked over the body once more. I noted that the tips of her fingers were black, that there was a slipper on only one of her feet, that her wedding ring bit onto the flesh of her finger as if she had never removed it. It was as much as I could bear to do, for that yawning, nightshade-filled mouth was one of the most hideous things I had ever seen. I could hardly keep my gaze from it. I wondered what the police would make of the berries. Would they implicate me? Who else, they would say, had access to such a supply, as well as the requisite knowledge of poisons? For a moment I was tempted to remove them, to empty that gaping hole and put every single belladonna berry into my pocket. But no doubt they would be lodged in her hypopharynx too, perhaps stuffed down into her oesophagus, and I did not fancy scrabbling about down a corpse's throat for poisonous fruits.

I wanted to go to the drawing room where we had first met the Christians, and where I knew Mrs Christian at least spent most of her time, so we made our way down the same gloomy corridors we had traversed not two days earlier. Our footsteps were muffled by the Persian runner that covered the darkly varnished floorboards, about us, the house resolutely silent. In the drawing room the curtains were pulled closed. The grate was black and cold and the room frigid. I had been under the impression last time that the fire had barely kept the winter at bay, and that as soon as the flames died and the cinders lost their heat then cold and damp would sweep in. The iciness of the place ate into our bones and our breath bloomed before us, spectral in the dark.

We threw the curtains wide. The sun's bloody rays revealed a scene of complete confusion. Books were thrown all over the place, pulled from the shelves and cast onto the floor. Some of them had fallen open, their spines cracked in two. I could see Mrs Christian's small neat handwriting clustered about the margins and overlaying the words, like black ants crawling over the pages. Many books were still on the shelves whilst those on either side of them had been flung aside, so that there seemed no logic to it at all, as if the books selected for scrutiny and rejection were entirely random.

'What chaos!' said Will. 'The place was so neat and orderly last time, everything laid out just so. Who on earth did this? If Mrs Christian did it she must have been frantic!'

I picked up one of the books that had been thrown to the floor, then another, and another. I looked at those still on the shelves. 'Whoever did this was looking for something and looking desperately. You see all the books that remain on the shelves have the author or the title marked upon the spine? All those that have been tossed to the floor have no writing on their spines. They were searching for a book that had no markings on the spine but might only be identified by the content of its pages. Would Mrs Christian do such a thing?'

'I don't know,' said Will. 'She knew what was in her own library more intimately that anyone. She had copied most of it out onto reams of paper.'

'So we might assume that someone other than Mrs Christian did this, and that perhaps they did not know what they were looking for, or what it looked like. And yet they have not done this to all the shelves but seem to have stopped at "M".'

'Perhaps they found it.'

'Perhaps they did,' I said. 'Whatever it was. But, let us look around some more while we can.'

Those walls that were not covered with bookshelves were hung about with botanical paintings, darkened by years of smoke, their once beautiful colours filmed over with a dim sootiness. They were beautifully executed, showing plants from far-away places, India, China, Ceylon, Burma, all the places the Christians had visited. Behind a screen decorated with painted leaves and flowers that stood before the left-hand wall, a pair of double doors, flung wide, led through to a library. The shelves lining the walls were filled with books on botany and *materia medica*, maps and charts rolled and stacked. A number of these books had also been cast aside. The place was dusty and neglected, as if it had been a long time since anyone had used it. I could tell from the whirling, choking atmosphere that the disruption of the bookshelves was recent, the frantic activity that had taken place sending up clouds of ancient dust that had yet to settle. A large workbench in the middle of the room was covered with the paraphernalia of the experimentalist – microscopes, flasks and dishes, test tubes clamped to stands, open cages that might once have contained dogs or rats but which now stood empty.

After that we went upstairs. The house exuded decay, indifference, loneliness. I had noted it on our first visit, but at least on that occasion the place had been the preserve of the living. We opened a door onto a room barely furnished and evidently little used. A nursery for a child that was no longer there. Dead, perhaps, rather than grown up? Bedrooms that appeared to be awaiting guests who no longer came. The room that had evidently belonged to Mrs Christian was cold, the small fireplace a black hole. The bed looked hard and uncomfortable, the drapery that surrounded it years old, dusty and faded. The furnishings were dark lumpen pieces, the walls hung about with the same botanical paintings we had seen downstairs. Even grimed with dust they glowed like jewels against the dark walls of that drab and cheerless chamber.

In the window stood an escritoire, the only item in the room that appeared to have been cared for, for if the rest of the room was neglected, this was the opposite: a place of industry and effort, strewn about with papers covered with a familiar tight-scribbled handwriting.

An ink bottle rolled empty upon the floor, a pewter inkstand with its lid flipped open bristled with pens, quills of varying size. A penknife lay atop a sheaf of yellowed papers, beside the scattered parings of whittled nibs and a stained, ebony-handled blotter. The drawers of the desk were open, the contents – more paper, maps, books – were disordered, as if hastily rooted through. I noted the location of the desk, positioned so that she might see out of the window at the driveway, and anyone who might be approaching, and also the door of the room, so that no one might enter unnoticed. 'It's the same sort of thing as we found downstairs,' said Will, looking over a few of the pages. 'Pages from the book she claimed to be writing. But this disorder, this is not Mrs Christian. Someone has been here too.'

My gaze travelled to the fireplace. Mrs Christian's corpse had smoke smuts on its fingers. Had she been up here, in this room, in the minutes before she had fallen from the balustrade? The fire had burned itself out long ago and the cinders were dark and cold. I bent closer. The ash was a mass of fine black flakes: paper burned away to almost nothing. And yet putting papers onto a fire was not as effective as one might think, especially if they had been burned in haste.

'What are you looking for?' said Will.

'I don't know,' I replied. 'I've no idea what's going on, but she burned something before she died. Something that it was evidently vital she got rid of.' I crouched at the grate, but the fragments there crumbled to dust immediately at my touch. I pulled out the grate and peered beneath, but there was nothing there but powdery dust and ash. I put my hand against the mantel, and stuck my head into the fireplace, squinting to peer up the chimney. I reached my hand up the flue. The soot was thick, at first fluffy to the touch but then greasy. Nothing. I seized the poker and jabbed about with it up the chimney. A cascade of soot. Nothing. I stood back and tossed the poker into the hearth with a clatter. My hands were filthy. I pulled out my handkerchief and wiped them. 'I suppose we'll never know.'

And then, just as we turned to leave, something drifted from the chimney to lie amongst the ashes. No bigger than a butterfly, it was a fragment of paper, singed at the edges, and streaked with black and brown. Half burned, incomplete and charred as it was, the writing on it was still visible. I plucked it up. The words '*ants away . . . urgent . . . garden*' were written in a bold clear hand I knew I had seen somewhere before. And further down, written with a flourish, the word '*she*'.

I took out my pocketbook and slipped the fragment inside.

How many minutes had passed since we had sent the housemaid to the neighbours? Perhaps ten? Fifteen? No doubt she was being calmed down with tea and brandy, a boy would have been sent for the constable, who would be here at any moment. We did not have much time. 'Come along, Will,' I said. 'We need to look at that balustrade on the top floor.' We climbed the stairs. The second storey was a place of loneliness and neglect. The paper on its walls was a dark, vivid green, but was peeling, blackened in places with water damage and hanging down like rotting vegetation. There were doors leading off to the right, but all of them were locked. The balustrade itself told us nothing – there was no blood, no evident scratches or marks. A single slipper lay against the balustrade, indicating the spot from which she had fallen. And yet there was something else on that top floor, something neither of us had expected to see. It was directly opposite the slipper, a door of dark oak, just like all the others – almost. But this door was darker. It had a greasy patina, as if it had been shouldered open many times. There were knocks and scratches to its surface, some recent, others clearly of long standing. A cheap tallow candle projecting from a pewter candlestick stood on a small table to the left. The wall behind bore streaks of black and brown, as if a lit candle had been left there regularly, its untrimmed wick trailing wraiths of soot. The door stood ajar; beyond it, a red glow pulsed. The smell from that one room had seeped out into the corridor like a physical presence: stale sweat, brimming chamber pots, dirty bedding. It was a smell that brought with it the memory of everything I had been glad to leave behind when they tore St Saviour's Infirmary down: unwashed bodies, neglect, sickness. And beneath it, always, the sweetish reek of opium. Will pulled out his handkerchief and pressed it to his nose as I pushed open the door.

At first, I could not make out what we were looking at, though the red glow we had seen was nothing more alarming than the crimson dawn striking through a gap in the heavy brocade curtains. The casement was open wide, the breeze that blew in making the curtains billow, bringing with it the familiar tang of the river and the stink of night soil. Will pushed past me and strode towards the casement, pulling the dusty drapes aside with a flourish. The dawn light flooded in, blood red, the bars that covered the windows a black silhouette upon the bare floorboards. There was an opium pipe in the hearth, long and thick, with a wide heavy bowl. Beside it, a low flame still guttering within, was the red lamp used to heat the opium. A bed stood against the far wall. It was narrow, iron framed, with a thin mattress not unlike those we had had at the Infirmary. Its sheets were rumpled and stained. Upon it, in a tangle of dirty canvas and greasy leather straps, was a straitjacket. A chain attached to its leather collar passed through a thick, heavy ring that had been screwed into the wall. A tray of food lay on the floor, upturned, as if knocked to the ground. 'This was Dr Christian's room?' said Will.

'I can't think who else might have slept here,' I said.

'What theory do you have?'

'That Dr Christian escaped from this room, flung his wife – intentionally or not – over the balustrade, and ran away.'

'Who filled their mouths with berries? Who wrecked the drawing room and library, Mrs Christian's desk?'

'I don't know.'

We were both silent for a moment. Then, 'The maid we sent out seems to be taking rather a long time,' said Will.

'Too long. I am beginning to wonder—'

'What?'

'Whether she was entirely what she seemed.'

'How so?'

I thought over the exchange we had had with the girl. It had been quick, and the hall gloomy. Will and I were distracted by the broken body we had found, by the need to stop the girl from looking at it, and it had not registered in my mind that she might be anything other than what she seemed. She had said she was a maid, she had looked like a maid, she had been carrying a brimming coal scuttle, and had acted with the usual cringing deference we expected from a servant. And yet . . .

'She did not ask who'd had an accident,' I said. 'It's possible that, as a servant, she hardly cared which of her employers it was, but she did not ask what type of an accident either. She exhibited fear at the sight of us, and dropping the coal scuttle was an excellent distraction as it allowed her to keep well back, to crouch down picking up the mess, to put her hands to her face in alarm, so that I have no idea what she actually looked like.'

'She was just a girl,' said Will.

'We have no real idea *what* she was,' I said. 'Was she a girl? Was she a woman, or a boy? Had she really just returned, as she said she had, or had she been there all along? Were there others with her, escaping out of the back while she distracted us from the front? One cannot leave the house without being seen from the front windows, and she would have been an excellent decoy.' I thought of the chimneys I had looked up at as we had approached the house. I had noted to myself that not one of them was smoking. I had known then that something was wrong.

Now, I wondered why on earth a housemaid would be carrying coals through the house when she had not even kindled the fire in the kitchen. What a fool I had been!

'You think she murdered Mrs Christian?' Will was saying. 'Or filled her mouth with berries? That she wrecked the house looking for a book?' He sounded incredulous. 'She was just a servant!'

'I have no idea who she was,' I said. 'Can you describe her?'

'No,' said Will after a moment.

'No,' I said. 'Neither could I, apart from a general impression. We never look at servants. The point of them is to be unobtrusive, and her costume was so drab, her appearance so average that we had no reason to pay her much notice, or to doubt her. Certainly I think she might *not* have been a servant. The note from the fireplace bears only a few words: "ants away . . . urgent . . . garden". It's not much to go on, I admit. But might it not be "send the servants away tonight. I have something urgent I wish to speak about concerning the garden", or perhaps "the physic garden", or even "the body in the garden"?'

'And who might "she" be?'

'I have no idea! It might refer to someone, or be a warning about someone. If I knew that, our next steps would be much easier. I admit to being a little disappointed, Will. If our opponent was the servant then she seems a very commonplace adversary, though a convincing little actress.'

'Perhaps she was not alone.'

Before I could answer we heard a noise. It sounded like a door slamming, and voices, far away in the bowels of the building.

'Perhaps we have spoken too soon,' said Will, 'and the girl was just as she seemed.'

We ran downstairs, towards the voices which were coming from the back of the house, the kitchen and scullery. In the kitchen a woman was standing beside the kitchen table tying an apron over her dress. 'You think they've managed without us?' she was saying. 'I'm more than happy to get a day's holiday and a sovereign for my pains, but will it be worth it when we see what a mess they'll have made of the place? She says she's kindled more fires than I've had hot dinners, but I can't see how.' She caught sight of my unexpected face in the doorway and let out a scream. The woman she'd been talking to, a scullery maid, stared at Will and me as if we were demons. I had caught sight of myself in a mirror as we passed through the house to the kitchen and I had to admit that with my crimson birthmark, now adorned with smoke smuts, I did indeed look rather alarming. I held out my hand. 'Please, madam,' I said. 'I'm here by invitation. I believe you're the housekeeper? We met the other day.'

'Cook, housekeeper, dogsbody,' replied the woman, the colour slowly returning to her flabby cheeks. 'Mrs Walker to you. And yes, I remember you.' She pointed to my birthmark. 'I'm not likely to forget *that*!'

'There's been an accident,' I said. 'We have already sent the housemaid to fetch the constable.'

'Housemaid?' she said. She gestured towards the girl with the lank hair and grubby apron who was kneeling in front of the fire with a box of kindling and a coal scuttle. 'This is the housemaid. This is Betty. You been back here earlier, Betty?'

'No, Mrs Walker,' said the girl.

I cursed myself. She was no more a servant than I was. How easily we had been duped! My only excuse was that the sight of Mrs Christian had so distracted me that I had been hardly able to think of anything else.

'What accident?' said Mrs Walker again. She sank onto a chair. 'Is it the master? I knew it. He's not been himself these past few days.'

'Did Mrs Christian send you away?' I said.

'Yes,' she replied. 'All of us away. Me, and Betty here and Samuels the coachman. She said it were time we all had a holiday. Told us to stay away till seven o'clock, that she would see to the master and herself until then. Went to see my sister, I did. Betty went home. Don't know about Samuels.'

'So there were no servants in the house at all?' I said.

'None,' she replied.

'And do you know *why* she sent you away?'

'Oh yes, sir,' she said. 'It's because someone was coming, she said.'

'Who?'

'Bathsheba Wilde. She was expecting Miss Bathsheba Wilde.'

Excerpts from the diary of Catherine Underhill.

10th July 1818

Bathsheba has asked me to stop writing my journal. She says that is not what she has employed me for. If I write, I must write what she has told me to write. It is the first time I have sensed her disapproval of me. I told her that I had lost my journal overboard that very morning when I was writing on deck, leaning on the rail. I am not sure she believed me.

25th July 1818

Bathsheba has been through my belongings. I suspect she was searching for my diary, though she did not say so. Instead she said she was checking to make sure I had brought the most appropriate travelling items. Fortunately, I had concealed my diary beneath my mattress. I decided it would be better not to object to her search of my possessions, whether her reason for doing so was convincing or not.

7ᵗʰ August 1818

Tonight, Bathsheba, Mrs Christian, Jane and I dined at the captain's table. I think it was not his idea, but he put a brave face on it. Bathsheba was very animated. One of our fellow diners asked what her interests were, and there was some general discussion about horticulture. The other ladies at the table wanted to talk about roses and lilies. Mrs Christian and Bathsheba wanted to talk about the nightshades, of which there are a prodigious number.

'That potato, captain, that you are mashing into your gravy with such violence is of the nightshade family,' she said. 'Likewise the tobacco you stuff into your pipe of an evening.' The captain looked as though he would like to tip both potatoes and gravy over Bathsheba's head, as she had earlier told him that the hull of his ship was riddled with worms and that he would be better served by the hardwoods of India if he wanted a ship that would last.

'Tomato,' she went on. 'Peppers, chilli plants, or "capsicums" as they are more commonly known. All common foodstuffs in various parts of the world, all part of the same family. But I prefer the more interesting nightshades, Atropa belladonna, Datura stramonium, *the* Mandragora. *Their effects upon the human brain and body are truly fascinating.' She went on to say that it was a fine line that separated medicine from poison. Tobacco being a prime example. 'One might smoke its leaves and derive only pleasure. But if those leaves are soaked and the essence is distilled, then it will kill you in an instant.'*

The company fell silent for a moment. Mr Rexman, a tax collector from the East India Company who was also dining with us that evening, made a comment about witches, and how perhaps the captain might consider burning Bathsheba at the stake if there were any unexplained deaths on board. Or, as a bonfire was not a good idea on a ship, perhaps a ducking stool might be fashioned from the captain's chair and a length of rope?

Everyone laughed, the captain especially, 'Though no one is throwing my chair overboard, even for such a good cause as that!' There was more laughter. Bathsheba smiled, and said Mr Rexman had better hope she was not a witch, as he would not reach Calcutta alive if she was. She said it with a smile and a merry laugh, but there was a glitter to her eye that I did not like. I think others saw it too, and it was fortunate that the ship's surgeon, who was already half drunk on the captain's brandy, said, 'Indeed, ladies and gentlemen, but we are to face some heavy seas over the next few days and you may soon all be begging Miss Wilde to put you out of your misery.'

9th August 1818

As the surgeon predicted, the weather has changed. Mr Rexman has been sorely afflicted by seasickness. This morning I watched him stagger up onto the deck after spending two days in his bed. I assumed he wished to get some air. He has not been seen since.

Chapter Nine

After asking us a number of questions, the police, eventually summoned by the genuine maid, let Will and me go – for now, at least. Dr Graves sent Bloxham on the corpse-wagon to collect Mrs Christian's corpse and take it to the mortuary. I followed in a cab. I had no wish to travel with Bloxham, though I was determined to help Dr Graves with Mrs Christian's post-mortem. I asked Will if he would come with me.

'Good Lord, no,' he replied. 'I never want to see either of them again. Two bodies before breakfast? That's a record, even for you, Jem!' He declined to take a cab back home, saying that he would stroll back as he needed some fresh air. 'Send a runner to fetch me when you're done,' he said. 'Or I can meet you in Sorley's. I don't mind where, I just don't want to be around any more corpses until after lunch.'

Dr Graves was not the only surgeon called upon by the magistrate or the police to conduct post-mortems, but he, or one of his henchmen, was almost always the first on the scene when a body was discovered. I saw some of his urchin informants now as I approached the mortuary. They recognised me – I am well known about the neighbourhood and my devilish face is hard to forget. Their ringleader was a skinny young lad with a bruise on his cheek and a filthy cap on his head. I tossed him a shilling.

'Dr Graves in?'

He nodded. 'He's arguing with a woman.'

I stopped. 'A woman? Who?'

'Don't know her name.' He jangled the coins in his pocket. 'No idea who told her about this latest one but she's in there now.' He grinned. 'Arguing.'

Even from outside I could hear the sound of raised voices. Inside, the mortuary attendant was wiping down one of the slabs with a filthy cloth, a bucket of murky water at his feet. He wore an old overcoat, grey and stained, and a battered stovepipe hat pulled down over his ears. He nodded to me. 'Join in, why don't you, Mr Flockhart.'

'Thank you, Sam,' I said. I slid a half crown onto the slab. 'Let me know if anyone else comes in asking about these two.' I gestured towards the shrouded bodies that Dr Graves and the woman were arguing over. Sam pocketed the coin. 'What's it about, Mr Jem?'

'I don't know,' I said. 'Let's hope we can soon find out.'

Dr Graves was looking furious. His face was crimson, his brow creased into a scowl. His eyes kept darting over to Dr and Mrs Christian, who lay side by side on two slabs at the back of the mortuary.

'Madam,' Dr Graves said. 'You cannot *watch* a post-mortem. It is not an appropriate spectacle for a lady.'

'You expect me to faint, sir? Or to scream? I have killed a snake with my bare hands, have sucked poison from a hornet's sting at the top of a man's thigh and cauterised spider bites on my own leg with a hot knife.' Bathsheba Wilde pulled her skirts up and showed him a tanned and muscular calf bearing two pale scars.

'Madam!' cried Dr Graves, recoiling from the sight as if he had been slapped, though I knew for a fact he was a regular at Mrs Roseplucker's Home for Young Ladies of an Energetic Disposition, a brothel on nearby Wicke Street, so this feint at modesty was purely for form's sake. 'Are you a lady? I cannot think you are if you feel it appropriate to engage in so shameless a display!'

'I have pulled worms from the soles of men's feet, lanced boils the size of quails' eggs – have you seen a tropical boil, sir? They are not like our own.'

'Indeed,' stuttered the doctor. 'I have no doubt—'

'Well then, man! Step aside and let me be seated. Why, I've stitched up wounds that made the Company surgeons blanch as white as a memsahib's arse—'

'*Lady!*' roared Dr Graves. '*If* you please! Whatever you have done, however many *arses* you may have seen, in *my* mortuary you will not "help". Ah Flockhart, there you are!' He plunged towards me and seized my hand desperately. 'Tell this . . . this *woman* that I am not to be trifled with.'

She looked at me and her mouth twitched into a smile. 'Mr Flockhart,' she said.

'Miss Wilde.'

'Tell her she cannot attend,' snapped Dr Graves.

'Why would you wish to attend, ma'am?' I asked.

'She was my friend,' she said. 'I have a right to know how and why she died.'

'And him?' I pointed to the shrouded figure of Dr Christian. By the collection of bowls and vessels laid out on the table at the back of the mortuary I knew his post-mortem had already been completed.

She snorted. 'I don't care a jot about him. Neither did she. I would guess that he died of a heart attack, brought on by the abuse of narcotics of various kinds. Opium. Aconite. Cannabis. Belladonna.' She glanced up at me, her eyes dark and keen, as if she expected that last word to elicit a response, an acknowledgement of some kind.

'We will inform you of the outcome, madam,' I said. 'But Dr Graves is correct. You are not permitted to watch the proceedings. No one is, who is a member of the general public.'

Dr Graves was licking his lips. Now that she had been defeated he was no longer interested in her. Instead, rather like Miss Wilde herself, he now seemed interested only in the shrouded corpse of Mrs Christian. He had set out his knives side by side, and, one by one, was buffing them lovingly on his shirt tail.

Bathsheba Wilde looked as if she would like to seize one of those knives and plunge it into his carotid. Instead she fished in her bag – a huge leather satchel – and handed me a *carte de visite*. Some three inches by four, it was bordered with a narrow strip of green, one side of it printed with an elaborate linocut of clustering fruits and flowers – purple hoods of aconite, golden trumpets of narcissus, oleander, frangipani, may apple – each was as beautiful as summer, and as deadly as a viper's poison. In the midst of these a name was printed in stark black lettering: *Bathsheba Wilde, Nightshade House, Islington Fields*.' She laid the card on the slab.

'I know who are you are, madam, and where you live,' I said.

'We start,' she said, 'at half past eight. Come tomorrow. I have some others attending too. You might find it a rewarding evening.' She turned to leave, but I had one thing I had to ask.

'Before you go, madam, may I ask whether Mrs Christian was alive when you saw her last night?'

She blinked. 'I did not see Mrs Christian last night,' she said. 'I saw her two nights ago. She came to see me, and I can assure you she was alive and well when she left.'

'By God, Flockhart,' said Dr Graves as the woman vanished up the mortuary steps. 'What a harpy! I never liked her.'

'You've met her before?'

'I have.' His tone was grim, his lips pressed together in a thin line. 'Though I wish I had not.' Dr Graves examined each of his knives in turn, picking them up and studying the blades. The Liston knife evidently failed his exacting standards of cleanliness, for he scraped at a bit of dried blood with a horny thumbnail. 'She is not without skill as a horticulturalist and a botanist,' he said. 'Spent some years in India, I believe.' He looked at me, but his face gave nothing away. The lamp was behind him, the window high in the ceiling showed dark winter clouds that added little illumination, and his eyes were dark shadows in his pale, gaunt face. He pulled a whetstone from his bag and drew his knife across it slowly. The rasp echoed from walls and ceiling. 'Yes,' he said. 'Kew took many of her finds. Edinburgh too. The Chelsea Physic Garden, and your own both benefited. Yours especially. Private collectors,' he shrugged. 'There were those willing to pay a high price. There always are. You'd be surprised, Flockhart, at the money an orchid will command, or a new species of rhododendron. Not that I have any interest in these things. But there has always been a disreputable air about her, about her behaviour. She knew Dr Christian and his wife very well. Christian was one of our physicians, of course. But physicians are an arrogant breed. They act as though their knowledge is some sort of rare, alchemical specialism, when in fact they do little more than slap on leeches and administer purgatives. Even you apothecaries can manage better!'

'Thank you, sir,' I said. 'I had no idea you rated my skills so highly.'

Dr Graves smirked. 'Look, Flockhart, there's little affection between you and me, but you're an honest man, and a capable one at that. You're wasted in that shop of yours. You have your apothecary's licentiate, you ran St Saviour's for years, so you're already a doctor, and better than most of them. Take your MD. Get out from amongst the jars and bottles and make some money, man. Your father would be proud. All the work you did with poisons shouldn't go to waste either. It'd make the perfect thesis. I know you'd almost completed it when Dr Bain was murdered. I'd take it somewhere away from this old place too. Edinburgh, perhaps, or Glasgow. Both fine places for a man of your ability.' He turned away. 'There,' he muttered. 'I've said it. I'll not be saying it again either, so you'd best remember it.'

'Thank you,' I said. Had he just given me a compliment? Some advice and encouragement? I had known the man all my life and he had not once acknowledged my skill, indeed, it usually seemed anathema to him that he even acknowledge my presence. 'Are you quite well, sir?' I said.

'Perfectly,' he snapped. 'Why?' He did not wait for an answer but stopped sharpening his knife and tested the blade with his thumb. 'But we were talking about that Wilde woman, weren't we? It's my belief she murdered her half-brother though I have no proof.' He shrugged. 'And then she took his body back and had it incinerated in the garden before anyone could do anything about it. Some say she took his heart out first, and keeps it in a box.' He laughed. 'Then she tried to publish his work under her own name. As if a woman could author anything intelligible!'

'Wilde's *On Poison*?' I said. 'I have it.'

'I should hope you do,' he said. 'It's an important book.'

'Well,' I said, 'it might have been important in its time, but it is somewhat outdated now, and based rather too much on old wives' tales, superstition and rumour rather than experimentation.'

Dr Graves grunted. 'She's a tartar! Money like you wouldn't believe. Her father was a friend of Clive, you know, so that'll tell you something about the kind of money I'm talking about. Arrogant nabob, if you ask me. The son – her half-brother – was just the same. She was the illegitimate sister, of course. She's a half caste herself, which might account for some of the goings on one heard about. I can tell you here and now, Flockhart, it's nothing a British woman would ever dream of doing.'

'What sort of goings on?' I said.

'Having an opinion and insisting she was right, for a start. You heard her when you came in! Christian was in awe of her, and his wife too. Can't think why. Can't stand an opinionated woman,' he muttered. 'All that *do this* and *do that*, and *I know best*. It's enough to make a man want to knock their heads together. Christian's wife was just as bad. No wonder Christian sought his pleasures elsewhere. Who'd get a cockstand with all *that* going on all the time?'

'That's it?' I said. 'A woman has an opinion and for that you condemn her?'

'That's the start of it,' snapped Dr Graves. 'Women can't hold opinions of their own, they are too weak. Their minds can't manage. That Wilde woman is a perfect example. But there were other things – her peculiar interest in native customs, all those women she used to have staying with her. Didn't eat meat! Can you believe it?' He shook his head. 'Of course, it's all of little interest to me, I was never a part of that set. The three of them used to go out together looking for medicinal plants. Mind you, Christian was never the same after he came back from India that last time, though perhaps it was just the malaria.'

'When was that?'

'Oh, years ago now. I believe he was the director of some botanic gardens or other out there for a time. Not that all that greenery and traipsing about outdoors holds any fascination for me. Give me a dead body over a bag of roots and leaves any day of the week! And I'll empty my bowels in a controlled fashion, thank you very much, and not while I'm shitting out the after-effects of some native potion I've drunk. Oh no, Flockhart. The risks I took were in the graveyard at night, with my spade over my shoulder and two students stuffing a corpse into a sack, ha, ha! Each to his own, eh?'

Dr Graves rubbed his hands together. 'I must say, you're rather spoiling me today, Flockhart! Is this second one from your home and garden, or from somewhere else altogether?' He made a noise which I knew to be laughter, but which sounded more like a rusty gate being swung back and forth. I explained how it was that I had come by Mrs Christian's corpse.

'She's not a pretty sight,' I said. 'She fell down the stairs. Well, over the banister at the top of the stairs, to be precise. Quite possibly an accident, though the exact nature of that accident is impossible to describe as there are no witnesses. But we will come to that. Before we do, what can you tell me about her husband? I know you've already done him. Can you tell me how he died?'

'Heart congestion,' said Dr Graves. He gestured towards the collection of bowls and other receptacles he had set out on a long, scrubbed deal table at the far end of the room. 'Take a look for yourself, Flockhart. It was bound to happen sooner or later – if the opium didn't kill him first, of course. In that respect I'm surprised he lasted this long. Everything points to long term use. I've taken his organs for the students to see. They might like them for their own collections.'

Dr Graves threw back the old man's winding sheet and peered down at his anatomised corpse. 'What a sorry state he's in,' he remarked. It was true. Stripped of his nightgown the man before us on the slab was a pitiful sight. His bones seemed to lie just beneath the surface, the ribs and pelvis painfully visible. His skin was as pale as a trout's belly, with a damp sheen to it, like curd cheese. His limbs and body were hairless, what remained on his head wispy and long, straggling across his pale bulbous skull. His wrists were bruised, as if they had been tightly bound, his neck chafed raw, no doubt by the leather collar of the straitjacket we had seen in his chamber. I could not imagine what terror had assailed him in his final moments on earth, but his face was contorted into an expression of fear and horror that had not been softened by death. His eyes stared in his head, the blue irises so pale as to be almost invisible, so that it looked as though two hard-boiled eggs were bulging from his eye sockets.

'Do you mind if I take a bit of lunch, Flockhart?' Dr Graves had set out a collection of cheeses, cold meats and relish amongst the post-mortem receptacles, and they shared table space with Dr Christian's brains, liver, spleen, heart and other internal organs. He rinsed the knife he had used to eviscerate the corpse in a bucket of red water that stood beside the drain, and then used it to saw at a leg of boiled ham. 'Want a slice? I have plenty. I must admit a post-mortem always makes me peckish.'

I shook my head. 'No, sir. But thank you.' The pale lumps of cheese and pink sinewy ham glistened. Beside them, a spoon projected from a jar of lumpy, bile-coloured pickle.

'I have oxtail, and pressed tongue? Do help yourself if you change your mind.' I noted a blanket on a chair, and wondered, for a moment, whether Dr Graves actually slept in the place too. Certainly his foodstuffs looked at home amongst the organs.

Dr Graves handed me a tankard of ale, drawn from a keg in the corner of the mortuary. 'Your father never liked him,' he said, gesturing to Dr Christian with his knife. 'Treated him with professional courtesy, of course, but there was never any fondness between them. Christian was something of a ladies' man. Hard to believe now, though it's evident from the lesions on his head that he's had the pox. Lack of teeth too – always a problem with mercury. Yes, apart from a fondness for whores, Dr Christian and I had little enough in common. His wife was a shrew. Treated Christian like some sort of Indian bearer. No wonder the fellow sought oblivion in the pipe. But opium is a reluctant servant at the best of times, and it's a powerful master once it has you. He's not the first of our illustrious profession to fall foul of the stuff.'

'Was there anything unusual about the body?' I said. 'Anything unexpected?'

'He was undernourished,' replied Dr Graves. 'Though it's common in opium fiends. Half-starved, I'd say. Twenty, thirty years an addict, it's hardly surprising. His entire body cavity reeked of the stuff, and I've smelled enough corpses to know. Lungs especially, as you might expect. Bowels costive. Poor chap. Practically witless in the end, no doubt, though whether from the pox or the opium it's impossible to say.'

'And what killed him exactly?'

'His heart gave up,' said Dr Graves. 'Simple as that.' Dr Graves turned to write his thoughts in a heavy ledger chained to a desk in the corner of the room. I could not disagree with his conclusion, though to me it was evident that Dr Christian had died of a terror so great that it had caused his heart to stop. His midnight flight through London, his running – I had observed the soles of his feet, as well as the pavement outside my apothecary and it was evident that the man had been on tiptoe. Yes, the night had been freezing, and anyone would be reluctant to put their whole foot onto the freezing earth, but the distance between the toe prints on the pavement pointed to a different conclusion: Dr Christian had not minced to our door on his tiptoes but had raced towards it like a man pursued by the Devil. He had died before he could rouse us, and had dropped his curious skull memento on the ground as he expired.

'And the berries?' I said, though I already knew the answer.

'Yes, that was rather peculiar.' Dr Graves picked up a bowl. The contents glistened purple-black. 'Just in the mouth,' he said. 'A few in the throat, but his tongue got in the way making a blockage, so it looked worse than it was.' Dr Christian's mouth was still open, his slack lips stained dark with juice.

'What do you make of it?' I said.

'Oh, that's your department, Flockhart. What did you say it was? Some sort of sloe?'

'It's nightshade,' I said. I was sure I had already told him. The man didn't listen. 'Deadly nightshade. The thing is, it's wintertime. There are no fresh berries at this time of the year.' I took one up between my finger and thumb. It was plump and shining, ripe and juicy. 'Preserved in something. Alcohol, by the look of it, definitely spirits of some kind.'

'An apothecary's little joke, perhaps?' said Dr Graves. 'You keep berries like this, I suppose?'

'I keep it in all its forms. Usually as a tincture. But I can't see what their purpose is here. They didn't kill him?'

'No,' said Dr Graves. 'They're merely a decoration, as it were. A later embellishment. But he was already dead, so whoever put them in there was guilty of nothing more than desecrating a corpse.' I could tell that Dr Graves was no longer interested. He had wiped his lips on a handkerchief and was approaching the slab once more. Mrs Christian was next in line.

'Did they have any children?' I asked.

'Not that I'm aware of,' said Dr Graves. 'Just the two of them in that big old house.' He stared down at the body. Rigor mortis was well advanced, pulling the muscles of the woman's face into a grimace. The nightshade berries, plump and ripe, had burst to form a thick black paste that coated her teeth and tongue and oozed from her open mouth. It dripped down her chin in a black and purple mulch. The sight was sickening, the pale dead flesh and milky eyes against the black sticky mass, the broken jaw making the mouth wider and more demented than anything I had ever seen. Her body remained in its twisted and broken position. Her eyes were grey and filmy, one knocked askew by the fall so that she simultaneously gave me an angry stare, whilst also watched the door for incomers.

'Shall I strip her?' I said.

'Be my guest,' said Dr Graves. 'Want some tart, Flockhart?' And he turned his attention to a large custard tart he had brought with him. I shook my head and took my knife to the dead woman's clothes.

Mrs Christian's dress was a stiff carapace of dark green watered silk, close-fitting at the bodice and tightly laced at the waist. The skirt was wide and heavy, the sleeves buttoned at the wrist, the collar high at the neck, so that she would have been forced to keep her head and body upright at all times. Her torso was held rigid by strips of whalebone that ran the length of her body from beneath her breasts to the top of her pubis. I used a scalpel to cut the clothes from her body, the stiff fabric parting beneath my hands like the shell of a pupa splitting open to reveal the soft white grub nestled within. I noted the compression at her waist. The organs inside would be squeezed and dislodged, forced upwards into the lungs and downwards towards the bowels. I noted the lines on her flesh where the corset had dug into her, the curious shape of her body moulded by years of tight lacing. Here and there the skin was broken, as if the rough weave of the corset's lining had chafed the skin. Usually, corsets were lined with soft cotton, but this? This one had been lined with a sort of fustian, which must have been so uncomfortable against her skin that she might as well have worn a shirt of nettles like a medieval monk. Dr Graves seemed hardly to notice, so intent was he on his tart, but I took my time, noting the damage she had inflicted upon her own body. Most startling of all was what I found about her neck; a chain of some dull, brownish metal, iron perhaps, which had marked her skin in an angry red line. The thing that hung from it was as pale and cold as her skin. An ivory skull, some two and a half inches in diameter but perfectly formed, its eye sockets darkened by time and years spent pressed between flesh and fabric, so that it had a macabre, almost living appearance. It was hidden beneath her bodice, pressed tight against the breastbone by her constricting clothes, so that it had created a large circular bruise as black and purple as the berries that filled her mouth. I had noticed when we met that, as she spoke to me, she had raised her hand to her breastbone continually. I would never have guessed the reason for it.

I took the thing from around her neck, my hands shaking as I tried not to look at the ruined face, the blackened glistening mass in the screaming mouth. I am not a superstitious person, I do not believe in ghouls and curses, but as I pulled it over her head I felt a faint stirring of the air about me, as though someone nearby had sighed, so that I shivered and looked around. But there was no one but Dr Graves, licking his lips as he cut himself another slice of custard tart. I slipped the skull into my pocket. 'Well, sir,' I said. My voice sounded thin and reedy in my ears, but if Dr Graves noticed he gave no sign of it. 'Shall we begin?'

Excerpts from the diary of Catherine Underhill.

15ᵗʰ August 1818

Mrs Christian and Bathsheba spend a lot of time in each other's company. They are together in Bathsheba's cabin for hours. Earlier today Jane and I found them both asleep on the bunk together. The air was thick with the smell of Bathsheba's 'herbal mix'. I wish I knew what it was. Even Jane says she does not know.

The other passengers do not like us. Any of us. Jane's reputation is the talk of the ship. The captain went to speak to Bathsheba about it. Bathsheba promised to speak to Jane, but I knew she had no intention of doing so. None of the other women aboard will talk to us. Even Mrs Christian is shunned. None of them appear to care. And, as strange as I find the company I keep, I don't care either. I would choose my unorthodox and unpredictable companions over any of the other women passengers no matter what. I wonder whether I have changed much on this journey. Would I always have made this choice?

17th August 1818

Bathsheba has been taking a tincture of Atropa belladonna *and* Strychnos nux-vomica. *Death by strychnine poisoning is terrible to behold. I have seen it only once, in a boy who had ingested some that his mother had been using to poison rats, and who was brought up to the Infirmary convulsed by the most terrible seizures. His teeth were clenched into a grimace, his little body jerking back into an arch as his muscles spasmed. There was nothing that could be done for him and he was dead within minutes. With such a death the possible outcome, why anyone would experiment with the stuff I have no idea. She tells me that it acts as a tonic, that it stimulates her digestion and makes her more alert. Certainly, she seems more attuned than ever to my presence in the cabin next door (I am obliged to write slowly, beneath the bedclothes, in case she hears). The belladonna is just as dangerous. She says it is the reason she has been entirely unaffected by seasickness, but I know it also has powerful hallucinogenic effects. She seems not to be affected, though her behaviour is not like that of other women. The last three nights she has left her cabin after midnight to prowl up and down the deck. I have seen her myself, dressed in her Indian silks, standing with her hair streaming out behind her, watching the moon.*

18th August 1818

Bathsheba has just entered my cabin unannounced. Thank goodness I had put my diary under the bedclothes and picked up a copy of Willard's Flora of the Himalaya *the moment I heard her door opening. She has left me some of her belladonna and* strychnos *tonic, and strict instructions about the dosage. 'Too little and it achieves nothing, too much and death is a certainty. And yet what would life be without risk? Hum-drum, tedious, ordinary.' She took me by the shoulders and looked into my eyes. Her pupils were huge and dark, as if she were absent from her body and I were looking into an empty shell. 'We have the chance to be gods if we choose,' she said. Her voice sounded strange, as if she were speaking the words of others. 'There are ways of opening up our minds and bodies to higher, better things. Those with the courage to see beyond the everyday will reap the rewards.'*

I don't know what she was talking about, or what she wanted. I fear I will be unable to meet her expectations.

24th August 1818

We have had a calm evening after a day of high winds. I have just come in after some hours on deck with Bathsheba. Despite her curious habits, her non-conformity and disdain for the mores of the drawing room (mores which, it seems to me, become more and more oppressive the further we get from home) her knowledge and enthusiasm are a delight. Tonight, she made me lie beside her on the deck, looking up at the stars. I have no idea what the sailors must have thought. But it was late and few of them were around. There were no passengers, as they seem all to keep to their berths after they have dined. I felt exhilarated, and although we are sailing across the wide ocean on a crowded wooden vessel, it was as though she and I were the only two people on earth. She asked if I had taken her belladonna and strychnos mixture. I said I had, though in fact I had done no such thing. She looked pleased, and said, 'Can you feel your muscles singing? The fire running through your veins, through your mind?' She laughed, not waiting for my answer, and whispered, 'I have taken it for years. I am invincible. I have always felt it.' She started to tell me of the places she had been, and the sights she had seen. They were sights that had left her in no doubt that she had been chosen, she said – though chosen for what exactly, she did not make clear – and I could not help but envy her.

She told me about the ghost orchids of Cuba which bloom between June and August. 'They grow solely in Cyprus trees, in whose branches they seem to float, like ghosts. They are pollinated by the giant sphinx moth,' she said, 'and depend upon a single type of moss to propagate. It was dark and still that night too, with the smell of salt on the air just as it is now.

'And I have seen the Lotus bethelotii, fertilised only by sunbirds, themselves a great rarity. And the jade vine, long and blue-green and as luminous as a summer sea. It is pollinated by bats, which hang upside down to drink its nectar. I have seen the bats doing that very thing right before my eyes!

'I have been blessed, Cathy, blessed to have witnessed such marvels.' She squeezed my hand as she spoke, and I felt a thrill of pleasure that she had chosen to confide in me. Her lips and teeth had a red tint to them, which gave her a diabolical air, though I knew it was simply because she had been chewing betel nut, which she had bought off one of the Dravidian deckhands. 'Of course, my favourite of all these wonders is the Amorphophallus titanium. Bodiless, stemless, leafless, rootless, it leeches on vines for sustenance and support. It grows six feet high and stinks of rotting flesh.' She was smiling, and I admit now that I felt a little disconcerted by the sight of her, with her wild hair, her crimson teeth, her dark, fathomless gaze. 'All that a flower is, or should be, the Amorphophallus is not. For that reason alone, I admire it. For being the opposite of what is expected, what is wanted, I applaud it. I have tried to grow it, *but without success. For its refusal to be captured, controlled, subjugated, I revere it.'*

30ᵗʰ September 1818

Tomorrow, we arrive at Calcutta.

Chapter Ten

❦

Will and I went to Sorley's for tea. I could not face the apothecary with its grisly jumble of bones and mementoes. Indeed, it seemed to me that the physic garden and my apothecary were tainted now, cast into shadow by mystery and death. I had to find out what had happened, what was *still* happening. Both places had always brought me closer to my father – had he not schooled me in all I knew? – and to my mother – had she not loved the garden much as I? It bore the stamp of her, had helped me understand how she thought, how she had seen the world. Now, it seemed that all she had thought about was the concealment of the most unspeakable of crimes. Spending time with Will too, now that he was out of danger, was something I had anticipated with a pleasure I had tried hard to hide from him. How relieved I was to see him well again, to have him by my side in a garden he loved. I had planted some of his favourite things – the camomile lawn was for him, the colourful everlasting *helichrysum* that surrounded it were also for him as he loved their bright colours and indestructible straw-like leaves. I used a distillation of their oils, combined with peppermint and camomile, as a mixture for mental exhaustion, and as an anti-inflammatory, so there were at least some commercial benefits to be found in the great number of them that were now growing there. I had not let on how worried I had been, had not told him how many nights I had sat at his bedside in case he needed me. That he had recovered at all was a miracle in itself, did he too not deserve to spend time in the garden without being pursued there by images of death and decay? Could we not have one place where we might be at peace? Now, everything was spoiled. I could not clear my mind of my resentment.

'Three corpses in five days,' said Will, who appeared not to have noticed my black looks. 'Let us hope there's not another one tomorrow.'

I nodded. 'Mrs Spiker knew who our first corpse was,' I said. 'That was clear enough. But if she won't speak there's nothing we can do. Perhaps I will go back tomorrow.'

'And say what?'

'I don't know. I could show her the other things, the skulls.' I felt my skin grow chill at the thought of those horrible rattling death's heads. 'Surely she would respond to that.'

'Either that or it will finish her off.'

'I don't care if it does. Horrible woman in her nasty lair. Like a rat in a nest. I'm surprised Dr Anderson gives her licence to do it, no matter how much she might pay to be in the place.'

Will looked at me, surprised. 'Since when did you care

what patients got up to at Angel Meadow?' He stuffed his pipe with tobacco and handed me the pouch. Sitting back, he blew a cloud of pale smoke into the air. He coughed. Tobacco aided expectoration, but he should not have been smoking so soon after his illness. 'Who else might we ask?' he said. 'Who else was involved in the physic garden back then? Thirty-two years ago,' he shook his head. 'It's a long time. Who would remember? Perhaps Dr Graves?'

'Dr Graves was never interested in physic,' I replied. 'He is a surgeon and an anatomist. In fact, he loves the dead – perhaps because they do not answer back. As far as I'm aware he hasn't operated on anyone since St Saviour's moved south of the river. He told me he prefers cold flesh to warm.'

'Well, we need to find someone to speak to.'

'Bathsheba Wilde has invited me to dinner tomorrow,' I said.

'Just you?'

'So it seems.'

He grunted. 'You should have a care, Jem. She is not to be trusted.'

'What else can I do? And we have that publican's token too. We must visit the North Star Angel, or at least find out what we can about the place.' I rubbed my hands together. 'We are making progress.'

'I'd hardly call two fresh corpses progress, Jem,' he said. 'Whoever those bones belong to, their appearance has resulted in murder of the most extreme and violent kind. I hardly think the post-mortem of two people connected with this case is a cause for celebration.' He shook his head. 'Sometimes I hardly know you, Jem Flockhart. Is it only the thrill of the chase that pleases you? The solving of the puzzle that puts warmth into your veins?' He coughed again, two circles of colour appearing on his cheeks once more. I was about to make a retort along the lines of how it was just as well someone was giving the matter some thought, as otherwise no one would, and if we left it to the police, we would never know what had happened or why. But I let it go. He was not himself.

'I wonder why it was so important to put the berries into the mouth,' I said. 'Of all three corpses. There is clearly a link. The death of Mrs Christian is especially disappointing as I was sure I would be able to get her to talk once she knew her husband was dead. It was a difficult post-mortem. Rigor meant she was still in that broken and twisted position. You know, whoever did this had actually broken her jaw to get the berries in. Knocked her teeth out in the process. So clearly we are looking for someone not afraid to get into the thick of it. I assume someone who didn't know her well, or who disliked her. I mean, could you do that to me? Could you stick a poker between my teeth and break my jaw apart just so that you could make a point with some deadly berries?'

By now Will was almost translucent. His eyes were huge and dark, his lips and cheeks quite bloodless. I saw he had his bottle of *sal volatile* clutched in his right hand, though he had not yet taken a whiff of the stuff. 'Was it not enough to just throw her down the stairs?' he said. 'Even *worse* they must desecrate her corpse before it was even cold. What monstrous crimes have we stumbled on here, Jem? Two days ago we were looking forward to working in the garden, to air, and light and growing things, and now what do we have? We have an old man dead of terror at our door, and a dead woman at the foot of the stairs, her limbs twisted like old rope, her mouth wrenched agape and pounded full of black poisonous berries.' He shook his head, and I saw then that his hands were shaking too. 'I'm more afraid and puzzled by these deaths than by all the others we have witnessed over the years. More afraid than ever and afraid for all of us – myself, you, Gabriel, Jenny. Who is doing this, and why? What do they want? We have no idea even now, and look how quickly the corpses have piled up. Are you not afraid? I don't see it if you are. Perhaps it's because poison is your metier, your world. You don't see it for the horror that it is, only for the puzzle it presents, a chance to show off how much you know. But I *am* frightened, Jem. Yes, your mother's name is on that list, does that mean that they will come for you? Poison is so furtive a means of murder. It might be administered without anyone being aware of it. I am beginning to wonder where we might be safe. It might be put onto one's food, one's drink, into clothes, the very air we breathe–'

'Will, stop this,' I cried. 'Listen to yourself. You can't help matters by becoming hysterical.'

'You might at least show a little compassion for the dead. For Mrs Christian.'

'Why?' I snapped. 'Why should I show anything of the kind? In what way will emotion help us here? For a start I didn't know her, and what I did know of her I didn't like. She was a cold, secretive, disobliging woman. I care nothing for her death and weeping over it will serve no purpose at all. What *will* help, however, is if we take in the facts of what we see before us, and *think*, Will, think about how this happened, who knew her, who could have reached her, who had the knowledge of poisons to achieve such an outcome, why was such a death selected. There are many other poisons to choose from, and why was more than death required, so much so that they were prepared to use violence, to break teeth and bone simply to administer deadly berries to a corpse? Tell me how emotion, empathy or an excess of compassion is going to help us to answer any of those questions?'

Will shook his head. 'You're not yourself, Jem,' he said. 'You're better than this.'

'Oh, I am very much myself,' I said. 'This is who I am. It is *how* I am. I save my tears for when I need them. If you don't like it you may as well leave me to it.' I expected him to sigh, and shake his head, to mutter something about how he despaired of me sometimes. But he didn't. Instead, he stood up from the table where we sat, and leaving his ale untouched before him he walked out of the chop house. 'Will!' I said, but he did not turn around. 'Will!' I paid for our food and went after him. He was walking as briskly as he could manage, though I had caught up with him in a few steps. I tried to take his arm but he shook me off. 'Will,' I said. 'Please. I'm sorry.'

'Are you?' he said. He did not look at me, his face stony as he kept walking. 'I've never heard you speak so cruelly. So callously. Are you so completely without heart?' He sounded shocked, and disappointed, as if all at once his view of me had been revealed to be a sham, his belief that I was a good person a mirage he had been foolish enough to believe in, that he saw me now for what I was: flawed, brutal, cold. I could not bear it. How would I manage without his good opinion? Without his belief in me?

'Will,' I said. I tried to make him stop, but he pulled away still. The loneliness that had once been my constant companion, but which I had been able to put aside since

Will had been my friend, swirled about me like the incoming tide of a cold familiar sea. 'Forgive me,' I said. 'Please. You're right. I'm *not* myself. All this . . . it is all too close. Too close to home. My mother, my garden – it matters too much to me. And you're right too about the risks. To me, to you and the others. *I* am all that remains of my mother. What if *I* am found dead with my mouth stuffed with deadly nightshade? It's unclear what's at stake here or why. You must understand—'

'Must I? Well, I don't.'

'Will, I *have* to find out. It's in my nature, now more than ever. This is *my* mother, *my* past. I have to—'

'You have to put yourself in danger by going to this Bathsheba Wilde woman's house?'

'Yes, Will. I'm afraid I do.'

'I see.' He still did not look at me. His walk had slowed now, though through necessity, rather than because he had any choice in the matter, as I could see he was wheezing.

I threaded his arm through mine as we fell into step, as we always did when we walked. 'Lean on me,' I said.

He smiled, but it fell away quickly. 'Am I so weak, Jem?'

'Yes,' I replied. 'But you will be strong again. And the quest to find out what is going on will distract you from yourself.'

'I think I am not myself either,' he muttered. 'I am always so tired. It is making me frustrated.'

'Shall we go to the garden?' I said. 'You always like it in the twilight and it's almost dark now. And there's an owl in the oak beside the wall at the foot of the garden. It might come out. You like owls.'

I did not really want to go. We had not been to the

garden since we had dug up the remains. I knew we had not yet filled in the grave and the ground was blighted by the yawning hole from which we had extracted the skeleton. The deadly nightshade would still be lying beside the hole, a guilty mound of wilting roots. And yet perhaps it was better to break the spell, to take ownership of the place and not leave it to horror and death. Perhaps the owl would even put in an appearance. I knew the thought of it would entice him.

'Very well,' he said, 'though it's the last place on earth I want to visit. Not that home feels much better. We still have the bones at the back of the shop. It's attracting the wrong sort of customers.'

I loved the garden in the cold months. The damp, loamy smell of the earth and the fallen leaves, the mist that hung about the place in the mornings, the long shadows, the gold and silver light. In autumn, the soil seemed to exhale a slow, easeful breath, perhaps in relief at the end of its labours. By January, there was a cold, hard feel to the place, as though it were readying itself, gathering its strength for a riotous springtime display. The walls protected it from all but the worst of the wind, so that the leaves in my garden were always the last to fall. In November I set Gabriel and Jenny to work with the rake and a basket, and we would burn the last ends of the summer in a blazing golden bonfire. In January and February I prepared the earth for spring, digging and hoeing, the soil holding its bulbs and shoots like jewels hidden in a black velvet bag. This year, everything was different. Spoiled. The garden seemed rotten and malignant. Instead of wet leaves I saw toadstools and black slimy fungus. Instead of the scent of burned twigs and wet earth, there was only the stink of cheap coal from the houses on St Saviour's Street. And the ground was scarred by that dark, open grave. My mother had known who lay beneath. Had my father known too? Had he known and yet said nothing, allowed a man to lie rotting beneath his feet while he and I passed back and forth overhead?

Will did not speak. He did not need to. He knew what I was thinking. I unlocked the gate in silence, the key turning in the well-oiled mechanism with a smooth familiar silkiness that I had always secretly enjoyed. There was a technique to it, and only I could open the gate without grating and jangling and muttered curses. I closed it behind us noiselessly and we skirted the lavender bushes. And that's when Will froze. He put his hand onto my arm and pointed into the gloom.

Before us, down the garden, at the hole from which we had dug the bones, was a figure. I could not make it out at first, though I had the impression of someone hunched and darkly hooded. I saw claw-like hands caked with dirt. The face I could not see, but I had the impression again of darkness, a visage so black that it seemed to shine blue in the light from its lantern, a white flash of teeth as it grinned and muttered to itself. It was in the grave, right inside it, bending and scrabbling and sifting the earth. Will and I stood stock-still. How might we approach, or apprehend the creature? Whatever means it had used to get in the garden, it would presumably seek the same way out. The gate was behind us, but I knew there were quick and easy ways to get over the high wall that separated us from our neighbours – if one knew the garden's secret places. And then, all at once, he – it – whatever dreadful apparition we were looking at, seemed to sense it was no longer alone. It stopped its crouched scrabbling. Quickly, it glanced up at us. And then it sprang forward, up and out of the grave, and in a flash it was racing across the camomile lawn, low and fast, its dark cloak billowing out behind.

'After it!' I cried. 'Will!' I had fire in my veins then. What was this dreadful creature, how dare it come into my physic garden, rooting and dancing in the earth that I tended? I bounded after it. Oh, but how quickly it moved, springing from the grave like a jack-in-the-box, leaping over the beds of poppies, sending their seed heads dancing, hurling itself left and right, through the rhubarb, past the glasshouse and down towards the dog-roses and comfrey that grew unkempt at the end of the garden. I knew it was heading for the wall, where it was easy to scramble onto the old lawn roller, half hidden by ivy, and over into the grounds next door. But I knew the garden better than anyone, my stride was long and I covered the ground quickly. And yet still the creature seemed to be moving away from me, faster than ever, as though its feet did not touch the ground. It hurtled through a bed of nettles, old and woody and winter-brown. I followed, the dead stems and leaves slippery beneath my boots. The creature had no lantern, the night was darkening, and yet it seemed to know the garden as well as I. It reached the wall, precisely the spot where I knew the lawn roller was located, scrambling up like a monkey. It looked back over its shoulder. Again I saw that midnight face, red rimmed eyes, a black hood drawn tight at the chin. I saw black-clad arms, and legs braced to leap, and then it was gone. Not two seconds later I was on top of the wall myself. I leaped down and bounded after it, already half vanished into the gloaming of the garden next door.

The house that had once stood there, Corvus Hall, was long gone, burned to the ground so that little but ruined walls and scattered roof slates remained. It had once been an anatomy school, and since its demise no one had been near the place. The creature I was after appeared familiar with the terrain, however, heading east, towards the tumbledown remnants of the Hall, zig-zagging between bushes of yew and holly, leaping over bits of charred and scattered masonry. Underfoot I felt the crunch of glass and the remains of burned bones, for when the anatomy school had burned to the ground it had sent a thousand specimens, animal and human, into the flames. Up ahead of me, the apparition stopped. It stood for a moment, a dark shadow on the jagged remains of a wall that jutted from the weeds like a row of blackened teeth.

Afterwards, when I considered what happened, I knew it had been waiting for me, that it had decided what to do, and rather than making off through the yew trees and out onto St Saviour's Street it had devised a far more horrible plan. But at the time I saw none of this. Instead, I thought that it was taking stock of the situation, seeing how far away I was before it bounded away from me again. And so I ran faster, for all that the dark, crouched and shrouded silhouette gave me the shivers I knew I could catch it.

My feet slithered on broken glass and loose stones. Brambles clawed at my legs and hands. Directly ahead lay the entrance to the dead house, a subterranean room, sunken into the earth so that its occupants, the bodies that had been used by the anatomy students who had studied at Corvus Hall, might lie on their shelves and trolleys until their time came to be dissected. It had once been accessed by a corridor that plunged into the earth from the direction of the main house. Since the Hall had been destroyed, its entrance was now nothing but a dark brick-lined hole in the earth, fringed with nettles and dock-leaves now black and slimy for the winter, and slippery with a layer of dark green moss.

Up ahead, I saw the figure slow for a moment, glance over its shoulder once more, and then plunge out of sight into the dark mouth of the subterranean tunnel. Thick knots of couch grass snared my feet and brambles reared in great spiked arches, hoops of thorns tearing again at my clothes as I plunged after it. I should have stopped. Something should have given me pause. The fear I had felt at the sight of that crouched, midnight-faced goblin-like figure, the speed at which it had fled from me, the knowledge I had of Corvus Hall and the dead room, that there was only one way in and out, each of these should have been enough to make me stop and think. All I had to do was wait and the creature would emerge – it would have to. But my reason had deserted me. I was thinking of – what? Nothing but the need to catch my quarry. My desire to know, to understand, to do *something*, overwhelmed me, and whereas I should have been afraid, and should have allowed that fear to temper my actions, I felt only a blind fury. And so I flung myself on, headlong, into the darkness.

Beneath my feet, the oxblood-coloured quarry tiles that covered the floor were buckled and uneven. The tunnel's walls felt damp to the touch, and sticky with the smoke that had poured down from the main building and coated them with a layer of soot. I could still smell ashes in the air, an acrid smouldering reek, tinged with sulphur, and mixed with the stink of drains and rotten leaves. After some six paces I stopped. Up ahead I could see only darkness. I sensed, rather than saw, a movement, for there was no light at all. I put my hand out – nothing. I glanced back. The entrance was a gash of night sky fringed with silhouetted brambles and couch grass. I was panting hard, and the sound of it filled my ears. I tried to hold my breath, but then all I heard was the sound of my own blood pounding in my head. I crept forward again. My foot kicked against something – a rat perhaps, or a twist of root? – and I stumbled, plunging forward so that I was on my knees in the dirt and darkness. The jolt seemed to bring me to my senses. What was I doing, pursuing this creature into the earth? I felt a movement behind, a stirring of damp air and the smell of old, stale earth, and wet winding sheets. Memories assailed me – of being buried alive, of lying next to a corpse in the dead house, of worms and putrescence, of small cramped spaces and an all-encompassing darkness, and I let out a scream. But the noise I made went nowhere, deadened by the walls, so that it sounded in my ears like the voice of someone entombed. Fear swept over me. I could not see, could not fathom which way to turn to leave that horrible place. And somewhere, not far away, my adversary was hiding. I tried to stand, to move forward, but blundered into the wall and cracked my head, sinking to my knees in pain and disorientation. 'Will!' I screamed. 'Will! Oh God! Will! Help me!'

All at once I heard the faint hiss of exhaled breath and something rushed at me out of the dark. It was no more than a shadow, a silhouette in human form, as if it had itself been fashioned from blackness. I staggered to my knees but it was too late, and I was down again. The air was punched out of me as I fell, my head striking the ground, so that for a moment I saw stars exploding in white flashes of light. The creature, whatever it was, sprang onto my back. The weight of it crushed me, so that I could not speak, could not move or draw breath. I tried to rise, but it was too heavy. I tried to reach around but my arms were trapped. I scrabbled at my neck, but its fingers were tight about my throat, squeezing harder. I felt its breath in my ear, an excited, shallow breathing, almost a laugh. My lungs screamed for air, my legs kicking impotently against the ground, toes drumming, stars and coloured lights exploding in my head. 'He can't save you.' The voice was a coarse whisper in my ear, wheedling at first, and then angry. 'No one can save *you*. You're the child of a murderer. A *murderer*.' The hands grew tighter. My eyes felt as if they would explode in my head. The words, filled with fury, were spat into my ear like poison: 'Blood. Speaks.'

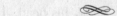

When I came to my senses I was lying on a cold wet floor in a dark damp silence. My throat and head ached, my breath catching in my throat as panic welled up inside me. Something moved against my hand, and I screamed. Somehow, I managed to blunder in the right direction, for all at once I was out of that dreadful dark space, the night air fresh on my face. A bramble lashed my face and I dashed it away, tearing my hand. I felt arms around me and heard a familiar and beloved voice whisper in my ear.

'Shhh, Jem.' He held me tight as I thrashed and cried out. 'Stop. Stop. You're safe now. All is well.'

'All is *not* well,' I shouted. I pushed him away. 'Where were you? You left me alone to run after that, that *thing*.' I seized him by the shoulders and stared into his eyes. 'Did you see it?' I could feel my eyes huge and staring in my head. 'Did you see it? What was it? An apparition? A demon? A man? It was black – no,' I shook my head. 'No, it was blue. Like midnight. Its face – Did you see? It was a demon. What else might it be?'

'Demons, Jem? Really? In London?'

'Yes, in London,' I snapped. 'In my garden, no less. I saw it with my own eyes. Didn't you?'

'You had a closer look than I,' he replied. 'It bounded away before I had a chance to see it properly, with you not two paces behind.'

'But its face!' I shut my eyes tight, and there it was again. Midnight blue, eyes red rimmed.

'I did not see its face.'

'What was it doing there? Was it dancing? Dancing on a grave? My God, Will—'

'Not dancing, Jem.' He shook his head. 'Let's get out of this horrible place. What on earth possessed you to run after it like that? And into this vile rat-hole too!' He looked at the ragged entrance into the earth with distaste. I could hardly blame him. The place should have been filled in when the house burned down, not left gaping in the ground like some sort of vacant open tomb.

'I followed it in here, I didn't think about what I was doing, didn't think that it was luring me in, though now I look back that's exactly what it was doing. It attacked me.' The night air was cold and fresh against my face. A whiff of the river tickled my nostrils. There would be a thick fog by the morning. Already the moon was stained brown by it, and I could taste the stuff, like sulphur, on my lips. 'Did you see where it went?'

'No.'

'What kept you?' I lapsed back into irritation. Had he moved faster, or at any rate kept up with me, he might have at least seen the direction in which the thing had escaped, might perhaps have run after it. Two of us together could surely have overpowered it? The owl hooted from amongst the ruins of Corvus Hall, a long low, mocking note.

'I couldn't run, Jem,' he said. 'You know that. I've been ill, have you forgotten already?'

'You could have tried.'

'What would you have me do? Save you from your rash and ill-conceived actions or accompany you headlong into them? You forget yourself, Jem – again! I'm sorry this has happened, sorry about the bodies, about the . . . whatever it is that's happening to the garden, to us. But blaming others, blaming *me*, is not going to make any of it go away sooner.' He coughed. His face in the moonlight was bone-white, his cheeks hollow and his eyes darkly shadowed. I could hear the breath wheezing in and out of him, the rattle of something deep within his lungs. He gave a sudden cough, sharp and painful, as the rising fog caught in his chest. Dear, kind Will. I knew he would follow me into the abyss if he had to. An accusing moon stared up at me from a pool of dirty water.

'You're right,' I said. 'I'm sorry.' We trudged towards the physic garden across the overgrown lawn. 'And now you will have wet feet too and will catch a chill. This grass is soaking.'

'I can have a mustard footbath when I get home.'

'Mm,' I said, absently. Then, 'Where did you get that lantern? And what did you mean when you said "not dancing"?'

'This is the lantern it left beside the deadly nightshade,' said Will. 'Beside the grave.'

'And the bit about not dancing?'

'It . . . he – whoever, *what*ever it was – was not dancing, Jem, they were looking for something.' All at once I noticed that he was wearing gloves, the ones I had made him put on when we were digging up the deadly nightshade and dumping it, roots, stems, leaves, beside that open grave.

'Were *you* in the grave too? Again? But there was nothing else to find. Nothing but earth. We scoured the ground for remains, clues, evidence of who he was. We took all there was. There was nothing more.'

'Yes, I was in the grave,' he said. 'I thought we had taken all that was to be found there too. But I thought our friend tonight was clearly looking for *something*.'

'And?' I said. I gritted my teeth, irritated once more. Could he not just spit it out? He was so slow these days.

'And yet the roots of the deadly nightshade held on to one last secret. I'll wager any money that what I have in my pocket is the very thing our curious visitor was searching for.'

'What?' I snapped. 'What is it?'

He slipped his hand in his pocket. He was about to draw it out, but at that moment a fox barked in the ruins of the Hall, a high-pitched cry, half yelp, half scream. It set my hair on end. I felt a cold creeping fear seep up my neck. Something was still not right. We were being watched, I was sure of it. I saw Will's expression change too, and all at once his gaze snagged on something behind me. He peered over my shoulder at the dark shadows of the yew avenue and held up his lantern. Was it my imagination or, as I turned to look, did something move in the shadows there? Something dark and shifting, something crouched, half-human in form, but with a bearing that was at once diabolical and beast-like. I could not see it, could not be sure, but I felt its presence, retreating, stepping back, but watching. Will withdrew his hand from his pocket slowly. 'Not here, Jem,' he whispered. 'Not here.'

Chapter Eleven

⚍⚎

We walked back towards the apothecary in silence. We did not look back, other than once, and there was no one there resembling the creature we had seen in the garden though there were plenty of other people about. Usually, I was glad to get away from the noise and bustle of St Saviour's Street. Now, I was relieved to be amongst my fellow human beings. Nothing could happen to us while we were on the Queen's highway, surely?

'Whoever that was,' said Will, 'I imagine they know exactly who we are and where we live, and so have no need to skulk after us through the streets to see where we are going.'

'No doubt.' I walked faster all the same. Usually Will and I were evenly matched, we were the same height, we took the same long stride. But Will was slow, and he seemed to be finding it hard to keep up with me. He pulled his scarf around his nose, for already the fog had veiled the city in brown, and the dark streets had taken on a dim, underwater appearance. I pulled him to a halt, removed my own scarf and wound it about his neck and the lower half of his face. 'Don't argue,' I said. 'You mustn't breathe this stuff in.'

He nodded. I could see that he was trying not to cough. His eyes watered. His 'Thank you, Jem,' was no more than a whisper.

At length we turned into Fishbait Lane. I could not resist a look back. There was nothing to see, I knew there would not be, and yet the feeling we were being followed still hadn't left me.

I could have found my way down Fishbait Lane to my apothecary in the dark, which was just as well as there was little enough to light our way. The lamps inside my neighbours' shops showed as dim yellow smudges. But mine glowed brightly, the bottles of coloured liquids that proclaimed my profession, golden St John's Wort, flame-coloured calendula oil, rosehip syrup a bold glowing crimson, marking out our windows with their warm gules of colour. I flung open the door and marched in. The scent of the place – hops, lavender, attar of roses – was a balm to us both, and as I shut out the night we exchanged a glance, and smiled.

'Sit here, Will,' I commanded. Pulling up a footstool, I bent to remove his wet boots. 'Gabriel, boil some water and get the mustard. I want some peppermint, rosemary and lavender in the water too.' I turned to Will. 'The rosemary and mint will help your congestion, the lavender will soothe your throat and lungs. Jenny, make some tea. And you, madam.' Mrs Speedicut watched me from her chair in front of the stove. 'Move your fat arse and fetch Mr Will a blanket, some dry socks, and a plate of bread and cheese.'

'Not that mousetrap stuff,' said Will. 'And can I have some brandy in that tea? Thank you, Jem.' His eyes were closed as I pulled off his wet boots and socks. 'I should convalesce more often.'

'There ain't no brandy,' said Jenny. 'Mrs Speedicut drank it.'

'It were medicinal,' said the old woman, her expression resentful. 'My gin were finished.'

'You drank a sick man's brandy?' Will opened his eyes. 'You thoughtless slattern!'

'A sick man? You heard *my* cough?'

'You mean that noise you make just before you spit brown phlegm into the fire? The one that sounds like a navvy shovelling rocks?'

'*I'm* at death's door and you don't care. I could die and *then* where would you be?'

'With one mouth less to feed, and more room to move about the place,' said Will. 'And I wouldn't have to smell that horrible tobacco anymore either. Where on earth do you get it? From the floor of a pig sty?' He closed his eyes again. 'Want to see what I've got in my pocket, Jem?'

'Is it a pheasant?' Gabriel tipped some mustard powder into a large enamelled bowl as the kettle reached the boil. 'Or some money for a pie?'

'A pheasant!' said Will. 'Yes, I caught it with my bare hands out in the lane just now! How did you guess?'

'Is it gin?' said Mrs Speedicut. 'We're out of gin. Did I tell you?'

I tossed Jenny a few coins. I had to get rid of them. 'Take Mrs Speedicut and Gabriel to Sorley's,' I said. 'Get something to eat and drink. I want you all gone for an hour. You're in charge, Jenny.' I was glad to see them go.

I could see Jenny was curious, Mrs Speedicut too, but I did not want any of them to see what Will was about to show me. It was for my eyes only, and they would be safer, I was sure, the less they knew about the events that were unfolding. Will's eyes met mine. His expression was serious now. He put his hand into his pocket.

'I didn't have time to look at it properly,' he said. 'I found it tangled in the roots of the nightshade. The chain is lost. Broken, perhaps. The rest—' He pulled out a handkerchief. It was clean but bore smears of dirt from where he had used it to pluck something from the roots of the belladonna. 'Obviously we missed it as we were looking in the soil, rather like our demonic visitor. But when I held up the lantern I saw it gleaming amongst the roots where the soil had dried and fallen away.'

Gold is always bright. It is almost as though it wants to be found, and I knew that the object he held out to me had no place hidden in the cold dark earth. Two inches high and an inch and a half wide, it was a large gold locket. Its hinge and clasp were caked with dirt, the whorls and curlicues, tiny engraved tendrils, fruits and leaves that covered its surface black with ingrained soil against the smooth gleaming background. It was beautiful; costly and exquisite – surely a keepsake, a memento filled with meaning and significance for both giver and receiver, made and gifted with love. It felt heavy in my hand, the gold cool to the touch but warming quickly with the heat of my skin.

'It's beautiful,' said Will. 'Look at the pattern. What are those flowers? Can you identify them?' He shrugged. 'Perhaps it's just vines.'

I rubbed it with a wet cloth. The soil would not come

out of the engraving, and the earth's dark tracery made the design easier to see. 'It's not just vines,' I said. 'It is foxgloves, oleander, jimsonweed, passionflower.' I was peering at it through my magnifying glass, though I could see well enough without it. 'Belladonna. Lily of the valley.'

'Do they mean something? Is it a code? The language of flowers, and all that? Rosemary for remembrance, pansies for unrequited love, or whatever.'

'It's possible,' I said, still peering through the glass. 'Though if I were you I'd not start communication by flowers any time soon or you're likely to scare the ladies off.'

'I don't have any ladies,' said Will. He coughed. 'What flower means "do you have any of that linctus to stop me from coughing myself to death?"'

I gave a bark of laughter. 'It's the stuff in the bottle next to the senna powder. Top shelf.'

'I can't reach it.' He sat back and closed his eyes. 'I will just have to die here while you pore over that locket. What flower means "neglected by friends"? Whatever it is I want one engraved on my tombstone. Perhaps it's the flower of the bitter cherry.'

I was about to retort that the flower of the bitter cherry actually meant 'get it yourself', but I noticed how pale he still was, the shadows beneath his eyes now dark as bruises.

'I'm not sure this is about the language of flowers,' I said, mixing a few drachms of liquorice and thyme linctus with a splash of hot water from the kettle. This particular batch I had mixed with spruce oil, which was especially good for thinning the mucus and reducing coughs. I put a dollop of honey in it to sweeten the mix. 'I think the flowers engraved here contain no message, at least not one that might be understood by any ordinary lady.'

'And an *extra*ordinary lady? What might *she* think of it?'

'An extraordinary lady might recognise all these flowers and know immediately that they have one thing in common: each of them is poisonous.'

'D'you think it belonged to the corpse?'

'It's a lady's piece, not a man's. Besides, I can't imagine such an item being in the possession of a crippled man who kept a monkey as a pet. Surely he'd either sell it or pawn it – if it was his.'

'That's true. Unless it was of some value to him. So, assuming it's not his, who might it belong to? How did it get into his grave? Perhaps it was dropped or fell in by accident. You'd not risk digging him up again to look for it once you'd realised it was missing. Or maybe it was thrown in deliberately? But if so, why?'

He was right. The only thing we could assume was that the creature, or whatever it was that we had seen sifting through the open grave, had been looking for this very object. When it had squeezed my throat, and I had put up my hands to tear its fingers away, I had felt leather gloves rather than skin. Leather gloves to protect it from the poisons. Evidently, it had knowledge of the bush's deadly properties. 'It said I was the child of a murderer,' I told him. 'As it gripped my throat and crushed the breath out of me by sitting on my back. It said no one could save me from that. "Blood speaks." That's what it said.'

'What does that mean?'

'That I'm wicked, just as my mother was. It is in my blood, as it was in hers.'

Will snorted. 'What rubbish. Though I suppose it's certainly one interpretation of the words "blood speaks" – if you choose to believe the view of someone who dresses up in a cloak and smothers themselves with blue paint. I'm not sure I'd accept their opinion as that of a rational and clear-thinking person. Perhaps there are some other interpretations?'

'Such as?'

'"Blood speaks" certainly sounds like a reference to consanguinity, though that itself might mean any number of relationships. Not just you and your mother, but perhaps the relationships of the dead man with another. The idea of blood speaking might also be a biblical reference. I am thinking of Cain and Abel, of course.'

'Of course,' I said. And then, when he did not elaborate, 'Forgive me, Will, my father preferred Culpeper to the Catechism. What biblical reference are you talking about?'

He sighed. 'What Devilish company I keep these days,' he said. 'It is fortunate I was brought up in a Christian household, Jem, so that I can keep you abreast of such matters. Cain murdered his brother Abel, even you know that.'

'I do, Will.'

'And the Bible tells us that Abel's blood spoke out.' He held up his hand and raised his voice like a preacher. '"And He said what have you done? The voice of your brother's blood cries out to Me from the Ground. And now thou art cursed from the earth, which hath opened her mouth to receive thy brother's blood from thy hand"!' He coughed. 'Or something like that. Of course, I'm not suggesting that the dead man's brother is upon us, merely that spilled blood cannot be hidden, and will be revenged, one way or another, no matter what. Perhaps that's what was on your attacker's mind.' He paused for a moment, and then said, 'In which case, they have probably given away more than they realised.'

I sat in silence for a moment, thinking over what he had said. 'I had no idea you were so knowledgeable,' I said at last.

'Oh, I recall one or two things. Anyway, what's in this locket? Can we see? Perhaps there is something inside that might illuminate matters further.'

The locket was tightly closed, its years underground welding it tight shut, so that in the end I had to use a blade to prise it apart, as if it were an oyster.

'Have a care, Jem,' said Will gently as I tried, and failed, to get the tip of my blade between the two halves. 'Perhaps it does not wish to be opened.'

I clicked my tongue. 'It's a locket, Will. It is without thought or feeling.' I put down the knife and looked for something slenderer. I took up a lancet from the bowl on the apothecary table and began to prise at the clasp, twisting and levering, so that when the blade slipped it stabbed into the cushion of my thumb. I felt the sharp pain at the same moment that the locket sprang open and I saw the face that had been trapped within for some thirty years or more. I cried out, my blood welling thick and dark, as if it had flowed straight from my heart.

Excerpts from the diary of Catherine Underhill.

3rd October 1818

Nothing could have prepared me for what this place would be like. The noise! The colour! The crowds of people! London's palette is grey and brown. It is dark and wet and cold. Here, the world is the exact opposite. The heat is so dense it feels as if one might cut it with a knife. The sun is huge and bright, the sky an endless blue. The bazaar, which we had to pass through on our way towards the Cantonment where the Europeans live, is filled with the most wonderful sights, smells and colours – animals, people, spices, fruit and vegetables I have never seen before, silks and calicos. The people swarm around us with their hands out for coins, or holding up wares for our inspection, live chickens, baby goats, cuts of meat, folds of cloth, bags of beans or brightly coloured vegetables. I cannot understand what they are saying, though Dora, Jane and Bathsheba bat them away, and shout phrases at them that send them scurrying. They are clearly delighted and excited to be 'home', as Bathsheba calls the place, and their enthusiasm is infectious.

There are flies everywhere, even more than there are people, as well as pariah dogs, stray cats, cows wandering at will through the streets. Here and there men lie at the roadside. Some appear to be dead, though I am told they are not. Some are bundled up in rags as if sleeping, with a bony foot or arm projecting. One has spent years with his right arm held above his head, so that it has withered away to a useless stick, another has long fingernails which, I am told, he has not cut for ten years so that they have grown back on themselves and have pierced his hands. These are what Dora calls 'religious medicants' or 'fakirs', and they are much revered by the local people, who look after them with food and other offerings.

Dora calls the Indian people 'the natives', as does everyone else. I am tempted to point out that as 'country born' women, Jane, Dora and Bathsheba might also consider themselves 'natives', but I say nothing, as there is evidently a distinct hierarchy. Where Bathsheba might fit is, as yet, unclear. Her mother was Indian, her father a Company official whose vast wealth she has inherited entirely. She combines the arrogance and entitlement he must surely have possessed with a strong belief in India as her birthright. She does not deny her dead mother, but celebrates her as a native princess, dark, exotic and mysterious. The white women here, the memsahibs, envy Bathsheba's wealth and disdain her dark face. I can see that she enjoys provoking them with both.

4th *October 1818*

We are staying with Dr Christian before we go up country as he has a large bungalow near to the botanic gardens. I am aware of

Bathsheba's contempt for him, but he does not seem too objectionable to me. He showed me around his gardens. He is proud of them, and rightly so, for he has worked hard to learn about the cultivation of native plants and has many Indian friends who share his passion. He cares nothing for their caste or colour, and it is only the plants, and the understanding and interest that a man might have of them, that concerns him. Bathsheba he admires a great deal. Mainly, I believe, because she is so knowledgeable. She is also one of the main benefactors of his gardens, and for this he is grateful.

I asked him what he knew of her and he looked at me keenly and said, 'Her name is not mentioned in respectable circles. You would do well to keep your connection with her to yourself if you wish to be welcomed into the drawing rooms of the Company memsahibs.' I said I had little interest in such places, as they generally seemed even more stultifying than the drawing rooms of home. He smiled at that, and said, 'Might I ask, what is your connection to her?' I told him that she had employed me as a companion. One who was knowledgeable about plants and keen to learn.

'Well, well,' he said. 'Perhaps you will last longer than the others.'

'The others?' I said.

He did not answer me. 'Have you considered remaining here in Calcutta?' he said after a moment. 'You might find yourself a husband easily, and there is plenty of amateur botanising to be done here in Bengal.'

I have seen the memsahibs and I do not envy them. It seems to me that they are either fat and languid, or thin and dried out. They sit beneath the punkah sipping tea and complaining about the servants, which they keep in extraordinary numbers, so that they don't have a single thing to do themselves (apart from play the pianoforte, and dance – a most ludicrous undertaking in so *warm a country). Their fat pale children are half-smothered in flannel and wool, no matter what the temperature might be, as if the manners of 'home' must be preserved at all costs – even if it means death by heat exhaustion. Usually, the boys get sent back to England to be educated, so that they can become as arrogant and boorish as their fathers. But the girls do not. Their minds left to rot, they become worse, even, than their mothers. All the women hate India, even though they will never leave it, and would be nothing without it. I will <u>never</u> become one of them.*

'Miss Wilde pays me,' I said to Dr Christian, perhaps more tartly than he deserved. 'She pays me for my knowledge, and my skill, which means I am <u>not</u> an amateur.' He inclined his head at that, but I had not finished. 'And if there is one thing that I have learned from her,' I added, 'it is that a woman does not need a husband to be happy, or successful.'

He smiled, and said he was glad his own dear Dora did not share my opinion, and that there were surely some men who encouraged and supported their wives. 'Though I admit,' he said, 'that it is not a common phenomenon.'

At that point, Bathsheba appeared nearby, talking to one of the native gardeners. Dr Christian saw her. For a moment he hesitated, and then all at once he leaned towards me. He kept his voice low, as if afraid she might overhear. 'Don't go with us,' he whispered. 'Say you are sick. Say it is the heat. Say anything, but do not go!'

Chapter Twelve

〜〜

As we set out for the East India Docks the sun came out, a rare sight in London, but one which raised my spirits. I was glad to be out of the apothecary, to be doing something that might take us a step closer to finding out what was going on. The night before, rather than provide us with answers, the contents of the gold locket had deepened the mystery still further. Inside, we had found a miniature, a small pale face with watchful dark eyes. The paint was stained and discoloured due to its time in the earth so that I was afraid to try to clean it in case it flaked away completely. The chestnut-coloured hair, the serious expression were familiar, the blue coat with its shawl collar and the high neckerchief were from an earlier time, but the face was recognisable.

'This locket was my mother's,' I'd said to Will after a moment. 'There can be no doubt about it. This picture is my father.'

'Are you sure?'

'I think I would know my own father.' I had felt tears of frustration sting my eyes. My mother's involvement with the dead man, had I ever doubted it, was now confirmed. But even as one small mystery was solved, another one presented itself, for within the locket, a lock of discoloured ribbon attached to its head, was a tiny key. Some half an inch in length, it was brown in colour, plain and uninteresting. Its imprisonment within the locket was the main reason that the miniature was discoloured, and it had left a dark mark against the image where it had been lying. I did not like to imagine what fluids had seeped from the corpse, through the seam between the two gold halves of the locket, to cause the key to oxidise and bleed like that.

'A key!' Will had held the thing up to the light. 'I love a key! It is at once perplexing, and yet optimistic. Where there is a key there must also be, somewhere, its lock. And what might lie behind that lock? Why, secrets revealed. Questions answered. We must regard this as a step forward, Jem, something with the potential to explain all. Now then, what might *this* key be for? Have you any idea?'

That night I had lain in my bed with the locket and the key beside me on the pillow. My mother's locket. My father's face. A tiny key. The bones, the silver bowl, the ivory skulls, the dead monkey and curious publican's token. The two dead bodies. The deadly nightshade. I could not sleep, and the connections between these apparently random items eluded me. I had no idea what the key might signify or what it might unlock, and no idea how and why it had found its way into a grave in my garden.

It was with a view to clearing my head, and perhaps being able to make some connections, that the following morning I set out for the docks with Will and Jenny. I left Mrs Speedicut in charge of the apothecary. Since she had helped me to nurse Will when he was ill, she now seemed to have inveigled herself into the place as a full-time resident. I had decided, therefore, that the least she could do while she was with us – and now that Will was so much better – was to look after the shop once in a while. I left Gabriel with her. I had still not forgiven the lad for his public lecture about the bones, and although I had to admit that his display had probably done something to further my enquiries, I did not like to have my apprentice taking matters into his own hands without my consent. A morning in the company of Mrs Speedicut, therefore, would be a just punishment for his misbehaviour. Even worse for him was my decision to take Jenny with us. I could see how pained he was that he was missing out on an adventure away from the apothecary. He loved the waterside, and his apology was so abject, his expression so miserable, that I almost gave in and told him to fetch his hat – but no. Jenny was more familiar with the riverside than any of us, and I hoped she might act as a guide and narrator. Gabriel would just be an added annoyance. So I pretended not to notice his mournful looks, and as soon as I had prepared the prescriptions for the day we set forth, without him, for the docks.

Jenny chattered on as she led us towards the waterfront, excited to have so important a role. She was a curious sight, for she wore her skirts at mid-calf with a pair of Gabriel's trousers on underneath, stout boots on her feet, and one of Will's stovepipe hats on her head – one he no longer wore because the nap had grown dull. She had wanted to dress as a boy entirely, but I had forbidden it.

She had no reason to hide who she was, and I would not have the choice of intimacy and family taken from her the way my father had taken it from me. I told her she ought to be proud of her sex, of what she might achieve as a woman, that she might do anything she pleased if she had a mind to do it. It was a lie, of course, for women had none of the freedoms of men. And yet times were changing. Who knew what possibilities there might be for her in the future? Jenny had been schooled in a brothel for the first twelve years of her life. She was under no illusions about how women might fare at the hands of men, how dangerous and fragile their happiness was. I hoped she would not always be so angry and distrustful.

The smell of the river was strong on the air, and the closer we got the worse it became. The Thames is no better than an open sewer, with all manner of effluent discharged into it daily. Its sluggish, tidal nature prevents the stuff from leaving the city. The ebb tide sucks it down the river, the flow tide brings it back again, and on it goes, gathering more and more filth, unable to ever purge itself, the stink of the water an offence to all, apart from those without noses.

'My God, the place reeks today,' muttered Will as we emerged onto the waterfront from the narrow slippery-flagstoned thoroughfare known as Cat's Hole. An ever-changing city of wood and rope stretched off to east and west. 'You know there really need to be some changes made to the river. It's too wide, too slow flowing. No wonder the water is choked with effluent. If the foreshore were built up, some sort of embankment say, it would squeeze the river into a narrower channel. It would then run faster, and, as a result, cleaner.'

'You should submit your plans to the Prime Minister,' I said.

'Yes, and no doubt he will use them to wipe his arse, and they will end up bobbing outside the windows of parliament.'

I had always liked the docks, though I went there rarely these days. The whole of the city teemed with noise and life, with bustle and movement and colour. It was never silent, the sound of street hawkers, hansoms, newspaper sellers, animals, provided a constant cacophony, hard and flinty as it echoed from walls and buildings. But near the river the noise had a different timbre. Overhead, crows and gulls wheeled and cried; on all sides were the shouts of men, from the loading and unloading of ships, the rattle of block and tackle, the rhythmic clang of a rope striking a bell, the creak of timber as it rose and fell on the water. The streets were narrower, the shops smaller and meaner, the public houses and lodging houses dirtier and uglier the more numerous they became. Beside the river, life was at its most raw and vibrant. The streets teemed with people of all kinds, here a black-faced stevedore, there the sallow skin of a Lascar. Many would be gone on the next tide, the same tide that would bring in others – a tall blond Scandinavian whaler, or a deck hand taken on in Calcutta to crew a tea clipper back to England. It was a whirl of noise and colour, and constantly changing palette of smells – fried fish, sewage, rancid fat, sweat, spices, at once overwhelming and unforgettable.

Jenny was still prattling on. 'I used to know all the victuallers and pot men from the Six Bells to the Blue Brazier,' she said. 'Mother Lovibond what used to run the House I worked at would send me out to get her gin. Course, she owed all of 'em money, so I had to go further east and west to find one whose patience she'd not worn out. Luggin' those great heavy bottles. Mr Aberlady, who I used to work for at the Seamen's Hospital, used to see me goin' past and sometimes helped carry my bottles for me.'

'What about the North Star Angel?' I said. 'Did you ever know that place? Sorley said it was up near the East India Docks. A bit too far for you, I think?'

'North Star Angel?' Jenny frowned. 'Can't say as I remember that one, Mr Jem.' She looked disappointed. I knew she badly wanted to please me, to justify her place at the apothecary and my faith in her. She had been with us for little over eighteen months, and she was the best apprentice I could have wished for. I had given her my name, so that she might be Jenny Flockhart, and see her own name over the door to the shop one day. I had given her a profession she could be proud of, and she was so quick to learn with such an enquiring mind that I was hoping to put her in for the examination at the Society of Apothecaries once her apprenticeship was complete. Her gratitude was boundless, and I saw her frown in concentration as she tried to find a way she might help.

'I know the Blue Angel,' she said suddenly. 'That's up by the Six Bells.'

'North Star,' I said, 'not Blue.'

'What about Solomon Saul,' said Will. 'Do you know him?'

She shook her head. All at once, she brightened. 'But Mrs Lovibond will! There ain't nothing goes on down here without Mrs Lovibond knowing what it is and who done it.'

'I thought you didn't want to go back to your old House,' said Will.

'Don't worry,' she said, grinning. 'I'm Jenny Flockhart, apprentice apothecary now, not Jenny Quickly, maid of all work what gets kicked up and down the stairs day and night. She better 'ave some respect, or I'll put stuff in her tea and give her the shits like she won't believe.'

She patted her satchel – it was one of mine with a broken strap that she had salvaged and repaired. 'I got all I need right here. She durst even *think* about treating me cruel and I'll see to her! I can give her the colic, the squits, or the burning wee. She better be afraid o' me!'

'Well, I most certainly am!' murmured Will. 'Lord preserve us from the squits and the burning wee.'

'Besides,' went on Jenny, 'I brought some herbs she might want for her girls. Just in case. Keep her sweet, like.'

'What have you created, Jem?' said Will. 'She is your creature through and through.'

'Mrs Lovibond's what you might call dramatic,' said Jenny as we walked. 'If you know what I mean.' Will and I nodded, though I could see from his face that he was as mystified as I was. Jenny led us down a dark narrow thoroughfare, not far from the Seamen's Floating Hospital. On both sides of the street were flat-fronted terrace houses, their yellow brick stained chocolate brown in colour. Jenny had lived at number three, a dire place at the dark end of the street. She marched up the steps and pushed the door open. 'Mrs Lovibond!' she cried. 'Mrs Lovibond!'

The place stank of fish and boiled cabbage. A flight of stairs, carpeted in something brown and sticky looking, but which was probably cheap drugget strewn with dirty sawdust, led upwards into the gloom. The hall to Mrs Lovibond's house was painted the offal-red colour beloved by brothel keepers. The places I had visited in the past

– notably Mrs Roseplucker's Home for Young Ladies of an Energetic Disposition on Wicke Street – had adorned their crimson walls with pictures depicting scenes of unlikely congress. Mrs Lovibond, however, had chosen an altogether different theme. I did not know whether the effect she had created was better or worse, but I began to get a sense of what Jenny meant when she described the woman as 'theatrical'.

'She were an actress,' whispered Jenny, seeing me peer at a playbill for Samuel's Hall which, judging by its fresh colours, had only recently been added. 'She were on the stage!' The walls had a moist spongy look to them. They were pasted from floor to ceiling with theatrical advertisements and playbills, which acted like a sling of glue and paper and seemed to be the only things holding the place together. The words and images, the heat and stink of that close little hallway made my head spin. A poster for Astley's Amphitheatre showed a man wrestling with a lion above the words BENGAL TIGER AND LIVING LIONS! Another for The Coburg declared ARTIFICIAL FIREWORKS, and the chance to witness MR BESWICK'S SPECTRAL VISIONS! They were layered one on top of the other, so that behind the most recent additions for Samuel's or the Adelphi, there were glimpses of past acts, faded and stained and long forgotten. EQUESTRIAN EXERCISES and THE HARLEQUIN PLAGIARIST peeped out from behind a striking line-drawing of a woman with dark hair and eyes, her slender arms outstretched below the words NOOR, QUEEN OF THE INDIAN DANCING GIRLS. She, in turn had her legs obscured by a playbill for Wexford's Supper Rooms, and the promise of SONGS! DANCERS! BEASTS! The effect was claustrophobic and overwhelming. Beside me, Will was examining an advertisement depicting a genderless figure who appeared to be running across a stage while holding aloft an enormous python. Below were the words CAPTAIN CLARK'S CHINESE SNAKE ACT! And underneath, in case there was any doubt on the matter, LIVE SERPENTS!

'I'd like to see this,' he said. 'D'you think it's still on?'

'It's from ten years ago, Will. I imagine the captain, and his snake, are long dead.' I rubbed my eyes. Was Mrs Lovibond herself somewhere on these walls? I had no wish to search them for her if she was. 'Where is she, Jenny? Take us through, can't you?'

We followed Jenny through a door on the right. It led into a small parlour. Lit only by a glowing fire of greasy coals and a pair of flickering tallow candles, it was as dark as a burrow. The windows were draped with crimson curtains, the air rich with the smell of urine and low tide. More theatrical images were pasted about the walls of this room too, though they were far fewer in number and depicted only bare-breasted women and dancers. The pictures, and the walls they were pasted to, were faded and peeling, as was the woman who sat before the fire. She rose with a leer as we entered, clearly in anticipation of custom, though her smile froze when she saw Jenny. I could not fathom her age, so ravaged were her features, and so heavily were they painted with what ladies liked to call 'enamel'. A layer of white paint, it was made up of lead and albumen, and was, in the long term, quite ruinous to the complexion. Mrs Lovibond had painted the stuff on thickly, and then drawn in her features and other embellishments. A tiny pair of red and watery eyes peered out at us through two black rings fringed with long brush strokes in a grotesque doll-like parody of eyelashes. Her lips were daubed with vermilion grease which had leached into the wrinkles about her sunken mouth so that it looked in the gloom as though she were sucking on a ball of red wool. Of course, the main problem with enamelling – apart from death by poisoning from the mixture itself – was that any facial expression caused the stuff to crack. I had the feeling that Mrs Lovibond had been wearing her enamel for quite some time, as her face had the appearance of a Renaissance fresco that was in dire need of attention. 'Good morning, madam,' I said.

She gave me a leer, but before she could reply, another voice interjected. 'Well, well, if it ain't Mr Flockhart and Mr Quartermain. Say "hello", Annie. You remember our friends from Fishbait Lane, don't you? An' you too, Mr Jobber. What do you say to an old acquaintance like Mr Jem, here?' Another woman was sitting in a sagging brocade armchair on the opposite side of the fire to Mrs Lovibond. She had been invisible to us when we entered, but there was no mistaking her now that she was leaning forward, and that harsh voice and rotten-apple face beneath its wig of curled horsehair was unforgettable.

'Mrs Roseplucker,' I said. 'What an unexpected pleasure.' Her henchman, Mr Jobber, was sitting behind the door in the shadows. At his mistress's command he had lurched to his feet, his great wide face moist and pale as an over ripe cheese. He swayed where he stood, but said nothing, as if he had already forgotten the reason he had stood up.

Mrs Roseplucker's most loyal tart, Annie, was not so silent. 'Hello, sirs!' she cried. She had been sitting beside

Mr Jobber looking bored, and she grinned up at Will and me like a child. 'What brings you young gen'men here?'

'Why! Don't the young bucks follow our Annie everywhere she goes!' cried Mrs Roseplucker before we could reply. She turned to her companion. 'You see, Poll? Our Annie's always pop'lar. *Very* pop'lar. She's not been here five minutes and here's her reg'lars! Mr Jobber, take the young gen'men's coats and hats and see they gets their money's worth.'

'I don't want him touching my coat,' cried Will. He pulled his topcoat tight about himself, as if he feared it might be physically torn from his shoulders. 'And don't you dare touch this hat. Don't you *dare*—' And then as Mr Jobber lurched forward, hand outstretched, 'Get away from me, man! Call him off, can't you?'

'Now then, Mr Jobber, my dear, don't menace the gentlemen so!' Mrs Roseplucker cackled.

The woman sitting opposite Mrs Roseplucker eyed Jenny balefully. 'My, if it ain't Jenny Quickly come back to see us. You owes me money, my girl. Leastways, this here "Mr" Flockhart does, for he's took you without my permission. That's stealing.' Her gaze flickered over me, so that I was reminded of Maximus the python that had once lived onboard the Seamen's Floating Hospital. 'You owes me money, Mr Flockhart. Jenny Quickly was mine. Trained by me in all manner of work. You think you can just take her away? Oh no you don't.' She reached out a skinny, flounce-draped arm and made to seize hold of Jenny. But the girl was too quick for her and skipped out of the way.

I smiled. 'Now, Mrs Lovibond, you know that's not true. Jenny works for me now and any payment for your loss has already been made. Besides, Jenny has brought something for you and your girls. I would say she is of more use to you in her current occupation than in her previous one. Your own personal apothecary, no less! Jenny?'

Jenny opened her satchel and handed over a package of wrapped oilcloth. 'Herbs to bring a girl on,' she said. 'Pennyroyal, carrot seed, black cohosh, raspberry leaf.'

Mrs Lovibond snatched the package and sniffed at it warily. Then, 'Got any salve?' she said. She put a hand to her crotch and clawed at herself through the greasy fabric of her skirts.

'Don't do that, Poll,' said Mrs Roseplucker. 'It only makes it worse.'

'Ladies,' I said. Looking from one to the other, a slow smile spreading across my face. 'Are you—'

'Sisters,' said Mrs Roseplucker. 'Yes. It were Poll here what got me that place I was in on Cat's Hole. You remember it, Mr Flockhart?'

'How could one forget?' said Will. 'The smell of the place. Like old kippers.'

'That weren't kippers. Mr Jobber won't have them in the house.'

We all turned to look at Mr Jobber, man mountain and cured fish expert. He was poking a finger into one of his ears, an expression of ecstasy and concentration on his face.

'Cat's Hole ain't so bad,' said Mrs Lovibond. She was a thinner version of Mrs Roseplucker, her cheeks sunken and lined, but with the same malevolent stare, the same grating voice, the same wide apart eyes on either side of a sunken nose – the 'saddle nose' so common in those who suffered from syphilis.

'We wondered if you could help us, madam,' I addressed Mrs Lovibond, realising as soon as I spoke that 'help' was probably not something Mrs Lovibond was in the habit of dispensing any more than her sister was.

But Will was still revelling in the women's siblinghood. 'I can't believe you're sisters,' he said, looking from one to the other with his hands on his hips. 'I suppose that's because I find it hard to imagine you having a mother, or being children. I always fancied you'd just been formed whole, Mrs Roseplucker, manifested out of darkness and shadow, like Mephistopheles.' He laughed.

'Mister who?' snapped Mrs Lovibond. The two women stared at him out of identical lizard-green eyes. On the mantelpiece a clock ticked. From upstairs there came a groan of release. A few seconds later we heard footsteps, and the sound of urine thundering into a chamber pot. Mrs Roseplucker pulled out a pocket watch from a secret nest hidden somewhere beneath the ragged lacy flounces of her bodice.

'Our Annie gets 'em to it much faster,' she said. 'You'll make twice as much.'

'You want help?' Mrs Lovibond turned her reptile stare towards me. 'Well, now, sir, that's more expensive than any of my girls.'

'I'm sure, madam,' I said smoothly. 'It usually is.'

'What kind of help might you be wanting?'

'Information,' I said.

'Information is it?' she grinned. 'Well now, that really *is* worth its weight in gold.'

'Information has no weight,' said Jenny. 'It's just hot air. Does that mean it don't cost anything?' She looked pleased with herself.

'Yes, well, *my* hot air is *very* expensive,' snapped Mrs Lovibond. 'And the ruder *you* get, my girl, the more costly *it* gets!'

'Shut up, Jenny,' I said. 'And you.' I jabbed Will in the ribs. He closed his mouth but slipped a hand into his pocket and jangled some coins. At the sound of it, both women leaned forward. Mrs Lovibond ran a mercury-blackened tongue over her lips. She turned and jettisoned a stream of foul saliva into a spittoon beside her chair. 'What is it you want to know?'

'Perhaps we can both help?' said Mrs Roseplucker, eyeing Will hungrily. 'You've always enjoyed my help, ain't you Mr Flockhart?'

'Oh no, you don't, Peggy!' said Mrs Lovibond. 'These gen'men have come to *my* house, it's me and *my* girls they want to see. Or, at least, it's *my* help they're wanting. Not yours.'

Will was staring at the woman's fearful visage in fascination. All at once he decided that flattery might be the fastest, and cheapest, way to get what we wanted. But there was little that was fast and cheap at Mrs Roseplucker's apart from the girls, and I knew her ghastly sister would be no different. 'How do you keep your complexion so clear, Mrs Lovibond, ma'am?' he said. 'It is surely the envy of the town!'

'I wash with opium water at night,' said Mrs Lovibond. She put up her hand to pat coyly at her giant wig of ebony horsehair ringlets. 'And I use ammonia every morning. A drop o' belladonna in my eye.' She simpered up at him, evidently enjoying the attention. 'Gives a girl an Italian look. Dark and mysterious. You won't find the like anywhere in London!'

'I have no doubt,' he replied. 'And your girls?'

'Whatever you desire, sir,' she said. 'Every one of 'em's theatrical, you know. All excellent actresses. Trained 'em myself in the arts of the boudoir.' She pronounced it *boo-doyer*. 'Their pleasure is most realistic. Everyone says so!'

'To be sure!' said Will. 'And you taught them all they know, I'll be bound?'

'I used to be on the stage, sir.' She made sure to enunciate every word with as much precision as she could muster. 'I'm what's known as "theatrical", and you, gentlemen, are lucky enough to have stepped into what's known by all the best gentlemen as "Mrs Lovibond's House of Theatrical and Performing Girls". Want to see? Beryl!' she screamed suddenly, her elocution slipping. 'Beryl! Get down 'ere.' From overhead there came the sound of a thud, as if someone had jumped, or fallen, off a bed, followed by the sound of a reluctant tread on the stairs.

'This is my lovely little Beryl,' said Mrs Lovibond as a thin girl with stringy hair and a face as enamelled as her mistress's came into the room. 'Ain't she a jewel?'

'A diamond of a girl, I can see,' said Will. 'But I'm afraid on this occasion, I must decline—'

'Shut up, Will,' I muttered. 'You're just making the whole business take longer.'

'They don't want girls, these two, they wants information,' said Mrs Roseplucker, her eyes fixed upon me. Her voice was as loud and harsh as a rook's. 'Weren't you listening? It's all they ever wants.'

'What on earth are you doing here, Mrs R?' I asked. 'Are you not content with Wicke Street?'

'I'm thinking of becoming a fortune teller,' said Mrs Roseplucker casually. 'Or a medium. I were here for some advice about the stage.'

'Are your novels not selling?' said Will. 'I thought *The Crimes of Dockside Dan* was a real page-turner.' Mrs Roseplucker had taken to writing penny dreadfuls when her brothel business had declined. Gabriel and Jenny were both avid readers of her oeuvre, though I had no idea Will had succumbed too.

'There ain't no money in writing,' she said. 'It's all "Dickens this", and "Dickens that". Can't think why. He don't half drone on! I need something else. I *understand* people, see? I've always been good at that, so I've decided to expand my activities and see into the future, or the past, depending on what folks is wanting. I can see Beyond the Veil, Mr Flockhart. Should be a nice little earner once I gets a few tips. I can have Mr Jobber in the audience, in secret, o' course, and I can pretend to tell his past and then people will feel much more *open* to it. People pay, you know! It's all just stories in the end, and I can do that! Stories is easy.'

'Who on earth would come to see an old villain like you?' said Will.

'Loads of people,' she said. 'Everyone's got a dead John, or James, or George. Don't you?'

Will laughed. 'I do, actually.'

'There you are then. After that I can just make it up. I'm good at makin' things up. Anyway,' she scowled. 'Worth a try. Times is hard and I'm *not* going back to that house on Cat's Hole.' All at once she closed her eyes and put her fingers to her forehead. 'Wait!' she cried. 'Wait! I can see it! You're . . . you're a-lookin' for something. For someone. Both of you is lookin' for something you cannot find. I see . . . I see . . . *bones*! Death. Ah, the Devil is on your shoulder, sir. But wait! *Wait!* The bones is talking to me. I can read 'em . . . '

'You mean you can read the *Police Gazette*,' I said. I folded my arms and grinned as the old hag continued.

'Christian,' she went on, her eyes still closed, her head thrown back, her fingers to her temples. 'I'm gettin' the name . . . Christian.' She cracked open one eye, regarding me through a slit between her painted lids. 'Though he ain't a Christian man.'

'You know him, madam?' I spoke more sharply than I had intended and knew straight away that the price for any information she might be able to supply had immediately gone up.

She opened both eyes now, staring at me craftily. 'Oh yes. And I know who those bones are too. But it'll cost you.'

Notes on the poisonous nightshades (Solanaceae).

ATROPA MANDRAGORA
Also known as mandrake, or Satan's apples.

Description
A perennial herbaceous plant, the mandrake's leaves are up to a foot long and some four inches wide. They lie open upon the ground in the form of a large, dark rosette. The flowers grow from the centre of the rosette on short stalks, like a primrose. Bell-shaped, they might be whitish, mauve or purple in colour. The flower is followed by a smooth round yellow or orange fruit the size of a small apple. They are filled with pulp and have a strong apple-like scent. The root is large, pale brown and often forked. It may be up to four feet long and resembles a bloated parsnip.

Toxicity
All parts are poisonous, though the highest concentration is in the root.

Symptoms

Like all the poisonous nightshades, ingestion of the mandrake results in blurred vision, dilation of pupils, dry mouth, dizziness, headache, vomiting, rapid heart rate, and hallucinations of a particularly vivid and troubling kind. Mania and death follow if the plant is administered, or taken, without care.

Antidotes

There are no antidotes for poisoning by mandragora. Emetics and purgatives are recommended, and the stomach washed out with a solution of mild vinegar, or salt.

Medical applications

Mandrake might be used as an emetic, for the treatment of stomach ulcers, and against constipation. It is effective for epilepsy and other convulsive disorders, for arthritis, and the whooping cough. It is used for the management of pain, and for sedation. Mandrake is considered an effective aphrodisiac.

Miscellanea

The mandrake is the object of many myths and superstitions, perhaps due to the resemblance the root has to the human form. The divided taproot often appears to possess legs, and sometimes arms, the short stalk and broad leafy rosette taking the place of neck and head. Superstition declares that no one might hear the cry of the mandrake as it is pulled from the earth, and live.

Old Anglo-Saxon herbals endow mandrake with mysterious powers against demoniacal possession. Folklore dictates that when digging the plant from the earth the digger must beware of contrary winds. It is considered useful for expelling demons, who are said to be unable to bear its smell. Dried mandrake root is often placed on a mantelpiece, to guard a home against misfortune. The plant was fabled to grow beneath the gallows of murderers, nourished and sustained by the blood and fluid that drip therefrom.

Excerpts from the diary of Catherine Underhill.

6th October 1818

Mrs Christian – she tells me I must call her Dora – and Bathsheba went to the bazaar today. When they returned the two of them were dressed in men's attire. Dora had chosen an Indian costume of loose trousers and a sort of longish tunic. Bathsheba, however, had chosen a curious mixture of Indian and British clothing. She was dressed in men's riding britches and boots, and had a linen shirt tucked in at the waist. On top of this she wore a jerkin of animal fur, clamped to her body with a thick leather belt. She walked with a swagger, her hair about her shoulders in writhing black snakes. Her gaze was distracted and unfocused, as if there were something else she was seeing that the rest of us were not privy to. Mrs Christian was the same, so that I wondered what else they had been doing in the bazaar. In her men's riding boots and with her hair unbound, Bathsheba towered over us all. Her face was dark, her eyes, rimmed with kohl, were as black as stones, her mouth and teeth stained scarlet with the betel she now habitually chews. She stood with her legs apart, a knife and pistol tucked into her belt. She held out her arms, admiring the figure she cut. 'Well?' she said, grinning. 'We are nearly ready.' Then she looked at me. 'It is safest to dress this way where we are going.'

I did not want her to think I was in the least bit surprised by her unorthodox appearance, so I simply nodded, and asked whether she would not be too warm in her jerkin of goat hair as the weather was rather hot still. 'And that knife will be excellent for slicing melons,' I added, for I have noticed a prodigious number of these huge, green, ball-like fruits stacked in the bazaar. 'Such a refreshing choice in the heat!'

She scowled and replied that the goatskin was both waterproof and warm, and that she would be glad of it when we were in the hills to the north, which was where we were heading. As for melons – she pulled out the blade and waved it in my face. 'This is for slitting the throat of anyone who crosses me. The melons I will leave to you.' She looked annoyed, as if she had wanted to shock me, and was furious that I had belittled her magnificence with my bland, facetious questions.

I tried on the clothes that she bought for me – a pair of loose trousers and a long tunic, like those worn by Jane and Mrs Christian. I admit it was a relief to take off my corset and dress, as the clothes of home are completely inappropriate out here. Why the Company wives insist on aping the fashions of London is a mystery to me, and the freedom afforded by a pair of men's leggings is delightful. I think I will take Bathsheba's advice and cut off my hair too.

The knife in my belt is long and curved, like something a badmash might carry. I certainly hope I never have cause to use it for anything other than fruit!

9th October 1818

This morning I was in the garden speaking to the head gardener, a young Indian man named Sandesh. He is an expert in his country's flora and fauna. Having seen Dr Christian in the garden on several occasions now it is my impression that it is Sandesh who does all the work. He directs the other gardeners, writes up his observations and findings for the Horticultural Society of London, monitors the health of the specimens they grow, and maintains a regular correspondence with botanists up and down the country. Dr Christian, on the other hand, does little that it useful or relevant. Perhaps Dr Christian was once a better man, for he seems to be highly regarded and is certainly knowledgeable. And yet without so able a man as Sandesh to run the place, the garden would be a ruin.

I was asking Sandesh about his cultivation of Datura metel, *its uses in Indian physic, its sacred properties and applications, when one of Dr Christian's bearers came running up to us. He said Dr Christian was sick, and that he did not know what to do. The fellow is new to the household I believe, the man who usually attends to the doctor's needs having accompanied Bathsheba and Dora on an afternoon botanising somewhere to the north. Sandesh and I went with him towards what looked like a windowless summer house in the corner of the garden. Inside, the place was laid out like an apothecary's shop, the walls lined with shelves filled with labelled jars and bottles. A long bench in the middle of the room was littered with the paraphernalia of the experimentalist – flasks, condensers, pestle and mortar, bowls of liquids, crushed leaves, powders. It was boiling hot in there. The stove was lit, and upon it, a saucer containing some sort of brown resin was smouldering, scenting the air with a rank, herbal smell.*

I could see Dr Christian crouching within. I was about to rush to his aid, but Sandesh put out a hand. 'Cover your mouth, Miss Underhill,' he said. 'And whatever you do, do not go inside, not while the Datura is burning.' He handed me his handkerchief and, covering his own nose and mouth with his sleeve, he dashed forward and extinguished the smouldering saucer with a pitcher of water. We stood side by side, outside on the veranda, waiting for the air to clear.

With the light streaming in through the open door, we were able to survey the scene: A large hookah sat beside a charpoi, hard up against the wall. A rumpled and stained blanket lay as if cast aside, and I had the impression that Dr Christian himself had not long before been lying upon it. I had not thought I was homesick, but the place reminded me so much of St Saviour's and the apothecary there that I felt a stab of longing. Dr Christian had scuttled into the corner and was curled up there like a frightened child. He held his hands over his head as if he were warding off blows.

'Oh,' I said. 'The poor man!'

'He won't come to harm while he is cowed like that.' Sandesh's face was impassive.

'What is it?' I said, for I could tell he had more to say. 'Please, you can speak freely to me.'

'He does this to himself,' he replied. 'There is no "poor man" about it. He abuses substances about which he has only the slightest knowledge. One cannot underestimate the Datura.' He shook his head. 'And you cannot go in. Not yet. Not unless you want to end up pursued by devils and demons more terrifying than anything you can imagine.' He told me it was not the first time he had come across Dr Christian in such a condition, that the doctor regularly smoked the most potent strains of Datura, but that he did not know what he might do to stop him. 'I am partly

glad he is going up country with Miss Wilde tomorrow,' he said. 'As no matter what I might think of her, it will at least get him away from here. The efficacy of the herb diminishes with use, and so he takes more and more. It is not a habit that can be sustained. And yet I admit I am concerned too. What other temptations will be put in his path once he is far from anyone who might hold him back? That woman is not to be trusted, and I fear for him every time he travels with her. These poisons should not be trifled with.'

By this time the air had cleared, although we each covered our mouths and noses again as we went inside. 'Do not speak harshly to him,' he whispered as we approached Dr Christian. 'Use your most gentle voice, as he will be in a waking nightmare and we will be a part of it.'

'Dr Christian,' I said, keeping my voice low. 'What on earth is the matter, sir?'

Dr Christian looked up at us. His face, usually so tanned due to the time he spent in the garden, was grey with fear. His eyes were staring. Even in the dim light of that apothecary I could see that his pupils were dilated, the blue iris completely invisible. He gazed at us in terror. And then all at once he seemed to realise who we were. 'Miss Underhill,' he hissed. 'Are you one of them? I think perhaps you are not, for here is Sandesh beside you.' He seized Sandesh's hand. 'Thank God it's you, sir! I can trust you, at least. Is she one of them, d'you think?'

'One of whom?' I said.

'Them,' he said. 'They are demons, all of them. Can you not see? Ask Sandesh. He'll tell you!' All at once he pushed me away, much harder than he intended, I think, for I cannot believe that he meant to harm me, and I fell against the table. A flask smashed on the ground and he let out a scream. 'They are here! Can you not see them! All around! Look at them dancing, out there! There, look!' He pointed over my head towards the door, though I could *see nothing but the bearer who had summoned me, and in the distance through the open door one of the boys who worked in the garden. Dr Christian screamed again and dashed his hands about his face, as if swatting angry flies, though again there was nothing there that I could see.*

'What's in there?' I whispered to Sandesh, pointing to a door in the wall at the back of the room. He replied that it was a cupboard, a box room in which sacks of herbs and dried leaves were stored. 'We must lock him in,' I said. 'If there are sacks all about then he will not harm himself. If we leave him here then I don't know what he will do!' The stove's gaping mouth of orange flame seemed now to exercise a peculiar fascination for Dr Christian, who was gazing at it with a fear and loathing I could hardly imagine it deserved. 'If you open the door to the store cupboard,' I whispered, 'I will shove him inside.'

Sandesh shook his head. 'No, miss. It is I who will do the shoving. Dr Christian is stronger and faster than you might think, and considerable force is required.' He grinned suddenly. 'I've done it before. He never remembers. Not even when I do it really hard!'

I opened the cupboard door, and then held out my hands to the doctor, enticing him to stand. 'Dr Christian,' I said. 'Come, let me help you.'

'I cannot get out,' he screamed. 'They are coming from the fire, one after the other, and blocking my way. Look at their claws and hooves! Their faces! My God, their bloody faces!'

'Come this way, sir,' I said. 'I will help you.'

Dr Christian snatched up a knife from beneath the blanket and brandished it before him. He crept sideways towards me. His eyes were fixed upon the stove and he thrust his knife towards it jerkily, as if stabbing at unseen creatures. 'There!' *he cried.* 'And there!'

As he stepped away from the wall Sandesh plunged forward. He shoved the doctor as hard as he could into the open cupboard.

Dr Christian fell sprawling on the floor. His knife clattered to the ground, and I kicked it aside as we slammed the door closed and turned the key. Once inside Dr Christian began screaming and sobbing and battering his fists upon the door, begging to be let out, shouting that they would come for him, that we had trapped him and sent him to his doom. I tried to pacify him, to calm him down, but it was no use. Even now, I cannot think what options we had. Should we have let him run mad about the gardens or the town? Should we have sent for one of his colleagues from the hospital, and had him forced into a straitjacket? I told the bearer to go to find Mrs Christian. I told Sandesh that I would wait where I was until she came, but that it might be better if he was not there. At first he refused to leave me, but I can be very persuasive, and I could tell he was relieved to be spared from having to explain, yet again, why Dr Christian was locked in a cupboard. I told him I would find him in the next day or so, and let him know what had followed.

It was almost nightfall before the bearer returned. He did not bring Mrs Christian. Instead, Bathsheba came with him. She seemed unconcerned by what had happened. 'Datura metel can be a useful aphrodisiac,' she said. 'I have tried it on Jane, and it was most efficacious. Like most men, improving his sexual performance is one of the only things Dr Christian ever thinks about. But there are severe consequences if too much is ingested. It is the same with all the Datura, all nightshades of that kind. The dose is crucial for the desired effect to be achieved. Jane has been driven mad by the stuff in the same way before now, though that was entirely my fault. The hallucinations haunted her for months afterwards. But Dr Christian should know better. He's a medical man, after all.' At the sound of her voice, Dr Christian started up a high-pitched screaming.

'Shall we let him out?' I said. 'He seems much calmer.'

But Bathsheba refused. 'The visions will assail him for a long time yet. Will he never learn what happens when he oversteps the mark? He has no self-control, no self-discipline. He is curious, I admit, and that's what I value in him. That and his knowledge of the Indian pharmacopoeia. He wants to know more, to find out what the limits of life might be, but he is a weak man, Cathy. Weak in mind and body. No wonder Dora despairs of him.' She barked out some commands in Hindi to the bearer and turned away. Dr Christian remained where he was, whimpering and howling, locked in his own cupboard.

11ᵗʰ October 1818

I saw Dr Christian at breakfast. It is the first morning he has been allowed out of the cupboard. He said nothing of his behaviour two days earlier. It was as if it had not happened at all.

Chapter Thirteen

❧

It cost me over a guinea to get the information from Mrs Roseplucker. It came in drips, each sentence paid for, so that she had emptied my pockets in no time. In the end, what she had to tell us left me with almost as many questions. But was worth every penny.

'I ain't always had Wicke Street,' she said. 'Before that I worked the streets like the rest. I was in demand, from all sorts o' high and mighty people. I knew the Prince Regent, you know! Asked for me personal, he did.'

'I don't think he did, Peggy,' interrupted Mrs Lovibond. 'It were *me* he liked. Always had an eye for a theatrical lady.'

'I'm sure the dear man was in love with both of you,' said Will. He always hated our encounters with Mrs Roseplucker. Her easy familiarity, the smell and look of her, the way the girls pawed at him, the looming bulk of the idiot-man Jobber – he despised it all. Once again, he hoped flattery might move proceedings along. 'There is not a queen on the earth who could hold a candle to either of you. But, to the purpose! Madam, you were a beautiful young girl who walked the streets near to the Infirmary, the men casting themselves into the Thames when you disdained their amorous advances. Pray continue.'

'I was and I did,' she said. 'And Dr Christian was one o' my reg'lars. He came to me every week. Said he was trying some medications to sharpen his appetites.'

'His appetites?' said Will.

'Don't interrupt or we will never be done. He was refer-ring to aphrodisiacs,' I muttered. 'It might have been any number of things, catuba bark, gokshura, cordyseps.' I turned back to Mrs Roseplucker. 'So, madam, I take it that he was in search of release?'

She nodded. 'Spring it was, and the sap were risin' in him like you wouldn't believe. The days were lengthening and as my route took me past St Saviour's physic garden I'd noticed the greenery coming out, buds and shoots and such like. There were a lot goin' on there too, comings and goings and voices and activity. Cart loads o' soil and plants, and people tramping in and out. Made my boots and the hem o' my dress all muddy. Well, one night I were making my way along St Saviour's Street when Dr Christian burst out o' the garden, right out o' the gate like a rat out of a trap. He runs straight into me. Well, seein' as he were one o' my reg'lars, I takes it upon myself to greet him proper-like.

"Why, Dr Christian," I says, seizing hold of him. "Ain't this a pleasure?" He were muttering and shaking, his face white as curds. "Why, sir," I says, "what on earth's the matter? Is it somethin' a lovely girl like your own dear Peggy can soothe?" And that's when he told me, though he was that a-feared he didn't hardly know what he was saying.'

'And you recall what he said?' Will sounded incredulous. 'After all this time?'

'Course I do,' she replied. 'It's what I had for breakfast that I can't bloody remember. Besides, it were too strange to forget.'

'And what was it, madam?' I said smoothly. 'What was it he said to you at the gate to my physic garden some thirty years ago?'

'*He should of stayed dead* is what he said. *He should of stayed dead.* Said it over and over, looking this way and that, and trying to wriggle out o' my grasp like a naughty boy runnin' from the strap. "Who, sir?" I says. An' that's when he told me. He looks me straight in the eye – I'll not forget the look he gave me either, for I ain't never seen a man more frightened – and he whispered as clear as day. *Delaney! Delaney, of course!* He said it strong-like, as if he expected me to know who it was he were talking about, though o' course I had no idea. And then he looked over his shoulder again. I looked too, and I saw the door o' the physic garden, nothin' but a black shadow in the darkness it was, though it seemed to be openin', slowly, slowly, like somethin' evil were about to come a-creepin' out. Well, at that he screamed and tore himself away from me.'

She sat back. The look of satisfaction on her face grew as she beheld the rapt expressions of her audience – Jenny, Annie, and the enamelled Beryl sitting at her feet, Will and I with our gazes fixed upon her, Mr Jobber with his hands to his face in horror. 'Run, Mrs Roseplucker, run!' he bellowed suddenly.

'I did too, Mr Jobber!' Mrs Roseplucker turned to the man-mountain. 'There now, don't you fret, Mr Jobber. I'm here, ain't I? Course I ran! I ran after Dr Christian, though I never saw the poor man again.' She shrugged. 'Thought he must o' died.'

'He has died, madam,' I said. 'But only yesterday.'

'This is just one of your tall stories,' said Will. 'Creeping evil and shadowy darkness? Save it for your penny dread-fuls.'

'I've used it already,' she said casually. 'In *The Cursed Pit.* You read that one, dearie? It were one o' my earlier stories.' Jenny shook her head. Like Gabriel, the girl was an avid reader of Mrs Roseplucker's vivid tales.

'But you've just made all that up!' said Will. I jabbed him in the ribs. Of course the woman had embellished her tale, she was a born story-teller and loved an audience. But did it not contain within it a kernel of truth? Did it not tell us something we had desperately wanted to find out? I had to believe that it did.

'Have I though?' Mrs Roseplucker held up the guinea we had given her, and then put it between her nasty brown teeth and bit down upon it, as if testing its metal. 'You can take it or leave it. It don't matter to me one way or the other. I don't know who Delaney is or was, I only know what Dr Christian said to me.'

'And you remember the name Delaney after all this time?' he said.

'I *always* remember their names,' she replied darkly. 'You never know when it might come in useful.'

'And you didn't ask what was going on? You didn't tell the constable?

'Of course not! What would I be tellin' him? Besides,

when did any constable listen to anything a girl like me might say? Even those what were customers!'

'Delaney,' said Will. 'Does the name mean anything to you, Jem?'

'No,' I said. I turned to Mrs Roseplucker. 'Why didn't you come and tell me this? If you knew we had found a skeleton, if you knew who was involved. It's not like you to miss an opportunity.'

'Why should I come to you when you've come to me? I'm a-tellin' you now, ain't I? Besides, I only read about it this morning. And I hear you've had a bit of interest already. Time-wasters, I imagine.' She grinned. 'Makes you realise my information's *always* worth a bit more, don't it?'

'What about *my* information?' cried Mrs Lovibond. 'You want what *I've* got? It's as good as hers, only seein' as you made me wait it'll cost you more than hers.'

I looked at Will. I had no money left. He sighed. 'Yes, yes, yes,' he said. He put his hand into his pocket and jangled his coins. 'Get on with it then!'

'Name of Saul,' I said. 'Owned the North Star Angel. What can you tell us?'

Mrs Lovibond held out a grubby hand. Her enamelled face glimmered like a grotesque parody of a child's doll. 'Cross my palm with silver!'

Will tossed her a crown. Information wasn't cheap when it involved Mrs Lovibond and Mrs Roseplucker. She held the coin up between finger and thumb for a moment, then with an artful flick of her wrist, it disappeared completely. She turned her empty hand from side to side for all to see.

Beryl and Jenny gasped. Mr Jobber pounded his hands together like an ape trying to attract the attention of its keeper. 'I love it when she does her tricks,' murmured

Jenny. 'She taught me once, but I were never very good. Said it were useful for thievin'.'

'Well, madam?' I cried. 'I've not come here for your stage tricks. What can you tell us?'

'Only that Solomon Saul is dead.' A terrible leer split her face like a crack appearing in a dirty chamber pot. 'See if you can't get Peggy here to contact him from Beyond the Veil.'

And then all at once the room was in uproar. Will plunged forward, his face furious. 'Well *that's* not worth a single penny of *my* money.' He pushed her against the back of her chair and rammed his hand into what looked like the greasy opening to a secret pocket in the woman's skirts. I saw the fabric rise and fall as his fingers sought to locate the coin.

Mrs Lovibond's eyes grew wide. 'Sir!' she cried in mock horror. 'Oh *sir*! Get your hands off my cunny *this instant*!' and then, as the tussle continued, '*That's* it, sir, let me help you,' and she seized his hand by the wrist and jammed it hard between her legs. '*Oh!*' she lifted her hips, rolling her eyes and opening her frayed scarlet lips in a moue of feigned ecstasy. 'Oh *sir*!' she cried. 'Sir, *don't*!' By now Will had realised his error and was trying to extract his hand. His face was crimson and sweating, but she kept a tight hold. 'Want me to unbutton you, sir? I think you might be ready now.' Mrs Lovibond came at him with claw-like fingers. A chunk of enamelling dropped from her cheek as she leered and cackled. Will screamed and wrenched his hand away, staggering backwards with such force that he almost bowled me over.

Mrs Roseplucker gave a great bellow of laughter, rocking back and forth in her chair and clapping her hands. 'Ain't that the best burlesque!' she cried. 'Ah, Mr Flockhart, Mr Quartermain, you gentlemen'll be the death of me. It's *you* what should be on the stage!' She wiped a tear from her eye. 'Old Solomon Saul might well be dead but his daughter ain't. She keeps the Blue Brazier on Parson Street, though whether she'll have anything to say about her father or the house he kept is another matter.'

Chapter Fourteen

The Blue Brazier was not two hundred yards from the Seamen's Floating Hospital. It was situated on a narrow thoroughfare, just off Parson Street between a chandler's and a pawn shop. The windows of both were filled with nautical items, seamen's jackets and boots, caps, carpet bags, brass compasses, wooden sea chests. The place we were looking for was no more than a dark door and a shallow bay window made up of small panes of thick glass separated by wide wooden astragals. It was mean-looking, but clean. I noted the scrubbed and white-washed step, the polished brass ship's bell at the door, the windowpanes wiped clear of grime as much as might be possible in so narrow and dirty a street. The name above the door was Rebecca Abelman.

Inside, a woman was wiping down a long trestle table. She had a leather cloth in her hand and a bucket of greyish water at her feet. The place smelled of beer slops and stale tobacco, the sweat of men, wet oilskins, river mud. But the sawdust on the floor was clean, and the woman herself was neat enough in a careworn, slatternly way. I wondered how much money she would want for the information she supplied, as we had nothing left between us but a few coins that might buy a pie and a couple of pots of ale. I asked for two of what she had, and a smaller one for Jenny. The woman recognised me straight away.

'You're that apothecary,' she said as she filled our tankards from a barrel behind the counter. 'The one that worked on the Seamen's Hospital. The one that found those dead girls.' She shook her head. 'Terrible business.'

I admitted that she was correct, told her my name was Flockhart, and that Jenny and I had worked on the Seamen's Floating Hospital for a number of weeks. For a while we exchanged pleasantries about the Hospital, the growth in river traffic in recent years, the stink of the mud at low tide. I gave her a salve, calendula and lavender mixed with beeswax and tallow, that I had in my satchel. 'It'll help your hands,' I said. 'Reduce inflammation, soften the skin, prevent cracking.'

'I don't need that,' she said. 'I don't have money for fancy things.'

'There's no charge, madam,' I said. 'And if you find it is of use then I am happy to supply more, also free of any charge.'

'Oh yes?' she said. She put the pot on the table before her. 'In that case, what is it that you *are* wanting?'

'Nothing,' I said. 'At least, I don't want any money. I wondered whether you might be able to help us. I have some questions—'

'Questions? What about?'

I put the token on the table. The words 'Saul' and

'Angel' engraved on that dark token were hardly visible in the gloom, but she flinched at the sight as if I had hit her. 'You know what this is?'

She did not pick the thing up. 'Well, well,' she said after a moment. She didn't smile, though her expression had hardened, and I saw her fingers squeeze the cloth she still kept in her hand. 'I've not seen one of these for a long time.'

'How long?' said Will.

'Ten, twenty years.' She shrugged. 'What of it?'

'It's from your father's place,' I said. 'I see you no longer go by the name of Saul, and yet there is no wedding ring—'

'Changed my name,' she said. 'Abelman will do. I certainly didn't want "Saul" over the door. And no, I didn't get married. My mother taught me well enough what marriage means for a woman.'

'And your father?'

'Is dead, and his grog shop and flop house are razed to the ground. He was a bad man and he came to a bad end.'

I sighed. It was such a long time ago. The woman I was talking to would have been no more than ten years old when the bones, the man Delaney and his monkey went into the ground. Any trail towards the truth would be stone cold by now. Still, we were here now and it was worth a try. 'Do you have many memories of the North Star Angel?' I said. 'I assume you lived above the place with your father?'

'Yes, sir,' she sighed. 'But none of those memories are good and I'll thank you not to make me re-live them. My mother, my father, my brothers and I were all above the pub. All dead now, apart from me. He killed them all. My mother he beat so often one day she didn't wake up.

My brothers it was the fighting and the drink. With him as a father who can blame them? They learned only bad things, bad ways, and it's a mercy on everyone that there's not a one of them alive to continue his name.' She leaned forward. 'My father was a bad man, Mr Flockhart,' she repeated. 'That's all I will say about him, and I *will* speak ill of the dead as he deserved it. I learned enough from him to know that I didn't want his name, and I didn't want no husband neither. Not ever. I'm my own master, and my own servant. It's a pity more women don't feel similar. Might save a lot of 'em from misery and drownin's.' She glanced at Jenny. '*She* knows my meaning. She used to be with that Mrs Lovibond, didn't she?'

'What sort of a place was the North Star Angel?' I said. 'Please, Miss Abelman.'

'It's Mrs. This ain't no neighbourhood for a "Miss" to do honest work.'

'*Mrs* Abelman. If you could tell us just a little—'

'Only the poorest wretches chose to stay there at the Angel, Mr Flockhart. It was a vile lodging house that he kept, stuck in an alleyway around the back of the pot house. Twenty people in one room, men, women, children. And in the Angel itself, right beneath where we slept, that was where all the drinking and the fighting happened. We were all terrified of him.'

It turned out that for a woman who said she was reluctant to talk about her father, Rebecca Abelman had a great deal to say about him, and I kept my interruptions to a minimum, directing her thoughts as simply and briefly as I could, until we had as complete a picture as we were likely to get. Did she recall any of her father's lodgers? Any of the men who frequented the place? One in particular was of interest to me. 'Delaney,' I said. 'Do you recall that name?'

She shook her head. 'I don't recall anyone called that though that doesn't mean he wasn't one of them.'

'He walked with a limp, most likely he had a crutch, possibly two. He had one eye. We believe he travelled with a monkey.'

She looked at me for a moment, shaking her head slowly. I could not read her expression, as she was sitting with the light from the open door behind her, but all at once I was sure I saw the hint of a smile on her lips. 'Wait,' she said. 'A monkey?' Her voice had changed, the hard, resentful edge softening a little. 'Thirty years ago? You know, I *do* remember such a creature. I was only a girl then. Perhaps ten years old. I don't remember much about the owner. A man, certainly, and possibly a cripple, but one-eyed crippled men were the sorts o' men I saw all the time at the Angel. Someone with a handsome face and all his limbs and features would have made more of an impression.' She lifted the edge of her skirts, and I saw the heavy black boot of a club foot. 'I'm less than perfect myself. But I do remember a monkey. My father beat me, my brothers beat me, the men that drank at the Angel beat me. That monkey were about the only creature what didn't lift its hand to me back then. I'd taken up hiding under the tables to get away from my father, but that monkey, well, he could always find me, no matter where I hid. And when I learned it liked raisins and nuts I was off to the docks to find some as fast as you like. I was as much of a thief as any street urchin back then.' She smiled. 'I hoped I could have a monkey for my own, but well, that weren't ever likely. And then one day it were gone. I remember wondering where it had disappeared to. Used to sit on his owner's shoulder with its tail curled around his neck. Can't say I have much of a memory for him though. He sat in the corner, in the shadows, as I recall. Couldn't see much of him. That monkey though! Got me into trouble that creature did, but I didn't mind. Used to steal things. It were always taking those tokens my father'd made. I used to feed it bits o' bread and dripping, along with the nuts and such-like. Tried to baby it, but it was a monkey, it didn't want to be wrapped in blankets and treated like a doll.'

'And the man?' I persisted. 'Can you remember anything about the man?'

'Not really. Like I say, a long time ago now. Crutches, I think. Two of 'em, like you say, now I think of it. He didn't stay for long, as I recall. Perhaps a week?' She smiled. 'Why, I ain't thought about that monkey, or those times, for years! It wore a little coat and hat. It was always worrying at the jacket, but that jacket were stitched on tight. I recall he said his wife had made the clothes to keep the monkey happy. *Got to keep Harry happy*.' She smiled. 'That's it! Harry. *That* was its name. Said his wife hated the thing. Couldn't abide it. My father were the same. Said the poor thing was vermin. Said he wanted it gone, that it were a nasty thieving creature.'

'He had a wife? Delaney had a wife?' I said.

'That's what he said. And o' course there was that woman what came after, so it were true and he did have a wife.'

'After?'

'After he'd gone. I remember him leaving too, as I'd stolen some fruit from the warehouses and got caught and the foreman had tanned my hide something awful. I'd only done it for the monkey. I'd seen him in the morning, a-riding on his master's shoulder, heading up towards the town. And that was the last I saw of either of them. Owed my father money for his bed and board too. O' course, no one ran out on Solomon Saul, and he went looking for the both of them everywhere, but never found him. I assumed he'd jumped aboard some ship or other bound for India.'

'India?'

'We were close to the India docks, Mr Flockhart. Most of 'em at the Angel were either coming or going.'

'Was Delaney alone?' said Will.

'I don't recall ever seeing another soul talking to him,' she replied. 'I didn't even know that were his name. He sat on his own in the corner, that's all I remember. The monkey though—'

'Did he state his business?'

'What man explains his business to a child? I have no idea where he went, or where he came from, or what he was doing here. It was his monkey I remember. D'you know there was this one time—'

'Can you remember anything else?' I said. 'What about this woman you mentioned? She came after, you said? Can you be sure who she was?'

'Why yes,' she said. 'I remember that for two reasons. One is that it were unusual. Usually it were men who came looking for people at the Angel. But this was a woman. It were weeks after he'd gone too. She said she'd a letter with the North Star Angel marked as the address. Like you, she asked if I'd seen a man with a monkey. I said yes, but that he'd gone away, and that she'd best get away quick as she could as he owed my father money and he'd take it out on her if he knew she'd come asking after him.'

'What happened to her?'

'How should I know?' She stood up. 'I were a ten year old pot girl. I remember him and his monkey, as what child wouldn't? And I remember her because she were beautiful. She looked like I wanted to look, slim and fine-looking, with dark eyes and dainty dancer's feet. Not like mine.' She looked down at her ugly leather boot. 'I always looked at feet in them days. Not so much now, but I did then. But she weren't like the usual slatterns and doxies you got around the Angel, though if she were married to him I doubt she'd have remained beautiful for long.'

'What do you mean?' said Will.

'He were a cripple,' she said. 'He had no money or why else would he be at the Angel? Good looks don't last long when there's want.' I noted a bitterness in her voice, but she was right. There were few beautiful faces to be seen in those dark and crowded streets. She began wiping the table once more, rubbing at sticky stains of spilled beer with her leather cloth. 'I recall the monkey, and the woman. That's about it.'

'Don't suppose you knew the woman's name?' said Will.

'Well, sir, yes I do! Her name was Nora. I only remember *that* because it were the same as my mother's, God rest her, though my mother didn't look a bit like her. I remember wishing she *was* my mother, though it pains me now to say it, for my own mother's life was as wretched as it was short and she deserved better, leastways from me who was her only daughter.' She dragged herself to her feet with a sigh. 'There were always people passing through, Mr Flockhart, always sad tales and misery, and wretchedness and disappearings. No one ended up at the Angel unless they had no choice, and it was the last stop before the grave for many.' She dropped her cloth into the grey water and wiped her hands on her apron. 'I were determined it wouldn't be mine.'

Excerpts from the diary of Catherine Underhill.

12ᵗʰ October 1818

Bathsheba left today. She said she has some business to attend to up country, and that we – Jane, Mrs Christian and I – should join her in a few days' time. Later, I came across Dr and Mrs Christian talking beneath the neem tree in the gardens, though they stopped immediately when they saw me. They exchanged a look I could not fathom and both of them asked whether I would be better off staying in Calcutta.

I refused. I am determined to go. I don't know why they keep asking.

15ᵗʰ October 1818

Today I received a letter from Bathsheba. It was dated some two days earlier, so there is every chance she is no longer where she says she is. It is little more than a note, and it came with a consignment of plants, all of which she has asked me to crate up and send back to England with a note to young Mr Flockhart, assistant apothecary and master of the physic garden at the Infirmary. She says that she trusts no one but him to look after them, and that it is only a shame they are to travel home alone. Young Mr Flockhart has asked her to bring home as many herbs from the India pharmacopoeia as might be grown in his physic garden, or its hot house. When we return, we are to work on that garden, with a view to bringing it more up to date and setting it out with plants that might offer new remedies. I do not know young Mr Flockhart very well (though his father is an old tartar), but he has a modern and exciting approach to the garden and its contents. I will include a note in the consignment from myself, containing details of my work so far, and what else we hope to find for him.

17ᵗʰ October 1818

We are leaving tomorrow morning. I have learned that Sandesh will be accompanying us for at least a part of the journey, and I am glad of it. He helped me to crate up Bathsheba's finds and send them to the docks, and I would never have managed it without his expertise, as he knows precisely how to ensure they will make the journey successfully.

This afternoon I was approached by Dr Christian's bearer, the one who came to Sandesh and me for help, and who will be staying behind in Calcutta. He handed me a small bottle and told me to keep it with me at all times, and to take three drops of it in a little water whenever I needed it. He told me it was something called dodheri. He also presented me with a little muslin bag of seeds, which he had attached to a leather thong. He told me to wear it

about my neck. Sandesh was watching. He told me that dodheri
*was a type of fern. 'It is said to guard against the evil eye,' he said.
'The seeds do the same.'*

'The evil eye?' I said.

*'Dark spirits,' he replied. 'Evil in general.' He shrugged. 'It
comes in many guises.'*

19ᵗʰ October 1818

The journey by dak *was something I was looking forward to.
I hoped we might make haste, as it is burning hot on the plains,
and I am eager to get to the mountains. But Mrs Christian said
we should take our time, that there was plenty to see along the way
that would interest me. Besides, she said, it would give me time
to learn how to use a pistol, as we were travelling into the wild
lands far beyond the reach of the Company, and there is always
the chance that it might prove to be my best friend at some point.*

*Dr Christian sleeps for most of the journey, though I have no
idea how he manages to do so, for the* dak *is insufferably dark
and hot when the screens are down, and insufferably dusty when
they are open. It appears that there is no compromise. Jane seems
hardly to notice. There is a handsome young Ensign travelling
with us, and she has eyes only for him. Sandesh travels separate
to us, which is disappointing, as his conversation is far more
interesting than Mrs Christian's.*

*I have had to write this when the others are asleep. I have
little privacy while we are on the road, and assume I will have
even less when we reach our destination. Mrs Christian watches
me all the time. Perhaps Bathsheba has told her I am not to be
trusted.*

23rd October 1818

We are lodged tonight in the dak bungalow of a cantonment some hundred or so miles north east of the Hooghly. Dr Christian, Dora and Jane went out to the bazaar earlier. I was suffering from a headache and so I said I would remain here and rest a little. I sat on the veranda with Sandesh, who is writing a monograph about the flora of Bengal. He is in correspondence with a Dr Curzon about the foundation of an Indian Horticultural Society. He is travelling with us so that he might meet the fellow in person. I asked him to teach me a little of his own language, not the corruption of it that the others speak, so that I might at least be able to utter some common courtesies. He is leaving us soon, however, and I fear I will be able to manage nothing but 'thank you' and 'goodbye' when the time comes for him to go.

Dora has returned. She is without Dr Christian, who she says has met an acquaintance in the bazaar.

Evening

Dr Christian has returned. He was carried into the dak bungalow on a stretcher. He is catatonic. Mrs Christian seems not to be worried about him, though she will tell me nothing about what has befallen him.

Jane came back last. She had gone out in her European clothes, corseted and tight-laced, with shawl and parasol. She told me she had gone up to the barracks, where she had heard that one of her conquests from the journey over was stationed. I could tell by her appearance – hair dishevelled, shawl gone, lips bruised, that she had been following her 'animal nature'. She still has the mixture Bathsheba had given her, the tincture of Devil's eyelashes mixed with ginger and mint. She has some of Bathsheba's 'herbal mix' *too, and she smokes as much of it as her mistress did. She is a highly sexed creature, and looks lasciviously at women as well as men, so that I think she does not mind who she goes with.*

25th October 1818

Sandesh has gone. He has given me a book about herbalism and Indian physic, which he had translated himself into English and had published privately with his friend Dr Curzon's help. I will miss him, and his conversation, a great deal. I have a feeling there was something he wished to say to me before he took his leave of us, but there was no opportunity for him to speak to me in private.

Chapter Fifteen

As we turned into Fishbait Lane I heard the sound of footsteps behind me and a voice cried out, 'Mr Flockhart! Mr Quartermain!' We turned around to see the porter from Angel Meadow hastening up the street behind us.

'What is it?' I said. 'Has something happened?'

'Dr Anderson asks if you can come up the Asylum directly, sirs. Come now. Come quickly.'

The man would not say why, only that there had been an accident. 'An unfortunate occurrence,' was how he put it. But who it concerned, and what exactly had happened, he was unable to say. Will and I exchanged a glance. We knew who it was, though nothing could have prepared me for what had happened.

Dr Anderson was sitting in his office, a dimly lit room on the first floor of the main building, with his head in his hands. 'I blame myself,' he said. 'I thought that if I left her downstairs, that she would tell me what she was so afraid of. That she would let me help her.' He said that he had left Mrs Spiker in her cell downstairs. She had screamed and shouted to be let out, to go back to her room, that she would be killed if she remained where she was. 'But she was locked in,' he said. 'She was quite alone. No one had gone down there, no one had seen her. And then, when the attendant went in with her evening meal she found—' He stopped and passed a hand across his eyes. 'Well, gentlemen, you might see for yourselves as there is nothing to be done about it now and you may have some insights.' He looked at me as he spoke. 'God help us, Jem. Angel Meadow is no place for this.'

He took us down a flight of stairs and along a dim passage lined with green tiles. The smell of drains was heavy in the air. Dr Anderson was still talking, his voice drifting over his shoulder as he strode forward.

'I saw the woman not two hours earlier. I saw her being locked up. Miss Spiker saw her too. Ask the attendants. It's impossible. Quite impossible. How can anyone be murdered when they are straitjacketed in a locked room in an asylum? It simply cannot be done.'

'Have you told the police?' I asked.

'Not yet.' He glanced at me over his shoulder. 'My predecessor Dr Hawkins told me that you had done your fair share of detective work when you were here as a patient, Mr Flockhart.'

'I was never a patient,' I said quickly.

'Well,' he shrugged. 'Whatever capacity it was, he said that without you . . . well, let's just say things would have turned out very different. For that reason, I would like you to see what you can do for Mrs Spiker. For Angel Meadow.'

'Was her door open?' I said.

'No.'

'Who has the key?'

'Myself. And Roger, of course.'

'Roger is the turnkey?'

'Yes.'

'Have you questioned him?'

'He says he did not open her door after he had closed it and saw no one go near.'

'And you are sure it is murder?'

'What else might it be?'

By this point we had reached the dead woman's cell. It was at the end of a long dark corridor, illuminated only by the lantern Dr Anderson had brought with him. Inside, the corpse was no more than a dark lumpen mass, a bulky form sheathed in canvas with a draggled mess of hair at one end and a pair of skinny ankles and dirty-soled feet projecting from the other. Another lantern had been left in the middle of the floor, and the shadows leaped and pranced upon the body and around the walls like goblins.

Mrs Spiker was even more hideous in death than she had been in life. Her cell was stinking and filthy, the mess within like nothing I had ever seen. The woman lay against the wall. No one had touched her, or touched anything, Dr Anderson said. But when I saw the dead woman's face, I knew he was wrong. She was still straitjacketed, the leather collar high at her neck, her arms trapped and pulled tight about her and laced tightly in a knot at her back. She had vomited copiously, a watery mess of greenish-coloured gruel, bits of the brush she had gnawed at so anxiously specking the mess like spots of algae. She had emptied her bowels too, a curious pale liquid, pink with blood, that had soaked into her dress and seeped out over the floor, so that I was reminded of the sufferings of cholera victims, whose fate it was to void quantities of 'rice water' stools until their bodies could empty no more. Mrs Spiker's face was turned towards us, a hideous sight with her dead grey eyes, her sunken cheeks. Worse still, from between her open lips I could see a black mass of shining berries. One had rolled out onto the floor, leaving a wet purplish trail across her cheek. 'Who found her?'

'One of the attendants,' said Dr Anderson.

'Roger?'

'No, the woman who brought her meal.'

'And she was found like this?'

'Yes.'

'With her mouth full of belladonna?'

'Is that what the poison is?' Dr Anderson blinked. 'But when? By whom?' He put his hands to his head. 'I cannot have this. I cannot let this get out. A poisoner in the asylum? It would be in all the papers. And what will the governors say? I will lose my position. We would lose patients, subscribers, benefactors, everything! I cannot let this become public knowledge. Consider my reputation, the reputation of Angel Meadow!'

'We must act fast,' I said. 'May I speak to the attendant? The one who found her?'

'Why yes, of course. Roger? Roger!' The speed with which the turnkey appeared told me that he had been listening at the door.

'Who brought this woman's meal down?' I said.

'Don't know, sir,' he replied. 'One of them. All I know is that she screamed and dropped the food she'd brought. Checked to see if the poor woman were alive—'

'How do you know this?'

'I were watching, sir. She were bent over the body when I stepped in.'

I frowned. 'You were not with her when she went in?'

'No, sir. She took the key and went in herself.'

'Aren't you supposed to unlock the doors down here?'

He blushed. 'My rheumatics, sir. Always bad in the winter. She said she'd do it. I didn't see the harm in it, as I were only two paces away on my chair at the end of the corridor.'

'And so she went in, screamed and dropped the food. You went to see what had happened, saw her examining the body. Then what?'

'Then I went to get Dr Anderson.'

'And she stayed with the body?'

'Yes, sir.'

'Was she here when you came back?'

'No, sir.'

'And where was she?'

'Don't know, sir. Went back to the women's wing, I suppose. That corpse ain't a pretty sight, as you can see, sir.'

'And the attendant's name?'

'No idea, sir.' He looked guiltily at the floor.

'Well, can you describe her?'

He shrugged. 'All looks the same to me, sir. Old. Ugly. Fattish. None of 'em worth lookin' at. This one were no different.'

'And where might we find her?'

'Don't know.'

'For goodness' sake!' I turned to the superintendent. 'Dr Anderson, who is in charge here? How can it be that

242

an unknown woman enters and leaves a patient's cell? Is it possible that you might find whoever it was that brought Mrs Spiker's meal down, and bring her to me? In the meantime, if someone might help me to take Mrs Spiker's remains to the mortuary, perhaps I might proceed with her post-mortem. I've undertaken many such procedures and am happy to help you in any way I can – including with my discretion in the matter. The governors need never know.'

'Yes, yes, Flockhart,' Dr Anderson waved a hand. 'Do what you must. I never like the feel of dead flesh myself. I could send for Dr Graves, but between you and me, Flockhart, the fellow has too much of the fiend about him for my liking.' He dabbed at his lips with the fold of his handkerchief. 'Come and find me when you have discovered what happened.'

Roger and two of his henchmen loaded Mrs Spiker onto a trolley and rolled her along to the mortuary. Will walked beside me with a handkerchief over his mouth and nose. 'Who did this?' he said when the attendants had gone. 'No one had been near her. No one could even get in!'

'On the contrary, a great many people have been near her. What better place to hide than in plain sight?'

'What do you mean? Are you talking about Miss Spiker? Dr Anderson? Surely you cannot think it is either of them who would do such a thing?'

'No one is above suspicion, Will, you know that. Whoever did this had a reason. A motive. Revenge? Jealousy? Rage? Greed? Fear? Money? The usual emotions should be our first consideration. Miss Spiker may well have reason to hate her mother, the woman showed her no love at all, she sent her away when she was a baby and ignored her in favour of newspapers and glue. Miss Spiker didn't receive a single kind word when we were in her mother's room with her, no matter how much she indulged the old woman's peculiar needs. If Miss Spiker wanted rid of her mother I think I would hardly blame her for it. And yet, we must also ask whether she knew Dr Christian and his wife? Is there a connection there? I think not, though we cannot be sure.'

'And Dr Anderson?'

'No, no, I cannot see a motive there. Mrs Spiker was generally an easy patient and her bed and board were paid every month without fail. And you saw how frustrated he was by her death. The lack of income, the implication of scandal. Besides, he is unacquainted with the physic garden, and I cannot see what connection he might have with Dr and Mrs Christian. It seems hardly likely.'

'Then we are out of suspects!'

'And yet we are surrounded by them.'

'You think it might be a patient? An attendant?'

'Perhaps not a patient. But an attendant? They are everywhere, Will. And we did not look at any of them, not really. They are like all servants – always present but rarely seen. I can only recall a number of bulky women clad in grey. A muddle of hands and arms, the smell of sweat and boiled cabbage as they wrestled Mrs Spiker into her straitjacket. Can you recall the face of a single one of them? I can't.'

Will shook his head.

'And that, my dear Will, reminds me of the disappearing housemaid.'

'At Dr and Mrs Christian's?'

'Exactly. We didn't notice her either, and I'm usually

so observant.' I shook my head. 'I fear I'm not thinking straight, Will. I cannot be objective. I'm too hasty, too involved. This whole business strikes at the heart of who I am. Who I *thought* I was.' I rubbed my forehead. I could feel the beginnings of a headache just behind my eyes. 'All this emotion – it's exhausting. And it's making me clumsy and inattentive. Hasty. I *should* have noticed. I won't make the same mistake again.'

'No one notices servants,' said Will, 'or attendants, especially when there are so many of them! Not unless they're uncommonly pretty, or peculiar to behold. But even assuming that it *was* an attendant, how was Mrs Spiker poisoned? She was in a locked room! Did the same person hang around waiting to stuff her mouth with deadly nightshade once she was taken to the mortuary?'

Will looked down at Mrs Spiker's body, still trussed up in its straitjacket. The dead eyes and gaping mouth stared up at him accusingly. 'Good Lord, Jem, what a stink!' he muttered. 'I think I prefer shit and piss to vomit, when all's said and done. Vomit is the very devil. Do I have to watch this post-mortem?'

'I'd rather you didn't. You know what will happen.'

'I am getting much better,' he said. 'I have not fainted for months! Even you must admit that. Besides, I have salts – I always have them with me since I met you.'

He would have stayed, he would even have helped, if I had asked him to. But I wanted to be alone. 'In case I am wrong, why don't you go and see if you can find this missing attendant?' I said. 'The one who found Mrs Spiker. She might be in the servants' common room sharing her tale.' We both knew it was a fool's errand, but he was relieved to go all the same. I waited until his footsteps had faded before I reached for my knife and slit the straitjacket from neck to hem.

I had conducted many post-mortems and witnessed still more, though this was the first time I had undertaken one on my own. I found I was quite happy with only the dead for company, as at least they kept their own counsel. I began by examining the woman's clothes, which I sliced from her body with the aid of a scalpel. I looked at her fingernails, and the whites of her eyes, her tongue, scalp, and the rest of her body from the outside. And then I took up another, finer knife. The dead flesh parted easily beneath my fingers.

As I'd been taught, I examined every inch of her, inside and out. Lungs, liver, kidneys, bladder, bowels, brain, the lengths of intestines, the rubbery sack of the stomach, and crimson mass of the spleen. It confirmed what I had already suspected, though I had one last test to undertake that would confirm my suspicions beyond any shadow of a doubt.

I heard Will's footsteps approaching. He had taken his time, though I could hardly blame him. 'Well?' I said.

'She's completely disappeared,' he said. 'No one's seen her, and it seems no one knows who she is either.' He spread his hands. 'What more can I do? It seems you were right, Jem. Our adversary is a fat slattern whom nobody notices.'

'How commonplace,' I said. 'And how clever. The mundane is so much harder to recall, or notice.'

'What about you? Are you finished?' He sounded hopeful.

'Not quite,' I said. His face fell. 'You're just in time to witness me performing the Marsh test. A particular favourite of mine as it reveals the wizardry of the chemist in the service of truth and justice. It is the enemy of murderers and inheritance-seekers all over the world.'

'Murderers?' said Will. 'Was it the belladonna?'

'It was not, Will, though the berries were certainly an interesting garnish. But, to our test. Fortunately, this mortuary is very well equipped.' I gestured to the row of flasks and bowls, the jars of acids, liquids, powders that might be used in the examination of a corpse. 'Dr Graves insisted upon it, since he is as meticulous as he is ghoulish, and it is he who usually does the post-mortems here – indeed I am surprised he has not appeared already. No doubt he will sulk for months because I did not invite him.'

'Never mind that, Jem, get to the point.' Will held his handkerchief over his nose. 'This may well be a well-equipped mortuary, but it stinks like the abyss.'

'Does it?' I said. 'I can't tell anymore.' It was true enough. What had initially been an olfactory assault of the very worst kind was now hardly noticeable to me.

'My God, Jem, how can you not notice it? I fear you are turning into Dr Graves.'

'Let's hope not.'

'Get on with it.' He was looking green. 'I see your apparatus, Jem. A flask, a stopper with a long pipe of some kind projecting from it, a porcelain bowl and a flame. Now what?'

'Open the door if you please. I would prefer a draught to blow away the poisons, rather than undertake this in a closed room. Imagine if Dr Anderson found the two of us dead on the mortuary floor. How on earth would he explain that to the governors?'

He did as I asked. It made little difference to the movement of the air, but at least the room was no longer so confined, and I would perform the test as quickly as I could. Between the tips of a pair of tweezers I held up a strip of scarlet flesh. 'I have here a sliver of Mrs Spiker's stomach. To save you from fainting at the very idea we will call it "the compound". Watch while I pop it into this flask. I will now add a little piece of zinc, and a few drops of hydrochloric acid, like so. See how it reacts?' The mixture began to froth and bubble. I quickly stoppered the flask with the cork, from which protruded a narrow glass pipe. 'Stand back!' I cried. 'We must be quick, as the gas you see bubbling here is extremely poisonous.' I put the flame from the candle to the tip of the pipe, igniting the gas that was escaping. Its flame burned a pale orange. Between my finger and thumb I took up the small porcelain bowl and held it against the flame. 'Look! You see the black deposit that it makes on the cold surface of the porcelain? Black, with a mirrored sheen to it. The gas is arsine gas, the deposit it makes is arsenic. There can be no doubt on the matter.'

'Arsenic?' said Will. 'Mrs Spiker was poisoned with arsenic?'

'Yes,' I said.

'And the vanished attendant is the perpetrator?'

'No.'

'No? But you said she was.'

'I said no such thing, Will. The attendant administered the belladonna, but Mrs Spiker poisoned herself.'

'But her arms were tied in a straitjacket, Jem. She could not possibly have poisoned herself. Where would she get the poison from for a start? Dr Anderson does not lock up his patients with poison lying about the place. Are you quite sure? Might your little test be mistaken?'

'My "little test" as you call it, is the brilliant Marsh test, devised by Dr James Marsh in 1836 in response to the acquittal of the murderer Bodle, who had poisoned his own grandfather, though he got away with it due to imperfect means of testing. It was used with celebrated effect in the famous French Lafarge poisoning case of 1840, whereby Madame Lafarge had poisoned her husband with arsenic, but like so many before her escaped justice due to lack of evidence. His exhumed body was found to be riddled with the stuff, a conclusion only arrived at thanks to the discoveries of Dr Marsh. This "little test" has changed the face of toxicology and called murderers to account all over the world.'

'Yes, but how do you *know*? How can you explain it?'

'The manner of her death for a start. The voiding of all that watery stool was indicative. It looked like the victim had died of cholera at first, but whereas cholera is a common visitor to these streets, it is not currently amongst us, so I saw no reason to suspect that was what killed her.'

'So it was definitely not the berries?'

'If it had been the berries then the manner of her death would have been very different, so despite her mouth being full of them there was no reason to think that they were anything but a later addition. You may recall her behaviour, Will, the way she chewed on her glue-brush like a child? The paint on the brush was green. If we did the Marsh test again using fragments of paint as the compound we would no doubt see exactly the same reaction. Would you like me to show you?'

'I think it essential that you do.'

I ran the test again, this time using fragments of green paint picked from Mrs Spiker's stomach. The zinc and acid mixture bubbled, the orange flame burned, the cold porcelain turned a mirrored black. 'You see? It is filled with arsenic. Not because of anyone tampering with it, but as a result of the manufacturing process. The stuff may well be fairly benign if one only uses the brush in the usual way, but when it is used all day, every day, when it is habitually chewed as its user pores over her work, then it's a very different matter. Mrs Spiker has been gluing for years, and I imagine the chewing is a habit of long standing. The doses she received from it may have been fairly small, or indeed she may have built up a tolerance to it, but nonetheless she has been poisoning herself for quite some time. I saw it in the sores about her mouth and nose, the loss of teeth, the bald spots, the lines on her fingernails, and the greenish tint to the whites of her eyes. She probably viewed the world through an emerald haze.'

'And the berries were added later?'

'It seems we are looking for a servant with her pockets full of belladonna.'

'Perhaps if we find her we will find our murderer.'

'And yet she has not murdered anyone yet, Will. Dr Christian died of a heart attack, his wife fell down the stairs, and Mrs Spiker poisoned herself. If it's death this mysterious woman is after then fate seems to be on her side so far.'

'Then what's the point of the deadly nightshade?'

'I can't be sure, but it's my feeling that the berries are a way of making her presence felt. Perhaps she *would* have killed, had not fate got there first. It might be a message or a warning of some kind, it might represent some sort of vengeance. Whatever it is, it raises these deaths above mere accident.'

'What message?'

'I have no idea what the message might be, nor at whom it is directed.'

'What about the language of flowers?' said Will. 'I know I keep mentioning it, but ladies love all that kind of thing. They seem to understand it well enough, and this whole business smacks of a woman's hand.'

'In the language of flowers the belladonna signifies silence.'

'You don't get much more silent than a corpse with its mouth stuffed with berries. Might she be warning others to remain silent, or is she punishing the dead for their silence?'

'Who can say? It might very well be both. At this point all we have is conjecture. But we will find out. One way or another. Now then, we must present our findings to Dr Anderson – and let us hope the accidental nature of Mrs Spiker's death will allay his worry about the subscribers and the governors. After that I would like to take a closer look at her room.'

'Ah!' said Will. 'I can help you there, Jem. I took the liberty of asking Dr Anderson if we might be permitted to look at the dead woman's room once you were ready. He seems to have the highest opinion of your abilities and still considers this to be a murder. Might I suggest that we don't tell him otherwise until after we have looked through Mrs Spiker's vile nest? He consented readily enough and has given permission to the turnkey to let us through, though once he knows Mrs Spiker's death is merely misadventure, he might well change his mind and strip the place of all its embellishments before anyone can say anything about it. I imagine it's the last place he would want his beloved governors to see.'

The turnkey who took us back through the asylum was a large woman, more of a housekeeper than a gaoler, tall as well as broad though with the build of a wrestler rather than a glutton. She strode forward with a speed and confidence that made me suspect she was not a person to be trifled with. I imagined she would be able to chase down any miscreant lunatics and wrestle them to the floor on her own if she had to, perhaps single-handedly getting them into a straitjacket and slinging their tethered bodies over her shoulder like a stoker carrying a sack of coal. She was more well-spoken than most of the attendants I had come across and seemed to have a great deal of authority about the place. With a jangling of keys she unlocked Mrs Spiker's door. 'Has anyone been in here since she was removed to the basement?' I said.

'No, sir. The room has been locked up the whole time. We'll be removing all the paper in the next few days.'

'Did she have any possessions?'

'Everything she owned is in there, sir. By all means look, sir, and if you have any ideas concerning what happened, I'm sure Dr Anderson would be grateful to hear them.'

I thought she might stay and watch us as we searched, but she didn't. 'I'll be nearby if you need anything,' she said, and she strode off to speak to one of the other attendants. The inmates watched her passage down the corridor, and some of them started up a low moaning. One of them sank to her knees before her and tried to seize her hand. I heard screaming, and the sound of a fist pounding on the keys of a piano. More attendants appeared, I could hardly tell where from for they seemed almost to emerge from the very walls of the place, bustling to and fro, as if determined to look busy. God save me from such a place, I thought, no matter how kindly my gaoler might be. If one was not mad on entering then one would surely end up so.

I closed the door behind us, shutting out the hubbub. The room had a curious, muffled deadness to it, and I noticed that Mrs Spiker had papered over the back of the door too, so that the whole room was inches deep in newspaper cuttings, ripped out and pasted, ripped out and pasted, one on top of the other, a great yellowing mass of crime, sorrow, despair. *Boy found drowned in well near Seven Dials . . . Body in Regent's Canal identified . . . Murder at Anderson's Cross, Glasgow . . .* I ran my hand down the wall. Such meticulous labour, undertaken for so long. There seemed little harm in it, from the point of view of the asylum superintendent, if it kept her biddable. I wondered whether Dr Anderson, and Dr Hawkins before him, had been curious to see how far the woman might go. Until she had completely papered herself up? I noticed again that Mrs Spiker had favoured some areas more than others. The walls were no longer flat, but had a topography all of their own, some areas thickened and raised in a wedge of death and mayhem, others a smooth whorl of calamity, the tragedies they contained blurred and indistinct with glue. It was like being at the heart of a giant organism, or a chamber in a calcified wasps' nest. The bed was narrow, with rumpled sheets and a plain threadbare counterpane blotched and stained with glue, the bedding smudged black from hands that pored over newsprint all day. It stood beneath the window, which had also been papered over, though the crimes were layered but singly here, the daylight behind glowing dim. I took out my penknife and picked at the edge of the stuff that covered the window, peeling it off like strips of dry flesh. The daylight was little better, seeping through yellow clouds and a veil of fine rain. But it showed up the texture and undulations of the walls, the stains of mould that had grown in places, the lumps and dips from her erratic pastings.

'My God,' said Will. 'What a horrible lair.'

'Shall we look through her things?' I was suddenly desperate to get out of the place. It was hard to conceive of a more unnerving and horrible room. How had she lived there without going still more insane? The bulging walls oppressed me, the words everywhere made my head spin. *Dead . . . Murdered . . . Crime . . . Hanged . . . Hanged . . . Hanged . . .* Was my father's death somewhere here? It had to be. A sudden, powerful urge to look for it swept over me. I shut my eyes and took a deep breath.

'In her desk, perhaps?' said Will, oblivious to my silence and pallor. 'Or that cupboard beside the bed? I can't think where else we might look.'

There was little to show for the life she had led, and we laid out our finds upon the bed: a bodkin, a grey corset, a dress of dark green that seemed to be made from some sort of tarpaulin, so thick and greasy was its fabric. A bottle of glue and a brush. Some pins for her hair. A Bible, though it seemed never to have been opened, for the spine cracked with a sound like a cabby's whip as I prised it open. Inside, gossamer-thin paper, letters as tiny as mustard seeds. I slipped it into my satchel for later. There was also a copy of *The Newgate Calendar*, though for some reason she had elected merely to annotate its pages, rather than ripping them out and sticking them to the wall. There was little else to remark upon. 'D'you think she really was a "Mrs"?' said Will.

'I think it unlikely.'

'There must be something more. Something we've missed.'

I looked about at those yellow undulating walls. The words seemed to seethe before me, like ants. I passed a hand across my eyes. My head was buzzing. I looked again. There was one area of the wall, to the right of the window, that was more repellent than all the rest. It bulged like a tumour, so that my eye was drawn to it again and again. Why would she focus on that one area, papering it over and over. *Found drowned . . . found stabbed . . . murdered by poison . . . murdered by violent means . . . suffocated . . . burned . . . beaten . . . clubbed . . .* And in the middle of it, freshly daubed, so that the paper was still dark and damp, '*body found in the physic garden of old St Saviour's Infirmary*'. I took out my penknife and stabbed at the tumour. It was hard to the touch, years of glue and paper having dried to a thick hard carapace, and the tip of my knife made little impression. I pressed the blade in harder. I kept all my knives sharp, and with some leverage and pressure it sank further into the papery mound. I pulled it out and began to whittle at the centre, layers of paper coming away as I gouged and stabbed. I saw a date at the edge of the hole I had made: 31st October 1841. I had dug through ten years. I had twenty more to go.

'Jem,' Will spoke behind me. 'What are you looking for?'

'I don't know,' I said. 'But why is this bulge here?'

'What?'

'This mass here. Don't you see it? The way the wall

heaves, as though something were buried beneath? There are undulations all over these walls, but this one is far bigger, far more protuberant than anywhere else.' *28th May 1835.* I scraped faster. Perhaps I was wrong. Perhaps there was nothing here at all and I was as deluded as the woman who had spent thirty years fashioning these walls. And then the tip of my knife struck something.

It was not the wall, I could tell that much. It was too hard, too jarring to be mere plaster and paint. I scraped at it, and wriggled my knife, heard once more the *chink* and scrape of the blade. I looked at Will, who pulled out his own blade, and joined me in my work.

What had once been a bulge now looked like a giant burst pustule, a ruptured abscess, layers of paper hanging down like shreds of skin. At its heart was a cavity, no bigger than a man's fist, inside of which was something pale and rounded, like the ball-joint of a shoulder. I pulled back some more of the paper, and, digging my knife in hard, I prised it out.

Excerpts from the diary of Catherine Underhill.

27th October 1818

We have arrived at a place far to the north. Mrs Christian tells me that this is as far as the dak *goes and that we must find alternative means of travelling from here. Bathsheba, it seems, is awaiting us somewhere in the jungle further to the west. We are in a province called Oudh. It is not quite a part of the Company's India, though Mrs Christian says this is unlikely to remain the case for long, and that all manner of violence will no doubt ensue, for it usually does when the Company is concerned. It is a wealthy place, she says, and the Company will do what it must to get its hands on its revenues. The place seems wild and remote, the people's faces fearful and unwelcoming. I cannot make out what they are feeling – do they hate us or love us? They fawn about us for rupees, offer us all manner of goods, from coloured stones to baskets of live chickens, but the look in their eyes tells a different story.*

31st October 1818

I have been sick again. Sometimes I wonder if Dr Christian has something to do with it. He seems determined to prevent me from continuing onwards and has suggested more than once that I might prefer to return to Calcutta. Now, for the last three days I have had a terrible headache that prevents me from travelling. Jane and Dora have continued onwards to catch up with Bathsheba. Dr Christian stays here with me and says we will continue when I feel better – unless I return south again. He spends much of his time in the bazaar, however, and more than once has been brought back here by his bearers, quite insensible, though from what I cannot say. I begin to wonder who is looking after whom. He has asked me to note down his symptoms, how long it takes him to recover, and so on. I believe he intends to put these observations into a book he is writing.

2nd November 1818

I am feeling much better – possibly because Dr Christian has been gone for two days in the bazaar, though he is back now, and seems to be quite himself. Two men have arrived at the dak bungalow. They are brothers, Dr James and Mr William Delaney. They are very personable. The elder, Dr James Delaney, works for the Company. He is doctor-surgeon to the garrison stationed somewhere to the south east of us. He says he is lucky the Company has not moved him on, for it is often the fate of Company surgeons to be moved from garrison to garrison, or from one cantonment to another. No one wants to be this far up country, he says, but what can one do? The Company is one's master, after all. He told us he has started a small botanical garden of his own, helped by his *brother, Mr William Delaney, a tall handsome man and by far the better looking of the two. Mr William Delaney is a botanist, and a collector and painter of rare plants. The garden is a joy to both of them, they say, and it may grow to one of the finest in the Company's India, mainly because we are in a more temperate part of the country. Such a garden is not possible on the plains, where the wind blows hot and merciless all summer, and the rains wash everything away in the monsoon. They have heard of Dr Christian, as his knowledge of Indian flora and fauna is highly regarded in certain circles, and they both seemed delighted to meet him. I could tell he was flattered.*

Dr James Delaney said he had obtained money to expand the garden, and his brother, Mr William, was spending much time and effort gathering the plants and flowers of the region so that they might be studied and understood by physicians and scholars from all over the world. They speak about their project with such enthusiasm it is a delight to listen to them both. Mr William Delaney tells me that there are high prices to be paid for rare plants and flowers, those that can be cultivated or propagated in England, especially. He talked at length about how he had recently come across Eulophia obtusa, *the rare ground orchid, but that it is not yet known in England and I said, 'Oh, but it is, sir. I have seen it. My employer has them in her glasshouse in Islington.'*

He asked who my employer was and I told him.

'Bathsheba Wilde?' He looked at me and smiled, though it seemed to me that there was an uneasiness to it. 'How do you know her?'

I told him I had met her in London, an acquaintance of my father. 'I am her travelling companion,' I said. 'Though I have been unwell and was forced to rest here while the others travelled up country. We will be leaving in another day or so to join them.'

There was an awkward silence for a moment. I felt my cheeks colour, and an unaccountable panic rising within me. He seemed to apprehend it, for he said, 'Well, well, I am sure it is interesting work.' He slid a glance at his brother, who was talking now to Dr Christian, inviting him down to see the gardens he had told us so much about. 'Miss Underhill,' he said, leaning towards me and keeping his voice low. 'I have heard such things – I hardly know how to tell you.'

'What things?' I said.

'About your employer. About her friends. Miss Wilde passed through here some weeks ago, and is now far up country, far from any influence the Company might have. Far from anything we might call civilisation—'

'What things?' I repeated. 'What things have you heard?'

'About Miss Wilde in particular, though her friend Mrs Christian,' here he glanced over at the doctor, 'also stands accused of not living up to her name. As for the other member of that party . . .' He shook his head. I knew he was referring to Jane Spiker. I said nothing, waiting for him to continue. But he simply smiled and said he hoped he might make my acquaintance again soon, that perhaps we might talk further then. I don't know what to make of it. I will encourage Dr Christian to go to see Dr Delaney's gardens, and to take me with him. Perhaps then I can find out more.

Chapter Sixteen

※

It was a skull. No bigger than a crab apple, carved from ivory, with a small hole in each temple. We looked at it for a moment, neither of us saying anything. And then I put it into my pocket. The turnkey who had brought us up from the mortuary was waiting for us out in the corridor. She did not bother to look into Mrs Spiker's room but locked the door and led us away. The din of the inmates, the pounding fists and screams from the sitting room as the third movement of the Sonata Pathétique reached its peak, seemed curiously reassuring to me. Perhaps this was how Mrs Spiker had felt in the end: safe, cushioned from the real world, alone in her paper nest while the mad screamed and gibbered at the edges of her consciousness.

We went to see Dr Anderson. I did not tell him that we had found an ivory skull embedded in Mrs Spiker's wall, but merely shared with him what he most wanted to know: that the woman's death had been misadventure, and that the nightshade berries were nothing to do with it. 'A practical joke, perhaps,' I said. The explanation was inadequate, but it seemed good enough for Dr Anderson.

'Thank God!' he said. 'I can't imagine who would think such an action might be droll, but, well, this is a dark place at times, who knows what goes on in the attendants' minds when they need a little levity. But at least it is nothing so serious as murder.'

'Has anyone informed Miss Spiker of her mother's death?' I asked, unwilling to dwell on what might pass for amusement amongst asylum attendants.

Dr Anderson shook his head. 'Not yet.'

'Perhaps I might be permitted to break the news. Having undertaken the post-mortem I'm perhaps best placed to explain what's occurred. And I'm sure you have much to do here. The paperwork alone for a death by poison—'

'By misadventure.'

'And I shall record as much on her death certificate. But if I might—'

'Oh, very well, Flockhart,' he said. 'I suppose my manner can be a little . . . robust for the bereaved, though to be honest it's a blessed relief to many of them. Besides,' he turned to root amongst the papers on his desk, 'I'm rather glad to be relieved of going to this place. Its reputation, you know.' He handed me a slip of paper. 'Miss Spiker's address,' he said. 'Good luck.'

Miss Spiker's home was far to the north, beyond the limits of the city, where the pavements petered out into a metalled road, and then almost a track. But its rural setting would not last much longer. Already the brick kilns were smoking on Maiden Lane, Islington Fields marked out here and there for new houses. The buildings we passed were large villas, new built with new money, surrounded by walls and gates, the saplings freshly planted in gardens not yet mature enough to screen their mansions from the covetous gaze of passers-by. Nightshade House, however, was a far older and grander building than any of its neighbours. The date carved in the stones above its front door declared the place to have been completed in 1765. Beneath it, a coat of arms – two lions rampant, a cross of St George, and the words *auspicio regis et senatus angliae* – told me that it had been erected by a grateful employee of the East India Company. It was built in the Palladian style, with a façade not dissimilar to the Company headquarters on Leadenhall Street in the centre of town. It stood on the brow of a hill watching the city's encroachment from its tall casement windows.

We paid the cabby to wait and climbed the steps to the front door. The place was so grand that I wondered whether we were supposed to have used the rear entrance, though I had no intention of scuttling out of sight around the back like a tradesman. I reached out for the gleaming brass knocker in the shape of a lion's head that surmounted the huge, oaken door, but before I could do so it eased open, noiselessly, on its great iron hinges. A woman I assumed to be the housekeeper stared down at us without smiling or speaking. She looked surprised to see two strange men claiming to be there to see Miss Spiker, but when I mentioned Angel Meadow she admitted us without even taking my card. If the house had looked grand from the outside, on the inside it was extraordinary. The hall, cool and lofty, stretched to left and right below a ceiling painted with azure skies, exotic birds, trees and clouds. Its walls were lined with console tables in teak and ebony, each one displaying the marvels of the Empire – a stuffed pangolin in a case of crystal and ivory, fat-bellied flasks encrusted with precious stones, a golden musical box, a hookah studded with what looked like diamonds and emeralds. There were cases of jewelled daggers, gold incense burners, rare and beautiful birds, stuffed and mounted in realistic settings and trapped forever behind glass and ebony. A maid – a small silent Indian woman – who had been summoned from the shadows by the housekeeper, led us east along the glittering corridor, past a wide sweeping staircase and into what she described as 'the Blue Drawing Room', where we were to wait while she fetched Miss Spiker.

Will and I stood beside the fire in awed silence. Beneath our feet was a fine Persian carpet swirling with azure, crimson and gold, behind us the tall casement windows were hung with swathes of midnight blue silk embroidered with flowers and birds. The faces of tigers, peacocks, doves, lions, stared up at us from embroidered cushions. The fire screen was a diorama of stuffed hummingbirds, the hearth a glittering mosaic of lotus leaves. I saw a nightingale in a crystal display case, a tapestry depicting a tiger hunt, another golden music box. The walls were painted a deep Russian blue and hung about with gold-framed paintings of women as fat and pale as grubs, wrapped in folds of silk and lolling on sofas. Every surface that I could see held a vase, an urn, a plate of some kind.

'Well!' murmured Will after a moment. 'This is almost as grand as our place.'

'Steady on,' I said. 'Our tapestries are much better than these.'

'Paid for by years of devoted service to the Company, I take it.'

'That's one way of looking at it. Looted, robbed and pillaged more like. The reputation of the Honourable East India Company has become somewhat tarnished in recent years.'

'I suspect it was always tarnished,' replied Will. 'They just hid it behind mountains of tea leaves and calico.'

I ran my fingers over a solid gold finial in the shape of a tiger's head that stood on the mantelpiece beside a huge ormolu clock. 'It is from the throne of Tipu Sultan himself,' said a voice behind me. 'A gift to Miss Wilde's father from Clive.'

Miss Spiker was standing in the doorway, her hands clasped before her. 'Good afternoon, gentlemen,' she said. 'You find Miss Wilde from home—'

'We are not here for Miss Wilde, madam,' I said. 'We are here to see you.'

'Me?' She swept forward and sat down on the edge of one of the silken sofas. She glanced anxiously at Will, and then at the door, as if she was afraid someone was about to burst in. Perhaps Miss Wilde did not like men in her house any more than she liked them out of it.

'Miss Spiker, we come from Angel Meadow,' I said. 'We do not bring happy news.'

'She's dead, isn't she?' Miss Spiker's face was bone-white against her dark quivering ringlets. She looked awkward in such opulent surroundings, as if she hardly knew how she had found herself there.

'Yes. She was found earlier today. She had been taken downstairs, as you know. She became ill. Her illness had all the appearance of cholera.'

'Cholera!' Miss Spiker's hand flew to her throat.

'But it was not the cholera,' I went on. 'It was poison.' I watched her closely. Her cheeks grew paler still.

'Poison?' she said.

'Arsenic.'

'But who would do such a thing?'

'She poisoned herself,' I said. 'Years of chewing on the end of that glue brush. The paint was full of arsenic. It might not have been so deadly to her if she had not been in the habit of grinding it between her teeth and ingesting the particles. You were quite right to warn her against it. But she would not listen and now she is dead. I'm sorry, Miss Spiker. I did Marsh's test for arsenic and there can be no doubt.'

'Oh.' Her face, and her voice, betrayed no emotion. 'Oh,' she said again. She sighed. 'She was never kind to me, sir, so I have little enough cause to regret her passing. And yet despite it, she was my mother.'

'Might I ask,' said Will suddenly, 'how is it that you are here? It is . . . it is not where we expected to find you.'

'And where did you expect to find me, sir? Am I not good enough for surroundings such as these?' I was surprised by her fervour. I could see that Will was abashed too, and he dipped his head as he made his apology.

'Not at all, Miss Spiker. But . . . it is not your mother's home, I think?'

'This is the home of Bathsheba Wilde,' I said.

'It is, sir.' Miss Spiker sighed and began to dab at her eyes with a handkerchief of lace and silk, though from where I was sitting it did not look to me as though she had shed a single tear.

'May I ask what your relationship is with Miss Wilde?' I said.

I thought she was about to tell me it was none of my business, but she didn't. 'My mother was companion to Miss Wilde many years ago. Miss Wilde has looked after her ever since.'

'Ever since what?' I said.

'Since they returned from India. Since my mother went mad, sir. A long time ago now.'

'Who, exactly, returned from India?' I said.

'All of them. Mrs Christian. Miss Wilde. My mother. She was never the same, Bathsheba says. She said it was the heat – amongst other things. *Dewanee*, she called it. Bathsheba has paid for my mother's upkeep at Angel Meadow for many years.'

Amongst other things? I wondered what she might be referring to, though it did not seem appropriate to ask. 'You were born in Angel Meadow?'

'I was, sir.' Her cheeks grew rosy, as if at the shame of it. 'But I was not mad, and I did not belong there. Besides, an asylum is no place for a baby, and my mother showed little interest in me.'

'So when the asylum superintendent decided it was no longer appropriate that you remain there, he brought you here?'

'Yes. Bathsheba – Miss Wilde – was happy to take me in. She paid for my mother's upkeep, and said she would always take care of her. I've lived here ever since.' She could not stop from glancing fearfully at the door as she spoke. 'I have much to be grateful for.'

'You said Miss Wilde is not home,' I said. 'Are you afraid she will be angry when she hears that men have been here?'

She smiled slightly. 'Oh, she knows all about *you*. She will be glad to hear that you have called.' She glanced at the clock. 'All the same, I think it would be best if you left now. She dislikes visitors, unless she has expressly invited them. Especially . . . ' She looked at Will, 'especially . . . those who are men.' It was said in a whisper, as if even to utter the word might work as an incantation to summon the furious spirit of Bathsheba Wilde from the air. From outside the door I heard a scuffling, and the sound of muffled laughter. Miss Spiker heard it too, and she sprang to her feet. 'That's Bella,' she said. 'Don't mind her. She's just curious. You must leave. Both of you.' She yanked on the silken bell-pull, and a moment later the maid appeared. We followed her down the hall towards the door. There was no sign of the simpering, giggling Bella. I found I was glad not to have seen her.

Chapter Seventeen

When we got back to the apothecary Gabriel met us at the door. 'There's a woman,' he hissed. 'She's been here for ages. Keeps asking about you.'

'Yes, well, I shall see for myself if you would let me get in,' I said. 'Ah, Miss Clara. What brings you back here?'

'Mr Flockhart,' she said, 'I believe Miss Wilde has invited you to Nightshade House this evening?'

'She has,' I replied. 'I'm looking forward to it.'

'Please,' she said. 'You mustn't come. You'll learn nothing to your advantage there.'

'Really?' I said. 'Surely I will only be able to judge that if I go?'

'But Miss Wilde is . . . she is not as she seems.' She coloured prettily, the blood in her cheeks chasing away their city-sallowness. 'I have been there for some months now and it is a . . . a most peculiar household.'

'Peculiar? How so?'

'I cannot say. She is . . . different from everyone else.'

'I can see that,' I said. 'But "everyone else" expects a woman to behave meekly, to speak quietly and not to have opinions of her own, a fortune of her own, the determination to travel where she will and say and do as she pleases. I would not condemn her for being the opposite of that, would you?' Clara Foster was silent, looking down at her gloved hands. She rubbed at a smear of green paint that stained the thumb. 'Why do you stay there?' I said after a moment. 'If the household is so peculiar to you? And I think . . . I think she is not always kind to you. I refer to the bruises on your wrists, Miss Clara.'

She tugged at her sleeves. 'It's nothing.'

'And Miss Bella?'

She sighed. 'She can be . . . unpleasant.' She looked up at me, her gaze fierce. 'Bathsheba pays well for good work. And she is . . . fond of me. But I am not here to talk about my situation, I am here to warn you.'

'About what?'

The woman started forward, her reticence disappearing. 'Since those bones were dug from your garden nothing has been the same,' she said. 'I read about the death of Dr and Mrs Christian. I heard Bathsheba talking to Mrs Christian not twenty-four hours before she was killed.'

'Mrs Christian?'

'She came to our house the day before she was found dead. She did not want to come, did not want to be there, I could see that. But something had made her overcome her fear. I heard her talking to Bathsheba. She seemed very agitated. And later I heard Sukey – Miss Spiker – talking to Bathsheba on the same subject.'

'You seemed to do an awful lot of eavesdropping,

Miss Clara,' I said. 'And what was the topic of all these overheard conversations?'

'Why, the bones, of course!'

'And what did she say?'

'Who?'

'Well, let us start with Mrs Christian.'

'She said, "What shall we do? His bones will betray us all."'

'And what was Miss Wilde's reply?'

She shook her head. 'I couldn't hear. But Mrs Christian was very agitated. Then she said, "I have some books of Cathy's. They came to me by mistake and I never sent them on. Perhaps it's there." And Miss Wilde said, "You have never looked? Not after all this time?".'

'And this time you did hear her?' said Will.

'She was shouting, sir. I could not fail to hear her.'

'Was there anything else?' I said.

'They moved away after that,' she said. 'They saw me look over to them, and Miss Wilde took Mrs Christian's arm and ushered her away.'

'I see. And what of Miss Spiker? What did Miss Spiker say that you overheard?'

'Sukey had come back from Angel Meadow. "Mother says there's a book," she said. "A book that will see us all hanged." And Miss Wilde said, "I am quite aware of *that*, Sukey. But no one knows where it is. No one will hang for something that cannot be found."'

'And who wrote this book?' I said.

'I have no idea. I thought perhaps that you might know.'

'I?'

'Your mother's name was on the plan to the garden. Along with Miss Wilde, Jane Spiker, Mrs Christian,

Dr Christian too. She was the "Cathy" mentioned by Mrs Christian, was she not?'

'How on earth did you know that?' I said.

'Your apprentice told everyone,' she said. 'That day when he was showing the bones to the crowd.'

'Of course.' Gabriel! I thought to myself. Had I been any other kind of master I would have beaten the lad for his conduct with the bones. 'And so if Bathsheba does not have this book, and neither does Mrs Spiker or Mrs Christian, then you – and she – assume that I must have it, from my mother. Did she send you to me, Miss Foster? I noticed she and Bella could hardly keep their gazes from scouring my shelves when they were here. They assume it is somewhere in my apothecary but that I don't know about it?'

'Yes,' she said. Her eyes flashed angrily. 'Though she did not send me here. I came of my own accord.'

'Why?'

'To warn you, of course! She is not as she seems. She believes you know something, and she is determined to get it out of you.'

'I can assure you, Miss Foster, that there is nothing in my apothecary that I don't know about. I hope you will convey as much to your mistress.' I thought of how Will had produced the plan of the garden, how I had had no idea of its existence. Perhaps there *were* things I knew nothing about, books, papers, diaries, letters, all hidden under my very nose and I had not the wit to see them. For a moment she stood before me saying nothing. Her dark eyes were fixed on mine. I thought that she was about to say something, for she opened her mouth to speak. But then she appeared to change her mind, for she closed it again, her expression thoughtful.

'Miss Foster,' I said, 'you do realise that everyone on that list is dead. My mother, Dr and Mrs Christian, Mrs Spiker, even my father.'

'Mrs Spiker is dead?' Her fingers flew to her mouth. 'But when?'

'Earlier today,' I said.

'How?'

'Arsenic poisoning.'

'Arsenic!'

'The body, like those of Dr and Mrs Christian, had been desecrated with deadly nightshade berries.'

She closed her eyes, her hand clamped tightly to her mouth. 'My God,' she whispered. 'Who would do such a thing?'

'I have no idea.'

'Poor Sukey!' she said quietly. 'Does she know?'

'Yes. And I can tell you that "poor Sukey" seemed singularly unconcerned at her mother's death. We have just come from Nightshade House. She took it very calmly indeed.' I stepped forward and took her hands in mine. 'Miss Foster,' I said, 'as Bathsheba Wilde is the only name left on that list who is not dead, how long might *she* expect to survive? Perhaps you might ask her that question and see what reply you receive.' She tried to pull her hands away, but I kept hold. 'Thank you for warning me,' I said. 'I will see you later this evening, when perhaps I will ask her myself.'

Excerpts from the diary of Catherine Underhill.

3rd November 1818

Today we went to see Dr Delaney's new botanical garden. Mr William Delaney was also there, and it seemed to me that Dr Delaney purposely led Dr Christian ahead so that his brother might speak to me in private. The look exchanged between the two men told me that they had arranged this between them, neither of them evidently trusting Dr Christian, no matter how much they might respect his opinion as a fellow botanist and medical man. And so it fell to William Delaney to tell me what he could.

'I have heard many things about Miss Wilde,' he said. His smile was uncertain, and his gaze slid away from mine, looking to make sure Dr Christian was far enough away not to overhear. 'What else might one expect? She had an unusual upbringing. You will know, of course, that her mother was a native, her father

– well, he might as well have been one too, though he was born and bred an Englishman and one of the Company's finest. He knew Clive, and Hastings, which might account for his behaviour.'

I knew as well as anyone what had become of Clive and Hastings – one little better than a robber, the other greedy and corrupt beyond all measure, their behaviour sanctioned by the Company, until Parliament started asking questions. However, in the hope that he would elaborate, I said, 'I don't know what you mean, sir. What behaviour?'

'Let us just say that Percival Wilde was the very worst kind of nabob. He took what he wanted, whether that was land, money, riches or people, with scant regard for the consequences. He already had a wife and family at home in England, though he had no hesitation in starting another one here. His half-caste daughter was given his name, and when her Indian mother died the girl Bathsheba was brought back to England as a "gift" his English wife was obliged to accept. Mrs Wilde loved gardening, and this at least was a passion she bequeathed to the cuckoo her husband had foisted upon her. It was in her capacity as a lover of gardens that I first became acquainted with Mrs Wilde, and her "ward" Bathsheba. I was a young man, newly graduated in botany, and my first ever commission was from Mrs Wilde. She wanted orchids, and rhododendrons. I supplied both – amongst other things now familiar to English gardeners. I met Bathsheba Wilde on a number of occasions at that time, and a sulky-faced, angry little minx she was.

'Bathsheba was always different. I heard that when she was some twelve years old or so, she was sent to Wissendene to be cared for by an aunt while her twin brothers were born. One Sunday she scaled the tower of St Olaf's, and mounted one of the gargoyles at the top. She sat up there all morning, shouting abuse in Hindi to the people below.' He gave a bark of laughter. 'It rather sums

her up, Miss Underhill. Profane, idolatrous, ungoverned. But fearless too. Reckless. Certainly not biddable. Not one to be told what to do or how to behave. As for Mrs Wilde and her young sons, all succumbed to the cholera in the summer of 1802.' He cleared his throat. 'Of course, there are those who doubt that it was the cholera, as no one else in the house was affected by it, not even Miss Bathsheba, and she shared the same rooms and spaces as all of them.'

'And what is your opinion, sir?' I said.

'Mine?' he laughed. 'I don't have an opinion. How could I? I was not there. I can only tell you what I heard. And there are poisons that might appear to mimic the symptoms of cholera.'

'But there was another brother, was there not?'

'Yes, the eldest boy, James, was away at Oxford. He followed his father into the Company soon after he completed his education and brought his half-sister back with him to India.'

'I understood this brother was also dead,' I said.

'And dead he is,' replied Mr Delaney. 'But not before he had made his illegitimate half-sister his sole beneficiary after their father passed away. They say James Wilde went mad.'

'"They"?' I said. 'Who are "they"? Either he went mad, or he did not.'

'I didn't see him,' he replied. 'But I was told by a man whose opinion I have no reason to doubt that Bathsheba Wilde's half-brother flung himself from the roof of the Residency in Barrackpur while she was not ten paces away taking tea. Is that the act of a sane man? He did not die – not then – though he neither walked, nor spoke again. She took him back to England and left him there while she came and went as she pleased – here, and in England. South America. Ceylon. China. Burma. When she was in India she was mostly up country. Oudh. Sikkim. Kashmir.' He shrugged. 'And now she is back again.' His voice was mild *when he next spoke. 'The Company takes no responsibility for what happens in places they have no control over. She is her own responsibility.'*

'Perhaps you say this because she is a woman,' I said. I knew I sounded shrill and ungrateful for the confidences he had shared, but I could not help it. 'She is independent, outspoken, intelligent. She is both English and Indian, and yet neither will own her. She is a law unto herself because the alternative is to be a memsahib, or what is condescendingly described as a "native". Neither is respected or taken seriously. For her, that is no choice at all.'

His glance darted nervously towards Dr Christian, who had stopped to admire something and was now no more than a yard or so away from us. 'I love India, Miss Underhill. I love its colours, its heat, its glorious seasons, its plains and mountains, its flora and its history. I love its people.' He smiled. 'Especially its people. But Bathsheba Wilde? I have no idea what perverse creature her inheritance has made her into, but from what I know of her she is not . . . not like anything you might find either here, or there, or anywhere.'

I tried to draw him on it, but he shook his head. 'Forgive me, perhaps I spoke out of turn. I was merely trying to warn you. But my brother and Dr Christian are waiting for us. Might I suggest we keep the contents of our conversation to ourselves? What I have told you is based on my own observations, and on rumours from people who know what they are talking about. It's a mixture of truth and speculation, but where one begins and the other ends I have no idea.' He pulled out his penknife and cut a yellow rose from a bush beside the path. He handed it to me, and said, 'Whether you believe me or not, I beg you, at all costs, to reconsider your decision to follow Miss Wilde any further.'

Chapter Eighteen

⤜❧⤛

I left the apothecary at seven o'clock. I had no idea what to expect from the evening, but I had taken especial care over my ablutions, using a pomade of verbena and sandalwood on my hair and bathing in lavender and oatmeal. Will had watched me boiling the water enviously. He loved a lavender bath. He was sick, he said, lolling hopelessly in his chair, he had scarcely the strength to lift the kettle. 'I need you to tend me, Jem,' he said feebly. 'Only you can make me well again.'

Of course, I took pity on him, and soon he was immersed in hot water softened with oatmeal and fragranced with citrus, bergamot and lavender. 'Do you have any rose petals?' he said. 'I like rose petals. They smell nice and I like to see them bobbing in the water.'

'Yes, but they're too expensive for you,' I replied. 'Besides, you'll smell like a courtesan's boudoir if you add rose petals too.'

'*I* want a bath,' said Mrs Speedicut. She puffed on her

nasty pipe, blowing out a cloud of grey-brown smoke. 'I want oatmeal and roses.'

'Take that wretched pipe outside,' said Will. 'The only oatmeal you deserve is in your porridge.'

I walked down Fishbait Lane, conscious that I was, at that moment, probably the best smelling person in all London. I noticed a few ladies raise their eyebrows as I passed by, and I grinned and tipped my hat at them.

On St Saviour's Street I flagged down a hansom and directed him north. The wheels of the cab rattled over the uneven setts, sending up a spray of filthy water, straw and ordure. I sat as far back as I could against the leather seats, and watched the dark streets go by. Nightshade House was some distance away, I thought, if anything should befall me out there I would be hard pressed to get back to the city. But it was too late to worry about such things now, and I contented myself with thinking about the evening ahead. What might I expect? The invitation had contained nothing explicit or specific. I had nothing but the warnings of Clara Foster, and the reputation of Bathsheba Wilde as a guide to what might happen, though as it turned out neither was enough to prepare me for the night ahead.

The tall iron gates of Nightshade House stood open. I noted that as he turned in between the gateposts the cabby lashed his horse, urging his nag forward, as if he were keen to get the whole business over and done with. The driveway was marked by coloured lanterns which hung from the trees, glowing jewel-like in the velvet darkness. The door opened the moment the wheels of the cab stopped turning, and I had barely had time to alight before the cabby was heading back towards the city.

I wondered how I might be expected to return home. Perhaps Miss Wilde would allow her coach to be used. Perhaps cabs had been ordered. Perhaps she did not expect me to leave at all.

The Indian housekeeper took my hat and topcoat, handing them to a maid who carried them off into the shadows. She said, 'Miss Wilde is expecting you,' then clicked her fingers to summon another maid, slightly older than the first, with the same dark, sleek hair, but this one with a lazy eye and dirty fingernails – I had decided I needed to pay more attention to the domestic servants, given my unfortunate recent oversights. All three women were dressed in Indian clothes, plain silk azure-coloured saris beneath which their limbs moved with ease and grace, their silken slippers inaudible on the marquetry floor.

I expected her to show me into a drawing room, but instead we passed the door to the blue drawing room and continued on down the passageway. Lamps stood here and there on the console tables, the glass faces of the display cases shining like oil. The glinting glass eyes of stuffed animals and birds made them appear more lifelike than ever, so that it seemed as if they were merely waiting for a command to leap from their boxes and set upon me. The air had a heady, smoky scent. I had noticed it last time, but it was stronger now, drifting in spectral blue wraiths across the hall. The aroma was familiar now too, and whereas I had struggled to place it the last time due to the bowls of pot pourri that had scented the blue drawing room, now I knew exactly what it was. Opium. There were new scents too, cardamom, jasmine, attar of roses, the woody smell of *Cannabis sativa*, as well as others still unfamiliar to me. And beneath it all there was a hint of something else, something sweetish, familiar and yet horrifying. It was the smell of rotting flesh.

From up ahead I heard the sound of laughter and voices. Bathsheba's confident drawl, the soft murmur of Sukey Spiker, followed by Bella's humourless titter. And then the maid pulled open a pair of tall wooden doors and I found myself on the threshold of what appeared to be a jungle. She held out her hand, to signify that I should step inside, and then silently swung the door closed behind me. It seemed odd that I should be left to find my way through this hot house jungle by myself, but it was an unorthodox household, and the only thing that one might expect, I said to myself as I stepped forward, was the unexpected. And so I plunged into the foliage, making for the sound of voices, and the lights I could see flickering through the greenery.

The place was crammed with overgrown plants of the most extraordinary size. A huge leaf slapped my face, another clawed at my neck. The roots of enormous bushes had burst upwards, lifting the iron gratings that formed an uneven pathway beneath my feet. I had no idea what many of them were, and some of the ones that I did recognise – moth orchids, stargazer lilies, hemp plants – struck me as hybrids. Overhead I saw the glint of light reflected off glass, and beyond that, the darkness of the night. I passed a cruciform wrought iron pillar entwined with leaves and tendrils. Beneath my feet pipes hissed and juddered, and from somewhere to my right came the sound of running water. I wiped my brow with the back of my hand. The air was as warm and damp as breath. And then all at once my boot caught on a great smooth root that lay across the path like someone's leg, and I lurched forward, arms outstretched, to sprawl blinking in the lamplight at the feet of Bathsheba Wilde.

'Ah, good evening, Jem Flockhart,' she said, staring down at me. 'But please, such abasement really isn't necessary.'

I heard laughter and looked up to see a crowd of about twelve women seated about a clearing on sofas and divans. Some were young, some older, all of them loosely clad in colourful billowing silks. Behind the women, the hot house jungle rose in a great curling mass, heavy leaves, thick, thrusting stems, pendulous flowers, petals as thick and sensuous as bare flesh. For all my experience in the physic garden, and as an apothecary, I recognised none of them. The party was illuminated by more lanterns of coloured glass – emerald, ruby, topaz – that had been hung about in the greenery. The coloured light they produced glittered off the fat bellies of jewelled hookahs to be reflected on leaves and flowers in dancing fragments, like fireflies. The effect was both startling, and beautiful.

I scrambled to my feet, suddenly more conscious of my britches, my waistcoat and boots than I had ever been. Everyone had stopped talking and was staring directly at me. Someone stifled a laugh, and I felt my birthmark smart, the way it always did when my face went red. All at once I wished I had not come. Was it too late to change my mind and make off through the foliage, back to the coolness of the corridor, the driveway, the road back to town and the familiar safety of Will and my apothecary? I felt the strangeness of my situation keenly. I'd spent my life disguised as a man, the woman I was crushed and hidden beneath my bindings. I had learned to master my fear of being discovered, unmasked, and I had learned to walk into rooms filled with men – surgeons and physicians, apothecaries, patients, students – without thinking anything of it. Now, faced with a group of my own sex, I felt nothing but a sense of dread, of displacement, and wariness. As if sensing that it was only a deeply ingrained sense of politeness that was stopping me from plunging back into the jungle, one of the women stepped forward and took my hand to help me up. It was Clara Foster. She smiled down at me. Her hair, undressed, hung almost to her waist, so that for a moment I did not recognise her. I had thought her plain, but now I saw that she was quite beautiful. I was about to smile back, to speak, to thank her, but another voice interrupted my thoughts.

'Oh, no, no, no, Mr Flockhart. This will never do! Sukey, my dear, take our new friend upstairs and see that he – she –' she waved a hand as if to say she hardly cared what I was, 'is suitably attired for the evening.'

Sukey Spiker was sitting beside Bella, both of them watching me from the shadows. The silk they wore clung to their bodies, loosely folded and pleated, revealing the soft shape of thighs, breasts and belly. Sukey's pose was languid, draped across cushions and bolsters as if she were fashioned from melted wax. Bella's eyes were two colourless pools, her face palely powdered, her expression haughty, her hair, unbound, falling in snaking waves about her shoulders. In the dim light her peculiar face was softened, the resemblance between her and the tall handsome Bathsheba suddenly more marked. At the same time there was something about her that unsettled me, though I could not say what. And then all at once she parted her lips in a smile, and I saw that her teeth and tongue were stained blood-red. It was as if I were looking at the face of the Beast and I felt my stomach lurch in horror. I looked away. I knew it was only betel, the leaves of which might be chewed to release a mild stimulant, the resultant mass staining the mouth crimson. And yet somehow the sight appalled me.

She jumped to her feet and hauled Sukey up to stand beside her. 'I'll come with you, Sukey,' she said.

I followed the two of them back the way I had come. 'Lakshmi was supposed to tell us when you arrived, not leave you to stumble your way towards us on your own,' said Sukey. 'I don't know what she was thinking.' Bella spotted the girl Lakshmi in the shadows as we emerged from the hot house, and she clapped her hands. '*Jao!*' she shouted angrily. '*Jaldi!*' The girl flinched, a look of fear on her face, and scurried off, her slippers scuffling and slapping on the polished floor.

'You've spent time in India?' I said.

'With Bathsheba? Yes. We both have.'

'You don't call her your aunt?' I said.

'Why would I?' replied Bella. 'She is Bathsheba. She is not my aunt.'

'But your father was—'

'Yes. Her brother.' She stalked forward. That conversation was evidently closed.

'And Miss Foster?'

'Clara? London bred. It shows too.' She wound her arm about Miss Spiker's waist, and the two of them led me down the passage towards the stairs. The walls were hung with gold-framed paintings depicting scenes of faraway places: lakes and mountains mostly. But also more of the chubby-cheeked women lolling on gilded sofas beside mounds of jewels, exotic fruit and coloured silks. The women had no lashes, and with their tiny blue eyes, plump pale faces and little button mouths they reminded me of pigs.

'Bathsheba's father's collection,' said Sukey, waving a languid hand. 'He knew Clive, you know.'

'Really?' I said without interest.

'Where else do you think all this came from?' Gold bangles chimed on her slender wrists.

'And her mother?'

'She is descended from the deities of the Hindu pantheon,' said Bella.

I glanced at her. Was she teasing me? But her expression was serious. Sukey too gave no sign that they were joking. Bella gave me one of her diabolical smiles, and for a moment it seemed to me that in her eye there was a glint of madness. But then she turned away and started up the staircase, her strong slender fingers trailing lightly against the polished ebony banister. Her scent was of sandalwood and jasmine, heavy and exotic. It made my head spin.

'We have some clothes laid out for you upstairs,' said Sukey. 'We'll leave it up to you as to which of them you might prefer, though you'll need some help if you choose the sari.'

'D'you have men's clothes?' I said.

'Yes. We thought you might prefer them. They're on the bed.'

All at once there was a commotion behind us, the sound of banging, of boots pounding against door, canes rapping, and men's voices raised. Bella squealed and stood still. 'What's all this!' She cocked her head, listening. The sound of banging came again, a cane hard and persistent against the door, a man's voice shouting. She turned to her companion excitedly. 'Intruders? The constables?'

'Perhaps it's some gentlemen up from the town, again,' said Sukey.

'I'm surprised they dare after last time. Shall we go down?'

'But Mr Flockhart—'

'She can find the way.' Bella grinned. '*Shabash!* Come *on*, Sukey!'

'At the top,' Miss Spiker addressed me. 'The first door on the right. You will find all you need laid out.'

As soon as they were out of sight I bounded up the stairs. The house was huge, and with so little time I knew I would achieve almost nothing. And yet I had to try. Will and Gabriel had timed their arrival perfectly. *Give me ten minutes*, I had said. *Ten minutes inside and then make your presence felt.*

'What manner of house *is* this?' I heard Will shout. He was inside now. There came the sound of smashing crockery, of footsteps running, the raised voices of women. I darted along the hallway. There were doors on either side. I tried one. Inside, a bedroom, the bed draped in coloured silks, the carpet thick underfoot, more pig portraits. But it was unused, and there was nothing for me there. It was the same with the next three doors I opened. Downstairs the hullaballoo continued. I tried another door.

This one was different. It was three times larger than the ones I had already seen. Lit with lamps and topsy-turvy with silks and coloured fabrics, it was heavy with the spicy, sickly aroma I still could not quite place. The tall windows were covered in long drapes of crimson brocade, like waterfalls of blood. In the centre of the room was a huge bed, shrouded with gauzy curtains and scattered with pillows and bolsters, the silken sheets rumpled as if someone had not long got out of it. In this room there were no portraits. Instead the walls were hung with botanical paintings, the leaves moist and lustrous, the petals and berries glistening and jewel-like. They were watercolours, and yet the pigments were so vibrant, so bright and vivid that the images seemed three dimensional, as if I might reach out and pluck them from the frame or lean forward and smell their fragrance. Four of them hung side by side opposite the bed: *Datura stramonium, Atropa accuminata, Mandragora caulescens, Hyosycamus niger,* though I was more familiar with their common names – Devil's trumpets, Indian Nightshade, Himalayan Mandrake, Indian Henbane. On the other side of the room were six more. I recognised *Strychnos nux-vomica,* though the others were unfamiliar to me, my knowledge of *materia medica* being limited to what I had learned as an apothecary in London. What might be found in an Indian dispensatory was a mystery to me, though the flowers of the Devil's trumpets, and the long roots of the mandrake would be familiar to even the laziest apothecary. The name of the artist, inscribed in a small neat hand in the bottom right corner, was Clara Foster.

The room was lived in and well-used. It had a staleness to it, the musty scent of old clothes, of silks gone to waste and the slow passing of time. Much of the furniture was from India, I assumed, the wood inlaid with ivory and teak in intricate patterns. Before the window stood a desk scattered with papers, letters to the Calcutta Botanic Gardens, the Bombay Botanic Gardens, the Gardens at Simla and Jaipur. Most appeared to be part of a longer correspondence. One, beginning 'My Dear O'Shaughnessy . . . ' was addressed to the senior medical officer in the Company's army. It made reference to 'a new Indian *Materia Medica*', and contained notes on the use of mandrake in Indian physic. What a mind the woman had! How much might I learn from her! I could have pored over those letters for days, but now was not the time, alas! and already I could hear that the commotion had moved to outside the house, and seemed to be almost beneath the windows of the room I was in. I heard Will's voice.

'I demand entry! You are holding Mr Flockhart against his will, I *demand* entry!' We had decided that five minutes of altercation and distraction would be the best he could hope for, but he had brought Gabriel with him, and the two of them were remarkably effective. I had a few minutes left, I was sure. I pulled open drawers – the usual mess of blotters, letter knives, sealing wax, scraps of scribbled paper. Nothing to capture my attention, to make me pause. Around the room on tables and chairs, more clothes, books, letters. And then all at once I heard a noise. Faint, but unmistakable, the swish of silk, the creak of a floorboard. And then – horror! – the doorknob was turning. I dashed through another door, a dressing room I assumed, perhaps I might hide amongst her clothes. But there were no clothes in this dressing room.

It was some twenty feet square. It had no window, only another door opposite the one I had just entered. There were no wardrobes, no mirrors, only row upon row of shelves reaching up to the ceiling some eighteen feet away, each one crammed with bottles and jars. A narrow ladder like the one I had in the apothecary stood to attention in the far corner. Where one might expect to see a dressing table there was a long workbench stretching the length of the room, upon it, a number of brass bowls, measuring scales, a pestle and mortar. Beside these, a blue stoppered flask, some five inches high. What it might contain I had no idea, but it being small and portable, and me being determined to have something to show for my adventure so far, I snatched it up and slipped it into my pocket. A candle had been left burning beside the pestle, its dim light reflected like eyes from the glassware. Each vessel bore a label, written in confident copperplate. From the long 's' and the self-assured tail of the 'y', the bold black colour of the ink, the thickness of the strokes, I recognised it as the same hand that had drawn the plan for the physic garden. All around me were the objects of my own profession; coloured powders, chopped and dried roots, dried petals, leaves, stamens. I recognised some of the names, but others I had never seen or heard of before. I saw jars of wet specimens – a whole mandrake root in a jar of clear viscous liquid; some sort of tuber, like a huge pale grub, or a diseased organ in an anatomical collection. On the workbench was a giant bottle of dark, glistening berries. Sloes, perhaps? Or elder? But I knew they were neither of those things. The label, fresh-stained with purple juice, confirmed it. It was a jar of berries from the *Atropa belladonna*, the deadly nightshade, preserved in spirits, and as fresh and moist as the day they were picked.

I had less than a second to make my escape. Already I could hear slippered feet crossing the carpet, the rustle of silk drawing closer. I plunged towards the opposite door. *Please, God, let it be unlocked,* I thought, *and no one on the other side of it.* I turned the handle, felt its mechanism move as smooth as butter. 'Is that you, Bella?' said a voice. Bathsheba Wilde herself! I slipped through, quickly and silently closing the door behind me.

The room I stepped into was dark. I fumbled for the key – I had not noticed it on the other side of the door – and there it was, cold and hard against my fingers. And yet the door had been unlocked. Would I not confirm her suspicions if I locked it behind me? And so I stepped away from it and groped my way along the wall a little until I felt the arm of a sofa. I crouched down beside it. The moment I did so the door was flung open. I turned away, so that she would not see my pale face glimmering like a moon in the darkness. She had taken up the candle from the workbench and she held it high, scanning the room. But I knew how hard it was to see beyond a candle, its flame dazzles the eye and its light shows nothing but jumping shadows. If I remained where I was, crouched and silent, I might escape her notice – if the beating of my heart did not give me away. I held my breath.

For a moment Bathsheba stood framed in the doorway. I heard her breathing, felt her eyes passing over familiar shadows, so that at any moment I expected her to cry out, to feel her fingers at my collar. But she said nothing. Instead, she merely clicked her tongue, and with a muttered curse she was gone. I put my hand into my pocket, my fingers curling around the stoppered bottle I had snatched up as I fled. I could not be found with it. I had to get back to the room I was supposed to be in and somehow hide it where it would not be found by anyone but me. I plunged forward in the darkness, towards that part of the room where, by the light of Bathsheba's candle, I had seen the door. I slipped out and ran silently back along the hallway to the room I had left not five minutes earlier.

I half expected Bathsheba, or one of the others, to be waiting for me, but there was no one. I tore off my clothes, so that it might look as though I had been busy undressing. From outside I heard the sound of Will's voice, and the vigorous clatter of his stick rapping on the door. I threw open the window. 'Will,' I shouted, so that everyone might hear me. 'For God's sake, stop this. I am here of my own accord. I don't need to tell you where I might go or why, and I don't need your permission for my actions. Go away. Both of you, go away. Go *home*.'

'I will not leave you here, Jem! Not amongst these . . . these *women*!'

'I will do as I choose, sir. It is no concern of yours.'

'But Mr Jem—' This time it was Gabriel.

'Enough!' I shouted. 'I will not be pursued and questioned by my own apprentice. How *dare* you come here, Gabriel Locke! Go away. Go away this *instant*. As for *you*,' I flung out my hand to point down at Will, releasing the blue flask as I did so. '*You* can pack your bags.'

'Jem, I—'

'I want you gone!' I shouted. 'From here. From my home. For *ever*!' and I slammed the window closed. From somewhere around the back of the house I had heard the sound of dogs barking. I hoped Will and Gabriel could run fast.

When I turned around Clara Foster was standing behind me. Her expression was blank. 'You're not dressed,' she said. 'Do you need help?'

'No,' I said. 'I've decided to wear the man's apparel. What d'you call it? The *kurta*.'

'As you wish.' I thought she was about to leave, but she stayed where she was. Then, 'Did you take something?' she said. 'When you were in Bathsheba's room?'

'No.' I felt my face grow hot. There was clearly no point in denying I had been there.

'She thinks you have.'

'I have not. Check, Miss Clara. My waistcoat and jacket are on the bed, you might look through their pockets, and search my satchel if you wish.' For a moment I thought my insistence has disarmed her. But it hadn't. She patted at the pockets of my clothes, and ran her hands over me, searching. She looked around the room. 'If it's here, I *will* find it,' she said, though I noticed she seemed to have relaxed a little, now that her search of my person was over. At the same time she seemed guarded, fearful even, though of what I had no idea.

'What were you doing in there?' she muttered.

I sighed. 'She knew my mother. But she says so little about her that I am none the wiser. I just wanted to see if there was something, anything that might tell me more.' I shook my head. 'And so I decided to pry. It was an abuse of hospitality, I admit, and I'm truly sorry.' I sighed again. 'I shouldn't burden you with my concerns.'

'You must find the diary,' she said. 'Your mother's diary.'

'That's the book you mentioned? It's a diary, is it?' I shrugged. 'Not that it matters. I don't know anything about it, so that's that. I certainly don't know where it is.'

'She believes you do know, even if you don't yet realise it. She'll get you to remember what you think you don't know.' She came over to me and put her lips to my ear. 'You are in dangerous waters, Jem,' she whispered. 'Have a care what you may find out tonight – about your mother. About yourself.'

For a moment we stood facing one another. 'Miss Clara,' I said. 'Why do you stay here?'

'For Bathsheba,' she said. 'She is very . . . persuasive.'

'And yet the other two are unkind. Bella hurts you.'

'She is a jealous, spoilt child.'

'Hardly a child, even if she acts like one.'

'She is not like other women. No one here is. You included.'

It was a phrase I had heard before, in another time, another place. It had not ended well. 'How so?'

'She is a woman, but like a child. Capricious, cruel, emotional. She cannot help herself.'

'But you can,' I said. 'I saw your paintings. You could easily make your way in the world, you don't have to stay.'

'I choose to be here.' She smiled a little. 'Just like you do.'

'You're Bathsheba's lover?' It was a guess, but I had struck home. She did not reply at first, but busied herself about the room, hanging up my shirt, passing me the *kurta*. It slipped over my head in a silent ripple of silk.

'What of it? Are you jealous too?'

'Of her or of you?'

'Don't answer my question with a question.' She stood close, adjusting the silken tie about my waist with expert hands.

'If you were not so ambiguous, I wouldn't have to.'

'The most ambiguous person in this house is you!'

'Oh, I think my intentions are very clear,' I said. 'You, however, remain a mystery.' I put my hands to her face and kissed her on the mouth. She was as soft as down, smelled of sandalwood and lily of the valley and tasted like heaven.

Excerpts from the diary of Catherine Underhill.

8ᵗʰ November 1818

We left the dak *behind some days ago, and have now entered lawless lands. The Company has no influence here, so Dr Christian tells me. I asked him how he knew where we were going, but he has been before, he says. Besides, Bathsheba and the others leave a trail of rumour behind them. Mostly it is evidenced by the local people talking behind their hands and pointing. On some occasions, though Dr Christian thinks I have not noticed, they make the sign of the evil eye.*

We have made camp near a village. We are at quite a high altitude now, and the air feels thin. The nights are cold, and I am sure Bathsheba will be feeling the benefit of her goatskin tunic. Dr Christian seems to know where we are heading, and he was vindicated in his choice of direction when, late in the afternoon, we passed a team of bearers carrying a consignment of plants boxed up for their journey south. They are from Bathsheba. Sandesh will take over when the consignment reaches him, so the plants will be in good hands. Bathsheba's finds included a number of dwarf rhododendrons, azaleas and orchids. They should do well at home, Dr Christian said, coming from these more temperate lands. It is not hot here, like it is in Calcutta, or dry like the plains. Dr Christian says it will get colder later in the year. I wonder how long he plans for us to stay.

12th November 1818

Four days have passed since my last entry. Four days of riding. The bearers walk, Dr Christian and I travel on ponies. The creatures are sturdy and biddable. We bought them when we left the dak. I am not used to riding, so it is as well that we go so slowly.

I have been practising with the pistol Mrs Christian gave me. I am becoming quite proficient and can blast a mango to pulp at twenty paces.

14th November 1818

Tonight, Dr Christian got out his hookah. I recognised the smell of Bathsheba's herbal mix. I do not like Dr Christian when he has been smoking. I have hidden his knife and pistol as he is not himself when he has been using the hookah.

15ᵗʰ November 1818

Dr Christian has been into the village. He has returned with something called 'bala' which the villagers use against fatigue. He says it is one of the Ephedra. *He has acquired some 'bala' plants, which he says he will take back to England. He has ordered a number of them to be sent to the gardens in Calcutta, where they will await him when he returns. Dr Christian has been testing the effects of the plant, a spindly, low-growing thing with attractive dark grass-like leaves.*

18ᵗʰ November 1818

Dr Christian has been awake for three days.

19ᵗʰ November 1818

I am beginning to wonder if we will ever find Bathsheba, Jane and Mrs Christian. I wonder why they brought me if they do not want me to join them. I said as much to Dr Christian, and he said we would catch them up soon enough and that I should enjoy being without them while I could.

22ⁿᵈ November 1818

This afternoon something unexpected happened. We have met no fellow travellers on our journey until today, when a Mr Norris, a missionary from the Church of Scotland, appeared as if out of nowhere. We are travelling along a path rather than a road, the greenery thick on both sides. We could hear him before we could see him, as the aged pony he sat astride was heavy footed, and the man's breathing was an anxious panting. He travelled alone, apart from one servant, a man named Harshad, who sat before him on the nag, Nr Norris clinging on to the man's back like a child. Mr Norris told us that he had had other bearers, but that they had left him two days before, had they not passed us?

'No, sir,' I said, 'but there are numerous paths through the jungle, and they may well have gone along one of those.' He did not seem convinced but looked at me as if I were not to be trusted. The man was sweating and red-faced. He had a rather hunted demeanour as if something pursued him, for he was forever looking over his shoulder or peering into the jungle as if searching for something he did not wish to find. We asked him if he would care to make camp with us that evening, as it was a lonely and inhospitable place and not one where a man might wish to sleep alone. He agreed, but said, 'Though I would rather travel alone than wait about in this godless jungle for the Devil to take me.'

I hardly knew what to say in reply. It was evident that he did not want to speak to me. He could hardly bring himself to look at me and made sure to stand as close to Dr Christian as he could. He seemed glad to meet us, and yet was clearly anxious, nervous and restless as if he was keen to find his way back to the dak *and leave the forest with its endless trees and narrow paths far behind. 'I am hemmed in,' he said, looking about him the way a convict might look up at the high walls of this prison. 'I cannot see them coming. I cannot see where they might be. My God, I never thought I would miss the plains, but I do.'*

'Who is it you think might be coming?' said Dr Christian.

'I don't know who they are,' he said. He looked at Dr Christian in surprise, as if he had never thought to ask.

Mr Norris made camp with us this evening. At first, Harshad sat with our bearers. I saw them talking together as if whatever it was that perturbed him and his master he was sharing with his fellow countrymen. Already our bearers are restless. They do not like being so far away from home. I fear our new guests are making them worse. After a few minutes, however, Mr Norris summoned Harshad to his side. It is as if he does not like the man to be too far away. Harshad has an intelligent look and a confident demeanour (in contrast to his master), and I have the feeling that without him, Mr Norris would be wandering around the forest in circles.

Mr Norris told us that he had been up country for a number of months. Initially he had had a curate, as well as more bearers. He was from the Presbyterian Missionary Society of Edinburgh and hoped to spread the word of the Lord. Dr Christian yawned when he said this. I have never once seen the doctor, or any of the others, go near a church, or pick up a Bible. I have not found it hard to follow suit, though I hope I would never yawn in the face of a clergyman. Mr Norris looked at him, scandalised.

'Mr Norris,' I said, before the man could express his outrage, 'what happened to your curate? Your bearers?'

'They ran away,' he said. 'We all ran away. And because we ran, we became separated. I have no idea where Johnson is now. I hope he escaped.'

'Escaped from whom?' I said. 'Ran away from what?'

Mr Norris's story is an extraordinary one. I will try to tell it as best I can, though the subject matter is so perturbing, so horrifying, I hardly know what to think. I must write quickly, as I suspect Dr Christian would stop me from recording it altogether if he knew what I was up to.

Mr Norris said he and his curate had been in the forest for some weeks. He was aware that they were well beyond the Company's official jurisdiction. He told us that they had lost their way somewhat, not being the best of navigators, and had not seen anything but the smallest of villages for days. He and the curate Johnson had set up camp. As night fell, they had heard noises coming from somewhere through the trees. To their surprise it sounded like women's voices, and women's laughter.

At first he thought it was a dream, but Johnson had heard it too. The bearers had also heard, and they were looking worried. 'The natives are a superstitious lot,' he said. 'And there are things in this part of the country, Miss Underhill, that would put the fear of God into the heart of even the strongest man. Bandits, Thugs, worshippers of the goddess Kali – heathens, every one of them. Perhaps we should have ignored what we heard, but we were lost and we had not seen another human being for days – of course I don't include the natives when I say that. Besides it was women we could hear. I thought they would surely recognise the authority of a man, especially a man like myself.'

I nodded. He is a pale and skinny runt, his red face peppered with mosquito bites, and I cannot imagine how anyone, man or woman, would look upon him as a figure of authority. But such arrogance and belief in themselves is the birthright of men, and so I kept my own counsel. Harshad, however, was not so diffident. Young and strong, his command of English as good as his master's, his appearance and confidence give the lie to Mr Norris's misplaced notions of superiority.

'You have no idea where you are going or what you are doing,' he said suddenly. 'Without me, Mr Norris, you would die here. What we saw that night, that was nothing an Indian woman would ever do.' He shook his head. 'Had I not looked after you they would have torn you limb from limb, along with Mr Johnson.'

Mr Norris's face turned red. I thought he might be furious, but instead he turned to the man and said, 'You are right, Harshad. I do not know what I would do without you. You have been a true friend to me, and I am most grateful.' His face drooped. 'This is a Godless place. I should have stayed in Morningside.'

A tear formed in the corner of his eye, and while he was fumbling for a handkerchief, I said, 'India is profoundly civilised, and religious, Mr Norris. It is just a different type of civilisation and religion to ours.'

Dr Christian nodded. 'When in Rome, do as the Romans do. I'm sure you remember your Saint Augustine, Mr Norris. Perhaps the people here do not wish to be turned into Christians.'

Mr Norris did not comment. He seemed to be concentrating on what he was about to say next, and I saw him take a deep breath in readiness. 'I hardly know how to tell you what we saw that night,' he said. He kept his eyes on the fire as he spoke, and as he told his story I could see why he could look neither of us in the eye. 'Johnson and I looked about, and sure enough there was a light some distance away in the trees. It was not very far, though far enough for us to lose sight of our camp as we made our way towards it. And yet we had lanterns, so we did not mind too much. As we drew close we heard the sound of voices and laughter. We smelled smoke on the air. It was not woodsmoke and I could not recognise the smell at all. Perhaps some fragrant bark or other. Dr Christian,' he said, leaning forward and clutching the doctor's arm. 'The women there in the forest, in the jungle, they were Englishwomen! Three of them. They were in a clearing. I could see walls and shelters about them like the remains of a temple of some kind, though it was too dark to see precisely what sort of a place they were in. But English *women, sir!* English! *Even now I can hardly believe what I am saying. Johnson and I saw them in a group. Harshad too!' He turned to the man for confirmation. 'Could* you *believe it?'*

'I could believe anything of the English,' replied Harshad.

'I have never seen a sight like it,' went on Mr Norris. 'Their clothes were awry, their bodies barely covered. One of them was tall, immensely tall, and completely unclothed. Completely! There in the forest! Her body was daubed blue. Blue, sir!' He closed his eyes tight, and then, as if assailed by horrible images, opened them again almost immediately. 'The tall blue one held what looked to be a pestle and mortar in her hands. She ground the pestle into the bowl and held it up. It was anointed with some sort of ointment. My God, sir! I cannot tell you what she did next. What they all did! Their faces in the light of the fire, red and grinning. Their eyes rolling. It will haunt me for ever.'

'Come, Mr Norris,' said Dr Christian, 'this is surely fantasy. Perhaps you were dreaming, or had taken an excess of laudanum.' He glanced up at me, and I saw that he knew who precisely it was that Dr Norris had seen, and that, like me, he feared the worst was yet to come.

'Fantasy?' cried Dr Norris. 'Laudanum? If only it were that, sir! But it was no such thing. I saw that blue demon with that pestle in her hand. I saw her reach between the parted legs of her fellow creatures and slide the thing inside. All three of them took it, one after the other. I could not believe what I was seeing, but it is the truth, the whole truth.'

'And you did not try to stop these . . . these English women, from performing this . . . this abomination?' said Dr Christian.

Dr Norris blushed. 'I did not. And after that . . . that ritual, it was as if hell itself had broken loose.' He closed his eyes. 'The noise they made, the sound of their cries, their screams. We ran, sir. We dropped our lanterns and ran. But we could not see where we were going. The jungle at night is filled with traps – low branches, brambles to tear the legs and snare the feet, fallen logs. We lost Johnson in the darkness. We have not seen him since.'

23rd November 1818

Mr Norris has gone. We awoke this morning to find that he and Harshad, along with all our bearers, have run away. He has taken our ponies too and left us with his exhausted nag. Dr Christian is furious, though he hides it well, and says, 'Never mind, Cathy. We don't have far to go now so it hardly matters, I hope.'

I am somewhat alarmed by it, however, as the two of us are alone here and we are miles from anyone we might look on as a friend. And I still have the feeling that we are being followed. I cannot say why. After what Mr Norris told us, I am afraid I may never see home again.

Chapter Nineteen

'Your friend Mr Quartermain is persistent,' said Bathsheba. 'He seems to think I have abducted you. Lakshmi set the dogs on him.'

I shrugged. 'I have no idea what he thinks. I'm not his keeper, though he is evidently under the illusion that he is mine.' I sank onto a divan scattered with heavy cushions and bolsters. The air of the hot house was more oppressive than ever, and already my new apparel was clinging to my damp skin.

Clara appeared unperturbed by what had occurred between us. She went to stand beside Bathsheba, who wound her arm about her waist and kissed her cheek. I saw Clara smile and lean in towards the older woman. She raised her glass, the wine inside as dark as blood, and said, 'To an interesting and enjoyable evening.' I did not know what to think.

And so it began. Even now, no matter how hard I try to remember the names and faces of the women I met that night I have only the haziest of recollections. Apart from those who were already familiar to me, Clara, Sukey, Bella, Bathsheba, I could say little about any of the others. They were all English, as far as I could gather, all clad in Indian silks, their wrists and ankles jangling with silver bangles, their hair studded with pearls and diamonds. Their feet were encased in silken slippers, or sandals of soft leather encrusted with tiny glass beads and laced with gold stitching. Their eyes were rimmed with kohl, their lips stained red with betel. They lay about on divans, charpois, piles of cushions, while maids in silk saris went in and out of the foliage bearing trays of small spiced delicacies, sweetmeats and glasses of alcohol. I took one. Absinthe. There was also gin, and champagne, and a concoction Bathsheba called *bhang*, which I did not try. At least, not at first. Everyone seemed to know who I was – and what I was – and after a few glasses of liquor I stopped feeling uneasy about it and sprawled on my cushions like the rest.

The place grew hotter. Overhead vines writhed and snaked, every now and then drops of warm water plopping heavily from the tips of thick, curling leaves. The chatter grew loud and raucous. I saw Bella sucking on the pipe of a hookah with her scarlet lips, heard the soft bubble of the thing as the smoke passed through. Faces swam before me. I felt the mouth of a pipe against my own lips, and for a moment I resisted, anxious still about what might follow. But already my limbs felt heavy and I found that I was listening intently to the noise of running water, once far away but now seeming curiously loud and roaring in my ears. I was sure I could hear the song of nightingales. I must have asked about them, as I heard a voice say 'Yes, we have four. Can you hear them? They say it's the most beautiful of all birdsong.' I saw a face framed with dark hair leaning over me. Clara. I smiled up at her. Might she kiss me? I closed my eyes in expectation, but it was only the pipe that touched my lips and this time I breathed in the smoke.

What followed? I can recall nothing but glimpses. Hands – mine and others. Bare flesh, soft and yielding beneath my fingers. My own skin, moist and slick; buttocks, shoulders, arched necks and wet, open mouths; eyes dark voids in which I saw myself reflected; a sweet saltiness on my tongue. From far away the nightingale sang, like a glimpse of heaven, but the instant I heard it, it was gone, obliterated by sighs and groans. And then all at once the ache of ecstasy I had felt deserted me, the fingers that traced across my skin burned like fire, and I saw that they were claws, not hands, and there was Bathsheba, as tall as a tree standing over us all, her hair, unbound, a mass of serpents about her head, our naked limbs writhing before her. Into my mind's eye came the book Dr Bain had given to my mother, only now it was without beauty of any kind, but was monstrous, filled with thick oozing roots and bloated pale petals. The foliage reared above me, dark and wet, a thicket from which there was no escape and I let myself be consumed by it, vines and tendrils furling around my wrists and ankles, pulling me apart and snaking between my legs until it was inside the very heart of me. I heard howls and screams, and my throat stung as my own voice joined that of the others.

When I awoke I found that I was entirely naked. My head was ringing and my tongue felt huge and dry in my mouth. I was lying beside an ornamental stream that ran between two moss-covered rocks, passed across the floor of the hot house and disappeared into the greenery. Sunlight glinted through the leaves overhead. One of the nightingales was singing. For a moment I stood like Eve in the gloom. I felt as though I could hear the moss sighing beneath my feet, the slow exhale of leaves, and the creak of petals unfurling. I listened for the sound of voices, but there was nothing.

Looking down at myself I saw bruises, what looked like fingerprints and bite marks on my inner thighs, my breasts and shoulders, the marks of bonds against my wrists. My arms and legs ached. I splashed some water on my face, but it was as warm as my own skin, and I felt no refreshment from it. I closed my eyes, but the visions I saw – a tangle of limbs, a red open mouth, a necklace of skulls – made me open them immediately. I cupped my hand to the water and drank.

In the clearing there was no sign of what had happened. All the little tables, the divans and charpois had gone. There were no hookahs, no silks, no cushions – nothing but a worn and sagging sofa of brown brocade. My clothes, the bindings I used to hide my breasts, my hat, topcoat and satchel were laid upon it. An easel and stool stood to one side, showing a half-completed painting of a blooming passionflower. As I looked at it, the thing seemed to come alive, the leaves sweating horribly, the tendrils reaching out like wire to snare my wrists. I cried out and stepped back – the illusion vanished, and I was staring at nothing more alarming than a half-finished painting.

I saw and heard no one. Not in the hot house. Not in the passage or the hall. As I walked down the drive, I looked back. The windows of Nightshade House were shuttered, as if the place was sleeping off its hangover.

It was over two miles back to the edge of the city, and I traipsed along the road between fields and smallholdings, enjoying the warmth of the winter sun on my face. And then suddenly the hedge at the side of the road started to rear and dance like a row of emerald fire, the green faces of goblins grinning and leering at me from amongst its leaves as my heart raced. I rubbed my eyes. Would I never be free of these monstrous hallucinations? And then I realised that the sound I had thought was my heartbeat was in fact the sound of horses' hooves coming towards me at a brisk trot, and the spell was broken once more. A hansom appeared around a bend in the road and a voice cried out. 'Jem! Thank God!' The cab came to a standstill and Will sprang down. 'Thank God you're here, Jem. I was prepared to brave the dogs again if I had to. Are you well? You look awful.'

'Yes, yes, I'm well enough,' I said. I climbed into the cab and closed my eyes. But I did not like what I saw when I did so, so I opened them again. Will must have seen the fear in my face.

'What's wrong?' he said. 'You look like you've seen a ghost.' He banged on the roof to tell the cabby to move off. 'So, what happened, Jem?' he said as we rattled our way back towards the town. 'Tell me everything. You've been gone for hours! We were getting really worried.'

But I would not be drawn. I did not want to relive a single moment of the night before. He did not press me any further, and I took a grateful swig from the hip flask he offered.

'Would you like to hear what I've been doing?' he said. 'Since you are unable to talk yourself. I have been into town this morning already.'

I glanced at him. He was looking tired again, despite the fact that it was not yet midday. 'You should be resting,' I said. 'Not gallivanting about the city.'

'Ah, but I have been gallivanting on your behalf,' he replied. 'You alone are permitted to visit Bathsheba Wilde and her strange coterie, but *I* have been making important enquiries.'

'May I ask where and why?' I kept my eyes fixed on the road ahead. I felt peculiar. Every now and then it seemed to me as though the sun were ten times its usual brightness. Will's face looked like the face of a corpse, and I dared not look at my own hands for fear of what I might see. He stared at me. I knew I must look terrible, but he did not remark on it.

'I went up to India House,' he said. 'Leadenhall Street. The shipping office there was most instructive. You know they have a record of every East India Company ship that comes and goes? Logbooks, journals, passenger lists, inventories. It's very comprehensive. I was there for hours.'

'And you found something?' My head cleared as my heart started racing.

'The date on the plan for the garden is 1820,' he said. 'Mrs Abelman at the Blue Brazier said she remembered it was spring when Delaney stayed at the North Star Angel – so we can assume he stayed there in February, March or April of that year. He, and anyone else he was with, would have arrived on an East India Company frigate before or during these months. According to Miss Abelman, most people staying at the Angel were coming from India, or returning there, so I assumed India House would be the obvious place to look.'

'Yes, and?'

'Well, I looked through ships' manifests, passenger lists and what-not, in search of names.' He closed his eyes. 'So many names, Jem. I can still see them, line after line burned onto my retinas.'

'And you found him?'

'I did indeed. On the *Minerva*, arriving from Bombay on 1st March 1820. William Delaney. Occupation: botanist. Plus wife.'

'Children?'

'None recorded.'

'Is that all?' I could not keep the disappointment out of my voice. 'I am impressed by your approach, but, my dear Will, we more or less knew this already.'

'Ah! But it is *not* quite all,' he said. 'The captain's journal entry contains information about an incident on board. I copied it out verbatim for you.' He reached into his pocket and handed me a folded sheet of foolscap.

'I cannot read it, Will,' I said as the words danced and scurried about the page. 'Would you be so kind?'

'Of course.' He cleared his throat, raising his voice above the rattle of the cab's wheels. '*On 21st January, inst. A third-class passenger by the name of Delaney assaulted another, beating him half to death with the aid of his crutch. The reason for the assault was as follows. Delaney, a man fallen on hard times and more well-spoken than his person and pocket might suggest, said that the victim had made himself an annoyance to his wife for some weeks now, to the extent that she dared not leave her husband's side. Yesterday afternoon while her husband slept, the man had attempted to make free with Mrs Delaney, causing her great distress and personal injury. She has something of the* nautch-girl *about her, and I had already advised Delaney to take up accommodation elsewhere on board. This he had refused to do, though it might have saved him, and his family, their agonies if he had done as I suggested. In the event, I deemed it not appropriate to punish Delaney for misconduct due to the extreme nature of the provocation, but instead advised him to keep to his area of the ship and his wife close by at all times. On speaking to the surgeon, I am informed that Delaney is in constant pain due to his crippled condition and as a result has developed something of an addiction to laudanum. Any other displays of violence from him, and I will not be disposed to act with such leniency.'*

'Rather an unusual way to discuss a woman,' said Will. 'Anyone would think she was little more than a chattel. I'm not sure what to make of it.'

'Indeed,' I said. 'But this is very interesting, Will, very interesting and adds much to our enquiries.'

'Does it?' he said.

'Oh yes.' I smiled. I had my own ideas, but I was not quite ready to share them. Not yet. I needed to think a little more first. Besides, there was something else I wished to ask him. 'Did you get the bottle I threw from the window?'

He nodded. 'It's at the apothecary.'

'D'you know what it is?'

'Jenny says it is some kind of woad. Perhaps copper-based, as woad itself burns the skin. She thinks it's been mixed with lamp black to give it a darker hue. It's in a tincture of sorts, but it might easily be mixed with a paste of oil and wax, and used to colour the skin blue.'

'Good,' I said. I smiled faintly. I could not manage more. He sighed. 'D'you know what's going on, Jem?'

'Not yet,' I said. I closed my eyes. 'But I do know where my mother's diary is.'

Excerpts from the diary of Catherine Underhill.

25th November 1818

*Dr Christian and I continue our journey on foot. Mr Norris's
nag is only good for carrying our luggage, though that is better
than having to carry it ourselves. I have thought about what
Mr Norris told us, about the pestle. I believe some medications
might be applied internally against the mucous membranes. I can
only guess what the mixture contained. I asked Dr Christian,
and he said that he thought it might be belladonna, hemlock,
jimsonweed. 'Perhaps ephedra, or something of that kind too. Or
mandrake.' I had suspected as much. I knew the plants he named
were all ingredients in what the old apothecary books call 'flying
ointment' – a preparation allegedly administered to the body via
the greased end of a broomstick. They are all poisons, all powerful
hallucinogens – if they do not kill you first. Dr Christian's face*

311

was stony. 'My God, Cathy,' he said. 'I have never sought to stop Dora from her friendship with Bathsheba, but this? This is beyond all imagining. We must find them before it is too late!'

26ᵗʰ November 1818

I am still convinced we are being followed. Perhaps it is because I am becoming so tired. There is little hope that we will find the others, and I fear we will die here, either at the hands of bandits or Thugs, or because our food and other supplies have run out. It is not what I expected from my travels. At night the forest is black, blacker even than the sky which at least has the stars and moon to illuminate it. The noises we hear – animals and birds, I hope – have taken on a terrifying aspect now that we are so alone, and they sound to me like the chattering of fiends and the grunts and pants of devils. They come from all sides too, as if we are surrounded. Sometimes we see curious flickering lights here and there in the jungle. Dr Christian says it is nothing to worry about, and is probably just marsh gas, though I do not believe him.

Date unknown.

My God! My God, what have we done? What have we become?

Chapter Twenty

❧

After his murder, Dr Bain's house on St Saviour's Street had been boarded up until his only son, my apprentice Gabriel Locke, was old enough to take possession of it. The doctor had never publicly acknowledged Gabriel when he was alive, but the lad's resemblance to his father was clear. Dr Bain's will had confirmed it. Until the boy came of age, however, the property remained in my hands. We did not tell Gabriel where we were going as I did not want the distraction of having to answer a barrage of questions from him. I hoped we would not be in the place for long, but as the house was large, and the thing we were looking for was small, it was anyone's guess how long it might take, or indeed, if we would even succeed. I was wary too, and jumpy. I was still experiencing the effects of the previous evening, and I felt watched, and distrustful of everyone. As we walked down Fishbait Lane towards St Saviour's Street, I kept looking back. There were people everywhere. None of them appeared to be following us, and yet had we not been deceived twice already? Perhaps our adversary was the watercress seller, sitting on the steps near the pump? Or the servant hurrying behind us with a package under her arm? There was a fog drifting in too, and the shapes of passers-by were vanishing behind a veil of greyish-brown. My clothes felt constricting, and rough against my smarting skin, as if they were lined with grit. Will took my arm, and I jumped.

'Come along, Jem,' he said. 'Let's get this over and done.'

The heavy iron key was stiff in the lock and grated horribly. As I swung the door open we were greeted by a breath of stale air, mouldering books and papers, dried ink, preserving spirits, dust and decay. I ushered Will into the unwelcoming darkness and locked the door behind us. For a moment we stood side by side in the hall. Will had known the doctor too. He had been with me when we had discovered the body, and he knew how badly my friend's death had affected me. He gave my fingers a squeeze, before fumbling for his tinderbox. The flames of our candles illuminated a flight of stairs that vanished upwards into blackness. Dr Bain's library and workshop were through a door on the right. With any luck it would be there that we would find what we were looking for.

The place had not been touched in the years since his death. The workbench where he and I had peered down microscopes was just the same; the cage in which he had kept the dog upon which mixtures might be tested stood open, as if waiting for its next occupant; bottles, pens, papers, books covered every surface.

'Has someone been searching here already?' said Will, looking around in surprise.

'No,' I said. 'It was always like this, don't you remember?' I used my candle to light the lamps, so that we could see what we were doing. I caught a glimpse of myself in the mirror above the fireplace and saw a face, horribly pale but with a splash of plum-coloured skin around the eyes and across the nose like a burglar's mask. My eyes were red rimmed and puffy, with black circles around them. I looked as I felt, sick and tired.

I took the locket from my pocket and opened it up to take out the key that was hidden inside. 'This picture is not my father,' I said. 'It is Dr Bain. She loved him – before she travelled to India. I suspect that's why she was sent out there in the first place, so that she might be encouraged to forget about him. I believe she still loved him when she came back. I was so sure this image was my father, I wanted to believe that it was, just as I wanted to believe that my mother loved him.'

'Perhaps she did,' said Will. 'She married him, after all.'

'Yes.' I sighed. 'Perhaps she did.' I would probably never know what had happened between my mother and Dr Bain. Who was there alive who might tell me? 'This key is the key to the diary, or to its whereabouts,' I said. 'And if it is not here, then I don't know where it is.'

Will started with the writing desk, a monstrous roll-topped affair that stood against the wall opposite the fireplace. It was mounded with books, and clearly had not been used for its intended purpose for many years. In all the years I had known him I had never once seen Dr Bain sitting at it. After that, Will said, he would move to the shelves on either side of the fireplace and I readily agreed. We had found Dr Bain's corpse on the hearthrug two years earlier, and I was glad to be able to turn my back on it and devote my attention to the workbench and the bookshelves against the far wall.

The more I thought about it, the more it seemed as though we were on a fool's errand. I had known Dr Bain for years. Why had he never mentioned that he had my mother's diary? I could not believe that he would have possessed such a thing, and yet said nothing to me about it. Unless he had not known that he had it. Perhaps she had hidden it there without his knowledge, assuming that she might be able to retrieve it should she ever need to do so. If she *had* hidden it, I said to myself, then where might she have put it?

The shelves were packed tight, a double layer of books crammed in in a disorderly fashion, with notes, sheaves of papers, letters, slimmer volumes stuffed in horizontal layers on top of them. The task of looking through everything would take all night. And yet if he, or my mother, had hidden a diary there, it was some thirty years ago. There would have been far fewer books and papers, perhaps even the semblance of order. I would have to dig down, through the layers of Dr Bain's life, the papers he had written and read, the experiments he had recorded, until I found the man my mother had known – young, optimistic, orderly, proud of his books and his knowledge and at the beginning of a glittering career. And so I pulled the first layer of books from the shelves. They were of no interest to me, of that I was certain. Unlike the haphazard accumulations of later years, the layer behind was alphabetised. Salford . . . Sexby . . . Stenhouse . . . Would my mother have put herself under 'F' for Flockhart or 'U' for Underhill? Taylor . . . Thomas . . . Timpson. And there, between Traynor's *Canine Physiology* and Vaughan's

Treatise on the Spleen was a small leather-bound book, six inches high and an inch thick, scuffed and worn, its bindings mottled with dark stains and perforated here and there by the depredations of moths. It was closed with a flap which wrapped around it so that the whole thing resembled a small leather box. In the centre of the flap-end was a keyhole.

I said nothing to Will at first, but stood with my back to him, my mother's diary in my hands. I ran my fingers over its smooth, dry covers, felt the tactile patina of old leather. I raised it to my nose but could smell only dust. How many times had I been in that room with Dr Bain? How many times had I taken books off those shelves? Why had I not seen it, not heard it crying out to me? And then I slipped the key into the lock and with a single click it was open.

Notes on the poisonous nightshades (Solanaceae).

DATURA STRAMONIUM

Also known as thorn-apple, jimsonweed, Devil's snare, stink-weed, Devil's trumpets.

Description

An aggressive invasive weed, Datura stramonium *is a foul-smelling, erect annual that grows two to five feet tall. The roots are long, thick and fibrous, the stem branching, the leaves irregular in shape and up to eight inches long. They have a bitter nauseating taste which remains even after the leaves have been dried. The flowers are beautiful, fragrant trumpets, white to violet in colour and resembling an unfurling handkerchief. They open at night and are fed on by nocturnal moths. The seed capsules are up to three inches across. When ripe, the pod splits into four chambers, each full of seeds. The seeds can lie dormant underground for years, germinating only when the soil is disturbed. Its preferred habitat is docksides and waste spaces, dung heaps, and other places where rank soil is created by the deposited refuse of humans.*

Toxicity

All parts of the plant are poisonous, especially the seeds. Neither drying nor boiling removes the toxin, though its potency decreases as the plant ages. Gloves should be worn at all times when handling the Devil's snare. Experience and knowledge of the plant is essential to minimise harm, as it is the most potent and fearful of all the nightshades.

Symptoms

Delirium, hallucinations, high temperature, dilated pupils. A pronounced amnesia is also symptomatic of poisoning by Datura stramonium. *Symptoms last between twenty-four hours and two days, but may endure for up to two weeks. It acts more powerfully on the brain than belladonna and produces greater delirium.*

Antidotes

There are no antidotes to poisoning by Datura stramonium.

Medical applications

Datura can be used to treat haemorrhoids, asthma, and some convulsive and spasmodic disorders. Its action is like the action of belladonna, but with more force, and without constipating. The leaves might be smoked in a pipe, alone or with other drugs, or burned in a saucer and inhaled. Like many drugs, after constant use the effectiveness is diminished, so that greater quantities are required to achieve the desired effect.

Miscellanea

The Devil's trumpets are said to aid the incantations of necromancers.

A sister species, Datura metel, *is considered sacred in India. When mixed with cannabis, as well as highly poisonous plants such as* Aconitum ferox *(Indian Aconite), it creates hallucinations* of such extreme horror and distress that those taking it have run permanently mad. The procedure is an aid to spiritual liberation. Smoking Datura, alone or with other intoxicants, is common in India, though the practice is not widespread elsewhere. The poisonous properties of the seed are well known in that country, where the Datura grows in profusion. It is rumoured that thieves and assassins there administer it to their victims to produce insanity and amnesia.

Excerpts from the diary of Catherine Underhill.

16th February 1819

This is the last entry I will make in this journal. I am back in the dak *bungalow. The others, Mrs Christian, Dr Christian, Jane Spiker and Bathsheba, are ahead of me on the road. We have plants, and Bathsheba is keen to get them to Calcutta. We have vowed, all of us, never to speak of what happened. And yet I cannot let it pass. I cannot let it slip away with no record, no confession as to what happened. I can absolve none of us from what occurred, even though I have no full or coherent idea of who did what to whom. With my own eyes I saw the three women, my travelling companions, commit murder. But was that fourth pair of hands mine? I do not believe I have it in me to kill, but who knows what primitive urges lie hidden within us all, kept out of sight and mind only by the veneer of rules we follow when in the society of others. My account of that night, from what I can recall, is as follows:*

Dr Christian and I had been in the jungle alone for many days. On the last day, as night fell, we heard the sound of voices. They came from up ahead. At first I thought I must be imagining it, that it was some sort of waking dream as we had heard no voices but our own for so long. But Dr Christian heard it too. It was just as Mr Norris had described, a flickering firelight, the sound of women's voices, women's laughter. We knew who it was. We had always known. Dr Christian led the way forward.

When we stepped into the clearing, I did not know whether to be glad or horrified. There were a number of women there, a half dozen or so Indian women, old and young, and I recognised none of these. I do not know where they had come from. Perhaps from hamlets hidden in the forest, perhaps from the hills to the north. Perhaps they had been gathered from the villages we had ourselves passed through so many days earlier. They were sitting on the ground in a semi-circle. In the midst of them, Bathsheba sat upon what looked like a throne made of stone. By the firelight I could see that we were in the remains of a temple of some kind. It had fallen into disuse, that much was clear, but there was a cistern nearby, so fresh water was available, and there were places to shelter amongst the tumbledown buildings.

Bathsheba was fearful to behold. Her hair was a wild tangle, her face darkly smeared with blue paint. She was clothed in a loose robe made of some sort of indigo calico. She sat erect, like Britannia, with her legs spread wide beneath her tunic and her bare feet planted firmly on the ground. Her lips and teeth were red, her eyes black-rimmed with kohl. Beside her, I saw Dora similarly attired, and Jane. Jane looked tired and had none of the air of confidence possessed by the other two. She looked sullen, her gaze vacant, as if she were drunk, or stupefied. But then as she looked up at Bathsheba, her expression changed into one of greedy anticipation, as if in expectation of something she greatly desired. The air was thick with the smell of roasting meat. There were lumps of the stuff, as well as pieces of fruit, and nuts, resting on leaves and stones about the fire. My stomach rumbled at the smell, for we had not eaten properly for a long time.

For a moment Dr Christian and I stood at the edge of the clearing. And then all at once Bathsheba jumped to her feet. 'Cathy!' She smiled. 'At last!'

I cannot recall how many days had passed since I last saw her, but when I look back in this journal I see that it was some two months or more. How she had changed! Dora too, and Jane, for they were all thinner. All of them had blood-shot eyes rimmed with kohl, their faces gaunt with sunken cheeks. Someone thrust a lump of hot goat meat into my hands. I could think of nothing but getting the food into my mouth. Dr Christian was the same. Bathsheba motioned to Jane to provide us with something to drink and an earthen cup was passed to me. I drank deeply. I could taste that it was not water, but I could not imagine my friends would do me harm, and so I drank without fear or hesitation as the salty meat had made me thirsty. I saw Dr Christian do the same, Bathsheba smiling at us as we drained our cups.

When I awoke later it was dark. I found I was lying where I had fallen, beside the fire. Someone had put a rough blanket over me to discourage the mosquitos. My head was buzzing. I felt confused and afraid.

On a rock beside the fire I saw the pestle and mortar. I would not have her come near me with that, I was quite determined. Bathsheba was standing over me and I said as much to her. She said she would not make me do anything I did not wish to do, though as she had drugged the water she had given me, I did not believe her for one moment. I asked her about Mr Johnson the *curate, whether she had seen him, but she smiled and said she had no idea who I was talking about. 'What are you doing here like this?' I said. 'What is happening? Have you taken leave of your senses? If you were lost you had simply to retrace your steps.'*

Her answer was the most bizarre reply she might have given, so that if I had not been convinced that she was mad before, then there was no doubt about it now. And yet it was clear that she believed every word that she spoke. 'I am a goddess,' she said. 'I am Kali, the embodiment of all nature's rage and tyranny. I am the mother of the earth.' She held up a bowl. It was silver, finely made. It was brimming with a crimson liquid. She looked at it as she spoke, her gaze fixed hungrily on its shimmering surface.

'Nature gives its gifts to those who understand its power,' she said. 'What gives life might also bring death. What offers wisdom might also lead to madness. It takes courage to tread the path that leads to knowledge, to illumination. One slip, and all is lost. I have devoted my life to understanding the fine line between one and the other, to seeking understanding of who and what I am. Only the initiated, those who have earned it, can step into the light. I see it clearly now, though I have never really doubted it. Man is master of the world, the highest of all creatures. But woman is higher still. Men cannot create life, cannot create another human being. Woman is life itself. The nightshades, belladonna, mandragora, Datura, have given me enlightenment, as I always knew they would.' She raised the bowl, put it to her lips, and took a long draught.

She seemed to grow taller as the shadows jumped and danced around her, throwing her head back so that her hair writhed and snaked. She passed the bowl to Mrs Christian, who drank, just as her mistress had. Dr Christian too did not turn her away. And then came Jane. She seemed hardly to know what she should do, she was so befuddled, but then she seized the bowl with both hands, her gaze fixed hungrily upon it as she drank.

And I? I closed my eyes. How long had we been up country? I had no idea. India was teeming with people and yet, apart from Harshad and Mr Norris, we had seen hardly a soul for weeks so far had we strayed from the path. My blood pounded in my head. London and my place in it seemed only the ghost of a memory. Those things I had once loved I could no longer recall – the feel of the garden's grass beneath my feet, the taste of strawberries, my father's face. My Alexander especially seemed lost to me, and I had to remind myself who he was, to tell myself that I did have those feelings still, for they had faded into nothingness. I was no more than a small, irrelevant part of this monstrous jungle we found ourselves in. Its darkness and greenery were all consuming, ungoverned, endless. I was lost, lost utterly, in a dark and lonely place, and the only release I might find would be in oblivion. I took the bowl Bathsheba offered me and, like the others, I put it to my lips. I could see from her face that she would not have brooked a refusal.

I have a little recollection of what happened next. My memory is no more than a series of fragments. Like scraps of paper blowing in the wind they turn this way and that, sometimes visible to me, sometimes not. I recall Dr Christian staring at the moon, his face rapturous. I recall him screaming and flailing as if fighting with an assailant only he could see. Beside him Dora lay naked, her hands between her legs. Dr Christian was oblivious to her. I saw him plunge into the jungle, and I do not recall seeing him again until the following morning. Given what occurred next, it is perhaps his good fortune that he fled screaming into the night.

There were noises all around me, though whether they were real or in my head I could not be sure. I saw Jane squatting beside the fire with the pestle in her hand. I saw Bathsheba standing upon her throne of stone, towering above everyone. She seemed taller than ever. She was naked, streaked and daubed in blue, a garland of ivory skulls about her neck. She was laughing, a knife in one hand, her silver bowl in the other. The Indian women were no longer present. I had noticed them slipping away into the night as if they wanted no part of whatever was about to take place, and in the light of the fire she was a lonely and terrifying figure.

And that was when everything changed. The moment they stepped out of the forest, the world turned upside down. If only they had not followed us. If only they had waited until daybreak. If only we had never met them, if only I had never told them who I was and where I was going. 'If only . . . if only . . . if only . . . ' two useless words that hold within them more regret than can ever be measured. I recognised them immediately. Dr James Delaney. Mr William Delaney. They had not taken two paces towards me before they were set upon. A rock to the head felled one, the other was attacked by Bathsheba herself. Dr Delaney (for it was he she had jumped upon) perhaps thought he might easily get the better of her. But she was strong and powerful. The mixture she had drunk seemed to have given her the strength of many, and she brought him down the way a lion might bring down a bullock. And then Jane and Dora were there too, leaping upon him, screaming, ripping, stabbing, tearing . . . Beside his brother, William Delaney struggled to stand. He had a great gash to his face from where the rock had struck him, and he fell back down. The noise was terrible to hear. I saw hands pulling at one of them, and I knew they were my hands. Was I trying to save him? To drag him away? In all truthfulness I cannot say whether I was or not. I know that I saw blood everywhere, that I was assailed by flashes of light and sound and a dull pain throbbed inside my head. The world was spinning and turning, so that I hardly knew which way was up. I fell to the ground and vomited, the liquid I had drunk burning my throat like bile. I saw Dr Delaney grow still beneath the writhing women, women I had once thought of as my friends, but whom I no longer recognised as human beings. I knew I had to stop them, had to get them off him, but I seemed unable to put this thought into action and instead I simply sat looking at my hands, so red, so sticky, glistening in the firelight, the screams and laughter of the others ringing in my ears. I lay back and looked at the stars and felt as if I were flying.

I will not describe in detail what I saw there the following morning. Dr James Delaney, a kind, delightful man, was nothing but mangled flesh and bone. His bowels had been torn out, his head had been cut from his body. His brother, once so tall and handsome, was lying some 10 feet away, a mess of battered flesh and broken limbs.

We left them where they lay.

Chapter Twenty-One

We sat there for some time, our heads together, poring over those brittle pages. Her writing was close and dense, each page crammed with words, though as time passed I noticed that her pen strokes became more scratchy and uneven, her letters more ragged and hurried, as if her hands were shaking. After we had finished, we closed it up and I slipped it into my satchel. We said nothing to one another, but left Dr Bain's house and walked back towards Fishbait Lane in silence. The city was invisible now, hidden by a thick brown pall of fog. When we reached the apothecary, I turned to him.

'She will strike tonight, Will,' I said. 'She knows I am on to her, and she has been following us. But we are prepared, and we will not make it easy for her.'

I sent them all to Sorley's. Will was reluctant to leave me, but I persuaded him. I needed to be alone, I said, and he could tell from my face that I would brook no argument. 'I need to think,' I said. 'And for that I need peace and quiet. Just for a while. Things are not as they seem – but I cannot think how. And if we are all here, she will bide her time. I need her to strike, Will. I need to force her hand.'

He nodded. 'If that's what you want. I will not be far away.'

I sat for a while, the lamp at my side turned down low. The stove door was open, the coals dark scabs on a mass of molten flame. Gabriel had asked me to put some potatoes into the embers, but I had not bestirred myself to do it, instead allowing myself to be lulled by the flicker and glow of the fire. I had still told Will almost nothing about what had happened to me the night before at Nightshade House. The bits I could recall I had not wished to relive. I was assailed by feelings of guilt, horror, surprise at whatever it was I had taken part in, but also a curious tingling excitement. The effects of Bathsheba's mixture had still not left me and I was gripped periodically by an all-consuming fear. It washed over me like acid, so that my skin and hair prickled and my eyes smarted. I thought of my mother in India, travelling alone up country, so far away from all she knew and recognised, no one but Dr Christian for company. *Had* she been one of those frenzied women who had attacked those two innocent men? Only Bathsheba could tell me now, though whatever narrative she might choose to recount would surely be unreliable. I sat before the fire, my mother's diary on my knee. I had read and reread it, hoping to find a truth that it did not contain, and all at once I felt tired to death. Despite my intention to stay awake and vigilant, despite what I had said to Will about the danger I felt was approaching, my eyes began to close.

I heard no footfall, felt no draught from the open door, did not notice the flame of my candle dance and flicker a warning. I was expecting her, of course. Her goals would be simple: to take the diary, to destroy it, perhaps to kill anyone who knew what it described. I thought I would be ready, I was so determined to entrap her I was sure nothing would distract me, and I had said as much to Will. But in the event my mind was too preoccupied to be vigilant. The deadly nightshade still coursed in my veins, and so when I opened my eyes and saw a blue-black face emerging from the shadows, I could not say whether it was a dream or not.

My hesitation was my undoing, and when she sprang at me, I was nowhere near ready. I felt her hands on my throat, her hot breath against my cheek. I tried to struggle but my arms were as heavy as lead. I was pitched off my chair, and felt hands pinning me to the floor. Strong fingers gripped my jaw as something hard and cold and tasting of metal and coal dust forced my mouth open. I saw the face above me, half shadowed by a hood and framed with snakes of dark hair, as berries, black and sticky, were shoved between my lips. I gagged and thrashed but a hand clamped over my nose. I tried to scream, but the mess in my mouth made sound impossible. I felt juice trickling down my throat, every instinct I possessed telling me to swallow. I retched and spluttered, and fought against that urge even as the room began to swirl and plunge around me, the mouth of the stove stretching and yawning like the gaping maw of hell.

And then I was spinning around, turning, lifted as if upon a sea of hands. I felt a burning sensation in my throat, the taste of salt against my tongue and a sickness in my belly. A mass of purple berries surged onto the floor before me.

'Spit, Jem!' screamed a voice in my ear. 'Spit them out!' Then I was on my back once more. My throat stung again, and I saw more liquid studded with black berries spew out of me. I lurched to my knees, my hand on my chair to steady myself. A woman was standing over me, as huge and broad as an oak, her great bosom sheathed in stained calico.

'Thank you, madam,' I rasped, my throat raw. I raised a hasty hand as she came at me again with her flagon of salt water. 'Please!' I cried, recoiling in horror. 'Mrs Speedicut, not again!'

Behind Mrs Speedicut the room was in turmoil. I heard the smashing of glassware, voices shouting, the sound of something banging against the floor. Will was wresting with a tall cloaked figure. Gabriel and Jenny were writhing on the floor, something heaving and squirming beneath them.

'Stop this!' I shouted. My voice sounded strange even to my own ears, and it stung my throat as if it had been scraped by wires. 'It is finished! It is all finished!' The cloaked figure, caught tightly in Will's embrace, turned her blue-streaked face towards me. She glanced at the fire and grinned as the dry pages and leather bindings of my mother's diary turned to flame. I cried out and plunged towards it, but Mrs Speedicut seized my wrist.

'Leave it, Jem,' she said. Her voice, for the first time ever, was gentle, sorrowful. 'There is nothing you can do. Let it go. Let her go.'

We left Mrs Speedicut and Jenny tidying up the apothecary while Will and I bundled Bella and Sukey into a carriage.

They sat side by side in a sullen silence. Bella's face was painted in a streaky mixture of blue-black woad, her eyes lined with crimson. She grinned at me, her stubby little teeth betel-stained and devilish. Sukey said nothing. Her pose was stiffly defiant, her fists clenched, her gaze angrily averted. Will sat beside me with Dr Bain's pistol trained upon the two of them as the carriage rattled and jolted its way through the fog to Nightshade House. I had sent Gabriel for the watch and told him where they should meet us. It would give us time for explanations, though now that my mother's diary was gone, there was no possibility of securing a conviction for anything but assault.

'Put that pistol away,' said Sukey. 'It's right in my face. What if it goes off?' She scowled at Will, her brow drawn down, her lips a thin sulky line in her round pasty face.

'You look just like your mother,' I said. I knew she would despise the comparison. Beside her, Bella twisted a strand of hair about her finger, as demure as a child. She looked up at Will coyly. She seemed to have forgotten that her face was smeared with blue paint, that she had recently been wrestling with him on the apothecary floor. 'So do you, Miss Wilde,' I said.

'My God!' said Will. 'Bathsheba Wilde is her *mother*?'

'And Bathsheba's half-brother, now long dead, is her father. No doubt that accounts for certain things.'

'I never knew my father,' snapped Bella.

'Your mother saw to that,' I replied.

'She despises men. She despised him.'

'I'm sure she had good reason to,' I said.

'How did you know we would come?' said Sukey.

'I knew I'd been followed when I left Nightshade House,' I said. 'I looked for you but I didn't see you, not at first, but I knew you'd be there. I didn't see you when we left the apothecary either. But when we came out of Dr Bain's house, then I *did* see you. The fog was rising. You were in a hansom and it made you bold. I sent everyone away from the apothecary so that you might be tempted to strike.'

'I didn't expect there to be two of them,' said Will.

'No,' I said. 'But things are often not as one expects.'

'Did Bathsheba send you?' said Will.

'No,' said Sukey. I didn't know whether to believe her or not.

The gates to Nightshade House were barely visible in the dark. The coachman must have been looking out for them, for all at once he swung right, and I felt the wheels bounce and jolt over the potholes that pocked the driveway. The house itself was no more than a hulking shadow in the fog, a lantern burning beside the door the only sign that anyone was at home. I paid the coachman double what the fare had been and said there would be more if he stayed where he was for the next hour. He nodded and pulled his coat up around his ears.

Bathsheba was in the glasshouse, sitting in the greenery with Clara. She was standing close to the younger woman as if she had just been bent over her, kissing her neck. She stood back as we appeared. Sukey and Bella flew to her side, Sukey kissing her hand and pressing it to her cheek. 'We did it for you,' she said. 'We did everything for you.'

'Don't be cruel to us, Mama.' Bella looked frightened, so that I wondered what punishments the two of them had been subjected to over the years to make them so fearful.

'Did you send them to murder me?' I said to Bathsheba. I could still feel the effects of the deadly nightshade they had forced into my mouth, a nauseous dizziness that made the foliage heave and sway before me. I saw faces peer out at me from amongst the leaves. One of them extended a long green tongue, and I flinched and batted it away with my hand. Bathsheba smiled.

'I see the *kali-puja* still runs in your veins,' she said.

I balled my hands into fists until I could feel my nails digging into my palms. 'That may be so,' I said. 'But I am its master.' I hoped I sounded more convincing than I felt.

Beside Bathsheba, Clara sat at her easel. She had set lanterns all about, so that her work, and the flower she was painting, were illuminated in a bubble of golden light. She looked surprised to see us.

'These two attempted to poison Jem,' said Will. 'Tried to stuff his mouth with deadly nightshade. If I had not returned when I did, they would have almost certainly succeeded.'

'We did it for you' said Bella again. She sidled up to her mother and took her other hand. 'You and Mrs Christian talked about a diary. We heard you. We knew you wanted rid of it. Mr Flockhart had it.'

'We burned it,' cried Sukey. 'It's gone for ever! Aren't you pleased?' How badly they wanted her approval, I thought. I looked at Clara. She was sitting on her stool, her eyes upon Bathsheba, her expression unreadable.

'I know what happened in India,' I said.

'Do you?' Bathsheba replied. 'I doubt that very much.'

'You thought William Delaney was dead. You left him where he lay and hoped never to think of him or his brother ever again. But he was not dead. He was scarred, blinded, crippled, but he was not dead. And, when he recovered, he came here to find you, to hold you to account for what you had done.'

She shrugged. 'Who would ever believe such a tale, then or now?'

'There would have been an inquiry,' I said. 'The Company's reputation was already in tatters. To have news of Englishwomen behaving like savages would have finished it off.'

She stared at me expectantly, as if waiting for me to say more, and indeed, I had plenty to tell. But I wanted her confession. If I remained silent, would she be able to resist the urge to talk, to tell us all how powerful and clever she had been? The silence ticked on. Then, 'I have no idea what the man wanted,' she said mildly. 'Revenge? Money? An explanation? An apology? Whatever it was I was not interested.'

'So you did not even hear his petition?' said Will. 'After all you had put him through?'

'I was not in the least bit interested in it. He was a loose end, that's all there is to it.' She sighed. 'He made it easy for us. We were working in the garden at that time, all of us – I insisted upon it. We were bound together for ever by what had happened. One day I found Delaney in the hot house – the gate was often left unlocked as we were coming and going. I thought perhaps he had been there all night. It was cold, anyone who has spent their life in India feels it when they return home. England is so damp and chilly. I found him by the stove in the hot house, asleep.'

I recalled the position of the corpse, its arched back, its bunched, claw-like hands. 'You poisoned him,' I said. 'Strychnine.'

'It seemed the easiest way. I had seen him outside this house, had seen him following me – it is hard for a cripple with a monkey to be inconspicuous. And so I had made my own enquiries about him. I knew who he was, though I had not expected him to come straight to us. The *strychnos* fruits love the cold season and were almost ripe. They were hanging right beside him. All I had to do was squeeze some juice into the bottle of laudanum he had beside him and wait. As it happens I did not have to wait long. When the others arrived he was already in a seizure.'

'You made them stab him, didn't you?' I said. 'Mrs Christian, Jane Spiker, Dr Christian. You all stabbed him so that you were all culpable, bound together in blood even tighter than before, because now your crimes had arrived on your own doorstep.'

'Your dear mother too,' she snapped. 'Don't leave *her* out of the equation. Only she had other plans. She made me throw my symbols of Kali into the hole we dug for him – oh yes,' she said, seeing the expression on my face, 'she was there that night. She made no objections to putting him into the ground in her own garden to save her own skin.'

'Who's Kali?' said Will.

'You brought those artefacts with you?' I said. 'Did you always carry them around?'

'They are the source of my power,' she said. 'Of *course* I brought them. I knew I would have work to do!' She threw back her head, her smile wide, her eyes glittering, and at that moment I knew she was completely mad. 'If Delaney and his brother had left us alone no harm would have come to either of them,' she said. 'I did not even know their names! It was your mother who brought them, she had met them in the *dak* bungalow, she had talked to them and told them where she was going. They followed her. We were none of us ourselves that night, and then all at once there they were amongst us! Where had they come from? They had no place there!' She shrugged. 'Knives, hands, sticks, we used whatever was to hand. We tore them apart. The next day we left. We left and we never spoke of it again. Not once, not ever.' She drew herself up, to her full, imposing height. 'What was done was done. It could not be *un*done, and I was not to be chased to ground for it back in England.'

We were all watching her. The younger women, all three of them, were crying; Bella and Sukey crouched at Bathsheba's feet, Clara still at her easel. 'We tried our best,' said Sukey, clawing at Bathsheba's skirts. 'We tried to take care of things for you.' Bathsheba ignored them both. Instead she was looking at Clara.

'My darling,' she murmured. 'It was so long ago. Don't let it worry you, they can't prove anything. We will put this behind us and be happy, you'll see.' But Clara could not look at Bathsheba. She had her head in her hands, I saw her fingers, wet with tears.

'Never mind *her*,' cried Bella. She tugged at her mother's skirts like a petulant child. 'She's not one of us.'

'I thought they were both dead when we left that place,' said Bathsheba. 'So much blood! It would have been better for him if he had been.'

'It might have been better for William Delaney,' I said, 'but it was not better for his wife.'

'I don't know anything about a wife,' snapped Bathsheba. 'What are you talking about?'

'The fate of his wife is of great consequence,' I replied.

'Is it?' whispered Will. 'You didn't tell me this.'

'You have as many of the facts as I, Will,' I said. I turned to Bathsheba. 'According to Mrs Abelman at the Blue Brazier, Delaney's wife was a girl with dancer's feet. She was right too, for Mrs Delaney had been a dancer. She was Indian, which is why the captain of the *Minerva* was so unconcerned about making references to her physical appearance, as if she were no more than a piece of meat to be pawed at by male passengers. I assume her husband left her somewhere less fearful than the North Star Angel while he went about his business of revenge. But once her husband was lost to her, and Mrs Delaney was left alone in a strange land, would she not return to the only life she knew?'

'Dancing?' said Will.

'Exactly,' I said. 'The theatre. You recall our visit to the theatrical Mrs Lovibond? The collage of playbills that adorned the walls?'

'I only remember Captain Clark and his snakes,' said Will looking sheepish. 'Sorry.'

'Yes, well, you are notably unobservant,' I said. 'Do you not recall the playbill for Noor, Queen of the Indian Dancers? The date on it was some six months after the *Minerva* docked.'

'So?'

'Noor,' I said. 'Mrs Abelman remembered "Nora" because it was "the same as her mother's" and because to a child's ears the familiar name "Nora" made more sense than the unfamiliar "Noor", which is what she actually heard.'

'Ah!' Will smiled. I could see he was impressed. But I had more to tell.

'We can trace the fate of William Delaney's wife,' I said,

'but what happened to his child?'

'What child?' said Will. 'Was there a child? No one mentioned a child.'

'Indeed,' I said. 'And the evidence that there was a child is thin, I admit. You recall that Mrs Abelman said the monkey wore a little coat and hat? But then she told us two entirely contradictory things. On the one hand, she said that Delaney's wife hated the monkey. On the other hand, she told us that Delaney's wife had made the coat to keep the monkey happy. But why would the woman who hated the monkey be the slightest bit concerned about its happiness?'

'I have no idea.' Will looked bemused.

I pressed on. 'What were Rebecca Abelman's exact words? That the coat and hat had been made "to keep Harry happy". She was very clear about that, for it was from those words that she had concluded that the monkey's name was Harry. But Rebecca Abelman was only a child. Monkeys are not happy to wear clothes. This monkey wanted to tear its jacket off, to the extent that it had been tightly stitched on. In which case, who might this "Harry" be?'

'A child?' he sounded unconvinced.

'Exactly. Wouldn't a mother do anything to keep her child happy, perhaps on a long journey from India when there is little to keep it entertained?'

The hot house had fallen eerily silent. All four women were looking at us in amazement. For a moment I doubted myself. Was it possible that I was wrong? But I knew I was not. I was only surprised it had taken me so long to realise the truth of the matter. 'Delaney had a child. Just because the name was not on the *Minerva*'s passenger manifest does not mean that child did not exist.'

'He would be over thirty years old by now,' said Will.

'He?' I said.

'Harry, of course!'

'Might Mrs Abelman have misheard that too? Might it have been "to keep Clarry happy"? Clarry – a father's affectionate name for his daughter?' I looked at Clara Foster. 'Delaney was your father, wasn't he, Miss Foster? And your mother was the Indian dancer, Noor.'

Clara Foster nodded. 'Yes, Mr Flockhart. You are quite correct.'

'Your mother died three months ago. You came here to find out what happened to your father.'

'This is all just speculation,' said Bathsheba. 'Anyone could make up stories like this.'

'It's not a story,' said Clara. She could not bring herself to look at the other woman, but held herself aloof, her head proud, her back straight. 'You killed my father,' she said. 'You have just admitted it. Or was that a story too? Please continue, Mr Flockhart. It's a history I prefer not to talk about, but you are welcome to do so.'

'Thank you, Miss Clara,' I said. 'Your father William Delaney went into his grave beneath the deadly nightshade, his widow returned to performing, as it was all she had. As for you? What might you learn in the theatre? To dance, like your mother? But Noor Delaney didn't want that for her half-English child. Instead she encouraged other skills she saw in you. Skills your father had too, but which had been taken from him that night in India, instantly plunging all of you into poverty. I believe that the theatre is where you learned to paint, perhaps faces at first, but then scenery, then plants and flowers, like your father who was a skilled botanical artist. Indeed, you showed such aptitude that you were able to find work. Respectable work. Better paid too, and without the taint of the theatre.

'Your mother died but always there was the question of where your father had gone. Whatever happened to him was shrouded in mystery. Even before he vanished, the attack that had crippled him and murdered his brother had been so violent, so horrific, that I imagine he scarcely remembered what had happened. As a result, your mother knew almost nothing about what had occurred that night when her husband's life was ruined. And so, you were brought up on whispered tales, half remembered snatches of words and events, faces and names, perhaps with nothing but the word "nightshade" to guide you in your quest to find out who was to blame for your father's death, for your mother's misery. When the time came for you to make your own enquiries, you could not use your father's name, and so you chose another.'

'Foster was the man who ran the theatre where my mother first worked,' she said. 'He was always kind to us. Everything you say is true, Mr Flockhart. My father disappeared, and my mother was stranded in London without him. He had said little to her about what had happened in India – I think he was hardly able to recall it for a number of reasons, though it haunted him for what remained of his life. I remember him waking up in the night screaming.' She closed her eyes for a moment and took a breath. 'My mother's sorrow at his misfortune, and then his disappearance, destroyed her whole life, and mine. I had little but the word "nightshade" to tell me where I might start. It meant nothing to me at first, but this house and its occupant have a certain reputation, and I was sure there had to be a connection. With my skills as a botanical artist it was not long until I was able to find myself a situation here.' She looked at me. 'What happens in this house is not to my taste, but I endured. I participated. I had no choice if I was to discover what had happened to my father, and I could not act until I was certain. I am not a murderer, Mr Flockhart, I simply wanted justice. And so I waited. I listened and watched, and I searched the house for something that might lead me to the truth. I *had* to know. And then you discovered his bones and all at once events began moving faster than I had expected.'

Clara looked at Bathsheba, Sukey and Bella, her face furious. 'I would have murdered every one of them, every one of *you* to find out what happened to my father that night. But it seemed that fate got there before me on every occasion. I heard Bathsheba and Mrs Christian talking about a diary. I heard her say "I still have books from Cathy, perhaps it is amongst those." So I went to see Mrs Christian. I wrote a note in Bathsheba's hand telling her to send the servants away as I had secret matters I wished to discuss. I knew she would comply. She was terrified of you. They all were. I could see it when she came here – her face, the way she looked at you, the way she cringed and wrung her hands.'

'But when you arrived things were not as you expected. Is that so?' I said.

Clara nodded, her expression defiant. 'It was my intention to—'

'I think we don't need to know your intentions,' I said hastily. I did not want the woman making reckless statements, not in front of the other three. 'What matters, I think, is what you found when you got there.'

'I knocked, crashing that big iron ring up and down on the door. I heard it echo through the house and in response came the sound of terrified shouting and babbling. Then I heard a voice, Mrs Christian's voice. It sounded as though she were trying to placate her husband, to calm him down. And then all at once there came the most terrible scream.' Clara put her hands over her ears as if she could still hear the sound. 'I pushed open the door. It was unlocked, just as I had asked, and at the very moment I entered, her body smashed onto the stairs in front of me. I rushed forward. When I looked up I saw Dr Christian staring down at me over the banisters. His face was wild, terrified. He scuttled down the stairs as I crouched over his wife. When he saw the open door behind me, he sprang over us both and ran through it. I went after him, but he was too fast. Perhaps he was driven by fear and madness, I have no idea, but whatever it was I could not catch him, not until he was at your apothecary, Mr Flockhart. And by the time I did catch up with him, he was dead.'

'But you stuffed his mouth with nightshade,' said Will. 'Why? Why not just leave him alone?'

'*Because* he was dead,' she said. 'His name was linked to your physic garden, to Bathsheba, to my father's remains. I knew he was guilty of something, even if it was merely complicity. So I filled his mouth, just as my father's mouth had been filled. I knew about *that*, Mr Flockhart, because your apprentice told half of London about it. I wanted it to be a warning. A sign to the others that I knew who they were, that I knew what they'd done. That I was coming for them and their silence would not save them.'

'But Mrs Christian's mouth was harder to fill, I think?' I said.

'Yes,' she muttered. 'By the time I returned she had grown stiff. I had to use the poker. Then I searched the house. I looked all over the place for this diary I'd heard about, but I couldn't find it. And then before I had even finished looking you two came.'

'You were disguised as a servant.'

'I learned more than painting in the theatre.'

'And you were the attendant who found Mrs Spiker.'

She shrugged. 'Some chalk and oil in my hair, a sullen expression and cringing manner, a few extra petticoats bunched about my waist. No one looks at a servant. It was easy.' She frowned. 'But she was dead too. What use was that? I learned nothing!'

'But you crammed her mouth with berries all the same,' I said.

She shrugged. 'Why not?'

'And the blue demon we saw that night?' said Will. 'Who was that?'

'That was Bathsheba,' I said. 'Was it not, Miss Wilde? What better disguise than that of Kali the Hindu goddess with whom you have always identified?' Bathsheba tossed her head and opened her mouth to speak. But I had not finished yet. 'You, Miss Wilde, were the only one who suspected there must be something else in the grave, something we had not yet found. Gabriel had informed everyone what we *had* found, you alone knew that there was something missing. Something else my mother had put there so that one day, perhaps, what had befallen Delaney might be uncovered.'

'You were looking for the locket,' said Will.

'You are just like her,' snapped Bathsheba, her gaze fixed upon me. She did not even look at Will. 'I knew that if you found it, you'd work out what she meant. Cathy always wore that locket at her throat. After we had buried Delaney I noticed it was missing. I saw her put her fingers up to touch it, the way she always did, and it was not there. And the way she looked at me, the smile she gave, I knew she had buried it with him. I knew the key to her diary was in that locket, I had never seen the diary itself, but I knew she had kept one throughout her time up country, even though I had ordered her to do no such thing.

'I asked her about it, of course, after we had buried Delaney. She said she would never say anything about what had happened in India, nor would she say anything to anyone about what she had done that night in the physic garden. She said she would make her own peace with both, but that she would not hang for it, and that she had stabbed Delaney through the heart as she could not bear to see him suffer.' She shrugged. 'Strychnine is, I admit, the very worst of deaths. Then she said, "But if William Delaney is ever found, then he deserves a chance of justice. I have given him that chance. And if God sees fit to unearth him, then he will have about him the means to tell the world what happened. And you need not come to me to look for it. I have hidden my diary too well for *you* to ever find it."' Bathsheba threw me a bitter look. 'Your mother could not come to terms with what she had been a part of, no matter what she said, and yet neither could she bring herself to tell the world what she had done. So instead she chose a path which, to her, seemed like a compromise. And she paid a pair of watchmen to sit in the garden too, so I could not even dig him up again! And then after a while it was too late. Besides, she proved as good as her word and said nothing about what had happened.' She frowned. 'She said I would betray myself in the end anyway, and that perhaps it hardly mattered.'

'And so you did,' I replied. 'I knew nothing about a diary until Miss Clara overheard you speak of it and mentioned it to me. It was you who told me what to look for and, with your taunts about my father, it was you who told me where to look. I would never have gone to search Dr Bain's house if you had not drawn my attention to his relationship with my mother.'

'What about the skulls?' said Will. 'The bowl?'

'Your mother made each of us keep one of the skulls from my necklace,' said Bathsheba. 'She said it was to remind us of what we'd done. The rest went into the grave. She insisted upon it. If I did not, she said she would tell everything. She would hang us all – even herself – if she had to, if I did not stop.' She smirked. 'What arrogance! As if she might stop *me*.'

'Mrs Spiker buried hers in the wall,' I said. 'My mother kept hers in her pocket. Mrs Christian wore hers like a penance. And yours, Miss Wilde?'

'That's not your concern.'

'Hers is on a necklace with numerous others just like it, Mr Flockhart,' said Clara. 'You saw it when you were here last night.'

'Did I?' I blushed. 'I cannot recall.'

'It's as well I told Lakshmi to let the dogs out, Mr Quartermain,' said Clara. 'Had you not been chased from the grounds that night you may well have suffered a similar fate to my father and his brother.' I felt the blood drain from my face at the thought. My mother had done the same as I, she had given in to temptation, and after that she had scarcely known what she was doing, or what atrocities she had taken part in.

'Why the nightshade bush?' said Will. He sounded utterly incredulous that such activities could have taken place at all.

'Because the deadly nightshade is one of the most poisonous plants in the garden. Who would choose to move it, when every bit of it is toxic?' I said. 'And besides, it loves a grave.'

'But why stuff the fellow Delaney's mouth with it too?'

'Why not?' snapped Bathsheba. 'Belladonna signifies silence. It gives powerful insights to those who know how to use it, but for those who do not it leads to madness and the grave.' She was looking at Clara now, an expression of such longing and sorrow on her face that for a moment I thought she might be about to apologise, to beg for forgiveness, say that she had been young and arrogant, misguided, was filled with regret for what had happened. But she said none of those things. Instead, the sorrow on her face melted like snow and was replaced by a haughty disdain. She looked imperiously down at her lover, who was still seated at her easel, and said, 'You cannot leave, Clara. I forbid it. You will stay here. With me.'

'Never mind *her*,' said Bella. She was still crouched at Bathsheba's feet, Sukey weeping at her side, her face streaked and smeared with blue dye. '*We* tried to help you. To save you. What about us?'

Bathsheba looked at her daughter with distaste as though seeing her for the first time. '*You?*' She spat out her words like poison. 'How could either of *you* be anything to me? Just look at you. What's that on your face? Who do you think you are? D'you think this is a *game?* Do you think I need *help?* From *you?*'

'Miss Clara,' said Will in an undertone. 'If you would care to collect your belongings we will take you back into town with us. We have a carriage waiting. Unless, of course, you wish to stay.'

'Stay?' said Clara. 'Here? Not for a single moment longer!'.

'The police will be along shortly,' I said to the three other women. 'I have told them what to expect from you. Miss Clara?'

'Thank you, Mr Flockhart.' Clara Delaney took my arm, and with Will leading, we turned and walked away.

Clara brought little with her from Nightshade House. Her bulging satchel, and a carpet bag of clothes and personal items was the only baggage she loaded into the waiting carriage. 'I'm sorry about your father,' I said, as we moved off. How inadequate it sounded. 'I'm sorry too that I can't absolve my mother from what happened to him.'

'It's not your fault,' she said.

'Why did she do it?' said Will. 'Why was – is – Bathsheba Wilde so adrift from all that's decent that she seems unable to see right from wrong? As for the blue dye, what in heaven's name was she thinking? In London too!'

'Bathsheba believes herself to be the goddess Kali,' said Clara. 'Or at least, the personification of Kali – that's the Hindu goddess of time, Mr Quartermain, the goddess of creation and destruction. She is a powerful and angry deity. For Bathsheba the similarity between the two of them was obvious.'

'But that's preposterous.'

'It might seem preposterous to you,' I said, 'but

Bathsheba said it so often it was clear she believed it. So did the other three. The mixture of *belladonna*, *Datura*, *henbane*, *ephedra* and *cannabis* she was in the habit of using made these convictions all the more real to her.'

'Do the goddess and Miss Wilde look similar?' said Will. 'I assume this "Kali" is blue?'

'Kali is known as the "dark blue one". Sometimes she's depicted wearing a tiger skin, sometimes she wears nothing but her necklace of skulls. Her eyes are red rimmed, her tongue prominent.' Clara shrugged. 'I suppose any woman might see similarities if she painted her skin and dressed that way too. But for Bathsheba there was no doubt. Of course, the goddess herself has four arms.'

'Four!' said Will.

'She carries a sword and a noose in two of her hands, and a severed head and a bowl to collect the blood from it in the other.' Clara sighed. 'At least my father escaped that.'

I squeezed her hand. I did not tell her that her uncle had not been so fortunate. 'Bathsheba Wilde's interpretation of who the goddess Kali is and what she signifies is completely muddled,' I said. 'She took whatever parts she needed from her mother's culture and discarded those she didn't. She is too lost and confused by her upbringing to know what she's talking about. Her father a nabob in the Company's India, her mother – I have no idea, but it has suited Bathsheba to believe herself to be a descendant of gods and goddesses on her Indian mother's side. Misunderstanding, lack of knowledge about Indian history and religious tradition, misguided use of Indian stimulants and rituals, combined with her English arrogance and sense of entitlement.' I held up my hands. 'She made her own interpretations, allowed her own vanity to grow

349

unchecked, to the point that she committed crimes so terrifying that her companions were scared out of their wits by her, or at least were never the same again. They all lived in fear of her.

'But to really understand, to really *know* what one is talking about, religious associations and connotations have to be learned, imagined, intuited via deep symbolic meanings embedded in nature and culture. She had none of this, or at least very little. A true hybrid, not unlike many of her own plants, she fitted neither here, nor there. And so she created for herself a world that took elements from whatever part of her upbringing she needed, a world where she made the rules. But such a place cannot, and does not, exist. Not in the end.'

Will and Clara were staring at me in surprise. I blinked. Had I been talking too much? Certainly, I had been thinking a lot as we jolted our way towards the city. Had I voiced *all* those thoughts? Suddenly I was not entirely sure. Perhaps the nightshade still possessed me, for the general dizziness I felt had now been joined by a warm sense of euphoria.

'Never mind the deep symbolic meanings and intuitive connotations, Jem,' said Will. 'To state the matter in its simplest terms, the woman is completely mad.'

'Robustly put, Will,' I replied. 'And, in fact, I believe you have put your finger right on the crux of the matter, as you so often do. Miss Belladonna Wilde is proof of it. There are certain things about that woman that are not as they should be. Her eyes, the bridge of her nose, her teeth – all point to congenital syphilis. The fact that her father and mother were half-brother and -sister cannot have helped matters, as the relation is too close in blood. I believe

Bathsheba Wilde was used by her brother, and possibly her father, for his own sexual purposes. Her antipathy towards him, and to men in general might support this hypothesis.'

'Don't make excuses for her,' said Will.

'I'm not making excuses, I'm trying to explain. Bathsheba was violated by him, she contracted syphilis from him and passed it on to the daughter she bore. And, although the disease is no longer manifest, I believe it still lurks within her, invisible to observers, but consuming her mind the way the visible lesions once consumed her flesh. Over time, it has turned her mad, compounding her hatred of men, and, with the aid of hallucinogens, making her believe herself invincible.

'This particular aetiological explanation is my own theory, I admit. I've shared my thoughts about the links between madness and syphilis with various doctors at the asylum on numerous occasions – so many case histories for those apparently suffering from incurable insanity contain reference to the pox caught years earlier, even if the symptoms of the original disease are no longer visible. The connection is obvious to me, though the mad-doctors seem unwilling to make the link themselves. Can't think why. Typical arrogance, I suppose.' I stopped. They were both staring at me again, so I cleared my throat and, resolving to say nothing more, muttered gruffly, 'Well, there it is. Perhaps she deserves a little of our sympathy, at least.'

Neither Will nor Clara gave me an answer.

Excerpts from the diary of Catherine Underhill.

21ˢᵗ March 1820

This book is the diary of Catherine Underhill, companion and fellow traveller to Miss Bathsheba Wilde, Mrs Dorothea Christian, Dr Robert Christian and Miss Jane Spiker. It is a true account of what happened to Dr James and Mr William Delaney. I cannot undo what happened that night, no matter how much I might wish it, though I have no doubt that fate, or vengeance, will catch up with us all one day.

I am ashamed to say it, but I cannot bring myself to put the hangman's noose about my own neck. And yet nor can I deny James and William Delaney the chance for truth and justice which they deserve. If it is God's will that the bones of William Delaney are found, I have left my locket, with its miniature of my once-beloved Alexander, with him. It will lead the finder, if he is astute and persistent, to this true account.

If this diary is found before then, I urge you, dear reader, to look beneath the deadly nightshade that grows in St Saviour's physic garden, and tell the world what I cannot: that James Delaney was murdered in India, and his brother William Delaney was murdered in England, by Bathsheba Wilde, Dora Christian and Jane Spiker, aided and abetted by Robert Christian and myself, Catherine Underhill.

Chapter Twenty-Two

~⁂~

Clara stayed the night at the apothecary. I put her in my bed, I would brook no argument from her or Will, and I spent the night beneath a blanket in my father's chair before the stove. It was not the first time I had slept there, and it would not be the last. In fact, I slept remarkably well, perhaps the result of the sleeping draught I mixed for myself, and I only awoke when Will shook my shoulder and thrust a cup of hot coffee into my hands. I saw from the apothecary clock that it was past eight.

'She's gone, Jem,' he said. 'But she left these for you,' and he put a note, and a rolled tube of thick artist's paper onto the table.

'Did you resist the urge to unfurl?' I said.

He grinned. 'I can never resist. And she is such a capable artist. I hope you still like the deadly nightshade, despite everything that has happened this week.'

I was sorry she had gone, sorry too that I had not had the chance to say goodbye, though I quite understood her

354

reasons for leaving. It was time for her to start anew. Her note showed that she thought the same and had laid down plans for her departure some time ago.

My dear Mr Flockhart, she wrote,

I have decided that my life in London is over, and the time has come for me to make myself available as an artist to any reputable botanical garden that will have me. For this reason, I applied for just such a position at the botanical gardens in Edinburgh, currently run by a Dr Balfour, who I believe is looking for someone with my skills, and who assures me I will not be disappointed, as his garden is second only to London in the magnificence of its collections. This note is goodbye. I'm sorry I could not wait for you to wake, but I did not want to be persuaded from going, and if anyone would have been able to stop me, it would have been you.

For what it may be worth, I do not believe that your mother ever meant to harm my father, or his brother. When my father came in search of his attackers in the physic garden that night, I imagine that any action she took was solely out of fear and desperation, perhaps in the belief that the blade was, in the end, a more merciful death to the one that awaited him. I believe she was, at heart, a good person. She has my forgiveness, as much as you, her beloved daughter, will always have my gratitude.

Your obt. Servant,

Clara Delaney.

Police Gazette, 23ʳᵈ January 1852
APPREHENSIONS SOUGHT
MURDER
£500 REWARD
ISLINGTON FIELDS

At 1:45 on the afternoon of Sunday 19ᵗʰ inst. a woman known as BATHSHEBA WILDE was found dead at her home of Nightshade House in the Borough of Islington. A reward of £500 will be paid by the commissioners of the City of London Police to any person (other than those belonging to the Police Force of the United Kingdom) who shall give information leading to the discovery and conviction of the murderers, believed to be two women: BELLADONNA WILDE, the daughter of the deceased, aged 35, five feet six inches high, of pasty complexion, light brown hair, blue wide-set eyes, a depression to the bridge of her nose, wearing a dark blue dress and black coat, and her companion SUSAN also known as SUKEY SPIKER, aged 29 years, five feet two inches high, of swarthy complexion, dark brown hair, brown eyes, round faced with a birthmark the size and shape of a sixpence below her right ear, believed to be wearing a bottle-green dress beneath a black coat. Both women are of respectable appearance and may be carrying luggage.

'I hope those two are apprehended and brought to justice soon,' said Will, tossing the *Police Gazette* back to Gabriel. 'I hate to think of them being at large. I'd put a rope around my own neck with my own hands if I thought I had to spend even a minute with either woman ever again.'

'Come now, don't exaggerate,' I said. 'Two minutes, certainly. But one? Even you could manage one.'

'Perhaps it was Miss Clara who did it, and neither of those two is responsible,' he said.

I laughed. 'Clara Delaney is not capable of murder, Will. That much was obvious.' I stood up and adjusted the picture that hung on the wall beside Dr Bain's skeleton. Gabriel and Jenny had picked it up from the framer on St Saviour's Street not ten minutes earlier and had put it up straight away. I was very pleased with what the man had done, for the painting was set off beautifully. Will leaned back in his chair, looking up at Clara's painting of *Atropa belladonna* in its frame of ebony and gold leaf.

'What an extraordinary talent she has,' he said after a moment. 'I know a thing or two about drawing, but that is astonishing. They are lucky to have her in Edinburgh.' He was right too. The leaves were dark and lustrous, their emerald stems tinged with mauve. Against that dark background the flowers appeared luminous, exquisite stars of purple velvet with tiny beads of white, like a necklace of diamonds encircling a thrusting orange-yellow stamen. Beside the flowers Clara had painted a cluster of berries, perfect spheres, heavy on their slender stems, and glistening like polished jet. The colours were rich and deep, with a moist, lustrous appearance, as tempting and succulent as jujubes. In the bottom right-hand corner was her signature, Clara Delaney, and in the other – Will sat forward. In the other was something entirely new. We turned and gaped at one another. 'Was that written there when you took it to the framers?' he whispered.

I shook my head. 'No! She must have . . . stopped by before going to—'

'To Edinburgh.'

'Of course.'

The words, added to the bottom left-hand side of the painting in a fine confident script, would forever remind me not to make judgements about what a woman may, or may not, be capable of: *Revenge is a dish best served cold. Nightshade House, 19ᵗʰ January 1852.*